RAW DESI_

Desire, Oklahoma 6

Leah Brooke

MENAGE EVERLASTING

Siren Publishing, Inc.
www.SirenPublishing.com

A SIREN PUBLISHING BOOK
IMPRINT: Ménage Everlasting

RAW DESIRE
Copyright © 2011 by Leah Brooke

ISBN-10: 1-61926-153-7
ISBN-13: 978-1-61926-153-2

First Printing: November 2011

Cover design by Les Byerley
All art and logo copyright © 2011 by Siren Publishing, Inc.

Printed in the U.S.A.

PUBLISHER
Siren Publishing, Inc.
www.SirenPublishing.com

RAW DESIRE

Desire, Oklahoma 6

LEAH BROOKE
Copyright © 2011

Chapter One

Desire, Oklahoma
Population 398

Blowing out a breath, Alison Bennett pressed a hand to her stomach to calm the butterflies. Reaching for the bottle of water on the passenger seat, she winced at the tight pull of muscle in her lower back.

Finding the bottle empty, she cursed and tossed it to the floor on the passenger side and stared at the sign again.

Well, she'd found it. Now she hoped she had the courage to see if it lived up to its name.

And hoped it was a good place to hide.

After researching the town, she'd acted on impulse and signed up for a seminar at the women's club, thinking that if she had an excuse to visit the town, no one would be suspicious.

Hopefully, while staying here, she could relax and shake off some of the aftereffects of the last several months and regain some of her former self-confidence. She'd let Danny's criticism regarding sex and her looks eat at her self-esteem, but instead of leaving him, she'd stuck around and tried to remake herself to please him.

Stupid.

In a fit of anger, she pressed down on the gas, alarmed when her old pickup sputtered and coughed, and sucked in a sharp breath when it jerked, tugging painfully at the tight muscle in her lower back. Almost immediately, a huge amount of thick smoke billowed out from under the hood, blocking her view of the road.

Swearing, she slowed and began to pull off to the shoulder, trying not to panic. A gust of wind blew enough of the smoke away to assure her that she'd managed to get the truck completely off of the road before it coughed again and died a shuddering death.

Slamming it into park, she hissed at the excruciating pull to her back and sat unmoving, taking several slow breaths before she carefully reached out and turned off the ignition, not moving any more than necessary.

Damn it, she didn't have enough money to fix her truck. She barely had enough for a place to stay, especially after a good chunk of her money had been used for the temporary membership to Lady Desire.

It had seemed like a good idea at the time, a chance to learn a few things to bolster her self-confidence and keep her next boyfriend from straying— something she was doing just for herself, but she'd already started to regret it.

Easing back with a groan, she wondered why she'd ever thought she could make such a long drive without stopping. It had been a stupid thing to do, but she'd been anxious to get here.

Now she would have what appeared to be quite a walk ahead of her to even get to town. To hell with it. She could do it. She'd dealt with worse.

Her stomach rumbled, reminding her that she hadn't had anything to eat since the breakfast sandwich she'd choked down while driving early that morning. She'd driven for hours without stopping, wanting to get as far away from Muskogee as she could as fast as possible. No matter what happened, she couldn't stay in her hometown any longer. She had to be prepared to get on with her life, and this seemed like as good a place as any to start.

First, though, she had to actually get there.

Thinking about what might be a long walk ahead of her, she reached into the side pocket of her purse for the plastic prescription bottles. Her medicine should be taken with food, but she didn't have that option right now and needed the pain pill and muscle relaxer before she could even consider making such a walk. Taking the small pills with the warm orange juice left in the plastic bottle she hadn't finished at breakfast, she stuck the rest of them back into the small purse she was forced to carry now. She missed her big carryall purses, but she tended to fill them, and the doctor warned her against carrying a heavy bag.

Alone, with no one else around to hear her, she didn't bother to hold back her pain-filled groan as she fought the temperamental door, wincing when the rusted hinges groaned in protest. Holding on to the steering wheel, she slid to the ground and had to take several deep breaths, waiting for the muscles to loosen enough for her to move again.

It took more effort than she could muster to slam the door the way she needed to in order to close it again, but she did the best that she could. Walking around the front of the truck to the grass on the other side, she wrinkled her nose at the smell of burning rubber and gave the smoking hood a wide berth.

Hearing a vehicle approach from the direction of the town, she turned, stilling when she saw the Sheriff insignia on the side of the SUV.

Hell, if it wasn't for bad luck, she'd have no luck at all. She and sheriffs generally didn't get along.

His lights flashed as he made a U-turn in the road and pulled in right behind her truck.

Watching him get out, she felt a moment of panic when she saw his size and harsh features, ashamed of herself for being such a wimp.

She wondered how many other women felt the same way after experiencing pain at the hands of a man she trusted.

Swallowing heavily, she kept her face blank, having already learned the value of not showing any signs of weakness.

Well over six feet tall, he couldn't be called handsome but had to be one of the most compelling and dangerous-looking men she'd ever laid her eyes on. She took an involuntary step back as he approached, wrapping her arms around herself against the chill that went through her.

He stopped abruptly and smiled, a smile that didn't quite reach those hard eyes, which remained sharp and full of suspicion. "Ma'am. Are you all right?"

Alison nodded, careful not to make any sudden moves. "I'm fine, thanks. I was just on my way to Desire when the smoke started coming out from under the hood. It coughed a little and died. As soon as I get to town, I'll call a tow truck."

She really didn't want to ride with someone who looked like he could break her in half with no effort at all, but she sure as hell didn't want to walk what could be miles. She could do it, though, if she had to. She'd learned that she could handle just about anything, and a walk to town paled in comparison. If only she could stay awake long enough.

Damn it, why had she taken that pill, especially on an empty stomach?

She shifted her purse to her other arm and winced at the pain that shot through her back and hip.

That's why she'd taken the damned thing.

The sheriff never took his eyes from her as he pulled a cell phone from his pocket and hit a number, the glint of gold shining from his ring finger making her wonder what kind of woman would be brave enough to take on such a man. "Can I see your license and registration?"

She dug both out of her purse and handed them to him, trying to hide the fact that her hands shook.

He spoke into the phone as he looked over her information.

"Talia, can you call Ryder and Dillon and tell them to come out to the road coming into town with the tow truck. Yeah, right where the sign is. Thanks."

Alison couldn't prevent a smile. "The road coming into town? Doesn't it have a name?"

The sheriff tapped her license with her registration. "It's Tyler Road, but everyone in Desire calls it the road coming into town. Alison Bennett. It says here that you're from Muskogee. Kind of a long way from home, aren't you?"

Alison shrugged and then regretted it when a muscle in her back protested the movement. "Yes."

His brows went up at her clipped answer. "What are you doing in Desire?"

Blinking at his suspicious tone, she looked away, too embarrassed to admit her reason for coming. "To shop. Maybe to stay a few days."

If possible, his expression became even harsher. He scowled, narrowing his eyes at her. "Lying to me is no way to get into my town."

Swallowing heavily again, she rubbed her arms with shaking hands. Determined not to let him see how much he intimidated her, she lifted her chin defiantly. "That's not very friendly."

A dark brow went up. "We're not friends."

His cold tone sent a chill down her spine, tightening her back even more painfully. She wanted nothing more than to get away from him, so she decided to tell him enough to satisfy his curiosity. "If you must know, I got a temporary membership to a club there. I'll only be in town for a week or two after that, and then I'm moving on."

His lips twitched. "Which club?"

Alison blinked again before she remembered what she'd read about the men's club and what went on there. "Oh."

His slow smile changed his face completely, but he still wouldn't be considered handsome. Lethal perhaps, but never handsome. "Yeah. Oh."

"I'm going to Lady Desire. Can you tell me how to get there?"

Shaking his head in amusement, he looked up as a tow truck approached.

"It's on the other side of town."

"Is there a place to stay nearby?"

"There's a hotel across the street from it."

Alison accepted her license and registration that he held out to her, and lowered her head to put them away, wondering how she would be able to afford moving on once she paid for the truck repair, in addition to almost two weeks at a hotel and food.

She looked up as the tow truck parked in front of her still-steaming truck. It backed up to it, not stopping until the two trucks stood only a few feet apart.

"I can't believe they got here so fast."

The sheriff shrugged. "It's a small town, and we all look out for each other."

Alison nodded, understanding immediately what it meant to be an outsider in a small town. Just as she knew what it felt like when the "good old boys" turned on someone they no longer liked.

Prepared for a couple of those good old boys with beer bellies to be riding in the tow truck, she took several steps back, wincing at the pull of tight muscles and surreptitiously rubbing her aching hip.

Her breath hitched when a strikingly masculine man slid gracefully out of the passenger side, his denim jacket doing nothing to hide his muscular frame.

Dark-blond hair framed decidedly masculine features, from a wide forehead to intense blue eyes that crinkled in the corner, a nose that looked as though it had been broken at least once, a square jaw and strong chin, and the firmest, fullest lips she'd ever seen on a man.

He smiled at her, the confident smile of a man who knew his place in the world, the smile of a man who knew what effect that smile would have on women.

A smile that somehow combined polite interest and blatant sexuality into something so alluring her jaw actually dropped.

Snapping it shut as he came toward her, she let her gaze rake over him, her fingers itching to trace over the muscular chest exposed as the sides of his jacket parted, a chest lovingly molded by a white T-shirt. His long legs, encased in faded jeans, ate up the distance between them with a speed and predatory stride that actually had her taking a step back.

His grin fell, his blue eyes darkening and raking over her like a caress.

"You don't have anything to fear from us." His overlong hair brushed the collar of his denim coat, the ends of it blowing in the light breeze and giving him a rakish look.

Alarmed at how easily he'd read her unease, she stepped back. "I, um...hello. Thank you for coming so quickly."

The blond man's grin widened, his blue eyes twinkling. "Not too quick, I hope."

Alison averted her gaze to hide her burning face and looked toward where another man approached from the other side of the truck, aware of the blond man's sharpened interest.

The other man had darker hair, and although he wasn't as muscular as the blond man, he stood just a little bit taller. Something in his eyes and the way he moved gave him a roguish look, and even though his movements were every bit as fluid as the blond man's, she sensed a restlessness in him as his gaze moved over her as though he would rather do away with pleasantries and get right to business.

His hair, much longer than the other man's, blew around his head, adding to the untamed look about him. His narrow face intrigued her, the cleft in his chin and his high cheekbones making her fingers itch to explore.

He shook his head when the blond man shot him a look, smiling in amusement.

"I'm not going to pounce on her, for God's sake! Hello, ma'am. Hi, Ace." He came forward, his brows going up when he glanced at her dilapidated truck. "I'm Ryder Hayes. This is Dillon Tanner. What's your name?"

A deep chuckle sounded from behind her. "Can you two behave long enough to get her to town? I was on my way to check on a lead."

Dillon's smile fell. "Anything to do with what's been going on at the clubs?"

The sheriff, Ace, nodded. "Yeah. Can you take her to the hotel once you tow her truck in? Show her how to get to Lady Desire."

Ryder's brow went up again, a speculative gleam in his eyes now as they met hers. Without looking at the sheriff, he smiled faintly. "We'll take care of her. Go do what you've got to do. We all want this guy."

Alison watched in fascination as the sheriff's expression darkened again. "I thoroughly intend to. I'm going to get that son of a—sorry, ma'am." He nodded toward her again. "Her name's Alison Bennett. Take care of her. I'll check back with you later."

With an absent nod in her direction, he got back into his vehicle and backed up several yards before making a U-turn in the road and taking off in the direction he'd been heading before he stopped to help her.

Left alone with Dillon and Ryder, she watched them work, becoming increasingly aware that the pain medicine she'd taken had begun to take effect.

She shifted her shoulders experimentally, and pleased to find the pain in her back lessening, she turned from side to side to stretch a little as she watched both men work on her truck. Pretending not to notice the looks they kept sending in her direction, she kept her eyes focused on their movements.

"When do you think you can give me an estimate?"

While Dillon worked to get her truck ready to tow, Ryder came to stand directly in front of her, blocking her view of Dillon, and waited until she lifted her gaze to his before speaking.

His glittering green eyes raked over her, a perfect foil for his olive complexion. They settled a little too long on her wide hips and ample breasts, making her wish she'd worn something other than faded jeans and a turtleneck under her baggy jacket. "Ace said you're going to Lady Desire. Is that why you came to town?"

She lifted her chin, wrapping her arms around herself again. In an attempt to keep her distance, she took a step back and answered coldly. "Yes. Although it's really none of your business. I need to have my truck back as soon as possible. Do you think you can fix it soon?"

She sure as hell didn't want to be caught with no transportation if she needed to flee.

Ryder shrugged, his eyes narrowing, making him look even colder than before. In the blink of an eye, his wild demeanor took on a dark edge, one that reminded her too much of Danny. "Maybe. Maybe not. It's an old truck. We'll have to see about parts. So, you're going to be staying at the hotel?"

Careful not to get too close to the truck, or to Ryder, she stepped aside and watched Dillon work. Ryder's sharp, watchful gaze put her on edge, and she felt better, safer, standing closer to Dillon.

Which made absolutely no sense at all.

Hoping a no-nonsense attitude would hide her nervousness, she lifted her chin defiantly.

"Yes, I'm staying at the hotel. I don't have a lot of money, so don't go padding the bill. I just want the thing to run. No extras."

Dillon straightened and winked at her, a slow wink that sent a wave of yearning through her. "We'll work something out." Not only sexy as hell and soft spoken, Dillon kept his distance, carefully sidestepping to avoid invading her space, the knowledge of her unease with them glittering in his blue eyes.

Ryder stared at her for several long seconds, unmoving, his fierce gaze drawing hers. Taking a step toward her, he smiled, a slow, predatory smile, stopping abruptly when she took a step back.

His smile fell, and without a word, he turned and went back to helping his friend, his watchful gaze lifting to hers with alarming frequency.

Shaken by her unwilling attraction to his bad-boy good looks, she concentrated on watching them work, careful not to meet their eyes.

It didn't prove to be difficult at all, especially with so many other delightful things to watch. Feeling loose and a little mellow now as the medicines kicked in, she smiled to herself and enjoyed the show.

They removed their jackets, giving her a tantalizing view of the muscles in their arms bunching and flexing as they worked as well as their firm bottoms each time they turned their backs to her. When they bent over the front of her truck, she couldn't take her eyes from them, fascinated at the most amazing men's asses she'd ever seen. Her own imagination ran wild as she thought about how it would feel to hold on to Dillon's wide shoulders and have those slim hips between her thighs and how it would feel to dig her heels into those tight buttocks.

No matter how much she fought it, though, her gaze kept returning to Ryder.

The tattoos on his arms didn't surprise her at all, the one that disappeared beneath the short sleeve of his shirt fascinating her. She wanted to see the rest of it, her imagination going wild at the thought of seeing him naked. Staring at his tattoo, she finally figured out it was an abstract design and wondered how far over his body it went.

With her fingers itching to explore, she looked up to find he'd caught her staring, and hurriedly looked away.

As soon as he got back to work, her gaze slid to his buns again, willing to bet they would be as hard and unyielding as the rest of him. She would also bet he would take a woman in that primitive, exciting way the look in his eyes promised.

What she wouldn't give for some of her former courage back and the chance to find out.

He shot another glance at her as they hooked up her truck, his brow going up when he caught her staring again. "So, what did you hope to learn at the women's club? If you're looking for volunteers, I'd be happy to let you practice on me. I'm sure I could teach you things you'd never learn there."

Mortified that they appeared to know about the club she would be visiting, she turned away, looking up and down the deserted road.

"There isn't much traffic here, is there? I guess I'm lucky the sheriff happened to be passing when my truck broke down."

Dillon straightened, frowning at her thoughtfully before nodding once. "Guess so. Are you all right?"

"Of course." She took another step back, uncomfortable under his scrutiny.

Ryder brushed off his hands as he straightened and came closer, leaning back against the side of his truck, his gaze narrowing in speculation.

"You don't like that question, huh? Interesting. You're shy but going to the women's club for the seminar this weekend. I happen to know they're teaching women ways to please their man. But no man worth his salt would let his woman come here alone, which means you don't have a man, do you? What happened, did some man break up with you because he said you were no good at sex? Did he cheat on you with another woman and now you want to use sex to get him back?"

Aghast that he'd figured her out so easily, she could only stare at him, trying to come up with something to say.

Crossing one booted foot over the other and his arms across his chest, he settled back as if he had all day.

"You know, it's probably his fault, not yours. Women don't have to do a hell of a lot to please a man in the sex department."

Dillon's steady look never wavered, the deep blue of his eyes sharpening as he studied her.

"Ryder's a little presumptuous, especially since we just met you." He gave Ryder a warning look. "He's too used to women at the club who fall all over him."

He took a step closer, pausing when she took a step back. The tenderness in his smile reflected in his blue eyes, making them glitter with silver.

"Since you're alone, we just don't want you mixing with men who might hurt you. The men's club is also having seminars over the next several weeks, and when your curiosity kicks in, we don't want you messing around with strangers."

Ryder pushed off from the side of the truck. "There's no ring on your finger, and I'll bet you're here because of a breakup with some boyfriend, aren't you? A woman scorned is careless. And dangerous."

The look in his eyes told her without words it was a danger he would be happy to face head-on.

He would be a demanding lover, and he exuded the same self-confidence Danny always had, thinking himself God's gift to women.

She suspected Ryder would be just as selfish as Danny in bed, and no matter how much he tempted her, she wouldn't subject herself to that again.

Shaken at the surge of lust their attention stirred up inside her, and alarmed at how quickly the fuzziness began to close in around her, she lifted her chin and planted her feet firmly to keep from swaying.

"It's none of your business. I'd appreciate it if you'd take me to the hotel, please."

She had to get there before she fell asleep on them, something that could happen in the next few minutes if she didn't hurry them along.

Ryder's grin fell, but his eyes danced with amusement as he opened the passenger door and waved his hand, gesturing her inside. "Sure thing, darlin'. Hop in. We'll take you wherever you want to go."

She shot a look at Dillon as she moved toward the truck, holding on to the door to steady herself as her head began to swim. Ignoring his look of concern, she slid inside and to the center of the bench seat on the older, but surprisingly clean truck.

She sucked in a breath when Dillon slid into the passenger seat beside her and closed the door, and watched with hungry eyes as Ryder circled the front of the truck toward the driver's side. What she wouldn't give to be the kind of woman who could tame such a man.

"You okay?"

Surprised by Dillon's question, Alison spun toward him, alarmed to find his face only inches from hers. Hurriedly looking out the front window again, she swallowed heavily, fighting the languid drowsiness that made her limbs heavy and her reflexes slow.

Even though he'd donned his jacket again, she would swear she could feel the heat pouring off of him. How wonderful it would be to be able to lay her head on his strong shoulder, have his heavy arm come around her to hold her so she could relax, warm and secure against him.

Shaken at her thoughts, she bit her lip, hoping like hell she didn't start blurting them out. Sitting straighter, she blinked her tired eyes, having more and more trouble keeping them open. She'd never had one of the pain pills affect her so quickly before, but taking it on an empty stomach had apparently made it work faster. Being tired when she took them probably hadn't helped much either.

"I'm fine. Will it take long to get there?"

Ryder slid into the driver's seat, making her jump when he slammed the door behind him.

"In a hurry to get away from us?"

She turned in her seat toward him, her lethargy making her clumsy as she leaned back to avoid touching him, and inadvertently pressed against Dillon. "I don't even know you."

Ignoring his hostile glare, she turned back to look out the front window, doing her best to put as much distance between them as possible without slumping against Dillon.

Ryder probably had women falling all over themselves to get close to him, his dark good looks making him impossible to ignore. Added to that, he had a quick grin, a devil-may-care attitude, and practically oozed erotic charm. That wildness she sensed in him, though, would be the biggest draw, a challenge to any red-blooded female to see if she could be the one to bring him to his knees.

Imagining him on his knees and all that wildness she saw in his eyes breaking free in the bedroom had lust slamming into her battered system with a force that staggered her.

On the heels of that came memories of the way it had been with Danny. She'd considered herself lucky that a man that had his pick of women would choose her.

By the time she walked away, she wondered what she'd ever seen in him.

Not about to let what happened with Danny keep her from having a loving relationship with a man, she'd quickly figured out what she had to do in order to be with one again.

She had to get her confidence back, and coming to Desire had seemed like a good way to do it. Ryder reminded her too much of Danny, but Dillon's gentleness pulled at her, and she found herself looking to see if he wore a wedding band. Seeing none, but knowing that mechanics sometimes went without them because of their jobs, she found herself hoping he was single.

She'd love to spend time with a man, a real man, before she left town again. The tingling of awareness beneath her lethargy and the way her nipples beaded each time they hit a bump and her arm brushed his proved to her that she could feel desire again, and an idea began to form in her mind.

Could she do it? Was she brave enough, desperate enough, to try?

Uncomfortably aware of their scrutiny, she searched her muddled mind for something to break the tense silence.

"The sheriff asked me which club I'm going to, and when I said Lady Desire, he smiled and said something about it being the women's club. So the other club is for men, and they're having seminars, too?"

She wished she had the courage to ask if men went there to learn the same kinds of things she hoped to learn, but figured she'd better not.

Ryder shot her a look of dark amusement. "Yep."

Something in that look had her shifting restlessly in her seat, alarmed that moisture soaked her panties. Clearing her throat, she stared again out the front window as several buildings and houses came into view. "Then why did the sheriff ask me which club I was going to?"

Ryder shot her a glance, the heat in it making her nipples tingle. "He didn't know if you were one of the subs that visit there."

Alison blinked again, wondering if she'd missed something. "Why would they want to do that?"

Jeez, Alison. Just shut up and stop asking stupid questions.

Dillon cleared his throat and shot a warning glance at Ryder.

Smiling tenderly, Dillon lifted her chin, his tender touch a sharp contrast to the intense scrutiny of his stare. "Because they get a chance to live out some of their fantasies in a safe environment with men who appreciate them."

The fingers holding her chin felt warm and firm, no hesitation or uncertainty in his touch. She felt safe with him, and at the same time a delicious warmth built inside her and made her yearn to discover what it would be like to make love with him.

He would understand. He wouldn't make fun of her or criticize her shortcomings.

She stared into his eyes, unable to prevent imagining pressing herself against him as he held her in his arms. Those big arms would come around her and hold her close, his touch firm, but gentle as he explored her, hold her while she slept.

With a start, she realized her eyes had closed and snapped them open, knowing she had to get to the hotel soon.

His beautiful blue eyes twinkled with amusement and something else she couldn't interpret. Lost in his stare, it took her a minute to remember what they'd been talking about. When she did, her face burned, but he wouldn't let her look away, tightening his hold on her chin when she attempted it.

Swallowing heavy, she lowered her eyes. "Are...are you telling me that women actually go there to meet men who—"

"Fuck them?" Ryder finished helpfully, but with an icy snap that startled her.

When Dillon cursed under his breath and released her, she whipped her head around to face Ryder, frowning in confusion to the underlying anger in his tone.

Ryder nodded once, but didn't glance her way. "That we do. Make them come until they're hoarse from screaming. They love it and keep coming back for more. Some spend their vacations in town just to be able to go to the club."

What would it be like to sit and watch?

Grateful that she hadn't blurted that out, she bit her lip and stared straight ahead.

The only time she'd ever seen men and women having sex had been in the porn movies Danny watched, but those had always seemed like acting to her. They taught her, though, how to fake an orgasm.

Trying to keep everything but curiosity from her tone, she shifted in the seat again, fighting her jealousy at the mental image of watching Ryder having sex with another woman.

No, she didn't mean Ryder, she meant Dillon. Staring up into Dillon's strong, masculine features, she felt herself melting under the tender concern in his eyes.

What would it be like to belong to such a man, if only for a little while?

Would he want her? Did she have the courage to find out?

Ryder shot her a glance, but she could read nothing in his hooded eyes. "Does anyone ever call you Ally?"

Thinking about the kinds of names Danny called her, she shook her head, a bitter laugh escaping before she could prevent it. "No. My parents always called me 'little bit' because I'm so short, and in school, everyone called me Alison."

After a long silence, Dillon gripped her chin again and turned her face toward his. His gaze slid over each of her features, lingering on her lips, before lifting to her eyes again. "Would you have dinner with us? We'll eat at the hotel."

It seemed strange for him to ask her that way, and she fought her lethargy, fighting to stay alert. "Both of you?" Why would he ask her to dinner with both of them? Had she missed something?

Ryder hit the brakes a little harder than necessary at a stop sign, shooting her a cool look when she cried out and grabbed for Dillon, who'd already caught her. "I guess that's up to you."

She couldn't even imagine trying to sit through dinner with Ryder, but she'd love to spend some private time with Dillon.

She'd love to have the opportunity to practice what she learned at Lady Desire on someone, and Dillon seemed to be the perfect candidate.

She'd bet anything she would be safe with him and that he would be a tender and patient lover, one who would treat her with kindness and respect.

It would also be nice to have someone to eat with, and she couldn't deny that it would also help her moneywise. Now that she had the additional expense of fixing her truck, she simply wouldn't be able to afford to eat very much while she was in Desire.

But she didn't want him to get the wrong impression, at least until she could make a decision without the fogginess that surrounded her. She had enough trouble right now just fighting the urge to wrap herself around Ryder...no. Dillon. Ryder reminded her too much of Danny and had to be avoided.

It kept getting harder and harder to keep her head from bobbing and to keep her eyes open, the harsh glare coming in the windshield making her eyes hurt. "Just dinner?"

Dillon smiled, cupping her face and running a thumb over her lips. "For now."

Hugging her small purse in front of her, she nodded once, licking her tingling lips and inadvertently touching her tongue to his thumb. With a shiver, she leaned closer without meaning to. "I'd like that, but just dinner."

Realizing what she'd done, she hurriedly straightened. "And it'll have to be a little later. I have some things to do first."

If she didn't get to bed soon, she would fall asleep at the dinner table. She smiled to herself imagining what they would think of that.

His smile grew as he settled back in his seat. "Just dinner then. We'll stop at the hotel first and get you checked in before we take your truck to the garage."

Trying to ignore how it felt to be wedged in between two such good-looking and masculine men, Alison looked from side to side as they drove into the small town, hoping she could stay awake long enough to get checked into the hotel.

The brush of their thighs against hers sent little tingles of awareness up her legs to gather at her center, dampening her panties and making her clit swell.

Damn, the effects of those pills would get her into big trouble if she didn't get somewhere soon to sleep it off.

If she hadn't been so tired, she probably would have offered herself to Dillon right then and there.

Sobering, she bit back a smile as they drove through town.

Fighting to keep her eyes open, she twisted in her seat, trying to see everything. Every place she passed appeared to be well maintained, and several people walked up and down the sidewalks, apparently shopping in all of the little stores lining the streets.

They stopped at another stop sign, and to her surprise, both Ryder and Dillon smiled and waved at the woman crossing the street pushing a baby carriage.

Two men flanked her, both with the physiques of men who did a great deal of physical activity. One of them would be considered gorgeous by anyone's standards, while the other looked too serious, his hard masculine features appearing almost cold.

Until he smiled at the woman.

The love in his smile as he helped the woman to cross the street could be seen even from this distance, and he didn't appear to care at all that it showed.

Danny would never have let anyone see what he called a "weakness" for a woman, and certainly wouldn't have demonstrated any softening toward a woman in public.

Alison watched, fascinated, as the woman cuddled against him, lifting her face for a kiss he readily provided.

Dillon waved to the threesome, turning to snap at Ryder. "Don't sound the horn, for God's sake. You'll scare Theresa."

He turned back, watching them with the strangest look on his face. Almost...yearning.

Ryder glared back before leaning out the window, his broad smile stealing her breath. "Hey! How's the angel?"

The handsome man laughed. "She's colicky. We're hoping a walk will help her sleep tonight. Plus, we also love showing our girls off. Who's that with you?"

Ryder didn't even glance her way. "Alison Bennett. Her truck broke down. We're going to check her into the hotel."

"You looking after her?"

Ryder shrugged. "Dillon is. She doesn't like me much."

The harder-looking man lifted the baby carriage over the curb, smiling wryly over his shoulder. "I have no doubt you'll change her mind."

Ryder waved, his smile falling as soon as the others looked away.

Alison watched in amazed shock as the other man joined the man and the woman on the sidewalk, running a hand over her the woman's hip as he bent to kiss her cheek.

Hardly believing what she saw, she looked toward Dillon. "Wait a minute. Which one of those men is that woman's husband?"

Dillon smiled, but his eyes hardened and cooled slightly. "Both of them. That's Boone and Chase Jackson with their wife Rachel and their new baby girl, Theresa."

Stunned, Alison looked back to the trio being stopped by another couple who bent and appeared to be making a fuss over the baby. "Are you telling me that a woman has more than one husband? Isn't that against the law? Does the sheriff know about them? How does she know which one is the baby's father?"

She knew her brain was fuzzy, but still, the idea of a woman having two men as husbands had her mind racing.

Had she fallen asleep?

Surreptitiously pinching herself to make sure she hadn't, she stared after the trio with the baby.

Ryder's brow went up, his own expression considerably cooler. "Ace is the one who rode to the hospital in front of them with the siren blaring when

Rachel went into labor at the women's club. And they're *both* Theresa's father. Anyone who says otherwise would be in a heap of trouble."

Alison looked from Ryder to Dillon, too tired to make sense of any of it. "I've never heard of such a thing before, well, I've heard of it, but never seen it in real life."

Ryder turned a corner and shot her a cold look. "Well, now you have, and if you don't want any trouble, you'll keep your opinions to yourself."

Stung by the reprimand, Alison shifted uneasily in her seat and stared straight ahead. "I wasn't criticizing. I've just never seen a woman with two men before. You can't blame me for being curious."

When Ryder said nothing, Dillon obviously took pity on her.

"In Desire, several people live that way. It's why they live here in the first place. We watch out for each other and especially for the women. Rachel's one of ours now, and so is little Theresa. We won't take kindly to any negative comments about them, and no one who lives in Desire will either. This town survives because of our support of each other. We don't take kindly to outsiders who bad-mouth our residents *or* the way we choose to live."

Bristling with outrage, Alison whipped around in her seat, her breath catching when her breast brushed his arm. Feeling clumsy and having more and more trouble with her coordination, she sighed tiredly and slumped back in the seat. "What kind of person do you think I am? I'm not about to say anything bad about them. I've never seen a woman married to two men before. Why would she do that? How does it work? Why would two men want to share a woman? Don't other people in town say anything to them? It's against the law, isn't it?"

Dillon's brows went up at her barrage of questions, and he smiled faintly as he glanced out the window. "We can talk about it over dinner. But suffice it to say that ménage relationships are accepted here. There are several others besides the Jacksons. There are all kinds of relationships here, and as long as the women are treated right, and are happy, no one interferes."

Intrigued, Alison tilted her head. "And if they're not?"

Ryder spoke from her other side. "Then we all interfere. The women of Desire are protected and cherished. We don't like strangers here, especially opinionated ones. They can come here and shop or, like you, visit our businesses, but once they cause trouble of any kind, they're tossed out of town on their asses."

Turning back to stare out the windshield, Alison shrugged, not believing a word of it. She knew that it didn't matter what kind of person you were, or if you were male or female, if the popular people in town didn't like you, you were through. "I have no desire to start trouble. I'm here to attend some of the workshops at Lady Desire. I'll stay for a week or so, and then I'm leaving. Well, as soon as my truck's fixed. If you want me out of town, get my truck fixed."

Ryder shot a look at Dillon before making another turn. "So you're going to take classes learning how to please a man in bed, and then you're going back to a man in Muskogee to use all your newfound knowledge on some poor unsuspecting sap?"

Alison laughed bitterly. "Isn't that what men do to women all the time? But to answer your question, no. And how do you know what classes Lady Desire is holding this weekend? On the website, I saw all sorts of classes. How did you know I wasn't taking belly-dancing classes, or self-defense classes?"

A sudden thought hit her, and she burst out laughing, so tired, her head lolled to the side. "Oh, God. Tell me you're not the men they use for the demonstration! That would be priceless."

This time both of Ryder's brows went up, his tone sardonic over Dillon's laughter. "No, we're not even allowed inside. We go to the men's club across the street and play with the submissives there looking for a good time. But I told you, for you, I'd volunteer my services. I can come over to the hotel after your class, and you can show me everything you learned."

His wicked grin didn't match the coolness in his tone at all.

"Consider it homework."

Alison knew she should have been offended, but the promise of pleasure shining in his eyes and his seductive tone made it impossible. When her head spun dizzily, she knew she couldn't have worked up the energy to be offended if she wanted to.

Ryder's quick glance down her body was as potent as a caress, making her wish she had the courage to take him up on his offer. Already she burned for him and clenched her thighs tighter together against the empty ache that settled there.

Vowing to become the kind of woman men like Ryder would fall all over themselves to be with, she took a shuddering breath, flinching when Dillon snapped at Ryder.

"That's enough, Ryder. Can't you see she's tired?"

Dillon sighed, his frustration apparent. "Alison, we all keep track of what's going on at the women's club. We have women to protect, and there's been a little trouble there recently. There it is." He pointed out his window as Ryder slowed the truck.

Alison sat forward, blinking to bring what he showed her into focus, her gaze following where he gestured. A petite, dark-haired woman hurried toward the front door of the brick building Dillon pointed to, carrying what appeared to be takeout food. She turned her head, smiled broadly, and waved to them before starting up the steps.

Uneasy now, Alison sat back. "What kind of trouble? I'm not going to get into any kind of trouble with your sheriff for going there, am I?"

Both men lifted a hand in greeting to the petite woman before Ryder started off again.

Dillon chuckled. "No, you're not going to get into trouble with the sheriff for going there. Did you see that woman?"

"Yes. Why?"

"That's Hope, she and her sister, Charity, own Lady Desire. She's married to Ace Tyler, the sheriff you met a little while ago."

Alison's jaw dropped. "I can't picture those two together. Lord, he's huge, and she looks so tiny and defenseless."

Ryder stopped at another stop sign and turned to her. "Hope might look small, but she's hardly defenseless. Especially when she opens that mouth. She was born here, and every man in town has watched out for her since the day she was born. Not about to stop now. She's one of us."

The emptiness she'd experienced ever since her fight with Danny and subsequent rejection of her from the town she'd grown up in grew even larger, filling her with a loneliness that brought a lump to her throat.

Swallowing heavily, she blinked back tears, thankful that neither one of them looked her way, and tried to focus on what Dillon was saying.

"Some asshole's been causing trouble around town, mostly at the two clubs." He pointed out his window. "There's Club Desire, the men's club. Since they're having another seminar, we're on the lookout for trouble there." He pointed to the building next door to it. "And here's the hotel. We'll get you settled before we take your truck back to the shop. We'll talk about your truck over dinner and give you an estimate tomorrow. Alison?"

Lulled by his tone, she'd been staring at his shoulder, imagining what a great pillow it would make. Mentally shaking herself, she cleared her throat and blinked. "You still want to take me to dinner?"

Dillon turned toward her again and frowned, his eyes narrowing on hers. "I thought we already cleared that up. Are you sure you're all right?"

Alison shrugged again. "Just tired. I've been driving all day. I just need to get some sleep." She could tell she slurred her words but couldn't do anything about it and smiled as some of the emptiness inside her filled with a warm, fuzzy feeling that she couldn't resist.

"I figured you thought I was a troublemaker and wouldn't want to take me to dinner anymore."

Ryder parked on the side, away from the other cars, and shut off the engine, his movements rough and jerky, nothing at all like the smooth gracefulness he'd displayed driving here. "We're responsible for you now. You won't cause trouble." He leaned toward her, his grin ominous. "We won't let you."

Not knowing how to respond to that, and too tired to argue with him, Alison followed Dillon out of the truck, pausing in surprise when he offered his hand. She stared at it blankly, surprised at the gesture. No man had ever shown her that kind of consideration before. What stunned her the most was that the move seemed as natural to him as breathing. He didn't appear to think about it. He just did it.

Careful not to move too fast, she slid across the seat and placed her hand in his outstretched one.

Even in her drowsy state, or perhaps because of it, she found herself unable to move as hot sizzles of awareness raced up her arm and through her body with a strength and speed unlike anything she'd ever experienced. Dumbfounded, she stared at her hand in his, her breath catching when he closed his hand around hers in the gentle way that men who are conscious of their own strength do.

The calluses against her skin should have felt rough and irritating, but instead comforted her, making her feel soft and feminine against his bold masculinity.

The strong hand of a strong man.

Dillon would be a steady man, one with patience, one who worked hard.

One who would be breathtakingly tender with a woman he cared for.

What would it be like to be that woman?

Lifting her gaze, she met his searching one, blinking to escape the erotic trance she found herself in. Fatigue had muddled her brain, and if she didn't get to a bed soon, she feared she'd fall flat on her ass.

Looking away to hide her burning face, she got out of the truck and attempted to pull her hand out of his, but he held on.

Ryder reached into her truck to retrieve her bag and moved to walk on the other side of her.

She reached for her bag, but Ryder merely shifted it to his other hand out of her reach as they started toward the entrance to the small hotel.

"I can carry that." She had to admit, being around men who knew their manners was nice, but not something she was used to.

Ryder ignored her and kept walking, flustering her with the speculative glances he kept sending her way.

As their eyes met, she stumbled, staggered by the predatory gleam in his eyes. She gasped as Dillon hurriedly released her hand and caught her with an arm around her waist, the shock of feeling his hard body against hers hitting her with a blast of sexual awareness that nearly *did* knock her on her ass.

It probably would have if Dillon hadn't been holding her up.

Dillon steadied her, staring down at her with eyes laced with concern. "Easy, honey. Are you sure you're all right?"

Determined not to give Ryder the satisfaction of looking his way again, she stared straight ahead and struggled to convince her rubbery legs to support her.

She needn't have worried.

Dillon held her steady, his arms strong and solid around her. Warm. Safe. Seductive.

She wanted it. She wanted to satisfy this burning need inside her, the need for reassurance that she was still a desirable woman.

She wanted to satisfy the hunger, the excitement of being well loved by a man, to be taken by a man who would make her *feel*.

She believed with everything inside her that Dillon would be the perfect man to accomplish both.

Turning in Dillon's arms, she smiled her best flirtatious smile, hoping it didn't look as stupid as it felt as she stifled an inconvenient yawn. "How could I not be all right with you here?"

Inhaling his scent, she snuggled closer. "Hmm, you smell good."

After a long pause, Dillon chuckled. "So do you. I'll bet you taste just as good."

Alison snuggled closer and closed her eyes, letting him guide her across the parking lot. "You don't have to bother with the lines. We can have sex after dinner. Oh!" Surprised at the yank on her arm that pulled her to a stop, she blinked her eyes open and stared up at him, wincing at the pull to her back.

Dillon's brow went up, his scowl making him look even sexier. "Excuse me?"

Ignoring Ryder's look of surprise, Alison looked around, belatedly hoping no one had overheard her.

Shaking off her stupor, and grasping for all the courage she could muster, Alison tried to adopt a seductive pose, stopping short when her back protested the movement. "You heard me. You want sex, and I want to practice what I learn at the club to make sure I get it right. I'll be gone in less than two weeks. In the meantime there's no reason we can't have a little fun."

Oh, God! Had she really said that out loud?

Dillon stared over her head at Ryder. "It appears she wants to use us to further her education after all."

To her surprise, Ryder grabbed her arm and yanked her around to face him, the action sending a sharp pain through her back, and she bit her lip to keep from crying out.

With his hands wrapped around her upper arms, Ryder lifted her to her toes. "So *now* you want to use us to practice on, huh? You don't think that's going to get you out of paying for the repairs to your truck, do you, because, honey, I don't pay for sex. Never have. Never will."

Embarrassed, insulted, and in pain, Alison clenched her fist at her side, wanting to slap that arrogant look off his face, but she didn't trust the look in his eyes daring her to do just that. "It had nothing to do with money or repairs to my truck, you asshole. I'm not a fucking whore. Just get away from me."

She reached for her bag, but he wouldn't release it, his brow going up in surprise when she fought for it as he held it just out of her reach.

She lunged after it, but found herself stopped short by the pain in her back even before the hard band of Dillon's hand wrapped around her upper arm.

Biting her lip against the pain, she took several deep breaths before speaking. "Give it to me, damn you. And leave my truck here. I'll get someone else to take care of it."

Dropping her bag on the asphalt, Ryder whipped an arm out, snagging her waist and lifting her several inches off of the ground, plastering her against him. His other hand caught hers when she lashed out to smack his face.

"Settle down before you hurt yourself. Settle down, damn it." He shook her once, the sharp pain forcing her to stop struggling.

"Listen, you asshole—"

"No, *you* listen." His green eyes flashed. "I don't know you. I met you less than an hour ago. You need repair work on your truck and after acting like you don't want anything to do with either one of us, you change your mind and within minutes you're offering sex. Just because we told you we go to the club, don't think we don't have standards. Every woman there is checked out before she's allowed in the door. I don't know you from Adam, lady, and until I do, I'm not buying what you're selling."

His grin sent a chill through her, making it difficult to breathe. "And by the way, there's no other place in town to get your truck fixed. You're just going to have to deal with us."

Alison hid her wince when he set her none too gently on her feet. Careful not to move any more than necessary, she poked him in the chest. "For you information, I'm not selling anything. I thought I made that clear. And it has nothing to do with you anyway. I was talking to Dillon. I wouldn't have you on a silver platter!"

Ryder gripped her chin, running his thumb over her bottom lip, a satisfied smile curving his lips when she shivered. With the other hand, he made a slow trail with a wandering finger from her chin, down her neck, stopping at a spot right between her breasts, making both of her nipples tighten unbearably and flare to life.

His low tone, laced with promise and intent, sent an answering surge of need through her.

"Real soon I'm gonna make you eat those words."

Dillon's gentle hands turned her toward him, shooting a look of impatience at Ryder over her shoulder. "Look, I can understand how hearing about the clubs and seeing Rachel with Boone and Chase have given you the wrong idea about our town. In Desire, we take sex and our women very seriously. But Ryder's right. We don't know each other very well. Let's get you checked in and we'll talk over dinner."

He ran a hand though her hair, his eyes alight with erotic anticipation. "One thing you should know, though. Just like Boone and Chase, Ryder and I share."

Chapter Two

Reeling from Dillon's announcement, Alison could only look from one to the other in stunned silence. She found it hard to believe that two men, so different in personality, would even consider sharing a woman.

"You're kidding, right?"

Ryder's eyes raked over her, cold and assessing. "No. He's not kidding." He smiled lecherously, a dark brow going up. "Scared?"

Dillon laid his hand on her arm, the gentleness in his touch making her yearn to cuddle against him and beg him to teach her the way it could be between a man and a woman.

He smiled when she looked up at him. The tenderness in it had a calming effect, settling some of her butterflies and making her inch toward him. "We'll see you to your room."

Walking through the parking lot, she turned to make sure no one could overhear. "Okay, let me get this straight. Neither one of you ever—"

"Fucks?" The unmistakable sarcasm in Ryder's voice had her moving closer to Dillon.

Nodding, she looked straight ahead. "Yes. Neither one of you *fucks* another woman without the other?"

Dillon wrapped an arm around her shoulders and pulled her closer. "Not usually. It's something we learned about ourselves a long time ago. We moved to Desire because of it when we were in our midtwenties. We're both thirty-six now. We know what we want, Alison. We want a woman to build a future with. We want a mother for our children and a partner, one who would embrace a ménage marriage and do what it takes to make one work."

Not daring to look at Ryder, she looked up at Dillon through her lashes and bent closer, keeping her voice at a whisper.

"I'd rather just see you. I don't think your friend likes me."

Dillon smiled, but it didn't reach his eyes.

"I have eyes, Alison. How long do you think that would last before you let him into your bed? You'd feel guilty for wanting him, he'd feel bad about intruding on what we had. No, Alison. We start as we mean to go on, or we don't start at all."

Sliding a glance toward Ryder, she sighed in regret that she wouldn't be able to have such a gentle, decidedly masculine hunk, but if it meant dealing with the wild and far-too-good-looking Ryder, she'd have to pass.

Ryder seemed to enjoy her discomfort, brushing against her far too often for it to be accidental, the masculine lines of his body hard and unforgiving against her feminine curves. His arm brushed the curve of her breast as he shifted his hold on her bag. While she checked in at the front desk, he leaned over her, his cheek brushing against her hair at the same time he flirted with the beautiful, young hotel clerk.

Turning to glare at him, she opened her mouth to tell him to back off, snapping it shut again when he lifted a brow expectantly. She turned away, determined to ignore him, not wanting to give him the satisfaction of knowing he riled her.

Her growing lethargy left her too tired to deal with him anyway. When the young woman held out her room key, Alison breathed a sigh of relief, anxious to get to her room and away from both men.

The young woman slid a sidelong look and slow wink at Ryder.

"Would you like me to escort you?"

Dillon snatched the key before Alison could take it, shooting a dirty look at Ryder over her head before taking her arm.

"No, thanks. We know the way. Come on, Alison. You look done in."

Deciding it would take less energy to let them take her to her room than to stand in the lobby and argue about it, she fell into step beside him, her lethargy growing with every step.

A poster caught her attention, an advertisement for a place called *The Bar*, which stated that Friday night was ladies' night and women could drink for free.

Interesting.

Since an affair with Dillon no longer appeared to be an option, she could go there after grabbing a quick bite somewhere. Who knew? She might meet another man who would be willing to help her with her research and not make her feel like a jerk afterward.

Flanked by Dillon and Ryder, and aware of their scrutiny, she stared straight ahead, letting the idea roll around in her head. The more she thought about it, the more she liked it. She wouldn't have sex tonight, of course, but it would give her the opportunity to meet other men, hopefully one like Dillon.

If she found someone interesting, she could meet up with them after the seminar tomorrow and see where it led. She just wanted one fling before she left, one chance to feel good again and shake off the lingering effects of her time with Danny once and for all.

While walking through the lobby, her back started to tighten up again, and she knew from experience that the only way to relieve it would be to lie down for a while. The medicine had started to take effect, however, and she had trouble keeping her eyes open. Her legs felt heavy, and each step seemed to take an inordinate amount of energy. Not wanting to slow down, she clenched her jaw and kept going, desperate to get away from both of them and to fall into bed as soon as possible.

She looked neither right nor left as she walked between them, just staring straight ahead and concentrating on putting one foot in front of the other as they made their way down the hallway.

Dillon finally stopped, tugging her arm when she would have kept going.

"Here's your room. Are you sure you're all right?"

Alison nodded once, regretting it immediately as the hallway spun.

"I'm fine. Look, about dinner, I think I'm just going to take a walk around town later and grab something. Thanks anyway."

Dillon paused in the act of opening the door and turned to frown at her. "I don't think so. We'll pick you up at six."

Not about to get caught up in an argument, she said nothing as Dillon opened the door and she went inside. Avoiding their probing stares, she stood in the center of the room.

"Thank you for coming to get my truck, and for the ride. I'd appreciate the estimate as soon as you can get it ready. If I'm not here, you can leave a message at the front desk."

Ryder stood with his hands on his hips. "Sure thing, doll." His flip answer didn't match the intensity of his expression or the assessing look in his sharp green eyes. "You don't have to worry about me at dinner. I'll grab something at the club so the two of you can be alone."

Alison watched Ryder leave the room, his long legs eating up the ground in an apparent hurry to get away from her, jumping when he slammed the door behind him and wincing at the pull of tight muscle.

Sucking in a breath at the cold blade of the inexplicable slash of pain to her stomach, she blinked to force back tears. She didn't understand why it mattered so much that he wanted to get away from her, especially when she'd been trying to get away from him from the moment she'd met him.

But she couldn't deny that it hurt.

Dillon stared after Ryder for several long seconds before turning back to her, cupping her cheek, his eyes searching. "Alison, look at me."

Lifting her gaze, she sucked in a breath, struck again by the tenderness in the eyes of such an overwhelmingly masculine man. Her heart pounded nearly out of her chest when his hands went to her waist beneath her jacket.

His palms left a trail of heat in their wake as they slid higher, not stopping until they reached the outer curve of her breast. Her nipples beaded, tingling for his touch and poking at the front of her cotton shirt.

Her breath hitched, a moan escaping before she could prevent it. She hadn't been touched with tenderness in longer than she cared to think about and definitely hadn't expected to respond with such heat to a man as gentle as Dillon.

God, she needed this. Needed to be touched. Needed to feel again.

Seeing the way he eyed the swell of her breasts, she stepped forward, flattening her hands on his chest and pressing her breasts against him. Perhaps he was shy and needed encouragement.

He lifted his gaze to meet hers at the same time he lifted his hand, pushing her hair back from her face and threading his fingers through it, brushing his thumb back and forth over her cheek. He stared down at her, his gaze raking over her features as though memorizing them, the tenderness and desire in his eyes laced with amusement.

She'd never been so turned on by a look. She would do anything he wanted if only he would keep looking at her that way. Pressing against the hand caressing the curve of her breast, she licked her dry lips, whimpering when his eyes flared.

"Dillon, touch me. Please."

He hesitated only a second or two, his eyes becoming hooded, before he shifted his hand and placed it over her breast.

"You're so incredibly beautiful, and you don't even realize it, do you?"

Even through her shirt and bra, the friction and heat of it shocked her. Crying out, she grabbed his arms for support, pressing herself harder against his hand to encourage him. She'd never been held so carefully, but with such purpose before.

He only touched her head and her breast but, with such little effort, somehow managed to possess her, not allowing her to look away and increasing her need with every caress of his palm.

"You're starving, aren't you, Alison? Starving for the kind of attention a woman like you needs. Starving to be taken to your limits."

Closing her eyes, she savored the image his words invoked. Opening them again, she sighed. "God, yes. Please, Dillon. Take me there."

Dillon's eyes narrowed, his lips curving. "You're surprised that you're responding this way. You're not as brazen as you let on. Hell, you couldn't even look me in the eye when you offered yourself to me. Don't mistake my tenderness with shyness or inexperience, Alison. I'm capable of tenderness, but there's a darker side to me that any woman who took me on would have to accept."

Alison cried out again as he pinched her nipple, the jolt of heat from it going straight to her clit, making it throb with delicious anticipation.

She had soaked panties, her body trembled with need, and he hadn't even kissed her!

She'd always known she needed a man like him—strong, yet gentle, but the reality of having both wrapped in one man proved to be more intoxicating than she could have ever imagined.

"I've never done anything like this before, Dillon. I swear. I've never met anyone like you before. I need you. If you're worried about Ryder, he doesn't need to know."

Dillon leaned closer, brushing his lips against hers, tightening his hand in her hair to keep her from following. "Do you know what I would do to you right now if you were my woman?"

His low, seductive drawl oozed over her like molten desire, sending her lust soaring.

Licking her lips, she gasped as he used just the tip of his finger to tease her nipple and fisted her hands in his shirt in an attempt to bring him closer. She needed his kiss, needed to feel his mouth plunder hers, whimpering in her throat when he denied her.

"What would you do?" Her voice, barely more than a whisper, came out breathless and needy. Oh, the possibilities. Her pussy clenched just imagining the kinds of things he might have in store for her, things she'd probably never even heard of.

"I'd shove those tight jeans down to your thighs." His lips moved over her face, brushing over her eyes, her nose, her cheeks, letting her feel the warmth of his breath caressing her features with each soft-spoken word.

"Do you know it makes a woman feel more exposed to have her pants pulled only partially down while the rest of her is covered? It makes her feel naughty when only her ass is exposed. Or breasts. Or soft pussy. It focuses all of her attention there. I'd do that to you."

Alison couldn't speak, the whimpers in her throat almost continuous now. She couldn't open her eyes because each time she tried, Dillon moved his lips over them again. Being unable to see him made her senses sharper, made each touch of his finger on her nipple more intense, each word he spoke more arousing.

His hand changed positions, the possessiveness in the hand that cupped her breast unlike anything she'd ever experienced. Not rough or demanding, the slow, soft caress like loving strokes over a prized possession.

The low rumble in his voice made her tremble. "I would rip your panties from that beautifully rounded ass so that it was bare. The sound of the material ripping would excite you as much as it would excite me."

"Oh, God, Dillon, you're killing me. I've never heard anyone talk that way before. Please, Dillon. Touch me again. Kiss me."

The sharp pinch of her nipple made her knees buckle, and only his hold kept her from falling.

Crying out, she rubbed her thighs together as the throbbing became unbearable. She couldn't get enough air in her lungs, breathing heavily against the need raging inside her. Her abdomen tightened with each clench of her pussy, her clit feeling so swollen and heavy as though it had taken on a life of its own.

"I'm not finished telling you what I would do to you. Don't you want to hear it?"

Licking her lips, she managed to nod while gulping in air. "Yes, oh, God, yes!"

Using his finger to tease her nipple again, he nuzzled her jaw, speaking so slowly that each word was like a stroke to her clit. "I'd put you over my lap, where I could look my fill. I'd run my hand over that gorgeous ass, listening to your moans and cries of anticipation. You'd try to cover yourself, but I wouldn't let you. I'd hold both of your hands in one of mine so nothing would get in my way."

Dillon lifted his head, not speaking again until she opened her eyes. "That ass would be mine, wouldn't it, Alison? For that moment in time, you would give yourself over to me, wouldn't you, Alison?"

Alison swallowed heavily before speaking, her voice huskier than she'd ever heard it.

"Yes. Yours. Please, Dillon. Just this once, let me be yours. I won't tell Ryder. I promise. Just you and me. No one else would ever know."

She didn't know where the words came from, but they spilled from her with ease. She wanted him more than she'd ever thought she could want a man.

He smiled, a cool smile, his eyes darkening into two chips of blue ice.

"If you were mine, and that ass was mine, I would give you a sound spanking that you'd never forget for trying to pit me against Ryder. And for your information, when I have you, I'm sure as hell not making a secret of it. I would make sure the world knew you belonged to me!"

His cold tone penetrated before the meaning of his words, but when they did, she gasped and tried unsuccessfully to pull away.

"You wouldn't dare spank me! You're nothing but a brute. You're not gentle or nice at all!"

She couldn't believe she'd been so stupid. The way he'd gone into detail told her that he would carry out his threat with no hesitation at all.

Later on she'd deal with the fact that those little details he'd mentioned had aroused the hell out of her.

Dillon looked down to where his hand covered her breast again, the possessiveness in his eyes and in his touch both irritating and arousing.

Alison turned away, her face burning, a little surprised, and more than a little disappointed that he released her.

That made her even madder. She didn't know how to handle him, didn't know what he wanted from her, but it became increasingly obvious that she didn't have the experience to deal with a man like Dillon, after all.

Taking several steps away, she wrapped her arms around her middle, willing the lust still raging through her to disappear.

"I'm rescinding the offer. I don't know what got into me. I thought this was a town where a girl could find some fun. Obviously I was mistaken. Thanks again for the ride. Now, if you don't mind, I'd like to be alone."

With a faint smile that didn't quite reach his eyes, Dillon nodded and moved to the door, turning at the threshold. "Sure thing. And if you're looking for fun, be prepared. In Desire, you just might bite off more than you can chew. If your goal is to get the upper hand with a man, no amount of classes you take at the club is going to make any difference here. You might want to think about that. See you at six."

He closed the door behind him before she got a chance to respond.

Damn it, she'd already told him that she no longer wanted to have dinner with him.

Hadn't she?

To hell with it. If he was too hardheaded to listen, it wasn't her fault.

She looked at her watch and winced. Now that Dillon had gone, it felt like all the energy had been sucked out of her. She only had a little over an hour and a half to get showered, dressed, and get out of here before he arrived. She lifted her bag to the bed, pleased to notice it didn't hurt much at all. It took more energy than normal, but finally she got undressed and into her robe, comforted by the warm, fuzzy softness.

She reached for the covers before remembering that she'd have to set the alarm on her cell phone so she could be showered, dressed, and gone before Dillon came back. Grabbing her purse, she took it back with her to the bed and tossed it to the other side.

She pulled back the bedspread and carefully climbed between the cool, cotton sheets and curled into a comfortable position, hardly able to keep her eyes open. After unzipping the purse, she rummaged inside until she found her phone and pulled it out, cursing when her prescription bottles came out with it, rolled to the other side, and fell to the floor.

Not about to get out of her comfortable position to retrieve them, she set the alarm on her phone and laid it on the bed beside her next to her purse, unable to keep her eyes open any longer.

She'd just started to doze off when her cell phone rang. Cursing, she reached out for it without opening her eyes.

"H'lo?"

"Where the hell are you?"

With a groan, Alison rolled to her back, dropping the back of her other hand over her forehead. "It's really none of your business, Danny. Don't call me again."

"Don't hang up on me, bitch."

Not bothering to open her eyes, she smiled. "You sound a little upset. What's wrong? Afraid the judge, your second cousin twice removed or whatever the hell he is, is going to put you in jail where you belong?"

He laughed coldly. "No, bitch. I called to tell you that if you show up to testify against me, I've got friends who'll say it was self-defense. You attacked me, bitch."

Her eyes popped open, and she struggled into a sitting position. "Self-defense? Are you crazy? You're a hell of a lot bigger than I am."

"Not including your fat ass, of course."

Alison grimaced, wondering why his insults still had the power to hurt her. "Of course."

"They'll say you came after me with a knife when you caught me cheating on you."

"I didn't give a shit. It's not like it was the first time."

"But who's my best cousin Larry gonna believe, you or me? Don't forget, I've got a witness. Tammy's gonna say you came after me with a kitchen knife. *You* might be the one who ends up in jail."

Alison sighed and fell back against the pillows. Her stomach tightening painfully at the thought of the kind of trouble Danny could cause. "Don't call me again."

She hung up before he could answer, jabbing her finger on the off button and tossing the phone aside, her weariness coming back with a vengeance.

Damn it. Trust Danny to come up with something like that. Maybe she should just walk away, refuse to testify, and get on with her life.

Hell, she couldn't think about it now, not when she couldn't even keep her eyes open.

As she started to fall asleep, she couldn't help but think about Dillon and the kind of woman he and Ryder would fall for. Even if she couldn't be that woman, she wanted to be *like* her.

Damn it, she would *not* let Danny continue to intimidate her.

Remembering the tenderness in Dillon's beautiful blue eyes, she wished he was in the bed beside her so she could fall asleep cuddled against him. His strong arms wrapped around her would make everything else go away, and she could rest.

God, she was tired.

Tired of humiliation.

Tired of being afraid.

Tired of always being on guard.

Tired of hurting.

She hadn't been able to relax for so long.

She shifted uncomfortably at the memory of Ryder's mocking grin. She didn't want to think about Ryder and his dislike of her. She wanted to think of Dillon.

He would be the kind of man a woman could depend on when she needed him. He wouldn't be the kind of man who had to put a woman down because he felt threatened by her strength.

Why the hell did Dillon need to share her, and why the hell did it have to be with someone like Ryder, a man who could easily finish what Danny had already started and break her?

She needed something else.

She needed someone just like Dillon.

* * * *

Dillon looked over at Ryder as they pulled into the hotel parking lot, impatient to get back to Alison. "You're awfully quiet."

It hit him suddenly that Ryder had been more pensive than ever since they left the hotel earlier, not speaking unless absolutely necessary. Preoccupied with thoughts of Alison, Dillon hadn't even noticed it until now.

Ryder parked the truck, and to Dillon's surprise, left the engine running. "I'll be at the club."

With his hand on the door handle, Dillon paused and turned back, meeting Ryder's gaze. His best friend's carefully schooled features didn't fool him for a minute. "Are you serious? I know you said you wouldn't come with us, but I figured you were just pissed off. I thought you would have changed your mind. We're *both* supposed to have dinner with her tonight. Don't you dare screw this up."

Ryder's lip curled in a way that could never be mistaken for a smile and turned back to stare out the front window. "I don't think that's what she had in mind. Look, you want her, and she already made it clear she wants you. I can go fuck a woman in the club without you being there, you know? I think you should be able to go on a date without me. Three's a crowd and all that."

Dillon couldn't help but laugh. "Since when the hell is three a crowd? Are you trying to say that you don't want Alison? I know you better than that. You couldn't keep your eyes off of her."

Ryder turned to him then. "Yes, that's what I'm saying. I don't want her. Now get out of here. Zach and Law are in town, and tonight's the auction. I want to get my choice of the girls before they get there."

The playfulness in his tone didn't fool Dillon for a minute. "Something's up. You liked Alison a hell of a lot more than you're letting on. She was probably just a little surprised to realize she'd be taking on both of us. Cut her a little slack. Everyone else, well, everyone but Boone and Chase, had the same problem. We do this as we mean to go on. We're both attracted to her. Let's get to know her better. Something's off with her and it's driving me crazy."

Ryder sighed and stared out the front window again, and Dillon knew he did it to hide his expression. "What difference does it make? Hell, Dillon, I just met her. I don't like or dislike her, but I've had naked subs in the club who didn't come on as fast as she did. If I want easy, I'll go to the club, which is where I'm going now if you ever get the hell out of the truck."

Dillon wanted to knock some sense into his friend. "Damn it, Ryder. Alison's not like that and you know it. She couldn't even look at me when she said it and couldn't say it without blushing. She's playing at bravado. She's sweet, Ryder. Hell, even *you* should see that."

Willing his cock to behave, Dillon leaned toward his friend. "Christ, she's so responsive. It's like she's starving for attention. I barely touched her and she was ready to come. She kisses like an angel and has this way of melting against you—"

Ryder slammed the flat of his hand on the steering wheel and whirled on him. "I don't want to hear about it! Go take your angel out to dinner and fuck her all night. Just leave me out of it."

Dillon clenched his jaw in exasperation at his friend's stubbornness. Alison had Ryder shaken, a phenomenon Dillon had never witnessed before.

"She really got to you, didn't she? I don't know why the hell you're fighting it so much. Aren't you a little tired of coming home to an empty house every night? Damn it, Ryder, I want a wife, a family. I thought you did, too."

Ryder shook his head, smiling coldly. "And you think she's the one? You just met her, Dillon."

"So did you, and she's already got you tied up in knots."

Ryder clenched his jaw, a sure sign he wouldn't be changing his mind. "Are you getting out or are you coming with me?"

Shaking his head, Dillon got out of the truck, knowing Ryder wouldn't talk about what he didn't want to talk about until he was damned good and ready.

Frustrated, Dillon blew out a breath. "Fine. Act like an ass. Have fun at the club."

"I will."

Dillon slammed the truck door and watched Ryder pull away, his brows going up at the squeal of tires.

No, Ryder wasn't nearly as unaffected as he claimed, but he'd have to work that out on his own.

Not about to let his friend's bad mood ruin his plans for the evening, he crossed the parking lot, turning to watch Ryder park the truck next door and get out, slamming the door behind him.

Mentally shrugging, he went inside and headed for Alison's room, wishing he'd had the time to knock some sense into Ryder. They'd been best friends since first grade, but not until they started high school and met Reese Preston did they ever even hear about ménages.

A new idea that dealt with sex intrigued both of them at first, a curiosity that soon became an obsession.

Walking down the hallway toward Alison's room, he smiled, remembering how fumbling they'd been and how competitive. Over time they'd learned how much pleasure a woman could get when she had the attention of two men and how eagerly she came back for more.

For two highly sexed young men, that kind of decadent power over women couldn't be ignored, and they'd taken advantage of it at every opportunity.

They'd heard about the town of Desire from Reese, and when the club opened years earlier, they'd joined and moved here, full of excitement and anxious for change. They'd quit their jobs as mechanics and opened their own garage and lived the dream.

They did the work they loved best and, while living in a town like no other, somehow became a part of it and enjoyed all the pleasures to be found there.

They'd always been careful. They'd only taken women who knew the score, and they'd made sure the women walked away with smiles on their faces.

Life had been good.

Until their friends started finding women, amazing women, to spend the rest of their lives with.

Women who made them happier than Dillon had ever seen his friends before—women who'd brought the town back to life and reinforced the way of life the founding fathers of Desire had set in motion over a hundred years ago.

It started with Jesse Tyler, now Jesse Erickson, and hadn't stopped since, each new marriage breathing life back into a town Dillon had come to love.

Seeing some of their friends and neighbors almost ecstatically in love with their new wives made Dillon begin to want more. He found himself watching them and wanting what they had.

Trips to the club had become more about talking with his married friends than competing with his single friends for the attention of the women there.

He'd also seen a change in Ryder, seen the way his best friend became fascinated by the relationships of those lucky enough to have found women who embraced their new lifestyles.

He'd sure as hell seen the way Ryder looked at Alison this afternoon. His friend hadn't been able to keep his eyes off of her, his gaze returning to her repeatedly when she wasn't looking. Even more telling, instead of laughing off her rejection, he'd been hurt by it.

Ryder never cared enough about a woman to be hurt.

No matter what Ryder said, Dillon knew he wanted to be with Alison tonight, but it was probably better that he stayed away from her until he could come to grips with his attraction to her.

He hoped like hell that the activities at the club tonight and being around the other men could snap Ryder out of his broodiness.

Arriving at Alison's door, he thought about his own growing need for a wife, a need that plagued him with loneliness. The desire to have a woman they could claim as their own grew steadily, a woman they could get to know intimately in more ways than just sex. Hell, he wasn't a fucking kid anymore.

He wanted a woman who would respond to his authority, who would trust that he would never hurt her, a woman whose body and moods he could learn as intimately as his own.

Only now, this woman had a face and a name.

Alison.

Filled with anticipation, he knocked on the door to Alison's room, determined to spend the time over dinner getting to know her better. His head tried to tell him to slow down, but his body wanted full steam ahead.

Although she tried to act the part, she didn't have half the sophistication other women he'd known possessed. She was so fucking cute he wanted to take a bite out of her.

He couldn't stop staring at her, from her dark, shining hair with bangs that accented her beautiful doe-brown eyes to a lush body that just begged to be taken. Her dimples showed each time she flashed that impish smile, so sweet and adorable it made his heart race.

And that ass. God help her when he finally got his hands on that ass.

He knocked again, frowning when he realized he'd heard nothing at all from inside. "Alison, it's Dillon."

After knocking again with no response, he clenched his jaw in irritation and started out. He'd almost reached the front door when he saw Ethan Sullivan, one of the owners of the hotel, in a conversation with the woman who'd been working at the front desk earlier.

Ethan grinned when he saw him and held up a finger in a gesture for Dillon to wait until he'd finished. Once done, he approached, still smiling.

"Hey, are you here to pick up that woman you dropped off earlier? I haven't had the pleasure of meeting her yet. Where's Ryder?"

Irritated that Alison had apparently left the hotel to get out of having dinner with him, Dillon snapped. "Ryder's at the club. I think I'll join him. I came to pick up Alison for dinner, but she's not here. Her truck broke down right outside of town and we towed her in. I was supposed to have dinner with her here."

He shrugged to hide his disappointment. "I guess she left. You didn't happen to see a woman leave here, did you?"

Ethan shook his head, his smile falling. "I didn't, but I can look on the computer and see what time she opened the door last."

Dillon blinked. "You can do that?"

Looking over his shoulder as he led Dillon to the front desk, Ethan grinned. "Lucas did it for us. Before we could only tell when a guest used the key card, but after all the meetings we've had about protecting the women, he designed this. He just installed it a couple of weeks ago. Not all of the rooms have it yet, but we make sure to put any single women who check in into one of the rooms that do. We can't spy on them, but in the middle of the night, we'll know if their door opened and can check the security cameras to see if they left or if someone broke in."

Standing behind the desk, he began tapping the keys of his computer and scowling. "Are you sure she's not in there? This shows that her door hasn't opened since she checked in. Hell, I'm going to have to call Lucas if this thing isn't working right."

A little prickling began at the back of Dillon's neck. "Nothing of Lucas's ever malfunctions. I'm going to go try again."

Ethan looked a little worried himself as he fell into step beside him. "Are you sure she's just not answering the door? Did you or Ryder piss her off or something?"

Dillon shrugged. "Or something. Look, if she doesn't want to go to dinner, that's fine, but I want to make sure she's all right before I leave. She looked a little pale earlier and really tired, but I don't know her well enough to be sure."

Realizing his anger at that was totally unwarranted didn't make it any less real.

Arriving at her room again, he banged on the door, this time hard enough to shake it on its hinges. "Alison, damn it, open this door."

Ethan sighed and shook his head. "We don't usually yell at our guests, or try to scare the hell out of them. Maybe you'd better let me handle this."

Frustrated and pissed off at Alison's apparent attempt to avoid seeing him, he folded his arms across his chest. "Fine. Hurry up, though. I want to get to the club while the night's young."

Damn it, how the hell did a woman he'd just met get to him so easily?

It was those damned doe eyes. And dimples. That damned attempt at sophistication she couldn't pull off.

The way she melted under his hands.

Fuck, he had it bad already.

Raising a brow, Ethan said nothing and knocked on the door again, this time not quite as hard. "Miss Bennett, this is Ethan Sullivan, one of the owners of the hotel. Are you all right?"

Hearing a low groan from inside, Dillon lowered his arms, fear making his gut clench. "Did you hear that? Get out of the way."

He stepped back, ready to kick the door down.

Ethan jumped in front of him. "No! Don't you dare go kicking my doors in! Jesus, how can someone usually so calm and in control fly off the handle so fast? I expect this from Ryder, not you. I have the master key."

Dillon cursed and tried to rip it out of his hand, but Ethan jerked it out of his reach. "Open the door, damn it. Something's wrong. I've got to get to her."

He didn't bother to ask himself why the thought of her being sick or hurt tied painful knots in his stomach. He just knew that it did.

Ethan glared at him over his shoulder and knocked again. "Miss Bennett, I'm coming inside."

Dillon shifted impatiently as Ethan used his own master key to open the door. As soon as the door clicked open, he pushed his way inside and raced to the bed where Alison rolled to her back and groaned again.

She blinked, raising herself to an elbow and pushing her long, dark hair out of her eyes, leaving her bangs sticking out in all directions. Groaning again when she saw him, she plopped back down onto the pillow and closed her eyes.

"Get out."

It came out thready and weak, tying the knots in Dillon's stomach even tighter. Moving her bag and purse from the other side of the bed to a nearby chair, he never took his eyes from her.

Ethan moved to stand at the foot of the bed. "Ma'am, are you all right? We've been knocking at the door and heard you moan. Do you need the doctor?"

Dillon ignored her one-eyed glower and sat on the edge of the bed where he'd made room, reaching out a hand to touch her flushed face. "Are you sick? Your face is flushed."

He tried not to think about how sexy she looked with her flushed cheeks and mussed hair, like a woman who'd recently been well tumbled. No matter how hard he tried to resist, his eyes kept going to the flash of leg exposed as she simultaneously struggled to sit up and pull the robe more securely around her.

Her movements were clumsy, her attempts to fight off his efforts to help her weak. "No, I'm not sick. I was asleep. What kind of hotel is this that a woman can't even sleep without someone barging in?"

Ethan smiled apologetically. "I'm sorry, ma'am. We were worried when you didn't answer the door and then when we heard a moan…"

Dillon laid the back of his hand on her forehead, not liking the glassy look in her eyes. "We're supposed to go to dinner, remember?"

She pouted, sticking out that full bottom lip in an entirely unpretentious way, probably not even realizing she was doing it. The naturalness of the gesture filled him with the overwhelming urge to roll her under him and kiss her until he'd branded her as his own.

Oh, hell. He had it *really* bad.

Pushing her bangs back, Alison stared at him, the unfocused look in her eyes jabbing an icy wedge into the pit of his stomach. "I said I didn't want to go out to dinner with you. You share and Ryder hates me."

Ethan lifted his brow at that. "Well, you certainly seem to know each other better than I thought. I guess I'll leave you two alone."

"No, take your friend with you. I want to sleep."

He turned, pausing as he stared at something on the floor. "Did you take something?"

Dillon looked up at that, his stomach dropping when Ethan bent and retrieved a prescription bottle from the floor. And then another.

Ethan frowned as he read the labels and looked up, meeting Dillon's eyes. "This is a painkiller, a strong one at that. And the other...I don't know." Kneeling on the other side of the bed, he touched Alison's shoulder, shaking it when her eyes started to close. "How many did you take?"

Alison sighed and started to slump toward Ethan, but Dillon wrapped an arm around her and pulled her toward him. "I only took one of each and they make me sleepy. Just go away."

Dillon snatched the bottles out of Ethan's hand and read them himself. "Are you in pain?"

Her words came out mumbled and slurred. "Not'nymore. Go 'way."

Alarmed, he tilted her head back, but her eyes had already closed again. "Do you usually fall asleep like this? Alison?" Dillon shook her, but other than moaning again, she didn't answer. He looked up at Ethan. "Look, I don't like this. I'm staying here with her. I'm going to call Doc and see what the hell these other pills are."

After a brief phone call with Dr. Hansen, Dillon felt slightly better.

"He said that it's a muscle relaxer and that if she takes these together, it could put her to sleep for several hours. Look, Ethan. I can't leave her alone like this. Would you really feel comfortable knowing one of your guests, a woman, was passed out from medication and all alone?"

Ethan sighed and raked a hand through his hair. "Of course not. But she's a guest, Dillon. I don't want to invade her privacy."

"I just want to make sure she's all right. She's new here, and if she has a problem, I need to call somebody. I'll let her sleep for a little while longer and then order something to eat. If she's taking pain medicine, I don't want her going all night with nothing in her stomach." Dillon laid her back gently on the bed, not having any idea what part of her body she'd taken the pain medicine for.

The realization that he knew so little about her, even though he'd started to feel protective and possessive toward her, hit him hard.

Ethan looked torn, rubbing a hand over the back of his neck. "Hell, Dillon. I hate letting someone in a woman's room, especially when she told us to go, but I don't want her left alone if she's sick or in pain. I trust you, but you promise me right now that nothing will happen here tonight, not even if she wants it to. She's taken prescription medicine and is obviously somewhat incapacitated. Promise me."

Insulted, Dillon came to his feet. "I don't rape women, for God's sake!"

Ethan straightened to his full height and glared at him. "I never said you did. You're awfully fucking touchy about a woman you just met."

Dillon shot a glance at the bed when Alison mumbled and stirred, lowering his voice. "She's in good hands with me. I'll watch out for her and order something for her to eat a little later. That's it. I can't just leave her alone."

When his cell phone rang, Ethan waved a hand and started out of the room. "I trust you with her. Let me know if you need anything."

He answered his phone, turning back to look at Alison again. "Sullivan. Yeah, Brandon, everything's all right. Hold on."

Holding the phone to his chest, Ethan smiled while Dillon laid his palm over Alison's exposed leg and, finding it cold, hurriedly tucked it inside the blanket. "Are you sure you're all right with her? Do you want me to call Ryder?"

Afraid she might get chilled, Dillon pulled the blanket up to cover Alison completely, tucking it in around her. "We're fine."

He forced himself to look up at Ethan, not wanting to take his eyes from Alison's sleeping form. She looked so lost and defenseless, nothing at all like the woman who'd fluttered her lashes and offered herself to him only a short time ago.

The possessive instincts he thought he'd buried long ago didn't just float gently to the surface. They seemed to all break free at once, bombarding his system until he couldn't breathe.

Surprised to see that his hand shook, he tightened it into a fist.

"I promise to call Doc if she needs him. I know painkillers can really knock you out." Turning back to Alison, he smoothed her hair back from her face, frowning at the small scar he found at her hairline that looked fairly new.

"I wonder what she's taking painkillers for."

"You'll have to ask her that when she wakes up. Dillon, uh, are you sure you don't want me to call Ryder?"

"I'm sure."

When Ethan's brows went up at his abrupt answer, Dillon sighed, straightening. "Ryder and Alison didn't exactly hit it off. I'll call him in a bit and let him know I'm staying here for a while."

Ignoring Ethan's speculative look, he pulled an empty chair closer to the bed. Without taking the time to consider his actions, he took Alison's hand in his, frowning at the series of tiny scars over the back of it. He wanted to look at the other, but she had it curled against her cheek, and he didn't want to wake her.

Ethan nodded once. "Call if you need me." Lifting the phone back to his ear, he resumed his conversation.

Dillon could hear him telling Brandon about Alison as he stepped out into the hallway, while closing the door quietly behind him.

Wondering what happened to her and why she needed to take painkillers, he clenched his jaw. Releasing her hand, he ran his fingers over her dark, sleek hair, smiling to find it as silky as it looked.

"Well, Alison, we're alone, but this isn't exactly the way I'd planned it."

He couldn't help but smile when she pursed her lips in her sleep and sighed.

He ran his fingertip over the outer shell of her ear, marveling that an ear could look so delicate. "Alison Bennett, what the hell is it about you that has me so turned inside out?"

Sitting back in the surprisingly comfortable chair, he toed off his shoes and settled back, lifting his feet onto the bed and staring at her. She'd seemed so shy and nervous on the ride to town and had blushed a deep pink when asking questions about Rachel's marriage to two men. Even in the parking lot when she'd propositioned him, she wouldn't meet his eyes and her face had turned bright red.

She didn't seem like the kind of woman who offered herself so readily, and her reaction to learning that he and Ryder shared their women would have been comical if Ryder hadn't gotten so bent out of shape about it.

After several minutes, he got up to turn on a low light, not wanting her to wake up to a dark room. Making himself as comfortable as he could, he turned on the television, muting it before digging his cell phone out of his pocket, staring at it as he contemplated calling Ryder, and then tossed it onto the nightstand.

With a sigh, he ignored the television and leaned back to stare at Alison.

As he watched, she shifted in her sleep, rolling to her left side and once again sticking her leg out from under the covers. The robe she wore parted when she moved her leg and slid completely off of her hip.

Dillon stilled, holding his breath. The belt of her robe had come loose, and her right side had become almost completely uncovered, only her arm in front of her holding the robe over her breast. Staring in fascination at the long expanse of skin now exposed, Dillon dragged his feet from the bed and knelt beside it, his movements slow and quiet so as not to wake her.

Only the bunched blanket kept her mound from his view, a view he desperately wanted to enjoy.

Unable to take his eyes from her creamy skin, he leaned forward, frowning at the scar on her hip. It looked fairly fresh, perhaps several months old. The pink line was straight, not curved or jagged. The faint outline around it appeared to be where stitches had been.

He couldn't help but run his fingers lightly over it, stilling when she moaned. Once she settled again, he bent to touch his lips to the scar as though kissing it would somehow make it better.

Anger at himself for not being with her when she'd been hurt made no sense at all, but it was there, gnawing at him.

He couldn't ignore the length of soft skin exposed, the need to touch her irresistible.

Keeping his touch light, he ran his fingers over her outer thigh to her knee. On impulse, he trailed his fingers around and over the back of her knee, smiling to himself when she moaned and rolled to her back, her arm falling to the side.

"You liked that, didn't you, baby?"

"Dillon."

He froze, staring at her in stunned delight.

He didn't think his cock could get much harder, and his hands literally itched to touch her.

He had no rights with her right now, but he vowed to himself that he would.

And soon.

As carefully as possible, he covered her again, tucking the robe and blanket around her. Grimacing as he moved, he settled into the chair again, adjusting his pants to ease the almost painful throbbing of his cock.

"Who are you, Alison Bennett?" Watching as she shifted in her sleep, he smiled when she stuck her foot out from under the covers again.

So, his little darling didn't like having her foot covered when she slept. He found it cute as hell, such a minor thing, but incredibly intimate. He frowned thoughtfully when his cock stirred, amazed that he found such a little thing so arousing.

Picking up his cell phone again, he ran his thumb over the numbers, thinking about the look on Ryder's face as he pulled away. He couldn't get over the feeling that his friend should know what was going on with Alison.

He started to dial, and just as quickly disconnected.

Ryder was probably knee deep in women by now and wouldn't welcome the call. Fuck it. If he didn't answer, Dillon would just leave a message.

Staring at Alison, he dialed, resigned to the fact that he wouldn't be able to walk away from her anytime soon. He smiled at the warm feeling that settled over him and the surge of anticipation at the hunt ahead of him and waited for Ryder to answer.

Chapter Three

Ryder sat at the bar in Club Desire, frustrated, pissed off with himself, and wondering why he'd thought coming here tonight would be a good idea.

No, he knew why he'd come and sure as hell wouldn't lie to himself about it.

He'd come with the sole intention of wiping the image of the look on Ally's sweet face when she offered herself to Dillon out of his mind.

She'd been red and flustered, her adorable attempt at acting the seductress more arousing than anything he could remember.

She'd fucking blindsided him.

Learning about Rachel's relationship with Boone and Chase, she'd been both embarrassed and intrigued.

The combination made him hard as a rock, the growing need for her making him ill tempered and restless. When she'd offered herself to Dillon, he'd had the almost uncontrollable need to throw her over his shoulder and storm off with her. After several hours of wild sex, she would be putty in his hands, and that sweet mouth and luscious body would be all his.

Fuck, he couldn't even stop thinking about her for more than a few minutes at a time.

He should have had some kind of warning.

How the hell was he supposed to handle having the rug pulled out from under him without having some kind of warning?

Determined to forget all about the adorable brat that had somehow wormed her way into his head and consumed his thoughts, he focused his attention on his surroundings.

The small stage had already been set up in preparation for tonight's activities, something he usually looked forward to.

Tonight, he couldn't seem to give a damn, which pissed him off even more.

What was Dillon doing to her right now?

Fuck.

He looked at his watch, only to see that only five minutes had passed since the last time he'd looked at it.

Dillon would probably end up spending the night with Alison, fucking her senseless, and wouldn't come home until morning.

"Where's Dillon?"

Sighing, he scrubbed a hand over his face and considered leaving. He'd been asked the same question at least a dozen times since he got here. He turned his head to meet Rio Erickson's gaze as he slid onto the barstool next to him.

"Dillon's on a date."

Rio's brow went up. He looked like he wanted to say something but snapped his mouth shut and nodded.

Staring back at the stage, Ryder took a sip of his beer. "We towed her truck in when it broke down just outside of town. She's staying at the hotel. Her name's Ally—Alison."

Frowning down into his beer, he wondered why the hell he'd volunteered that information, and tried not to think of how the way Ally's name just rolled off his tongue. "Where's Clay?"

"Right here." Clay took the seat on the other side of him and ordered a drink for himself. "Jesse and Kelly are busy setting up a display at the club for tomorrow's demonstration. We drove her over and carried all the stuff in, so we thought we'd come over and have a beer while we wait for her. Where's Dillon?"

"On a date." Ryder gritted his teeth together and slumped his shoulders, leaning over his beer, and stared straight ahead, watching in the mirror as Clay and Rio shared a look over his head.

After a pregnant pause, Rio took a sip of his own beer. "You not interested in her?"

Knowing Rio and Clay's history, Ryder didn't get offended at the question. They'd shared women for years until Clay met a woman Rio couldn't stand. When Clay got her pregnant and married her, it had been the beginning of a long road of unhappiness for both of them. They'd each married and had children, but neither could get over their desire to share a woman.

Once their boys got older and they divorced their wives, they'd both thought it too late to find the happiness they'd missed.

Until Jesse came to town to visit her sister.

They'd taken one look at her and fallen head over heels.

He'd never really believed it had happened so fast.

Hell, she'd probably blindsided both of them, too.

Women like that should have some kind of warning attached to them.

Now Jesse was married to both Clay and Rio and Ryder had never seen his friends happier. Even now their desire to get back to their wife was evident in the way they both kept glancing toward the window, and the fact that they both kept checking the display on the cell phones they'd placed on the bar in front of them.

He didn't doubt for a second that as soon as the phone rang, they'd jump on it and light out of the club as if their asses were on fire.

Lucky bastards.

This restlessness each time he saw his married friends with their women had to stop. He had no intention of losing his freedom, especially to a shy little brat with big brown eyes and cute little dimples and the curviest ass he'd ever laid eyes on.

Fuck.

Ryder took another sip of his now warm beer and grimaced. "We didn't exactly hit it off. It's no big deal. She won't be in town long, anyway."

Clay shrugged. "You've dated other women separately before, fucked them separately here. Just don't make the same mistake we made and settle for anything less than what you really want."

Ryder shrugged, saying nothing. There really wasn't anything to say.

A half smile played at his lips when King came into the room leading four women, naked except for the masks over their eyes, to play the game they all looked forward to each month. Their hands had been tied behind their backs and, despite their squeals and struggles, they were eager participants.

The identities of the women changed from month to month, the waiting list for this particular game longer than anyone could have imagined, but the game remained the same. The women got to live out a fantasy, and the men got a beautiful and willing woman to enjoy for the evening. Each woman had the same safe word for this game. Bull's-eye.

For the men who played it, having the same word each time made it easier, and there was never any confusion.

The women would have been stripped by King, Royce, and Blade, blindfolded, and had their hands tied behind their backs in preparation of the auction that would be taking place in just a few minutes.

The women would then be turned over to the man or men who'd won them.

They would be "inspected" on stage and in front of an enthusiastic audience in a way guaranteed to arouse them. The men enjoyed that part as much as the women, teasing the women until their juices coated their thighs and their arousal had been raised to a fevered pitch.

Rio leaned on the bar, his lips twitching at the boisterous crowd, and had to raise his voice to be heard. "What's she look like?"

Shrugging again, Ryder pushed the warm beer aside and ordered another. "She's cute. Long, dark hair. Short. Curvy. She's got big, sad eyes and..." Realizing he'd already said too much, he snapped his mouth shut and took a sip of his fresh beer.

Clay nodded and leaned closer to be heard. "Those sad eyes'll get you every time. When Jesse first got here, hers damned near broke my heart."

Ryder snuck a look at his watch again. "I think I'm going home now. Not much going on tonight anyway."

Clay raised a brow and looked pointedly toward the stage. "You're kidding, right? You and Dillon usually bid on one of these girls together. You're not going to bid solo tonight?"

"No."

Clay and Rio exchanged another one of those looks and settled back to watch the show.

Rio chuckled. "Law and Zach are here tonight. Hunter and Remington. Lucas, Devlin, and Caleb. Logan's here. John and Michael. Hell, even the Madisons are here. Not enough girls to go around, which means King arranged everything this month. He loves the excitement of having the men worked up and fighting over them. The bidding's going to be fierce."

Ryder shrugged and said nothing. As soon as the other men got into a bidding frenzy, he could make his escape and no one would even notice.

He watched in disinterest as Royce and King secured each of the women to a post in the semilit back of the stage and Royce brought the first woman forward into the light.

His interest reappeared when he saw that the woman had long, dark hair that fell in a silk curtain down her back, much like Ally's.

His eyes automatically trailed down her body, taking in her lush curves as his gaze slid to her bare mound. He reached for his glass, taking another sip of beer to ease the dryness in his mouth as he wondered if Ally kept her mound bare.

Irritated at the direction his thoughts had taken, he looked away. It didn't matter to him. She preferred Dillon and would be gone soon anyway.

Assuring himself he didn't give a shit what she did, he turned back to see Hunter and Remington move forward.

Hunter could always be counted on to rile up the men and usually prolonged the bidding by demanding that each part of the women be displayed and inspected. He had a hell of a dark side, which would increase the excitement in the room even more. He and Remington wouldn't bid seriously until the last woman had been led up on stage and then would play with her mercilessly before they finally topped the highest bid.

Hunter stepped forward, leaning against the raised stage, his usual place at the auctions, and scanned the table of items set up for their pleasure. "Are her nipples sensitive?"

Royce grinned, knowing the women couldn't see it and used his coldest tone. "It's your job to inspect the property you're bidding on."

Hunter picked up the small whip from the table, one that had just a flat piece of leather at the end. To the delight of the crowd, he reached up with it and traced the piece of leather over one the woman's nipples.

Her reaction, although expected, excited the crowd.

She cried out and twisted, trying to escape Royce's grip, her excitement at the game evident. "No. Don't touch me."

Royce lifted her to her toes. "Behave yourself or I'll paddle your ass right here in front of everyone. Now stick those breasts out and show them what they're getting."

"Go to hell."

Hunter brought the tip of the whip down on her nipple with a snap, but remained silent so she wouldn't know who'd delivered it.

Not knowing where it came from, or even if her future master had delivered the stroke, would make her nervous and increase her level of excitement.

At her cry, King lifted her chin from the other side. "You've been told to behave. Do you really want to set a bad example for your new masters?"

Even from where he sat, Ryder saw her shiver. It had already become obvious that she wanted to be dominated, to have a master who would overcome her struggles.

She wanted a fight and wanted to be taken.

Remembering the fire that flashed in Ally's eyes, he groaned at the rush of blood to his cock, engorging it and making sitting here downright painful.

Shifting his position, he took another sip of his beer and watched the stage.

As he'd expected, Devlin raised the bid.

"I want to see her clit."

Even from here, he could hear the woman's gasp of excitement over the sudden silence in the room.

As Royce held the woman still and hooked a foot around hers, King used his own foot to pull the other toward him, effectively spreading her legs so wide her thighs trembled. Reaching down, King separated her folds, exposing her clit and pussy to the crowd.

The men smiled and looked at each other when she whimpered, and her knees gave out.

Royce smacked her ass, making her jolt. "Stand up straight so you can be inspected. Stick that pussy out. These men want to see what they're buying."

Her skin glowed beneath the bright light shining on her, the glistening of her inner thighs clearly visible. Her limbs shook with the effort to stand still as Hunter teased her clit with the tip of the whip.

Remington leaned back in his chair, propping his feet on another in front of him, clearly enjoying himself. "Turn her around. Let's see her ass."

Grinning, Royce turned her to the excited yells of the crowd.

Clay chuckled from beside him. "These guys sure know how to get the woman all worked up. Look how hard she's shaking. I wouldn't be surprised if she comes right there on stage."

Rio laughed softly from his other side. "They won't let her. It's not like anyone in this room, other than the Madisons, hasn't had enough practice. They're just as worked up. It wasn't so long ago that we would have been right in there with them."

Clay shook his head and looked at his phone again. "Christ, Jesse's taking a long time."

Ryder's cock throbbed as he thought about exposing Ally in the same way as the woman on the stage, and no matter how hard he fought it, the vision just wouldn't go away. With her innate shyness, it would be more of a thrill to make her expose herself to him. He'd bet his truck that her false bravado would melt at his demands, but if he taught her the pleasure she could receive by obeying him, she would do it.

His cock jumped painfully, and he swallowed a groan along with another sip of beer.

A voice called from the crowd. "Bend her over. Spread her ass cheeks. I want to see that tight hole."

Ryder's lips twitched at the distressed cries from the other women standing bound at the back of the stage. The knowledge that they would be subjected to the same kind of treatment would heighten their arousal, one of the reasons they all did it.

So the other women would know.

And anticipate.

If he ever had a woman of his own, he'd make sure to let her know what he had planned for her, teasing himself, Dillon, and her. The image of a naked Ally between him and Dillon flashed through his mind, and he quickly took another sip of his beer and pushed it away.

Sobering, he sighed and looked away from the crowd by the stage.

For years, Dillon had talked about finding a woman and the two of them settling down with her. He'd gone along with it, never believing it would happen.

He'd been right.

Dillon had already started to fall for Ally, and the two of them seemed to get along better without him in the middle.

Restless now, he looked back at the stage in time to see Caleb squirting a healthy amount of lube onto his middle finger.

"I want to see how tight her ass is before I bid again."

Oh, hell. The mental image of bending Ally over and lubing her for his exploration of her luscious ass had moisture leaking from his cock.

The woman's squeal brought him back to the present, and he looked, smiling as she fought Royce and King's hold. She cursed and screamed but never used her safe word and actually arched her back and spread her legs wider.

Caleb grinned deviously as he approached her and ran a hand over her ass before separating her cheeks with a firm hand, lifting them, and exposing her puckered opening. With no teasing, he pushed past the tight ring of muscle and into her.

The silence that followed was filled with erotic tension as she stood on her toes and whimpered, only to shudder on a moan when Caleb began to move his finger, fucking her ass with it for the enjoyment of the audience.

"Oh, yeah. She's tight. She'll take my cock real good. She likes having her ass filled. It'll be used well tonight." He put in the final bid and slid his finger from her.

To thunderous applause, Caleb led the flushed woman off the stage toward where Devlin and bored-looking Lucas stood waiting.

As they led her to one of the rooms set up for tonight, Ryder fought an irrational surge of jealousy. The dark-haired beauty reminded him too much of Ally for comfort.

Disgusted with himself, he came to his feet with the intention of leaving. When his cell phone rang, he dug it out, hoping it was work related. Seeing Dillon's number on the display, he cursed and actually considered not answering. Staring at the phone, he took another sip of beer to ease his suddenly dry throat.

"You gonna get that?"

Without looking up at Clay's question, Ryder sighed and took the call, lifting the phone to his ear. "You finished already? Did you even feed her before you fucked her?"

Ignoring Clay and Rio's almost identical looks of surprise, Ryder headed for the door just as the bidding started for the next woman.

Dillon paused before answering, his tone cool. "No, we haven't eaten yet. That's why I'm calling."

Ryder kept walking in an effort to get away from the noise. "Why, to tell me how good she was?"

He hated the bitter words as soon as they came out of his mouth but couldn't seem to help himself.

Another long silence followed, making him feel even worse, before Dillon spoke again.

"Look, I just called to tell you I'm spending the night here. I'll see you some time tomorrow." Dillon disconnected before Ryder could say anything else, which was probably a good thing.

Cursing, and even more disgusted with himself, he went through the door Sebastian, the butler, held open and started down the steps just as Ethan and Brandon appeared at the bottom.

Brandon's smile fell when he saw him. "Don't tell me the auction's over."

Shaking his head, Ryder started past them. "No, they're on the second woman now. You'd better hurry. It's a full house tonight."

Ethan nodded. "So you're leaving to go sit with Dillon. Good, he looked really shaken. I told him if he needs something to call me. When I checked on them a few minutes ago, she'd already gone back to sleep."

Ryder stopped in his tracks, spinning to grab Ethan's arm. "What the hell are you talking about?"

Furious that Ethan had obviously spent time with Ally, he clenched his hand into a fist at his side. Reminding himself that he had no reason to be angry, he took a deep breath and let it out slowly.

"I don't give a damn. Fuck her all you want to. I'm going home."

Releasing Ethan's arm, he turned away again, only to have Ethan grab his arm and pull him up short. He was so angry that he actually started to swing, but came up short, even before Ethan moved to block his punch.

No piece of ass was worth losing a good friend.

Ethan released his arm, but got in his face.

"What the hell are *you* talking about? Fuck her all I want to? Are you out of your mind? I let Dillon in when she didn't answer the door, and he hurried up and covered her leg so I couldn't even see that. She took some pain medication and muscle relaxer, and it knocked her out. It scared the hell out of Dillon. He's sitting with her to make sure she's all right. Hell, he's like a fucking watchdog with her."

"What?" Ryder's stomach dropped. "Pain pills? She's hurt? Why the hell didn't he tell me that?" He spun away, racing to his truck. With squealing tires, he made the short ride to the hotel next door, one that seemed longer than normal, cursing himself as he recalled his conversation with Dillon.

Tense with fury, he strode to her room. Banging on the door with more force than necessary didn't make him feel any better. As soon as Dillon threw the door open, Ryder stormed inside.

"What the fuck's going on? What's wrong with Ally?"

* * * *

Alison woke from a sound sleep to the sounds of yelling and banging. Wondering if she'd fallen asleep with the television on, she rolled to her back, breathing a sigh of relief that once again she'd defeated the pain. Recognizing Ryder's angry tone, she frowned and opened her eyes just in time to see him storm past Dillon into her hotel room and toward her.

"What the hell's wrong with you?"

Blinking at the attack, she searched her memory for something that would explain why he and Dillon would be in her room. Alarmed at the fierce look on Dillon's face as he shut the door and came to sit on a chair that now sat at her bedside, she met his searching gaze before slanting a look at Ryder.

"According to my ex-boyfriend and you, any number of things."

Not liking how vulnerable she felt lying in bed with Ryder looming over her, Alison struggled to a sitting position, pulling her robe tighter around her and trying unsuccessfully to avoid Dillon's attempt to help her.

She looked around, immediately remembering everything and patted the bed beside her. "What time is it? Where's my phone? Where's my purse?"

Damn it, why hadn't her alarm gone off? She groaned inwardly when she remembered she'd turned her phone off after Danny's call.

Now she found herself alone in her hotel room with Dillon and Ryder and only a robe for protection.

Dillon nodded toward the other chair. "Your purse is over there. Your cell is on the dresser." He picked up her prescription bottles from the end table next to him and shook them.

"And your pills are right here. You want to tell me what these are for?"

Memories of what happened right before he left the room came flooding back. She'd almost convinced herself that it had been a dream, but the look in his eyes said otherwise. Filled with knowledge and a possessive intimacy that increased her sense of vulnerability, his gaze proclaimed ownership as it swept over her.

Reminding herself that her previous response meant nothing—after all, her mind had been fuzzy at the time—she pulled the blanket and robe more tightly around herself and lifted her chin, ignoring Ryder, who stood glaring at her from the end of the bed.

"None of your business."

Reaching out, Dillon brushed the hair off of her face, frowning at her forehead. "It's a little after eight. You stood me up. What's this scar from?"

Embarrassed, she slapped his hand away and fluffed her bangs back over her forehead.

"Again, none of your business. Now if the two of you don't mind, I'd like to be alone."

After making sure the robe covered her, she flung the covers aside, swung her legs over the side, and got to her feet.

Ryder shot a questioning look in Dillon's direction, one that Dillon ignored.

Reaching out a hand to steady her when she trembled, Dillon crowded close behind her. "Tough. Answer me."

She shook his hand off, almost falling on the bed in the process. Still too groggy to deal with either one of them, she decided she needed a shower, hoping it would wake her up. She didn't even look up at Ryder as she passed him, moving straight to her suitcase, and started pulling out clothes. "No. Get out."

She turned, almost falling again when she ran smack into Dillon's wide chest. She tried to step around him, but he caught her by the shoulders. Sucking in a breath, she looked up at him through her lashes. "Excuse me."

With a small smile, he gestured toward the clothes in her arms. "Good idea. Get a shower and get dressed, and we'll go get something to eat. Or better yet, get a shower and put your robe back on. We'll go get something from the restaurant and bring it back here. When was the last time you ate?"

When Ryder moved in behind her, she felt a momentary flare of panic and tightened her hold on the clothing she held in front of her. She pressed her thighs together as a rush of heat raced through her and settled at her slit, the sensation of being surrounded by such raw masculinity almost too enticing to resist. Staring at Dillon's chest, she shook her head, desperate for both of them to go and leave her alone.

"No. I want both of you to leave. I'm fine. If you could just contact me when you know how much it'll cost to repair my truck, I'd appreciate it. When I come out of the bathroom, I want both of you gone. If you're still here, I'm calling the sheriff."

Brushing past Dillon, she went into the bathroom, relieved that neither one of them tried to stop her.

As she started the shower, she grimaced when she heard Ryder's voice raised in anger and hoped they would be gone by the time she got out.

Damn it, she'd been so sure that Dillon would be perfect for her until he showed her that other side of him. If she couldn't even please Danny, she'd never be able to handle a man like that.

She'd also seen the look on his face when he saw the scar on her forehead and could only imagine how he would react when he saw the rest. Scarred and fat, her body disgusted her, but as soon as she lost more weight, she could regain her confidence and be back to her old self again.

Back to the person she'd been before Danny came into her life.

On that depressing thought, she looked over her shoulder to double-check that she'd locked the door, unbelted her robe, letting it fall to the floor, and stepped into the shower, all without once glancing in the mirror.

She took her time, shaking off the last of her lethargy and letting the warm water wash away the tension of the day.

Everything would turn out just fine. She'd made the decision to start a new life, and she wouldn't let something as insignificant as a lack of money hold her back.

As soon as this mess with Danny was over, she could start fresh.

She would find a job. She would lose weight, and she would become so good in bed that men wouldn't even pay attention to her hideous scar.

As she turned off the shower, she listened for any sound coming from the other side of the door. Hearing nothing, she started to hurry, realizing they must have gone to the restaurant to get food.

She reached for one of the fluffy towels folded neatly on the shelf and hurriedly began to dry off, still thinking about her money problem as she threw on jeans and a sweater, not taking the time to go back into the room to get the bra she'd forgotten.

She brushed her teeth, raced through putting on mascara and combing her wet hair back before cautiously opening the bathroom door. Looking around, she breathed a sigh of relief when she saw no sign of either one of them and hurried into the room, pleased that neither her back nor her hip protested at all. She slipped on her shoes and grabbed her purse, determined to forget all about Dillon and Ryder and enjoy the evening ahead.

A Friday night at the local bar with free drinks sounded like fun, and she hadn't done anything just for fun in a long time. Of course it would be lonely, but she hoped that she'd be able to meet another man as gentle as she'd first thought Dillon to be.

Someone tender and sweet to have an affair with before she left again.

Reaching for the doorknob, she stopped as the implications of what Danny said earlier hit her. What if there was already a warrant out for her arrest? What if the prosecutor no longer believed her, or what if he'd been bribed or threatened by Danny's friends and family?

Okay, now she really needed that beer. Once she escaped from Dillon and Ryder, she'd sit down to think and figure out what to do. Maybe she should just leave town as soon as they fixed her truck and—no. She had to find out if Danny had already filed charges against her, or she'd spend the rest of her life looking over her shoulder.

Every time she thought her life couldn't get any worse, it did.

As she left the room and went down the hall, the delicious smells and the sound of low conversation and soft laughter momentarily startled her. She'd forgotten that she had to pass the restaurant on the way out.

Her stomach rumbled, reminding her just how long it had been since she'd eaten, and she forced herself to ignore it. The peanuts or pretzels at the bar would have to be enough for tonight.

To her surprise, the hostess came from around the small counter and approached, moving to stand in front of Alison and effectively blocking her escape. "Good evening, Miss Bennett. I thought Dillon said the dinner order was to go. I'll just let him know you're here."

Alison smiled politely and started to back away, intending to work her way around the woman. "No, thank you. I'll just—"

She backed hard into a wall of muscle, but before she fell, two strong arms came around her. Resigned, she turned to look up into Dillon's smiling face, shivering when the fingers that tucked her hair behind her ear lingered and trailed down her neck.

"Good. Your color's a little better. Now you just need something to eat. Your hair's still damp. You didn't plan to go out in the cold with it that way, did you?"

Alison forced a smile as the hostess excused herself, waiting until she'd gone before pushing against Dillon's chest. "I keep telling you, what I do is none of your business! Let go of me."

He'd caught her hand against his chest and, with the other, drew her closer. "I'm making it my business. Something tells me you're even more fragile than I first thought."

Yanking her hand away, she stepped back, relieved that he'd let her. "I'm not fragile at all. Don't make the mistake of underestimating me." Each day she felt stronger than the day before and more determined than ever to get her life back on track. She was *not* fragile.

A tall, dark man approached, his friendly smile making her heart skip a beat. "Hello, Miss Bennett. I'm Brandon Weston, one of the owners. I see Dillon got to you first."

He sent a smile over her shoulder at Dillon before winking at her. "Probably afraid you'd take one look at me and send him packing. Are you feeling any better?"

Alison blinked, not sure she'd heard him right. "Excuse me?"

Frowning, he gestured for her to precede him into the restaurant, and she responded to the authority in the gesture without thinking. "Ethan told me that Dillon was worried when you didn't answer your door. He let Dillon in to check on you. Ethan and I own the hotel together."

Shaking her head, she grimaced, wrapping her arms around herself defensively. "I didn't even get a chance to find out how he got in my room. There won't be any need for that in the future."

Brandon raised a brow at that, his amusement apparent in his glance at Dillon. "I'll make a note."

Slowing her steps, she looked around, surprised at the number of people filling the restaurant and trying to keep her eyes from the darkly handsome hotel owner. He had kind eyes, tender, but with a trace of wickedness that she found enormously exciting.

"I didn't realize you'd be so busy, especially for such a small town. I really didn't want a big meal. I was thinking about getting a sandwich or something."

He smiled, his eyes lighting with mischief. "This place is usually busy on the weekends, especially when the clubs are having seminars. It's a real popular town in some circles."

She didn't ask, afraid she didn't want to know what he meant.

She caught the grin he shot Dillon before he touched her arm to turn her down a row of tables, a touch that felt warm and ...*nice*, but didn't give her the shivers Dillon and Ryder's did.

Damn it.

He shrugged at her polite smile, inclining his head.

"We have sandwiches here, too, if you prefer, but after what Dillon told me, I'd think you'd need something a little more substantial."

Noticing the number of tables where one woman sat with more than one man, she thought back to the trio she'd seen with the baby this afternoon. Trying not to stare, she followed Brandon, her eyes widening when she saw Ryder stand as they approached a table he apparently occupied.

Dillon pulled out a chair. "Thanks, Brandon. Now that you've assured yourself that your guest is safe with us, I think we can take it from here."

Avoiding Ryder's gaze, and taken aback at the anger under Dillon's sardonic tone, Alison turned to Brandon and shook her head. "I'd prefer to eat alone."

He smiled apologetically. "Sorry. There aren't any other tables available."

Aware of the attention she was getting, she pointed to three that sat empty nearby. "What about one of those?"

Brandon shrugged, not quite hiding a smile. "They're reserved. Won't you have a seat?"

Dillon held out her chair for her, standing behind it and holding out his hand. "We just want to have a nice dinner with you. No pressure."

Ryder's eyes narrowed. "Look at it this way. If we pay for your dinner, it leaves more money for you to pay for your truck repair."

Out of the corner of her eye, she saw that several people looked their way in amusement, a few of the men even chuckling. "What's this dinner going to cost me?"

Crossing her arms over her chest, she turned toward Dillon. "If this is about my earlier…lapse, just remember that I was under the influence of prescription medication."

Dillon inclined his head, his lips thinning. "I figured that would be your excuse. Once you've got that all out of your system, I'll have to prove differently. Tonight, however, all we expect from you is conversation. Now please sit down before I sit you down."

The steel in his otherwise polite tone convinced her that he meant it.

Her stomach rumbled, which was embarrassing enough without Ryder's knowing smile.

"Fine." Ignoring Ryder, she plopped down into her chair, stiffening immediately in anticipation of shooting pain.

When none came, she smiled broadly in relief, murmuring her thanks and accepting the menu from Brandon.

She couldn't resist wiggling in her chair, delighted that she could move so easily. Her hip didn't even hurt.

Opening the menu, she lifted it high enough to block Ryder's glower and turned to Dillon.

"Brandon told me that you'd been worried about me when I didn't answer the door. I appreciate your concern, but sometimes I sleep hard. There's no need to worry, and there won't be any need for you to barge into my room again."

Dillon lifted a brow. "Sleep hard? Is that what you call it when those pills knock you out? Why do you take them? Is it really for pain or are you doing it for kicks?"

Initially taken aback at his disapproving tone, she stiffened, about to jump up from the table and leave. The concern in his eyes, however, stopped her. Except for the episode right before he left her room earlier, he'd been nothing but solicitous and kind.

If Ryder had been the one to ask the question, she probably would have told him that it wasn't any of his business, but Dillon's warmth touched something inside her, and she found herself answering him.

"I had an accident about five months ago. I guess I drove too much today. In case you haven't noticed yet, the shocks on my truck are shot and it made my back sore."

Dillon frowned. "Your *back*?"

Ryder reached across and plucked the menu separating them from her hand and dropped in onto the table. "Those shocks are ridiculous. I noticed a lot of other things wrong with that truck, too—including the tires. They're not even safe to drive on. I'm surprised Ace didn't give you a ticket for it. He must be getting soft. Whoever's supposed to be taking care of you certainly isn't doing his job."

Bristling at his arrogance, Alison folded her arms in front of her, leaned forward, and smiled sarcastically. "Congratulations. You've won the award for saying the most sexist thing I've ever heard in my life."

Ryder leaned forward, too, getting right in her face, his beautiful green eyes glittering with anger. "You're not driving it again without new tires. I won't allow it."

Shaking her head, she sighed and picked up her menu again. "I stand corrected."

Hiding a smile at his low curse, she slid a glance sideways as Dillon buttered a roll and stuck it on her bread plate. Purposely looking away from it, she sighed. "No bread or butter for me."

Dillon ignored that and started buttering another roll. "What kind of accident?"

Aware of Ryder's intense scrutiny, she took the roll from her plate and placed in on Dillon's. "Car accident. I think I'll have the chef salad."

Closing the menu, she put it aside and looked up at Ryder. "Don't you know it's rude to stare?"

Ryder smiled coldly, his eyes sharp. "You're a real looker. I'm sure you're used to being stared at. Your nipples are poking at the front of your sweater, so don't tell me you don't like me staring. You don't think I'm sitting here wondering how they would feel on my tongue? You just ooze sex, lady, and you know it."

She choked on the water she'd been sipping and looked around to see that several of the diners looked their way and smiled. Uncomfortable being the center of attention, she averted her face, her cheeks burning.

Oozed sex? What the hell did that mean?

Setting her glass down, she automatically glanced at Dillon, comforted to see that he glared at his friend. Drawing a deep breath, she met Ryder's gaze. "Somehow that didn't sound like a compliment."

Ryder took a sip of his beer, saluting her with the glass. "Smart, too."

"That's enough, Ryder."

Alison blinked at the underlying steel in Dillon's tone and lowered her gaze. The hard edge sent a chill through her, reminding her a little too much of Danny.

Uneasy now, she started to rise. "I think I'll—"

Dillon touched her hand. "Sit down, Alison. Or I'll put your ass back in the seat myself."

Unwilling to make a scene, Alison took her seat again, this time more gingerly than before, aware of Dillon's unwavering scrutiny.

The thought of what that kind of strength, determination, focus, and patience would be like in bed would probably keep her awake tonight.

Looking up at Dillon again, she twisted the napkin she held in her lap, trembling with the need to find out. The soft sweater she wore brushed against her nipples every time she moved, making them even more sensitive. Wishing she'd taken the time to put on her bra, she shifted restlessly, pressing her thighs together against the tingling of her clit, but it didn't help at all.

Ryder grinned and sat back, apparently aware of her predicament. "My money's on Dillon."

"Shut up, Ryder." Dillon placed another buttered roll on her plate, his eyes daring her to refuse it.

Fisting her hands on her lap, Alison snuck a glance at Dillon out of the corner of her eye. "I don't like threats."

Dillon raised a hand to signal a waiter. "I don't threaten. I stated a fact. I'm just trying to save you some embarrassment. If you try to get out of that chair, you won't make it. Now how do you want your steak cooked?"

"I don't want a steak. Just a salad."

Dillon's brows went up. "You're a vegetarian?"

Looking toward the bar area, she noticed three men deep in conversation, who smiled in their direction. Two of them looked enough alike to be brothers, and both stood well over six feet tall, as big and muscular as the sheriff.

The other man, almost too handsome for words, had an air about him that was almost mesmerizing and a lean, muscular frame much like Ryder's. As one of the taller men spoke, the too-handsome man shook his head, unsmiling, and turned away, looking almost relieved when two women came out of the ladies room and headed toward them.

Both had the kind of beauty that made Alison feel just a little more insecure. As the two men turned and reached for the woman on the left, her face lit up, transforming her from beautiful to stunning.

Watching them surreptitiously, Alison realized that the two men must share the woman, much like the threesome she'd seen earlier with the baby.

As the other man reached for the woman on the right, she smiled, but even from this distance it looked forced. The man looked frustrated and preoccupied, but never stopped touching the woman. He kept an arm around her waist as they walked, and once seated, he caressed her arm, her shoulder, her hand, almost as if he couldn't bear to be parted.

The woman leaned toward him several times, watching him closely as though searching for something in his expression.

"Stop staring."

She whipped around, her face burning as she met Ryder's angry gaze. "I'm sorry. I didn't mean to stare. It's just that...I mean we saw those people today, and when I look around here, I see a lot of women with more than one man. Is it very common—oh my God! That's why everyone's smiling. They think we're—oh, hell. I've got to get out of here."

When she shot to her feet, Dillon placed a firm hand on her arm to keep her from escaping. At her glare, he slid his chair a little closer to hers and bent toward her, keeping his voice low.

"I warned you."

When several other diners turned in their direction, Alison sank back into her seat.

"They think I'm sleeping with both of you."

Dillon inclined his head, waving away the waiter who approached. "Most of them are our friends and are curious about you and why we're together. There are a lot of ménage relationships in Desire, and everyone's hoping there'll be several more."

Alison's face burned even hotter. "What do you mean by *everyone's hoping* there'll be several more?"

Dillon sat back in his chair and regarded her steadily, his body tense as though prepared to leap at her if she got up again. "Alison, the reason we live in this town is because we want what they have." He inclined his head toward the table she'd been watching, taking her hand in his.

"Jesse came to Desire last year to visit her sister, Nat, the other woman sitting there. Clay and Rio met her and fell hard for her."

Ryder grinned. "I remember the day they came into the shop to get Nat's car fixed. Every time I so much as spoke to Jesse, they were ready to tear me apart. When I flirted with her, you could tell that both of them wanted to beat the hell out of me, but didn't want to do it in front of Jesse. They stood between us so I couldn't see her. Yeah, they had it bad."

Dillon glanced at the other table, smiling wistfully. "They still do. Worse than ever. Jesse looks more beautiful every day, doesn't she? Clay and Rio can't stand to be away from her." Shrugging, he reached for his beer. "There's a lot of us who want what they have. It's breathing new life into this town."

Alison reached for her glass to ease her dry throat, unsurprised to find that her hands shook. "I can't believe people actually live this way."

Ryder sneered. "Don't knock what you haven't tried, darlin'."

Plunking her glass back down on the table, Alison glared at him. "I'm not talking to you."

Ryder raised a brow and grinned, leaned closer. "You take on one of us, you take on both of us, baby."

Ignoring the look of surprise and satisfaction on Dillon's face, Alison shot to her feet, scared to death of the riot of emotions racing through her and her own uncontrollable lust for two men who were obviously way out of her league. "I'm not taking on either one of you."

Dillon came to his feet just as fast. "Sit down, Alison."

When she hesitated, he moved to stand behind her, his breath warm on her neck as he bent to whisper in her ear.

"I'm not worried about making a scene, and Ryder lives for them. You're going to sit back down in that chair one way or another."

Swallowing heavily, she glanced around to see several of the diners staring at them, including the three men she'd noticed earlier, the two tallest ones seeming inordinately amused.

Ryder shook his head and jerked a thumb in their direction. "That's what we get for laughing at all the trouble they had with Jesse."

Alison wanted nothing more than to escape. Taking a steadying breath, she crossed her arms over her chest to cover her beaded nipples, which Ryder appeared to find fascinating, and looked up at Dillon over her shoulder.

"Look, I appreciate that you came to get my truck, and I appreciate that you came to check on me, but I really have some things to do."

Dillon's smile didn't reach his eyes. "Eating is one of them. The sooner you sit down, the sooner that waiter over there can take our order. I cancelled the other when I saw you leave your room."

"How did you see me? I didn't see you."

"It's not important. Sit down."

If she tried to leave, Dillon would just grab her again, and she was a little tired of being entertainment for the other diners. "Fine. But after dinner, I really have to go."

Dillon waited until she seated herself before calling the waiter over. "You need more than just a salad. How do you like your steak?"

Despite her objections, he ordered her a steak, salad, and baked potato.

She hated arrogant men, but had to admit she was hungry.

As soon as the waiter left, Dillon turned to her and continued in a conversational tone as though they'd been discussing the weather. "There are a lot of reasons that men want to share a woman. As for getting married, it's true that a woman can't legally marry two men, but in Desire she marries the oldest and is considered married to all involved."

"All involved? You mean there can be more than two?"

Dillon's lips twitched. "You're new here. You would have to be here awhile to understand."

Alison shook her head. "I'm leaving soon, so I guess you'll have to give me a crash course. What happens if one of the men who marry this poor woman without really marrying her decides later on that he doesn't want to share with anyone anymore and wants to marry a woman of his own? What if one of the men gets mad because he doesn't know if his *wife* is pregnant with his child or someone else's and leaves them?"

Both men looked at her like she'd lost her mind.

Ryder's lips thinned. "That doesn't happen. In Desire, we take our relationships seriously, and we don't hurt our women. Marriage is marriage, no matter how many people are involved."

Leaning over, he reached out an arm, his short-sleeved shirt riding up his bicep and giving her a tantalizing view of part of his tattoo.

Distracted, she didn't have a chance to avoid him as he grabbed the arm of her chair and yanked her toward him.

"And our woman would be so satisfied she wouldn't go looking anywhere else, and smart enough to know that if I ever caught her even thinking about fucking another man, her ass would be so red she wouldn't sit down for a month!"

Alison couldn't help it. She laughed. "Please. When I was getting information on the women's club, information for the men's club came up. It looks like a lot of slave-and-master crap. I understand a lot of the men in this town are members, right? Are you members?"

Dillon nodded, his jaw clenched tight. "Yes, we—"

She laughed humorlessly, thinking about Danny and his big talk. "I know. Your cocks are made of gold, and you're the best. You make women scream in ecstasy. If you're so good that you can keep your women in line with sex, why would you feel the need to threaten a spanking?"

"Women are just things to you, aren't they? They're not people. You like to hurt them because you can. Men are bigger and stronger as it is, but that's not enough for you, is it? No, you have to attack them two or three at a time. You're brutes, all of you!"

Furious that the last sentence came out as a sob, Alison jumped up from the table, ignoring their almost identical looks of shock, and ran from the restaurant. She started toward her room but figured they'd find her there faster, so she made a quick left and headed out the front door.

She'd stick with her original plan and find another man she could enjoy for the weekend.

Someone safe.

Men did it all the time, after all. How hard could it be?

* * * *

Dillon jumped out of his seat and started after her, but Ryder was faster and shot out a hand to stop him.

"Let her go. She needs to cool down a bit. We'll follow her to make sure she's all right."

Furious, Dillon whirled to glare at him, shaking off his hand, his own hands fisted. Catching the sight of Clay and Rio Erickson coming to their feet and starting toward them, he sighed and waved them off. He wouldn't start a fight here in the restaurant, especially with all the women present, but Ryder was pissing him off.

He shoved his best friend, some of his anger easing when he managed to knock Ryder back into the chair.

"*She* needs to cool down, or you do?"

Ryder sighed and inclined his head. "A little of both."

Dillon watched Alison's ass twitch as she hurried out of the restaurant, noticing that she moved easier now than she had earlier.

"I wanted her to eat, damn it, and I wanted to find out what the hell happened to her. You acted like an ass."

A muscle worked in Ryder's jaw, his eyes dark with what appeared to be concern. "I'll apologize to her once we both cool down."

"*You?* Apologize?" After tossing some bills on the table, Dillon started after her with Ryder right beside him.

Brandon came through the kitchen door just about the time they passed it. He moved quickly to stand in front of them, looking madder than hell.

"What happened? Is she crying? Is she hurt? What the hell did you do to her?"

Shaking his head, Dillon stepped around Brandon. "She's not hurt. Don't worry. We'll take care of her. Can you cancel dinner for us?" He hurried toward the door, not wanting to lose Alison in the dark parking lot.

Once outside, he caught sight of her as she ran under one of the large streetlights and quickened his steps, impatient to get to her. He knew that the look on her face, and the sob that broke free at the end of her tirade would haunt him for quite some time.

Ryder caught his arm again. "Slow down. You're going to spook her, and she won't talk to either one of us after that. Look, she stopped. She's digging through her purse. Is that her phone?"

Dillon slowed his steps, making sure to stay out of the light. "She looks pissed. She's yelling, but I can't make out what she's saying. Can you?"

Ryder stared in her direction, his eyes raking over her. "No. She hung up. Is she still crying?"

Dillon hurried his steps. "Did you see her face? What the hell happened in there? What's your fucking problem? Nobody asked you to stick around. If you don't like her, fine. Just leave us the hell alone." Even in this poor light, he could see Ryder's jaw clench, his face lined with guilt.

"So it's like that, is it?"

Dillon shot him a look, not about to let Alison get away. "It is. You just had to keep it up, didn't you? I was trying to get her to talk and find out what's wrong with her. Those bottles of pills were half empty, and there are still refills on it. They're strong, Ryder. I wanted her to eat something, damn it, and talk to us."

Ryder swore inventively, his steps quickening.

"I know that, damn it! Do you think I meant to do that? She's got me so twisted around. I don't know what the hell I'm doing. Fuck. She's signed up for a seminar on how to please a man, but seems to both hate and fear men. She comes on to you within minutes of meeting you after she did her best to keep her distance from both of us. Even when she's propositioning you like a damned hooker, her face is bright red. She's got a temper, but won't let loose, and she's got the saddest fucking eyes I ever saw. What the fuck, Dillon? One minute I want to turn her over my knee and paddle her ass and the next I want to throw her over my shoulder and take her somewhere I can fuck her brains out. Then one look from those brown eyes and I want to just grab her and put her in my pocket and tell her everything'll be all right. What the fuck's going on with her?"

Dillon glared at him. "That's part of what I wanted to find out before you scared her off. Hell, she stopped in front of the bar. Looks like she's going in, damn it. She can't drink on top of that pain medicine."

Ryder rubbed his hands together, his eyes lit with anticipation. "Then I guess we're just gonna have to stop her."

Dillon had already started after her, when to his surprise, Ryder stopped him again.

"What?"

The bleak look on Ryder's face knotted Dillon's stomach.

Scrubbing a hand over his face, he nodded toward the front of the bar Alison had just entered.

"She just rubbed me wrong, but I was rough on her and I'll apologize, but then I'm leaving. You two seemed to have hit it off, and that's fine. Just don't expect me to sit around and watch."

Following Ryder, Dillon hurried across the street to the bar, shaking his head in frustration.

"Damned women. I can only imagine what it'll be like when we find the one that'll turn us into lunatics like the others."

Ryder cursed. "If it's anything like dealing with Ally, forget it. I'll stick to the club. It's much easier."

"It sure as hell is."

Ryder grinned and shook his head. "Then what the hell are we doing chasing after her? You know, I don't think I'm going to leave, after all."

"That's what I figured."

Chapter Four

Alison stared up at the blue neon sign and smiled. They'd actually named the place *The Bar*.

No pretense at all.

Pausing, she took a deep breath and blew it out slowly, gathering her courage before she walked through the front door. As soon as she crossed the threshold, she stopped, a huge knot forming in her stomach when every eye in the place turned in her direction.

"Well, hello, darlin'. You must be new in town."

Alison turned her head to the left, in search of the owner of the sexy drawl, getting her first look at the outrageously gorgeous bartender.

Holy hell, he was beautiful!

She couldn't tear her gaze away from him as he moved away from the far corner of the bar where he'd obviously been watching a sporting event on the huge television with the others and toward her, bracing himself at the end of the bar closest to her. His black hair shone beneath the bar lights, his blue eyes dancing with mischief and interest as they raked over her.

Her pulse raced with both nerves and excitement, and moving closer to the bar, she searched for the courage to start a conversation with him. She'd done it so many times before she met Danny, but didn't remember it ever being so hard.

His brilliant blue stare left her momentarily tongue tied, and it took an embarrassing amount of time before she found her voice.

"Hello. Um. Yes, I'm only here until next week."

Keeping her gaze on his and ignoring the looks of interest from the other men, she smiled and stepped up to the bar, gripping the edge of it with both hands. Keeping her smile in place, she curled her toes inside her boots, wishing she could have worn her high heels.

Keeping his voice at a seductive whisper, he leaned closer. "Well, we're going to have to make sure you have a good time while you're here. What would you like to drink?"

Wondering why his seductive tone didn't do to her what Dillon's or Ryder's did, she vowed to herself to give him her undivided attention.

His flirtatious grin and playfulness didn't have the hard edge to it that Ryder's did. His body had the same hard, leanness as Ryder's, but he wasn't quite as tall.

He appeared to be about the same height as Dillon, but didn't have the same muscular physique. His eyes, although so blue they sparkled, didn't have the same tenderness gleaming from them that Dillon's did.

Frustrated with herself, she forcefully pushed aside thoughts of Dillon and Ryder and focused on the almost outrageously gorgeous creature in front of her. Trying to imagine him naked and eager for her to practice on him, she smiled again and tried to smooth her hair, mussed and probably tangled from the wind. Sliding onto the barstool, she glanced at the others and smiled politely, hoping they would turn back to their game and give her a little privacy so she could talk to the handsome bartender.

She hugged her jacket more tightly around herself, her still-damp hair and nerves making her chilled. Reminding herself that she wanted to entice him, she inwardly cursed and let it fall loose, hiding a smile when his eyes went to her cleavage.

Instead of his look exciting her, it made her uneasy, so much so that she wanted to cover herself again. Annoyed with herself, she pasted on a smile.

"This is a nice town. I've never been here before."

His smile turned into a grin when he glanced over her shoulder. "We'll have to see what we can do about trying to keep you in town a little longer. What's your name?"

"Alison. What's yours?"

His grin widened, and he looked like he was having a hard time holding back a laugh, straightening and lifting his hands as though in surrender. "I'm Michael. It's nice to meet you. Well, Alison, what can I get you?" He poured a fresh bowl of peanuts and set them in front of her.

She didn't see what the hell he found so amusing, and tried to think of a drink other than her usual beer in an effort to look sophisticated. "A screwdriver, please."

"Make that a virgin one."

At the sound of Dillon's steely tone, she whirled on the barstool, her arm hitting the bowl and sending the peanuts flying.

Ryder chuckled and dropped onto the barstool to her left, crowding her. "Hello, honey. Miss us?"

Dillon came up behind her on her right, effectively surrounding her and trapping her there on the stool.

Turning away from them, she hurried to clean up the mess, her hands clumsy. "I'm so sorry, Michael. I'll clean it up."

Over her apologies, Michael grinned, but his eyes sharpened and searched hers. "No sense crying over spilt peanuts." He wiped them up from the bar and poured a fresh bowl. "It's not the first time, and I'm sure it won't be the last. One glass of orange juice coming up."

Ryder scooped out a handful of peanuts, shooting her a wry grin, and waving a hand at the men who tore their attention away from the game to call out greetings. "I missed my dinner. Michael, I'll take a beer."

Dillon leaned over her and grabbed one of the plastic menus that had been propped against a napkin holder. "I'll have one, too, and we're gonna order a couple of sandwiches." He opened the menu and plopped it down on the bar in front of her. "You're going to eat something, or I'm going to shove it down your throat."

Michael grinned. "I take it the three of you are together."

"No."

"Yes."

Dillon and Ryder spoke over her, crowding her even more from both sides as they looked over the menu they'd placed in front of her.

Alison squirmed in her seat, overwhelmed by their closeness and hard bodies brushing against hers. When Ryder shifted on the stool next to her to remove his black leather jacket, she leaned as far to the right as she could to avoid him, shaking so badly she inadvertently fell into Dillon.

Jolting at the contact, she teetered on her seat and grabbed for the bar, grimacing as Michael whipped the bowl of peanuts out of the way just in time to keep her from knocking them over, too.

Dillon caught her easily and settled her back on the stool. "Easy, honey. Are you feeling all right?"

Yanking her arm from his grasp, she looked back up at the incredibly handsome bartender and leaned toward him, doing her best to turn her back to both Dillon and Ryder. "I'll just have a beer, too, please. A light beer."

"No alcohol." Dillon's flat, arrogant tone infuriated her, reminding her too much of Danny.

She glared at him over her shoulder, hardly able to believe that the man who glared back was the same man who'd been so sweet and kind to her only her only hours earlier. She didn't appreciate the arrogant attitude now any more than she had with Danny.

Turning her back to him, she smiled broadly at the gorgeous bartender, ignoring the glares burning her from both sides. "I can order my own drinks, thank you. May I have a light beer, please?"

Wrapping his arms around her from behind, Dillon rested his chin on her shoulder and poked his finger at the menu, his warm breath on her ear sending a shiver of delight through her. "Pick something to eat and then we'll go get a booth."

Alison stared down at the menu, fighting the urge to relax against the wide chest at her back. The shivers making her tremble now had nothing to do with the cold and everything to do with the hard, muscular heat surrounding her.

Her stomach muscles clenched tight and quivered beneath the hand Dillon used to caress her. She would swear she could hear the thumping of her heart when Ryder's hand dropped to her leg above the knee, the slow caress of his fingers over her inner thigh moving higher and higher.

Amazing need washed over her in waves, each stronger than the last. Her nipples beaded, poking against her sweater, the soft material caressing them with every ragged breath she took.

The little tingles grew, spreading throughout her body and to her center, making it difficult to remain still. Her clit felt swollen and heavy, the sharp jolts of pleasure from each brush of her sweater over her nipples making her pussy clench, dampening her panties.

Disconcerted that even the gorgeous bartender didn't stir her the way Dillon and Ryder did, she stared at the large hand Dillon braced against the bar and shifted restlessly.

Dillon's warm breath against her ear sent another shiver through her, creating an intimacy she wouldn't have believed possible in the middle of a bar. "She's still got pain medicine in her system. She passed out at the hotel and slept solid for two hours. She didn't even hear me come into the room. She hasn't eaten anything at all."

His low, caressing tone washed over her, his touch reminding her of the tenderness he'd shown her in her hotel room. This time, however, he pressed his cock against her, leaving her in no doubt of his intentions.

Without meaning to, she pressed back against him, closing her eyes. The hand at her stomach moved lower, and thankful that the bar blocked the view of Dillon and Ryder's hands on her, she automatically parted her thighs, making room for the strong fingers that pressed against her slit.

Dillon's hair brushed against her cheek, teasing her into turning her head toward him. Catching her lips with his, he nibbled lightly, stroking her bottom lip with his tongue until she parted her lips. Leaning toward him, she jolted in alarm as the men from the other side of the bar all cheered at once, breaking the spell.

Embarrassed, she slid a glance at them, only to find them engrossed in something that had happened in the game and paying no attention to her, Dillon, or Ryder at all. Clearing her throat, she straightened in her chair, sucking in a breath when Dillon's hands came down on her shoulders and massaged gently.

"Have you, Alison?"

"What? Have I what?" She took a shuddering breath as he slid the collar of her jacket and sweater aside and his lips brushed an amazingly sensitive spot between her neck and shoulder. Fisting her hands on her thighs, she jolted when Ryder's devious fingers pressed against her clit with an accuracy and firmness that stunned her.

Dillon's soft chuckle next to her ear sent another wave of delicious tingles through her, the sensation made stronger when Ryder pressed again. Biting her lip, she stared at the bar, shoving Ryder's hand away.

"Don't worry. Ryder won't make you come in here. We wouldn't want anyone else to hear the sounds you make when you come."

Ryder leaned closer, lifting her chin.

"Do you scream when you come, Ally, or do you bite your lip to try to hold it in the way you're doing now?"

Bristling at the arrogance in his smug smile, and knowing, *knowing*, his intent to rile her, she smiled serenely to hide the surge of panic.

"That's something you'll never know. Besides, even if I went to bed with you, what makes you think you could make me come?"

She turned away, watching Michael exchanging pleasantries with the other men before disappearing through a doorway to what she assumed to be the kitchen.

Ryder threaded his fingers through her hair, fisting his hand in it to turn her toward him.

He bent, leaning over her, the ends of his silky hair brushing her cheek. His smile faded until his expression showed no trace of amusement at all. Instead, his eyes held promise and the same possessiveness she'd seen in Dillon's eyes earlier.

"Darlin', I absolutely *know* I can make you come." Leaning closer, he moved his fingers over her denim-covered slit, somehow managing to find just the right spot, a spot Danny couldn't find with a map.

"Over and over. So many times that you'd beg me to stop because you couldn't take any more. With my mouth. With my fingers. With my cock. And I sure as hell wouldn't let you try to hide it."

Dillon rubbed her shoulders, causing even more of those mind-numbing shivers.

"Easy on her, Ryder. She's still a little off from the pain medicine. We need to get something in her stomach and get her back to normal. I hate not knowing how much of her response is caused by the medicine."

Ryder pressed once more at her slit before releasing her, leaning against the bar. His eyes sharpened as they slid over her features.

"I'm very curious about that myself." Patting her thigh, he grinned. "But we're going to find out, aren't we, Ally?"

Pushing his hand away, she looked up as Michael came back from the kitchen, wishing that with his stunning good looks and flirtatious smile, he affected her the way Ryder and Dillon did.

He would probably be a lot less trouble.

After the phone call from Danny on her way here, she found herself even more determined to have one last fling before she left town.

She'd never be able to find someone with Dillon and Ryder following her, so she had to find a way to get rid of them.

"I have no intention of sleeping with either one of you. You're both too arrogant and pushy. Now, go away."

Dillon bent low again, wrapping his arms around her from behind and sliding his hands up her inner thighs. "Why? So you can find someone else? You already offered yourself to me, remember?"

He applied pressure, pulling her thighs wider. "And, as for being arrogant, don't try to tell me you don't appreciate authority in the bedroom. We both know better, don't we, Alison?"

Alison shuddered as the same seductive tone he'd used in the hotel room washed over her, the silky possessiveness in it making her clit swell. Wiggling against the erotic feel of it, she attempted to squeeze her legs closed, but Dillon's firm hold didn't allow it.

Her breath caught as the sexual tension between them soared.

He seemed to know every button to push to earn her unwilling surrender, something she couldn't allow, not even for the short time she'd be in town. Never again would she allow a man to control her in any way.

From now on, she would be the one doing the controlling, and sex was a powerful weapon. The next several days might very well be her only chance to use it, and she didn't want to waste a minute.

"I won't be controlled. Now, get lost. I want to find someone who's not so bossy."

Ryder's brow went up. "In Desire? Good luck with that. In Desire, darlin', we call it being a man."

Averting her gaze from Ryder's assessing green eyes, she watched Michael move away from the bar, enjoying the sight of his firm, jean-covered ass as he bent to retrieve a container of orange juice from the small refrigerator behind the bar.

Dillon pressed against her slit, the shock of heat sending her gaze shooting to his.

Smiling in satisfaction, he nodded once and tapped the tip of her nose with the same finger.

"That's better. It's not polite to ogle one man when you're here with others. I'd love to know what's going on in that head of yours. Ryder's right. It'll be interesting to see the real Ally. So far you've been distracted, defensive, brazen, shy, curious, opinionated, and downright adorable. You don't really expect me to walk away from that without a fight, do you?"

Ryder touched a finger to her shoulder and trailed it down her arm, his eyes never leaving hers. "One minute you're coming on to Dillon like a cat

in heat, and the next you're outraged that two men want you. You're taking
a class to learn how to please a man and leave your hotel room not wearing
a bra, and yet you fight off the attention of two men who have already
shown their interest in you. So, what's your angle?"

Alison squirmed on the stool, breathing a sigh of relief when Dillon
removed his hands and leaned against the bar on the other side of her.

"I don't have any damned angle. Why don't you go find some other
woman to bother and leave me alone?"

Dillon straightened slightly as Michael approached.

"We'll watch over you while you're in town."

Michael poured her a glass of orange juice and set it in front of her, his
flirtatious grin replaced by a worried smile. "You'll feel better after you eat.
You two taking care of her?"

Dillon nodded and took a sip of his beer. "Yep." He ordered
cheeseburgers and fries for all of them, lifting a brow at Alison, silently
asking if that was all right. At her nod, he finished placing the order and
made himself comfortable on the seat next to her as soon as Michael moved
away.

He kept his eyes glued to the game on the television, but she could feel
his attention on her.

"So, tell us about the pain medicine."

Alison checked to make sure the other men had their attention focused
on the game before answering.

"I really don't think this is any of your business. And it certainly isn't
the business of everyone else in the bar. Why don't you go fix my truck and
leave me alone so I can do what I came to Desire to do?"

Dillon turned to her and smiled. "If what you came to Desire to do is to
learn a few things about sex, we can sure as hell help you with that." His
gaze sharpened. "Something tells me, though, that there's more to it than
that. Come on. Let's go get a booth."

* * * *

Ten minutes later, Alison found herself sitting in a booth with Dillon
and Ryder and eating the best cheeseburger she'd ever eaten in her life. She
wiped her mouth and took another sip of the ginger ale they'd ordered for

her after she'd gulped down the orange juice. "What is it with you two? What's with all the questions? I'm only going to be here for a few days. I've got enough problems, and I sure as hell don't need you two creating more."

Dillon handed her another napkin to wipe the juice that dripped down her chin, slipping his hand to her thigh and apparently enjoying watching her eat. "Tell us about your problems. After that we'll work on your lessons."

Alison choked on her burger, alarmed at the jolt of lust that raced through her.

Dillon rubbed her back, his concerned frown making her feel like an idiot.

"Are you all right?"

God, she had to get rid of them before she had an orgasm right here in the booth.

She took another bite of her burger and almost choked again as several men came through the door, almost immediately walking over to join the others. A few were absolutely gorgeous, some too masculine looking to ever be called handsome, but each of them with a presence that made them impossible to ignore.

If women knew men like this lived here, the town would be overrun!

Hurriedly taking a sip of her ginger ale, she checked out each and every one of them as they came through the door. She'd never seen so many heartbreakers in one place in her entire life and wondered if the medication had made her delirious.

Several women came in right behind them as if they'd been waiting for the bar to fill before coming inside.

If the bar filled like this, she didn't blame them a bit.

Alison grimaced when she saw that the women had all dressed for seduction, wearing short skirts that barely covered them and sexy tops that exposed ample amounts of cleavage. Looking down at herself, she sighed. Wearing jeans and a loose sweater, she didn't stand a chance.

She should have taken the time to dig something sexier out of her bag, but she'd grabbed what had been on top, in a hurry to get away from Dillon and Ryder.

Blaming them for what looked like would turn out to be a wasted opportunity, she set her glass on the table with more force than necessary.

"I'm fine, and I don't need your help. Thanks, anyway. Look, I appreciate all you've done for me, but I really would like to be alone."

Ryder pushed the fries closer to her, grimacing when she took one and dragged it through the ketchup until it was soaked. "Why are you taking a weekend full of seminars at the women's club about pleasing men if you hate men?"

She blinked and swallowed the fry. "I don't hate men."

Ryder shrugged. "Okay, so why are you taking the seminars?"

Since Ryder sat right in front of her and Dillon sat next to her, she had nowhere to look to hide her burning face. She'd never considered herself a prude by any means, but she'd never before had a conversation with another man about her lack of knowledge in the sex department.

Except Danny, and those hadn't really been conversations.

Thankfully, the noise the others made during the game kept them from overhearing their conversation, or she just might have crawled under the table.

"None of this is any of your business."

Resting his arm over the booth at her back, Dillon let his fingers dance over her shoulder. "You made it my business, remember?"

Alison looked up from dredging another fry. "I took it back, remember?"

Dillon raised a brow at that and leaned back, adopting a conversational tone. "I'm glad a lot of women go to the club. I think it's a good idea for women in ménage marriages to have others to talk to, and I know they have a lot of fun there. It's a safe place for them to go instead of heading out of town. Of course, none who are claimed are allowed to touch the men there, so it works out just fine."

Alison had a feeling he wanted her to ask what they meant by *claimed* and resisted asking, not wanting to fall into one of his traps.

Ryder sipped his beer and nodded. "Yeah, they're always laughing when they come out. They're probably all plotting ways to get even with their men about something."

Dillon's fingers on her shoulder moved slightly, working under the neckline of her sweater to stroke the sensitive area on her neck.

"I just don't understand why women feel the need to learn any tricks to please their men. They're already fascinating creatures. So soft and warm. So giving. So damned sweet."

Ryder leaned back in his seat, his hypnotic green eyes flaring. "It makes a man want to take his time learning each and every sensitive spot on her body, and how she likes to be handled. A slow, soft touch? Maybe a little harder? Firm or fleeting? How does she respond to being touched with my fingertips? With my tongue?"

Alison gulped and reached for her drink, trying to block the image of being naked and Dillon and Ryder exploring her, using their mouths and hands to touch her everywhere.

Ryder's gaze kept going to her nipples poking at the front of her sweater, kept beaded by the friction of her sweater moving back and forth over them due to Dillon's light tugs of her neckline. After taking a sip of his beer, he grinned.

"Why they would feel the need for tricks is a mystery to me. Basically they have the equipment to drive men nuts as it is. We're pretty easy to please."

Not sure how much more of Dillon's teasing she could take, she pushed his hand away and sat forward, crossing her arms over her breasts, glaring at both of them.

"That's bullshit, and you know it. Men want women who know all the tricks and want to sit back and let the women do all the work. Then they have the nerve to bitch about what they don't like."

"Harder."

"Faster."

"Slower."

"Take it easy."

"You're not touching the right spot."

"Don't you know what the hell you're doing?"

She glared at both of them. "You're all assholes."

She dragged another fry through the ketchup and lifted it, pointing it at Ryder.

"God forbid a woman says she doesn't like something. Then she's frigid. But men like to complain about what they like and don't like and as soon as they have their fun, fall asleep leaving a woman wanting."

When Ryder jerked upright and opened his mouth to speak, she held up a hand to stop him.

"Yeah, yeah. I know. Men try to please women. But that's only at the beginning. Once they're comfortable, that's it. After that, it's a bunch of quickies during halftime or jerking them off or giving blow jobs while they're watching TV. If a woman even manages to get them to bed, it's over in two minutes, and she's listening to his snoring in the dark and wishing she'd just used her vibrator instead. No, thanks. What the hell do men want anyway? You're all a bunch of assholes who want something until you get it and then don't want it anymore. I think all you guys care about is the conquest. *And* variety. Nope. My vibrator is the best lover I've ever had."

She popped the fry in her mouth and chewed angrily, thinking about how many nights she'd tried to please Danny only to go to bed unsatisfied. Picking up the ketchup bottle, she squeezed a small lake of it on her waxed paper and reached for another fry. Aware of the long looks passing between them, she shrugged.

"But that's not going to keep me company *or* keep me warm at night. I don't think love's in the cards for me, but I don't want to be alone. Why are you looking at me like that? I would think men like you would want a woman to learn all about pleasing them. Isn't that what men want—a woman who knows how to give them what they want in bed? It seems that's the most important thing to them."

Dillon stiffened beside her. "That's not true at all."

Alison smiled sarcastically. "Sure, it's not. Men really like a woman's sparkling personality. Get real. All they care about is that she's got a perfect body, no imperfections, and that she knows how to get him off without wanting anything in return. The rest of it is all bullshit."

Ryder's eyes narrowed thoughtfully, his hands clenching into fists on the table. "So that's why you want to take those seminars—to please a man who cares about nothing but coming?"

Alison waved a hand dismissively and reached for another fry. "That's all of them. Look, this is none of your business. Just fix my truck so I can be ready to leave when I have to."

The men she'd met since coming to Desire just reminded her of her own shortcomings and made her more determined than ever to learn what she needed to in order to have the upper hand in her next relationship.

Damn, she really wanted that beer now.

Dillon slammed his beer mug down on the table, drawing the attention of the men watching the game. He clenched his jaw and waited until the others looked away again, bending low.

"You made it my business when you came on to me in the hotel parking lot. Aren't you looking for someone to practice on while you're here?"

She hadn't thought it possible for her face to burn any hotter, but she'd been wrong. Sneaking a glance at him, she reached for her ginger ale, forgetting that she'd already finished it.

Each second of the long silence that followed strung her nerves tighter and tighter.

When Dillon finally spoke, his voice low and intimate, she couldn't quite hide her shiver.

"I think you're lying to yourself. There's nothing wrong with having needs, Alison."

She had to get out of here. Pushing against him, she kept her eyes lowered. "I already told you that I made a mistake. I don't know what I was thinking."

With a firm, but gentle touch, Dillon settled her back in her seat. "Stop jumping around before you hurt yourself."

Dropping her head in her hands, she wondered what her chances were of getting out of this booth anytime on the near future. "I wasn't thinking. I'd taken the medication, and my brain went on vacation. I just wish my mouth had done the same."

Looking up through her fingers, she nearly groaned at the looks of intense interest on both of their faces. She didn't want to interest them. She thought they'd be bored out of their minds by now and would have moved on to someone easier, someone less…damaged.

Knowing that interest would never last, she straightened and placed a hand on Dillon's forearm, trying not to notice the hard muscle shifting beneath her fingers. Snatching her hand away, she unobtrusively rubbed her tingling palm against her thigh.

"Please let me out. Call me at the hotel when you know how much it'll cost to fix my truck."

She didn't know what she'd do if it cost more than what she had in her checking account.

Dillon didn't budge. After shooting a look at a stone-faced Ryder, he frowned down at her. "You're not planning on making that offer to anyone else, are you?"

The rough edge of fury in his tone made it clear what he thought of that.

Not about to let either one of them intimidate her, well, not about to let either one of them *know* they intimidated her, she sighed and fisted her hands on the table, inwardly wincing when she saw that she'd shredded her napkin into tiny little pieces. She kept her attention on the paper, her hands shaking as she gathered it into a little pile. "I keep telling you that this is none of your business. Let me out. I want to go back to the hotel."

Ryder sat forward, capturing her hand in his and folding his around it. "Look at it this way. You have the chance to have two willing, able-bodied men to practice all of your new sexual talents on."

Lifting her chin, Alison glared at him, trying not to imagine what it would be like to have Dillon and Ryder letting her have her way with them.

She liked them, damn it, despite her determination not to. She'd already fallen under the spell of Dillon's tender strength and knew in her heart that he would make the perfect lover. Even now, with his thigh touching hers and his hand caressing a wide pattern on her back, her entire body tingled with awareness, and she had to fight her desire to lean against him.

Damn, he drew her, his chest and arms strong and inviting. She found herself having to make a conscious effort to resist him.

Swallowing heavily, she licked her dry lips, drawing a deep breath and working up her courage before glancing at Ryder. Catching the hard glint in his eyes and his knowing grin, she yanked her hand out of Dillon's and reached for her purse, cursing when she realized she'd left it in the hotel room. Grabbing her jacket, she looked for a way out.

"I don't appreciate being made fun of. I already told you I made a mistake. Just leave it at that."

Dillon shot a warning look at Ryder. "No one's making fun of you, Alison. We take pleasure very seriously here in Desire, but even if it doesn't appear that way to outsiders, we value honesty and fidelity even more. The women at the men's club are available for the men who are members, and we take a lot of pride in being able to sexually fulfill them. The women love it because they're protected and get to live out their fantasies. In the women's club they sometimes have men there that the women can experiment on and try out all the new things they're learning."

Alison nodded quickly, wanting this conversation to be over. "That's fine then. If I need to practice, I'll do that."

Ryder sat forward, his grin gone. "No. You won't."

Alison raised a brow at his arrogance. "Again, none of your business."

Shooting his friend another one of those looks, Dillon shook his head before his expression cleared, and he smiled down at her. "Wouldn't it be better to let us help you? We can guide you, and you'd have two men to give you the attention you could never get there. We'll be available and willing to answer all your questions."

Looking from one to the other, Alison narrowed her eyes, not trusting them at all. "Why?"

Ryder grinned. "I'd love to get my hands on you. And my mouth. I'll bet you're as sweet as pie. I'd like to get my mouth on that soft pussy. Once I did, you'd want more. We could take you together and give you more pleasure than you ever dreamed of."

Butterflies took flight in her stomach at the thought of those wide shoulders between her legs, that silky brown hair tickling her inner thighs. Not wanting him to know how his words affected her or how the erotic intent in his sparkling green eyes sent her pulse racing, she struggled to keep her face blank.

"I thought you preferred to go to the club and beat up on women."

Ryder's brows went up. "Beat up on a woman? Are you nuts? Honey, any pain I give a woman is designed for pleasure."

Alison smiled sarcastically, while her insides twisted. "Pain for pleasure. That's a good one. I'll pass."

Rubbing her shoulder, Dillon tilted her face to his, the hard glint of fury in his eyes sending a chill down her spine. "Even though you don't know us very well, I'd hoped you understood us better than that. Beating a woman is inexcusable. That's not the kind of pain we're talking about. Haven't you ever played in the bedroom? Experimented?"

God, she'd wanted to, but Danny got insulted the one time she mentioned it and accused her of criticizing him, which she found rather ironic.

Going on instinct, and lost in the tender indulgence in Dillon's eyes, she told them the truth. "I wouldn't know where to begin."

Running his thumb over her bottom lip, Dillon stared into her eyes, his smile tender and amused. "There's no such thing as doing it wrong. What works for some people won't work for others. That's the fun of learning your partner." His voice dropped, almost as though he was thinking out loud.

"You experiment and over time learn another person as well as you know yourself, that is, when you're with a person you care about—someone more than a one-night stand." Shaking his head, he released her and sat back, reaching for his beer. "A big part of that is play. Anytime there's something you'd like, all you have to do is say so, but I don't want you worrying about that now."

Pushing the mug aside with the back of his hand, he turned in his seat toward her, reaching up to tuck her hair behind her ear. "Ryder and I take pleasure and play very seriously, Alison. Most of the men in this town do, which is one of the reasons we all understand each other so well."

Ryder reached out a hand and trailed it down her arm to her hand, which he cradled in his in an affectionate move she never would have expected from him. "I would love to teach you how to play. There's no reason to be embarrassed, although I love to watch you blush. My cock is hard as a rock just knowing that we'd be the first to show you that part of sex. Tell me something, Ally. Have you ever been spanked?"

The low, deep cadence of his tone seduced her into leaning closer, until the meaning of his words penetrated the sensual fog.

Yanking her hand from his, she licked her lips and reached for her empty glass, shifting in her seat as Ryder yelled an order for refills over his shoulder.

When he turned back, his eyes no longer glittered, remaining flat and assessing.

"So, Ally, you never played before. Wouldn't you like to know what it feels like to be spanked?"

Lifting her chin, she caught several of the men at the bar looking her way, one in particular eyeing her strangely. Uncomfortable at the interest, which seemed more suspicious than romantic, she automatically turned toward Dillon.

"I've been spanked before. Once. It hurt. I didn't speak to my daddy for days, and he never did it again."

Dillon's eyes danced with amusement.

"That's not the kind of spanking I'm talking about. In Desire, a spanking is punishment for a woman who disobeys her men or jeopardizes her safety."

At a call from the bar, Ryder slid out of the booth and leaned over the table. "Spankings are also a form of play. The only difference is that with the punishment spanking, you won't get to come."

He walked away before she could respond and came back only seconds later with fresh drinks.

"Well?"

Alison snorted inelegantly, taking the drink from Ryder with a murmured thanks and ripping the paper from the straw. "Nice. Beat up on your women."

Ryder leaned closer and pushed her drink aside before sliding his hands up her arms and slowly pulling her toward him until their noses almost touched. His hooded eyes held a decadent danger she wished she had the courage to explore.

"Darlin', if I had your naked ass—"

With a gasp, she looked around to make sure no one had overheard and tried to pull away. "Naked?"

He held her easily, his grin pure sin. "Naked. If I had your naked ass over my lap and spanked you, I wouldn't let you up until you were drenched with your own juices and begging me to fuck you. We don't give spankings to hurt. They're designed as a reminder of who's in charge."

"In charge?" Alison pulled her arms from his grip and huddled into the corner of the booth. Crossing her arms over her chest, she rubbed them against the sudden chill.

"You men are all the same. Bullies and always having to be in charge. That's one of the reasons I'm taking the seminars. Women who are good at sex have men eating out of their hands. Men are pigs. Just because you're bigger—"

Dillon leaned over her, crowding her space. "And stronger. We protect our women. We can't do that unless we're in control. Face it, Alison, in general, men are better equipped to protect women than the other way around. It doesn't have anything to do with not respecting women. It's because we absolutely *cherish* our women that we're so determined to protect them. No matter what it costs, or how much we have to argue about it. A woman's safety is very important to men here."

Astounded at the passion and caring in his tone, she looked over at Ryder to see him nodding, his expression somber.

Wrinkling her nose, she laughed. "Yeah, well, maybe hundreds of years ago—"

Sitting back in his seat, Ryder nodded once, looking very much like she pictured an outlaw from the old west would look. From his long hair, to his sharp, unwavering gaze, to his long, lean build, he would look right at home with a six-gun on his hip.

"The laws of this town were created over a hundred years ago, with women in mind. Those women appreciated the protection, especially when the lack of women out here made it almost necessary for men to share their women."

Stunned, Alison turned to Dillon for confirmation, her jaw dropping when he nodded.

"Are you saying that—?"

Reaching for his beer, Dillon inclined his head.

"This town was founded by two brothers who loved the same woman. They didn't want her to be subjected to ridicule, so they used their poker winnings to buy this whole place. They lived here with her, and since they were the bosses, they could make any damned rules they wanted. Women were scarce, and they made it possible for men to share them, but it only worked if the women were protected. Hell, women wouldn't have even dreamed of coming out to a place so primitive if they hadn't been assured they would be protected."

"What about love?" Stunned at what had just popped out of her mouth, she waved her hand and reached for her drink. "Forget I said that. I don't know where that came from. Blame it on the lingering effects of medication and exhaustion."

Gripping her chin between his thumb and forefinger, Dillon leaned in closer. "You'll never find men who love their women as deeply as the men in Desire do. Our women are the most important things in the world to us, and we'd do anything to make them happy."

Alison tried to pull out of his grip, but couldn't. "Yeah, like spanking them."

Dillon shrugged. "If necessary. It keeps them safe. A woman would think twice about doing something that may put her in danger if she knows her husband, or husbands, would put her over their laps for it."

"Excuse me."

Startled, Alison looked up to find a man standing next to their table, the man who'd been sitting at the bar and staring at her suspiciously.

As tall as Ryder, he had the same black hair as the bartender, but instead of blue eyes, his were a deep, dark chocolate brown. The trace of concern in his smile made her uneasy.

Taking her hand in his, he shot a look at Dillon, one that Alison couldn't hope to understand. "Hello, my name's Devlin Monroe. I hate to interrupt your conversation, but I really need to speak with Dillon or Ryder for a minute."

Smiling her most winning smile, one she hoped didn't look as fake as it was, she ignored Dillon and Ryder's dirty looks. "Hi, I'm Alison. Do you think you could help me get out of this booth? These two don't seem to understand that I need to go."

Devlin shook his head, releasing her hand. "I'm sorry. Dillon and Ryder are good men and wouldn't hurt you for the world. If they did, I'd get involved and gladly beat the hell out of them or anyone else who did."

Ryder frowned. "Hey, Devlin. What the hell's going on? What do you need to talk to us about?"

With another look at Ryder, Devlin turned away. "I'll be at the bar."

As soon as Devlin left, Ryder shared a look with Dillon. "I'll go see what he wants and get us some more drinks."

Alone with Dillon, Alison thought this might be her best chance of getting away. "Look, I really do want to go. I'm tired, and I want to get an early start in the morning. Do you know of anyone around here who's hiring?"

Dillon's brows went up, and although she could see he gave her his attention, he slid several glances toward the bar where Ryder and Devlin stood talking.

"So you've decided to stay here after all?"

Alison shrugged and looked to where Devlin stood next to the bar, working busily on his laptop, his face a mask of concentration. "No, I have to leave, but I didn't count on the truck breaking down. I could use some money. I have a feeling the repairs are going to wipe out my account, and I'm going to need money to move on after…afterward."

If she didn't go to jail.

Dillon pushed his and Ryder's empty glasses aside before eyeing her thoughtfully. "As a matter of fact, we're hiring."

Wary now, Alison glanced toward the bar where Ryder and Devlin were deep in conversation, getting a funny feeling in the pit of her stomach. It didn't look like a friendly conversation, and she had a strange feeling they were talking about her.

"Hiring for what?"

Shrugging, Dillon gathered their now-empty baskets of food and stacked them. "For the garage. Ryder and I love working on just about any type of vehicle, but we hate doing paperwork. We have to stop working every time the phone rings, which can be a pain. You can work for us. You can deal with the phone, call in orders for parts, and help deal with filing away paperwork. Billing. Stuff like that."

Not quite trusting him and a little concerned at the look on Ryder's face, she shifted uncomfortably in her seat, suddenly finding it difficult to breathe.

"Are you serious about this, or are you playing with me?"

Dillon leaned close, sliding a finger under her chin, turning her attention from the two men at the bar to him. "If I was playing with you, Ally, you'd know it."

His eyes narrowed, moving over her face. "What's wrong with you? You're really pale."

Wanting nothing more than to get away from his scrutiny, she nudged him. "I have to go to the ladies room and put some cold water on my face. Let me out."

Apparently distracted by Ryder's loud curse, Dillon slid out of the booth, shooting Ryder a questioning look as he stepped aside.

Taking advantage of the fact that his attention had been diverted, she hurriedly slid out of the booth and started toward the back of the bar, surprised when the men watching the game cleared a path, moving aside and lifting their feet out of the way without any grumbling at all.

In fact they smiled at her.

Passing the bar, she looked up in time to see Ryder lift his head, the fury in his eyes unmistakable. She stumbled, catching herself before she fell and turned away, not wanting to see the pity she knew would follow.

He knew.

She had to get out of here.

Now.

Walking down the narrow hallway to the restrooms, she caught sight of the red back door with a lit exit sign over it and fought the urge to run for it.

Pausing at the door to the ladies' room, she looked back to see that Dillon had joined Ryder and Devlin at the bar, both of them hunched over Devlin's laptop.

Damn it, none of this was any of their fucking business.

Passing the door to the restroom, she raced to the other door, her heart pounding nearly out of her chest, scared they would came after her any second.

With her hand on the doorknob, she looked back one last time as she turned the knob and raced into the night.

Chapter Five

Ryder's anger increased with each word he read of the report until he literally shook with fury. He'd been mad before, but usually he could do something about it. In this case, the damage had already been done, and Alison had already taken care of it. Alone.

But he *could* make sure it never happened again and that she wouldn't be alone anymore.

Scrubbing a hand over his face, he fought the frustration clawing at him. He couldn't even promise himself *that*. He found it hard to believe he'd just met her, when he felt as though he'd known her forever. Something with her just clicked with him the way it never had with a woman before.

She would be leaving very soon, and he didn't even know why or where the hell she would be going. He had to find out. He had to stop her.

He had to talk her into staying here in Desire so they could get to know her.

The knowledge that she had a similar effect on Dillon filled him with a sense of inevitability that couldn't be shaken, one he didn't really ever think he'd experience. In fact it grew stronger each minute he spent with her, but this overwhelming need to have her near and protect her that hit him now slammed into his gut with the force of a sledgehammer. Gripping the edge of the bar, he closed his eyes and bowed his head, struggling to come to grips with the emotions battering his system.

He stilled as the image of Alison's face when he'd grabbed her outside the hotel flashed through his mind. The fear on her face, the momentary flash of panic in her eyes made more sense now.

Slapping his hand on the bar, he raised his head slowly and turned toward Dillon, who appeared to be waging his own inner battle. "If I ever get my hands on him, I'm going to show him what it feels like to be defenseless."

Devlin nodded in understanding, his demeanor calm, but his own eyes glittered with anger. "I thought you should know. You looked like you were coming on a little strong, and I saw the panic on her face when you and Dillon surrounded her. She was trying to flirt with Michael, but looked jittery as hell when she smiled at him."

Dillon finished reading and lifted his head, his eyes flat and colder than Ryder had ever seen them. "How do you know about this?"

Devlin shrugged. "She applied for a membership at Lady Desire. We screen all applicants thoroughly for Hope and Charity. Ace looks them over, too. The women hang out there, and we don't want any trouble from strangers."

He shrugged, closing the file on his laptop. "It stuck. I've thought about it several times since then. I'd planned to somehow bump into her while she was here, just so I could see for myself that she was all right. I'm going to track down a picture of him. I don't think he'll ever show up here, but stranger things have happened, and it would be nice to be prepared. I don't know about you, but I'm getting a little tired of being one step behind when women in Desire are being targeted."

Understanding the rage and frustration in Devlin's tone, Ryder slapped a hand on the other man's shoulder, fighting to get his anger under control before Alison came out of the restroom. "Thanks. Please keep this to yourself."

Devlin looked insulted. "I don't usually spurt out everything I know. Privacy is a big part of our business. I wouldn't have told *you* if I hadn't seen your interest in her. I remembered her. Like I said, it was kind of hard to forget. Ace recognized her and told me about her breaking down earlier, and he had a feeling you two would be watching out for her. I understand she's just staying in town for a week or two."

Ryder wasn't the least bit surprised that Devlin knew so much. He, Lucas Hart, and Caleb Ward had their own security business and did work for most of the places in town. Even when they had jobs that took them out of town, one of them usually stayed behind. They took protecting the town just as seriously as Ace and his deputies did and would definitely know about a woman they'd already approved for the club.

She needed him, *them*.

How could he let her leave, knowing she might be in danger?

How could he let her leave when he wanted her so badly he could taste it?

Devlin jerked his thumb in the direction of the back hallway. "Once you settle down, you might want to go get her. She went out the back door."

Dillon cursed and started toward the back. "Ryder—"

Ryder waved a hand, not waiting for him to finish. "I'm on the front."

Grabbing his jacket, he raced out the front door, a niggling little voice in the back of his mind telling him that this woman would completely change his life.

He was already smiling in anticipation of the hunt when he went through the front door.

* * * *

Keeping to shadows and ducking behind trees, Alison worked her way back to the hotel. She'd ended up taking several wrong turns, one which led her down a dark alley. Pausing at the entrance to get her bearings, she saw Dillon and Ryder on the street, obviously searching for her as they headed in the direction she'd realized she should have been going.

She couldn't deal with them any more tonight. Tired and emotional, she just wanted to be alone.

She also didn't want to face their pity. If they knew what had happened to her, they'd also know what an idiot she'd been, and she just didn't want to be reminded of it tonight.

It was none of their fucking business.

Figuring they would be going to the hotel, she followed them, staying hidden by ducking between cars and trees. She almost got caught a few times when they paused and scanned the area, but managed to duck in time. As they approached the hotel, they turned again, and she hurriedly hid behind a mature tree, trying to quiet her breathing. Her heart beat so loudly in her chest, she feared they would hear it and had to stifle a groan when she accidentally hit her hip on the rough tree trunk.

Closing her eyes, she fought back the pain, grateful for the lingering effects of the medicine still in her system.

She waited several minutes before daring to peek out again, breathing a sigh of relief to find them both gone.

Their truck still stood in the hotel parking lot, huge and shiny under the glare of the streetlights, but she didn't see either one of them anywhere. Hoping she'd managed to avoid them, she snuck through the front door of the hotel, intent on getting to her room as quickly as possible.

"Alison! Thank God."

She whirled toward the direction Dillon's harsh shout came from to see both of them turning from the front desk and starting toward her.

Ignoring the pain in her hip, she turned and raced down the hall, hearing the heavy tread of their boots on the tile floor getting closer and closer as they came after her. "Just leave me alone."

Dillon caught up to her first and with a hand on her arm, pulled her to a stop, his hands gentle on her upper arms, but firm enough to keep her in place. "We just want to make sure you get back to your room. Where have you been?"

Shrugging, she pulled away and dug the key card out of her back pocket. "I got lost."

Ryder fell into step with her on the other side as she headed to her room. "Are you okay?"

"Peachy."

Dillon's warm hand on her back caressed gently, sending a myriad of sensations through her. It provided comfort while at the same time making her nipples pebble as the electric little sizzles from his touch spread everywhere.

"Are you in any pain? If you're going to take another of those pain pills, I don't want you to be alone."

The combination of soothing and arousing at the same time overloaded her already battered system, and she knew she had to get away from them as soon as possible. Shooting him a dirty look over her shoulder, she started to walk faster.

"I'm not taking any more pain pills tonight. When I do, strange men break into my room."

Dillon kept up with her easily, running a hand over her hair. "I resent that."

"But you can't deny it. Look, it's been a long day, and I just want to get some sleep. Thanks for dinner." Reaching her door, she kept her eyes averted and stuck her card into the slot.

Nothing happened. Fumbling with it, she managed to get it in the slot again. Still nothing.

With a hand at her back, Ryder took the key card from her shaking hands and stuck it in the slot himself. Of course, for him, it worked the first time. "Get a good night's sleep. We'll see you tomorrow."

Alison watched in resignation as Ryder opened the hotel door and went inside, tapping the keycard against his hand.

Dillon nudged her into the room, following close behind. "And if you need a pain pill, call us so you're not alone."

"I'm going to be busy with the seminars tomorrow. If you could just leave a message at the front desk to let me know about my truck—"

Dillon pulled a card from his pocket. "You start work Monday." He went to the nightstand desk and used the pen the hotel provided to write something on the card. Turning, he handed it to her. "Our cell phone numbers are on there, too. If you need something, get scared, or are in pain, just call one of us, okay?"

Shaking her head, she tossed the card onto the dresser. "I really won't need—" Her words ended in a gasp when Dillon wrapped an arm around her waist from behind and bent, tilting her head back to give her a brief searing kiss before releasing his hold and nuzzling her neck. The bombardment to her senses left her trembling and shaky, and it took tremendous willpower not to give in to the need to curl against him.

His warm breath tickled her neck. "I won't leave here until you agree to call us if you need us."

She involuntarily tilted her head to give him better access, closing her eyes on a moan when he took advantage of it. Sizzles raced down her neck and shoulders as his warm lips brushed over them, making her nipples tighten and tingle with awareness against the soft material.

The slow caress of his lips up and down her neck from the neckline of her sweater to her earlobe weakened her knees and made her grateful for the support of the strong arm around her waist pulling her back against him. She trembled as Ryder stepped closer, his eyes flaring with heat and something else she couldn't identify.

The hard bulge pressing insistently against her lower back filled her with trepidation and, to her surprise, a rising excitement that she could have that effect on such a man.

The rush of confidence made her dizzy.

Ryder reached out to tuck her hair back behind her ear, a totally unexpected gesture. "You don't know anyone else in town. You need to call us if you need something. We're responsible for you."

Bristling at his arrogance, Alison gave him a dirty look.

"That's your fault. You wouldn't let me talk to Michael at the bar. Oh!"

Dillon's teeth sank into her neck, his low growl like little fingers dancing over her skin. "I'm not going to stand by and watch you hit on another man, Alison."

Doing her best to appear unaffected, she shrugged. "Nobody told you to watch."

Dillon's hands slid to her breasts in a move that surprised her so much, she froze. "Don't push me tonight, baby."

Lust hit her hard, her breasts seeming to swell in his hands. Amazed at the moisture that leaked from her and dampened her panties, she whimpered in her throat, her breath coming out in choked gasps.

Caught up in Ryder's green eyes, she had trouble forming a reply. "I never asked you to follow me to the bar. I can do what I want, and I sure as hell—oh God, sure don't need, umm, your permission."

Ryder lifted her chin, running his thumb back and forth over her lips. "You're in Desire, baby. You'll do what we say in order to keep you from getting hurt."

Twisting her head, she dislodged Ryder's hand. "Kiss my ass. I don't live here. I'm not subject to your archaic rules."

In a totally unexpected move, Dillon kissed the top of her hair and released her. "You're here for now. That's all that matters."

He and Ryder exchanged a long look, one that she couldn't read, but that made her very nervous.

Gathering her close again, Dillon wrapped his arms around her and pressed his cheek against her hair. "Do you want to talk about it? And don't try to pretend you don't know what I mean."

Embarrassed to have something so personal out in the open, she averted her gaze to hide her burning face and tried to pull away from him, but he held firm.

"No. I want you to forget you ever heard about it. It's none of your business, or anyone else's."

Even though her kept his hold gentle, she couldn't escape the hand that swept down to cover her right hip, caressing the scar hidden beneath her clothes. Although he would have no way of knowing the ugliness under his hand, his touch warming it brought tears to her eyes.

"We'll let this go for now, but we will discuss it. I don't know why you're embarrassed about something that happened to you, but Devlin won't say anything, and neither Ryder nor I will ever tell your secrets."

The sense of security and safety surrounding her brought a lump to her throat, the warmth and strength of Dillon's embrace difficult to resist.

She shrugged, attempting to look unconcerned.

"It won't matter. I won't be here long enough for it to matter."

Dillon ran a hand down her arm.

"Yes, you will. Don't forget about your new job."

Ryder looked momentarily surprised before he smiled and nodded. To her enormous shock, he tweaked her nose and smiled playfully. "Don't go chasing any other men. We'll see you tomorrow after your seminars. If you're going to practice on anyone, it's going to be us."

She watched them walk toward the door and hated the thought of facing the night alone. She knew if she asked them to stay, they would, which made it even more difficult to resist asking.

When Dillon turned the knob and the door swung open, she had a momentary surge of panic and leapt forward.

"Dillon!"

She stopped abruptly, taking a shaky breath when he paused, and rushed to get the words out before she lost her courage.

"If we have sex, I don't want this subject brought up again."

Both turned, sharing a look. Ryder looked like he wanted to say something, but Dillon shook his head.

Facing her squarely, he nodded once. "We'll do it your way. For now. We'll pick you up for breakfast."

Chapter Six

Tightening her hands on her purse, Alison started into the large room where several other women had already gathered.

Just inside the entrance and to the right, a serious-looking woman sitting at a table removed her glasses and turned to laugh over her shoulder. The accompanying male chuckle had Alison looking up, meeting the amused gaze of the man from the bar the previous night.

Devlin.

Damn it.

She started to step back with the intention of coming back after Devlin left, but the woman turned back, smiling politely and coming to her feet.

"Hello, I'm Charity, one of the owners. Welcome to Lady Desire. Are you signed up for the seminar?"

Seeing no way to escape without being rude, Alison sighed and approached the table. "Yes, I am."

Charity shot a resigned look at Devlin. "May I see your ID please? I'm sorry, but he's here to make sure I check them."

Devlin lifted a brow at her sarcasm and grinned. "That won't be necessary, Charity. This is Alison Bennett. She's with Dillon and Ryder. I can vouch for her."

Devlin held out his hand to her. "Hello, Alison. It's nice to see you again. Charity's just mad because we screen who comes in here. It's for the safety of the women, but none of them want to hear that. Don't worry. I won't be staying."

"No, they kick us out."

Another man approached from the side, a dark-haired man with glittering eyes so dark they appeared to be black, and so handsome she couldn't stop staring. His gaze lingered on Charity. Frustration, amusement, and some other emotion glittered in his eyes, making Alison feel like an intruder. His hands fisted at his sides as though he fought the urge to touch Charity as he turned to Alison. "Hello. I'm Beau. So, you're with Dillon and Ryder? I've got to give you credit for your courage. Ryder's a wild card. He keeps everybody on their toes."

Both Devlin and Beau had that air of authority about them, that indefinable aura that Dillon and Ryder possessed in abundance, but neither one of them made her insides tighten into knots or made it difficult to breathe the way Dillon and Ryder did.

The sense of inevitability that she'd experienced ever since she met them became even stronger.

She wouldn't, *couldn't* let it matter.

Alison watched in fascination as Charity began to fiddle with items on the table, much to the amusement of both men. She felt sorry for Charity, who seemed to do everything in her power not to look at Beau, her eyes darting around as though searching for an escape. Stepping forward, Alison shook her head, smiling faintly.

"I'm not *with* anyone. I'm only in town for a week or two, and I just met them when my truck broke down. Devlin saw me at the bar last night sitting with Dillon and Ryder, but I hardly know them."

Beau lifted a brow and shot a look at Devlin, before nodding.

"If you say so, darlin'. Charity, I finished with the tables. If I catch you trying to lift them again, you know what'll happen."

Charity whirled on him, her brown eyes narrowed dangerously.

"Beau Parrish, I'd appreciate it very much if you'd keep your threats to yourself."

Closing her eyes, she took a deep breath, missing his satisfied smile. Opening them again, she turned back to Alison and gave her a strained smile, gathering several sheets of paper and handing them to her.

"This is the itinerary for today. Sandwiches, snacks, and drinks are available at the bar. Enjoy yourself and if you have any questions, please let me know."

Alison knew damned well it was none of her business, but curiosity ate at her to know the relationship between Charity and Beau. Thanking Charity, she accepted the papers and turned away, stepping into the large room, and found herself surrounded by noise and laughter.

Pausing, she looked around, feeling more than a little out of place when she saw several of the women standing in groups, talking and laughing with a familiarity she hadn't been a part of in a long time.

The loneliness that she'd managed to push aside for months hit her hard, making her stomach tighten.

She didn't belong here.

Adjusting her purse higher on her shoulder, she turned with the intention of leaving. She would never fit in here and, after meeting Dillon and Ryder, knew she didn't have the courage to use any knowledge she might get anyway.

"Hi. Welcome. I'm Jesse."

Turning, Alison stared into the face of one of the women who'd been standing in one of the laughing groups and swallowed heavily, taken aback by the woman's beauty. Recognizing her from the restaurant the previous night, she eyed her curiously, wishing she had the courage to ask the barrage of questions that raced through her mind at the thought of a woman being shared by two men.

One thing she couldn't deny, Jesse looked happy. She'd never in her life seen someone so *radiant.*

Jesse's friendly smile put Alison at ease almost immediately.

"Please, come join us."

Alison found herself smiling back, determined to at least give this a try. She desperately missed the company of other women and thought of the women she'd used to consider her friends.

"Thank you. I'm Alison. I guess you could tell I don't know anyone here."

Jesse slipped an arm through hers and led her farther into the room.

"Believe me, before tonight's over, you'll know a lot of people."

The next several minutes became a whirlwind of activity as Jesse introduced her to several other women, each as friendly as the last. It quickly became evident that the group of women who lived in Desire seemed to be especially close.

Several minutes and at least a dozen introductions later, Alison had started to feel a little overwhelmed by all the attention. After excusing herself, she made her way to the bar where an assortment of finger food and sandwiches had been set up.

She'd been so upset at Danny's early morning phone call that she hadn't eaten breakfast, and she was starving. Not about to give up free food, she helped herself to a sandwich and ordered a beer, determined to enjoy herself.

Warmed by the camaraderie of the women she'd met, she couldn't help but smile as she watched others come up to the bar and help themselves to food and drink. Settling back, she exchanged pleasantries with them, enjoying herself immensely.

To her surprise, a beautiful woman she hadn't yet met came to sit on the stool beside her, turning to her immediately.

"Hi. I'm Charlene. I haven't seen you here before. Which men are you after?"

Blinking, Alison almost choked on her sandwich and had to wash it down with a sip of beer.

"Excuse me? Men? What men?" She looked around, her stomach clenching, hoping like hell no one expected her to actually do anything with a man. After what Dillon and Ryder said, she didn't think she'd be required to, but she'd ask Jesse just in case.

Charlene laughed, a tinkling feminine sound that Alison would give anything to duplicate. Fluffing her hair, she sent her long, dangling earrings swaying and tapped her blood red nails against the bar.

"No, silly. Not the men they use for the demonstrations. I'm talking about the men who live here. None of the men in Desire are allowed to come in here, well, not during the demonstrations, anyway. Did you get an eyeful of Beau? Yum. He only has eyes for Charity, but if she doesn't let him catch her soon, someone else will. And Devlin? Jeez, sex personified. I know several women who would love to have Lucas, Devlin, and Caleb in their bed."

Alison paused in the act of raising her glass to her lips. "What? Devlin shares women, too? With *two* other men?"

With an enthusiastic nod, Charlene finished her drink and ordered another. "Yep. Not that they come to the club very often, but I've seen them at the auctions. They're dreamy. Lucas is a little too serious, but in that really sexy way. Devlin's an absolute hunk. Caleb's playful, but you can never tell what he's really thinking. He's almost as wild as Ryder."

Meeting Charlene's gaze again, she smiled faintly, fighting back a surge of irrational jealousy that this woman knew Ryder. "I met Devlin briefly last night at the bar. I really didn't talk to anyone, and I don't think I'll get the chance to before I leave. The only men I've really had much contact with are Dillon and Ryder, and that's only because they're fixing my truck."

Leaning forward, Charlene nearly spilled out of her tight camisole, her eyes alight with laughter.

"Ooooh! Dillon and Ryder. Dillon's like a sexy teddy bear, and Ryder's an orgasm in boots. They're always really popular at the men's club. I've never been with them myself, of course, because I go after Hunter and Remy."

Charlene's bright smile disappeared, and a hard look came into her eyes.

"If you run across Hunter or Remington, I feel it's only fair to tell you that I've been subbing for them at Club Desire off and on for months now, and I consider them mine. I've been learning quite a few tricks to please them, tricks they seem to like."

Recognizing the insecurity behind the hostility, Alison finished her beer and stood.

"I don't know Hunter or Remington, or you, for that matter, but I'll give you some advice, something I learned the hard way. Fighting for a man is a waste of time and energy and only makes you end up feeling worthless. If they want you, they'll pursue you until they get you. As soon as they find someone prettier, sexier...whatever, they'll get rid of you."

Sliding her purse to her shoulder, she smiled humorlessly, clenching her jaw against the remembered pain.

Charlene smiled faintly, lifting her brow as she reached for her drink.

"If you really believe that, why are you here? Why are you so anxious to learn about pleasing men if you don't think there's anything you can do to keep them?"

Alison shrugged, more certain than ever that she'd made a mistake by coming here. "Good question. One I've been asking myself ever since I walked through the door."

Turning, she almost ran straight into Jesse, whose smile didn't quite match the concern in her eyes.

"Oh, Jesse! Hi. I was just—"

"It sounds like you were thinking about leaving. Come with me. I'd like to talk to you."

Alison didn't have the heart to pull away when Jesse looped her arm with her own and led her through the throng of women and across the room to a table on the far side.

Sitting around the table, three women she'd met earlier, Nat, Kelly, and Erin, appeared to be deep in conversation, but all three smiled in welcome as Jesse led her to the table they all shared.

As the lights dimmed, Alison scanned the room and saw that the other tables had begun to fill. The woman she saw on the sidewalk the other day, the sheriff's wife, stepped forward on the small stage with a microphone, introduced herself as Hope, and began to speak.

Alison listened with half an ear as Hope welcomed everyone and talked about what they would hope to accomplish this weekend.

She jumped, startled, when Jesse leaned close and whispered in her ear.

"I understand your truck broke down on the way into town, and Dillon and Ryder have been following you around ever since."

Uncomfortable at learning she'd been the topic of conversation, Alison shrugged and looked toward the brightly lit stage where a woman led three men to the center.

"They're just helping me with my truck."

Unable to keep her curiosity at bay, she turned to Jesse.

"I saw you in the restaurant the other night with two men. Your sister, Nat, was there with one man. When I first came to town, I saw a woman with two men pushing a baby carriage. Does everyone have two men? Does your sister have another man somewhere? Does every woman have to have two men? The woman I spoke to at the bar said that Devlin shares women with two other men. How do the men decide who's going to share a woman?"

Jesse laughed, touching Alison's arm.

"I'm pretty new here, but those were the same kinds of questions that baffled me when I got here. Come closer. We'll talk while we watch the show."

Smiling her relief that Jesse didn't seem to consider her questions as stupid as they sounded, Alison moved closer, wishing that she could stay in town. She had a feeling that she and Jesse would have become good friends.

"I was a little afraid you'd be insulted. It's nosy, I'll admit, but when I saw the way those two men were with that woman with the baby, it just brought up all sorts of questions."

With a smile of understanding, Jesse lifted a shaped brow.

"I'm not insulted at all. Thank God I had my sister here. I know it must be confusing for someone who doesn't have anyone to ask, especially when Dillon and Ryder started coming on to you. The same thing happened to me the day after I came to town to visit Nat. By the way, that woman you saw is Rachel, Erin's sister."

Swinging her gaze to Erin, her chin dropped. "Really? What does she think about that?"

Erin obviously heard her and sat forward, smiling. "I hated it at first. I figured the people in this town were crazy, perverted, and only cared about sex. But once I saw how much both Boone and Chase loved her, well, I had to accept it. Even when she was pregnant, I was trying to get her to leave town with me. I figured that marriage would fall apart in no time."

Knowing that others had a reaction similar to her own made Alison feel even better.

"They seemed really happy and in love when I saw them. Have you changed your mind since then?"

Nat and Jesse both laughed hysterically, as a red-faced Erin looked on.

Jesse caught her breath first.

"Erin is married to *three* men. She got her mind changed for her in a hurry."

"Shut up, Jesse. It wasn't *in a hurry*." With a sly smile, she studied her nails and accepted the chocolate cock Hope handed to her, eyeing it with interest.

"They had to work *very* hard to get me. I didn't give in easily, and I could never have respected a wimp."

Jesse grinned. "And Jared, Duncan, and Reese could never be called wimps."

Hardly able to fathom such a thing, Alison stared at Erin in shock. "How in the world—"

Erin laughed and twirled the cock by the stick.

"Don't ask me. I still don't understand how it works. It just does. We *make* it work. God knows I couldn't live without any of them." She paused, smiling, before blowing out a breath and turning back to Alison, her expression thoughtful. "I used to worry about it a lot at the beginning, especially when they argued, and told them so. They told me to stay out of their disagreements and to make time for each of them. I do, and it works. When they argue about something, I stay out of it. It can be frustrating, believe me, when the three of them agree on something and decide they can make a decision for me, but I have to tell you, it's nice to have men to count on. It's like it frees me somehow."

Jesse nodded immediately. "I know what you mean. When I was married to Brian, I had to do everything. He didn't want any responsibility at all. I always felt as if I had a huge weight on my shoulders. Now with Clay and Rio, I have two husbands to take care of things, ones who don't wait around for me to do it. They're a hell of a lot different than Brian."

Erin sat forward, a dreamy look on her face. "There are fewer fights than I expected, too. Jared's so bossy, he can make me crazy, and he won't budge at all. When I get pissed at him, I go find Duncan or Reese. Duncan loves to argue, and I vent my temper on him a lot of times."

She laughed, blushing. "We usually end up in bed, of course, but he usually makes me see Jared's side in a different light. It's frustrating as hell when they get bossy and domineering, but once you learn to get around them, it can also be a hell of a lot of fun."

Fascinated, Alison propped her hand on her fist, absorbed in the conversation. "I guess that's what these seminars are for, so you can learn how to get around them. My ex-boyfriend was like that. Bossy, domineering, always having to have everything his way. It didn't really matter what I liked or didn't, everything had to be his way. I guess when you get good at sex, you can get around them."

All four women stilled and looked at each other. Jesse shared a look with the other women before turning to her and touching her arm.

"I think we've given you the wrong impression, and for that, I apologize. The men in Desire are different. No, I know what you're thinking. I thought the same thing, but they are. If you care about them and they care about you, sex doesn't need any technique. Hell, technique usually flies right out the window with us. Our men love us and will do anything to make us happy. You want to get around Dillon and Ryder? Pout. Blink as if you're going to cry. They'll cave like a house of cards."

Trying to picture either Dillon or Ryder caring enough about her that a simple pout would affect them proved impossible. Men, in her experience, cared only about themselves.

Kelly sat forward. "Alison, my ex-boyfriend was a nightmare. I don't want to go into details, but it was bad. I was scared to death to trust another man again. Then I met Blade."

Shaking her head, she grinned. "Trust me to fall in love with one of the owners of Club Desire. A Dom. Talk about controlling. But we love each other, and that makes all the difference."

Alison's jaw dropped. "Weren't you scared? I mean, don't men like that like to inflict pain?"

Kelly laughed, her face flushed. "Some, but only the good kind. Please don't ask me to explain that. We both enjoy it *very* much. But let me tell you something that might help you understand. A little while ago, I had a miscarriage."

Her eyes filled with tears as the other women smiled sympathetically.

"Blade held me while I cried. He took me into our bedroom and sat in the chair and held me on his lap. All night. Every time I woke up, he had his arms around me, holding me. We stayed that way until morning. He didn't go to the club the next day like he was supposed to. He made me stay in bed, and he brought me meals and stayed with me all day. When I wanted to talk, we talked. When I didn't, he just held me. When we could finally make love again, he was so gentle, gentler than he's ever been. It was wonderful."

Sharing a smile with Jesse, she played with her straw. "But it stayed that way. I missed him. I missed what we had before. I had to practically threaten him before he would even spank me again."

Alison blinked. "Wait! What? You *wanted* him to spank you?"

Jesse laughed and patted her arm. "If you hang around Desire much longer, you'll understand. I'll tell you a little secret. The men think spanking keeps us in line, when in reality, most of the time we use it to get their attention."

Not knowing how to respond to that, Alison looked up as Hope approached the table, wearing a grin. Staring at her, Alison tried, and failed, to picture the petite effervescent woman with the huge, grim-faced sheriff.

Plunking a bucket of what appeared to be chocolate cocks, each wrapped in cellophane, in the middle of the table, Hope wagged a finger at them. "Control yourselves, ladies. They're for the demonstration."

Alison laughed at some of the comments the women made, surprised to find she'd begun to thoroughly enjoy herself. It felt good to laugh again, and she couldn't help but think about Dillon and Ryder.

After a phone call from Danny this morning, she'd been so angry, she'd walked around town to cool down, thinking about what she should do. She knew Dillon expected her to have breakfast with them, but she hadn't been able to face them.

As soon as she left the seminar, she would go in search of them, but first she wanted to enjoy herself with her newfound friends. Still finding it hard to believe that people could actually live this way, *nice* people, people who appeared to be smart and mature, Alison leaned forward, eager to learn more.

"Erin, have you been married a long time?"

Erin shook her head. "Not even a year yet, but my mother-in-law has been married to my three fathers-in-law for close to fifty years."

Alison paused with the drink halfway to her mouth. "You're kidding!"

Shaking her head, Erin rummaged through the bucket, measuring the chocolate cocks against each other. "Nope. Kind of blew me away, too."

Tapping her fingers on the table, Alison weighed her words carefully. "Dillon said that the oldest actually marries the woman but that the other man"—she shot a look at Erin—"or men consider themselves married, too. Do they really?"

Thinking of Ryder, she hoped the semidarkness hid her red face. "What if one of them met someone else? I mean, what if they decided not to share anymore?"

Nat sat forward and grabbed one of the chocolate cocks, ripping the bow and paper from it. "Not all men share."

A strange look came over Nat's face but disappeared just as quickly. "The men in this town are faithful. They don't wander. If they do, they're run out of town."

Alison's brows went up as she watched Nat slide the chocolate past her lips and so far back Alison feared she would choke.

"Do you have more than one husband, too?"

Jesse eyed her sister and grimaced. "Show off."

As Nat slowly drew the creamy chocolate from her mouth, she licked her lips and stuck out her tongue. "I've had years of practice. Pay attention to what that woman says, and you can do it, too. Clay and Rio would be thrilled."

Jesse stuck her tongue out at her sister. "Bitch."

When Nat simply laughed and did it again, Jesse turned back to Alison.

"No, Nat only has one man. Sometimes she has trouble handling him. I can't imagine what she'd do with two."

A little taken aback by the sadness that appeared and went just as quickly in Nat's eyes, Alison cleared her throat and started to unwrap her own erotic treat.

"So every woman doesn't *have* to be shared?"

Kelly had yet to unwrap her chocolate, laying it on the table and smiling serenely.

"No. Nat and I are each married to one man, and believe me, mine's more than enough."

Not wanting to ruffle any feathers, but curious about how anyone would be able to handle having their husband constantly surrounded by women such as Charlene, Alison leaned toward Kelly.

"How do you do it? I mean, how can you know that he's surrounded by all these beautiful women every day, and he's not—forget it. I'm just thinking about Danny."

Jesse slid a look at the others before leaning toward her.

"You don't have to be embarrassed because some man was stupid enough to treat you like dirt. This club is here so we all have a place to talk about things like this. Kelly trusts Blade because he loves her. If you saw them together, you would understand. He absolutely adores her, just as much as she adores him. The kind of relationships here in Desire *demand* trust, not only from the men you're involved with, but from the entire town. It took me a long time to understand that. It took me an even longer time to believe it. I think that's why we're all so close."

Alison grimaced. "It's a little hard for me to understand. I trusted Danny, and realized what a fool I'd been. I don't think I'll ever really trust anyone that way again. Men are just so consumed with sex that when the opportunity presents itself..."

Shooting a glance at Kelly, she cursed. "Hell, I'm sorry. I didn't mean you."

Kelly nodded and smiled. "I know what you meant. Before Blade, I would have thought the same thing, and I never would have believed I'd trust another man."

Jesse smiled and patted Alison's hand. "You will trust again, especially if you fall in love with someone from this town."

Alison shrugged, depression settling over her once again. "I doubt it. I won't be here long enough, anyway. Dillon offered me a job at the garage. I may have to take it in order to pay for my truck repairs, but I'll be leaving soon."

Jesse smiled. "I know it's none of my business, but if you and Dillon and Ryder hit it off, why don't you think about staying?"

Seeing the friendly interest on their faces, Alison set aside her chocolate and sat forward, glad to finally have someone to talk to. The knot of tension in her stomach turned cold as she thought about the weeks ahead.

"I can't. I have some things to take care of, and then I don't know what's in store for me. I can't make any plans right now."

She tried to laugh, but the fear of being arrested if Danny followed through on his threat made it come out more like a sob, and she found she couldn't talk after all. "I really can't talk about it."

Kelly licked the tip of her chocolate, seeming unconcerned with following the directions from the woman standing at the microphone and instructing them on giving blow jobs.

"So, you're going to work at the garage?"

Alison listened with half an ear to the instructions, wanting to get this right, but too involved in conversation with the other women to give the lesson the attention it deserved.

"I think so. I was supposed to talk to him about it this morning, but I left my room early and spent the day walking around town. I didn't want to run into them, but I almost did when I found the garage by accident. I had to duck around the corner so they wouldn't see me."

Nat licked chocolate from her lips again.

"Oh, if they want to talk to you, they'll find you. Ladies, if you want to learn how to suck cock, you're going to have to pay attention. Kelly, I can't believe the way you do that. Didn't Blade teach you any better?"

Kelly colored and giggled. "Blade likes the way I do it just fine."

Jesse sighed. "Hell, these things always make me horny. How long is this thing scheduled to last?"

Nat laughed. "You've got three more hours, sis. Then you and Kelly can give your demonstration, I can help Erin show some of the things from the lingerie store, and we can all go home and get laid."

Jesse patted her sister's arm. "That's because Jake knows how much these things turn you on. He's probably sitting over there at the club with the rest of them wondering what we're doing in here."

Kelly set her chocolate aside and reached for her water.

"That's true. Blade was laughing about it one day. He said that when Hope has a meeting here, the club's unusually busy with all of your husbands."

Jesse unwrapped her treat and eyed it thoughtfully. "Hmm. Nice size on these, huh? Yeah, the men all must be standing around the windows. Alison, you've got to watch this. The minute Hope or Charity opens the door, men pour out of the men's club like their asses are on fire. It's funny as hell."

Erin's brows went up. "I've never seen you complaining when those big lugs come over to get you."

Jesse beamed, her smile full of love, her eyes sparkling with it. "Are you kidding? Clay and Rio both give me extra attention when I've been to one of these things, and they know that submissive men are here. I think they're jealous."

Kelly shook her head and recapped her water. "Like they have a reason to. Jesse's crazy about those two."

Licking her chocolate, Jesse surprised Alison by tearing up.

"I shudder to think of what my life would be like without either one of them."

Nat grinned. "Told ya."

Unable to fully comprehend this way of life, Alison nevertheless enjoyed the conversation, feeling more and more a part of it.

"Jesse, you said that you had a demonstration. What are you teaching?"

With a smile, the other woman gestured toward a table where a variety of what appeared to be creams and lotions had been set up.

"Kelly and I own Indulgences, where we make scented creams, lotions, shampoo, things like that. Erin and Rachel own the lingerie store. Since

Rachel's home with the baby, Nat's going to help Erin with that. I'd love for you to try our products. Is there a particular scent that you like?"

Shifting restlessly in her seat, Alison shook her head, her face burning. She used nothing but the cheapest drugstore brands for shampoo and conditioner and hadn't been able to afford lip balm or lotions for years.

"No. I'm sorry. I don't have money for—"

"Shush. Consider it a welcome gift. Once you try our products, you'll be back for more. Dillon and Ryder can buy them for you."

"But I'm not staying."

Kelly grinned. "If Dillon and Ryder are after you, you'll stay." She shrugged. "If not, consider it a 'good luck on your adventures' gift. Jesse, what scent do you think suits her?"

As all four women discussed fragrances, Alison tried to follow the instruction of the woman on stage and nearly choked when she pushed the chocolate cock too far into her throat.

"How the hell does she make that look so easy?"

Nat immediately sat up and reached for her, rubbing her arm with a familiarity that touched Alison's heart. "No, honey. You've got to relax your throat."

Laughing through her embarrassment, Alison shook her head. "Women are actually supposed to know this stuff? How the hell does anyone learn this without a place like this?"

Hope came by the table again with another handful of the chocolate cocks and refilled the bucket at the center of the table. "That's what I always said. I knew this table was going to need extras."

Kelly giggled. "Blade taught me what he likes. God, it was so..." She turned red, the faraway look in her eyes intriguing Alison.

She'd been embarrassed at varying degrees since she walked through the door, but with these women it had become a *comfortable* embarrassment, one that all of them seemed to share. Enjoying herself immensely, she smiled at Kelly's look.

"Wow."

Giggling again, Kelly seemed to snap back to the present.

"Yeah. Well, sometimes I do it wrong just so he'll teach me again."

Nat nodded. "Yep. Probably get belligerent so he spanks you, too."

Kelly beamed, something Alison noticed these women did with remarkable frequency. "Absolutely. I love when he gets firm and takes me in hand. Oh, hell. How much longer is this thing?" She wiggled in her seat and reached for her chocolate again.

Alison couldn't help but laugh at her new friend's obvious hurry to get back to her husband and envied such closeness. She'd never known such intimacy with a man could exist, and she hoped she'd have a chance to see these women with their husbands before she left.

She desperately wanted to believe it could happen.

She'd seen glimpses of it with Rachel, the women with the baby, and with Jesse at the hotel restaurant, but at the restaurant, Nat hadn't looked quite as happy. Alison didn't know the other woman well enough to be sure, but the way Jesse kept touching her sister's arm and looking at her in concern told her something bothered Nat.

Smiling at Kelly, Alison cursed the fact that her face burned again and leaned forward, keeping her voice low so as not to be overheard.

"If I'm being too nosy, please tell me, but please try to make me understand this town's obsession with spanking. Dillon and Ryder have both threatened me with it, and to tell you the truth, it scares me to death."

All conversation at the table ended as all four women turned to stare at her.

Very afraid that she'd overstepped her bounds, Alison wished she'd never brought it up, but curiosity had gotten the better of her. Not wanting to insult any of them, Alison decided to be truthful.

"Dillon asked me if I'd ever been spanked and made it sound like something I'd like, although I can't imagine that. Ryder actually sounded like he looked forward to it, which I can understand because we rub each other the wrong way, but I thought Dillon seemed to like me."

Shrugging, she toyed with the stem of her half eaten chocolate candy. "I've never heard of it being...I didn't know people..." Blowing out a breath, she tossed her chocolate on the table.

"I guess I just don't understand why they would threaten it, and at the same time tell me how much I'd like it. Why the hell would I want to be hurt? There must be something I'm missing."

To her relief, the other women looked amused by her question, their tight expressions relaxing again.

Kelly giggled again. "I'll make you a deal. I'll explain it to you if you tell us all about you and Ryder rubbing each other the wrong way."

Toying with the tablecloth, Alison shrugged.

"There's not much to tell. I insulted him, and it kind of went downhill from there. He...scares me a little. Dillon scared me for that matter, when we were at the hotel room. Jeez, I thought he was gentle and a real teddy bear until then, but he got so...domineering."

Nat took a sip of her drink and sat forward.

"Oh, Lord. Dillon? Impossible. What did you do? What did *he* do? I've *got* to hear this story. We'll tell you anything you want to know about being bare assed over your man's lap as soon as you spill it."

Laughing, and relieved that she hadn't insulted anyone, Alison unwrapped another chocolate cock. "Okay. We were towing my truck into town ..."

* * * *

Dillon groaned and turned away from the hidden opening in the wall of Lady Desire, his cock so hard it hurt.

"I can't watch anymore."

Despite his claim, he looked again.

Ryder shoved him aside to look through the opening himself and cursed. "Oh, hell. She has another one. She just plays with it. Licking the tip, sucking on the end—"

"Shut. The. Fuck. Up." Dillon wanted Alison so badly he ached. Watching her ineptness at trying to suck the chocolate cock had to be the most arousing thing he'd ever seen in his life.

On top of his anger that she'd avoided him this morning, and his tossing and turning all night, unable to get the image of her ex-boyfriend tossing her down a flight of steps out of his head, he was ready to chew nails.

The desire to sink into her, to explore every inch of her body and give her pleasure like she'd never known had grown to the point that he walked around with a raging hard-on and couldn't concentrate on anything else.

Her innocence behind the sophisticated façade she tried so hard to portray fascinated him. He wanted to see her smile, wanted to see the pain and wariness in her eyes replaced with passion, with need, with love.

Hell, he had it bad. She stirred something in him that had never been stirred before, something damned uncomfortable. He felt as if he'd known her forever—as though he'd just been putting in time waiting for her to arrive. She fit so perfectly in his arms as though she'd been made just for him.

He showed up at her hotel room early this morning, hoping to take her to breakfast, only to find she'd already left. He'd searched all day for her, the image of her naked ass draped over his lap becoming more and more appealing by the hour.

He'd been worried all day, picturing her lying hurt somewhere with no one to look after her. He'd almost fallen to his knees in relief when he saw her walk into the club, watching from a bench on the corner where he'd been sitting for the last hour waiting for her to show up.

He'd almost approached her. He'd even come to his feet, but remembering the look on her face when he'd gotten angry before, he'd stayed away and had to stop Ryder from approaching her, not trusting the gleam in his best friend's eyes.

Thank God Ace had taken pity on him and unlocked the special access door Boone and Ryder had installed when they remodeled the club for Hope and Charity.

Watching her gradually warm up to Jesse and the others, seeing her laugh and smile, he'd stood there staring, mesmerized by her smile. Even in the dimly lit room, her face lit up.

Damn it, he had to find a way to make her stay.

Groaning, he finally managed to straighten and looked up to find Ace watching both him and Ryder in amusement.

"I'm glad you think this is funny."

Chuckling, Ace fingered the keys to the padlock that held the small steel door closed. "I've had more than my fair share of frustration watching Hope. I'm a little surprised no one else is here."

Ryder looked back over his shoulder and grinned. "Yeah, Hope has one of those chocolate cocks now. She's up on stage, and the men can't take their eyes off of her."

Ace's smile fell. "Move." He shouldered Ryder out of the way to peer inside himself.

Dillon shot Ryder a look, shaking his head at his friend. Ace was still touchy about his wife owning such a club, and most of them were careful about the subject around him. Of course, Ryder would pull a lion's tail.

"Ace, thanks for unlocking it. What do you know about the men who are scheduled for today?"

"That they're going to be naked in a room with our women."

Spinning when he heard the deep voice coming from behind him, Dillon met Reece Preston's fierce expression and saw Rio Erickson coming up fast behind him.

Ace straightened, an unholy gleam in his eyes. "They all know better than to touch. By the way, Hope was only handing them out. Alison must love chocolate."

Dillon beat Ryder to the small opening again, his jaw clenching. It nearly dropped to the floor when he saw Alison lick the head of the chocolate cock, listening intently to the woman on the stage.

Dressed in revealing leather, she had to be the Dominatrix that he'd heard Hope had here frequently, one who appeared to have complete control over the three men dressed in nothing but loincloths and kneeling behind her.

Unlike several of the other women who laughed and appeared to be joking with each other, Alison appeared to be listening intently to the instructions, her brows furrowed in concentration as she took the chocolate cock deep into her mouth.

Dillon's back teeth ground together, his cock pushing insistently against his zipper, almost as if he could actually feel her tongue moving over it. If his cock had been in her mouth and she had that look on her face, he would do whatever it took to change that look into one of pleasure and to make her forget all about what she was doing.

She didn't need any fucking instructions. Just being inside her—her pussy, her mouth, her ass—would be enough for him.

But if she wanted instructions—fuck, his cock leaked moisture, so close to release he couldn't stand it. He'd give her all the fucking instructions she wanted.

Watching her take the head of the chocolate cock into her mouth, he groaned as his cock twitched, so hard now it throbbed like hell and ached to be set free.

Ryder tried to shove him aside, but he managed, just barely, to stand his ground. "Damn it, Dillon, move out of the way. What's she doing?"

Dillon shot him a dirty look and glanced meaningfully in Ace's direction, not wanting to talk about Alison giving a blow job to a chocolate cock where anyone else could overhear.

Turning back, he bit back a groan as he watched her try to take more of the chocolate cock down her throat. Imagining that soft mouth on his own cock, he swallowed heavily, enthralled by the way she so diligently worked to take the chocolate cock deeper.

Each time she pulled the cock from her mouth, she paused to lick the underside of the rapidly melting chocolate head, the sight of her pink tongue curling against it making his cock throb.

She concentrated so hard on listening to the woman on the small stage speak, that she forgot to use her tongue, her frustration in herself plain to see.

God, she was adorable. So fucking adorable and sexy that his stomach knotted every time he thought about her leaving.

Just imagining what it would be like to guide her had his cock leaking more moisture. "Fuck. How much longer is this seminar scheduled for?"

Christ, he was going to embarrass himself and come in his fucking jeans.

Rio leaned against the side of the building, crossing his arms over his chest. "Too long. Jesse's always wound up when these things are done, and Clay and I can't wait to get her home. Clay's home now, breaking a horse and trying to get rid of his frustration."

Dillon nodded. "I get it now. How the hell do you stand this? Because of their stores, Jesse and Erin are in there all the time. Hope's constantly in there. Why don't you just put your foot down and tell them they can't go?"

Reese exchanged a smile with Rio and Ace.

"Uh, first, these women are no pushovers, and the last thing you want to do is piss them off unnecessarily. They know the rules. No touching."

Rio grinned. "No touching for the ones who've already been claimed. You just met yours. You sure as hell haven't had time to claim her yet."

Ryder straightened, lifting a brow. "How long did it take you to claim Jesse when she came to town?"

Inclining his head, Rio grinned again, a predatory gleam in his eyes. "Touché."

Ace chuckled. "In another hour or so they'll take a break. After that they have a talk about flirting and ways to seduce your man, and then Nat and Erin are going to show different lingerie for different body types."

Dillon stepped back when Reese shoved him and took his place by the opening. Rubbing a hand over his face, Dillon grimaced, remembering all the times he'd made fun of the others for spying on the women.

"Do I even want to know what the classes scheduled for tomorrow are about?"

Ace chuckled softly. "Probably not. I know Jesse and Kelly are showing products today and tomorrow, and I think I remember something about demystifying anal sex."

Ryder lifted his head, frowning. "What the fuck's the mystery?"

Dillon tugged Reese's arm to have one last look before they went to order the parts for her truck, stilling when a loud crash sounded from inside.

Ace was already moving, shoving all of them aside. He looked through the hole, turning away with a string of violent curses and took off running just as another crash sounded and the women started screaming.

"Fucking bastard!"

Not knowing what was happening, Dillon ran after Ace, the others hot on their heels. His boots skidded on the stones as he rounded the corner and smelled smoke. They got to the front just in time to see flames shooting out the window.

He fought the terror that clenched his stomach tight and kept running, hardly able to believe the sight before him. He saw a man running down the street with Devlin and Caleb in hot pursuit. Men poured out of the club across the street and ran toward them, their horrified expressions clear from even this distance.

The fire alarm inside went off just as Ace cleared the front door. Seconds later Dillon followed, his heart in his throat.

"Ace, get out of here. We've got this. Go get that bastard."

Ace appeared torn as he searched the crowd, before nodding once, the anguish and fury in his eyes as they met Dillon's edged with trust.

"Get them out of here."

"We've got 'em. Go!"

Cursing soundly, Ace raced back out the front door.

Surrounded by the others, Dillon ran into the club, holding an arm over his eyes as flames licked at the curtains and raced toward the women already running for the door.

Rio's shouts were the only thing that could be heard over the women's screams, his deep voice barking out orders and getting the women in a single file heading out the door.

Dillon saw him scanning the room repeatedly and knew his friend was frantically searching for his wife, some of the terror easing from his face when he caught sight of her.

With his eyes burning against the smoke, Dillon helped evacuate the women, growing more terrified by the second.

He couldn't find Alison.

He grabbed one of the fire extinguishers, while Reese grabbed another and started extinguishing the flames from what appeared to have been a Molotov cocktail.

Ryder was busy hustling the women out the door with Rio, steadying several of them who stumbled, some apparently unable to see through the smoke.

Blade Royal, Jake Langley, Beau Parrish, and Lucas Hart raced in and started tossing tables and chairs aside to make a clear path for the women to escape.

Hope came running toward the front carrying another fire extinguisher, just as King Taylor from the men's club across the street ran in with two more.

He tossed one to Ryder, who immediately started putting out the last of the fire and yelled over the noise. "Is everyone out?"

Charity ran forward with Beau right next to her carrying Alison. "She's the last one. Everyone else is out."

A furious-looking Ace growled from across the room. "Beau, get Hope and Charity out of here."

Beau strode across the room with Alison in his arms. "It's that same son of a bitch again, isn't it?"

Ace nodded. "Yeah, and this time we got him. Linc's taking him in now. Is everyone all right?" His eyes raked over Hope several times as though looking for blood.

Dillon raced forward, taking Alison from Beau and started out the door with her, just as several other men ran up to the building.

He met the eyes of a terror-stricken Jared Preston as he hurried up the front steps.

Jared shot a glance over his shoulder toward where Reese held their wife, Erin, securely in his arms. "Is anyone else still in there?"

Dillon knew he referred to the women. "Hope and Charity. Ace and Beau are inside. The fire's out."

Jared gestured toward Alison. "Is she all right?"

Dillon tightened his arms around Alison, alarmed that she trembled. So did he, for that matter. "I don't know yet. I'm taking her to see Doc." Unable to resist, he bent and kissed her lips, tasting chocolate and Alison.

When the soft fullness yielded beneath his mouth, he sank into her, tasting heaven. Without meaning to, he swept her sweet mouth with his tongue, the relief of having her safe and in his arms so overwhelming it almost brought him to his knees.

Lifting his head, he stared down at her, a surge of possessiveness filling him to see her lips wet and pink from his kiss, a blush slowly spreading over her cheeks. "You taste like chocolate, honey. Be still. I don't want you hurting yourself."

To his surprise, Alison pushed at him. "I'm fine. Put me down. I just hit my hip on a table and fell. I'm not going to any doctors."

Dillon shot a look at Ryder, who raced over. "She fell. We've got to get her to Doc."

Hope extricated herself from Ace's hold and came toward them.

"Tell Doc Hansen to send me the bill for all of the women who were here. I have a list of names I'll send him as soon as I get to the computer. Alison, please go get checked out. I heard you were hurt before, and I want to make sure you're all right."

Jared smiled and looked down at Ally. "I promise you this isn't how we normally welcome new people to town. Let your men take care of you." He met Dillon's eyes again briefly and slapped him on the shoulder. "Congratulations. They'll drive you to drink, but they're worth it."

* * * *

Alison struggled to come to grips with the events of the last few minutes. Still in shock, she tried again to talk Dillon out of taking her to the doctor. She'd had more than enough of them.

"It's just my hip. I hit it on the table when I jumped up, and I fell back into the chair. It just took me a minute to get up again, and by then Charity was already there helping me. Beau just scooped me up and ran. You don't have to carry me. I can walk."

Embarrassed at being held, Alison looked around, amazed at the number of men rushing from all directions toward the club—and the number of women being carried.

"Please put me down. This is embarrassing."

Ryder, who'd been in a heated discussion with the sheriff, joined them, his angry strides eating up the ground as he came up beside her. "Are you all right? Where are you hurt, damn it?"

Wincing at the sharp tone in Ryder's voice, she pushed against Dillon, wanting nothing more than to get away and go back to her hotel room.

Dillon paused on the sidewalk, still holding her in his arms. "You like to run away and be alone whenever you're upset or hurt, don't you? Tough. Am I hurting you by carrying you?"

Touched by his concern but disconcerted that he seemed to read her so easily, Alison flattened her hand on his chest, loving the feel of hard muscle shifting beneath her palm. "No, but please put me down. I told you, I just hit my hip. I'll feel better if I can just walk it off a little."

Out of the corner of her eye, she saw the sheriff coming toward them fast, his arm still wrapped securely around Hope. His eyes never stopped shifting, taking in everything. With a kiss to Hope's tousled hair, he patted her bottom and walked away, striding toward Alison.

"How is she?"

Alison started to speak, but Dillon beat her to it.

"She hurt her hip. I'm going to take her to the hospital now for an X-ray."

Trying unsuccessfully to push out of his arms, Alison winced. "No. No hospital. I hate hospitals. I don't have insurance, and I know that I can walk just fine if this big lug would just put me down."

Dillon's brows went up. "Big lug?"

Ace nodded once and eyed Dillon and Ryder questioningly. "I assume I can count on the two of you to take care of her?"

Ryder looked offended. "Of course. You got him, huh? I'd love to have a few minutes alone with that bastard."

The sheriff's expression hardened. "Not a chance. Nothing's going to get in the way of me getting this asshole convicted. I appreciate the help. I couldn't have gone after him if all of you hadn't gone in for the women. I'm going to have nightmares about that decision. It could easily have gone the other way."

Dillon stared down at Alison, his eyes searching her face, smiling as he apparently found what he was looking for, before looking up at the sheriff again. "You knew you could count on us, just like we count on you. No one in this town is on their own. You knew there were plenty of others running across the street to help. Don't second-guess yourself. By getting this asshole, you probably saved lives. His attacks were getting more violent." Lifting his head, he clenched his jaw. "Just let us know what the hell all this was about. We'll all be over tomorrow to clean up the club. Just tell Hope and Charity to leave it alone."

"Neither one of them will set foot in there until I okay it."

Alison blinked at the vehemence in the sheriff's icy tone, but the sheriff was already walking away.

The number of people who approached Dillon and Ryder to ask if she was all right staggered her. Dillon paused several times, keeping her in his arms as Ryder ran his hands over her, apparently checking for injuries, but also sending sizzles of awareness through her.

Trying to ignore the warm, tingling feeling that lingered from Ryder's hands, Alison laid her hand on Dillon's chest, unable to resist such an inviting, wide chest to pillow her head against. "Please put me down. I need to walk."

The worry in Dillon's eyes eased, his blue eyes warming as he looked down at her hand against his chest. Moving slowly, he lowered her to her feet, his hands out as though to catch her if she stumbled.

Ryder did the same on her other side. "I still think we should take her to the hospital."

"No." Alison stepped away from Dillon, gingerly putting her weight on her right leg to find her hip only slightly tender.

The men on the sidewalk parted, making a path for her, most offering advice to Dillon and Ryder about how to take care of her.

"Get her to Doc's so he can take a look at her."

"Get some ice on that hip as soon as possible."

"Make sure you get her legs up."

Alison headed across the street toward the parking lot of the hotel, relieved that they didn't try to stop her.

"It doesn't look like I'm going to get those seminars I came for."

Ryder grinned, taking her arm to help her cross the street, while Dillon took her hand on the other side.

"Doesn't look like it. I'm not quite sure what you're trying to learn, but I'm willing to teach you."

Alison didn't answer, the surge of heat at his words making it nearly impossible to speak. Once they got to the parking lot, they led her in the direction of a shiny red pickup truck and paused beside it.

Dillon's arm came around her from behind, carefully now as though afraid he might hurt her. "We both are. We want you, Alison. I've made that clear from the beginning that I wanted you."

Ryder grinned. "And you won't even have to pay for it. You can still work at the garage to save money, and in the meantime we'll teach you all you want to know about sex…and pleasure."

God, even after what had just happened, his devilish smile and slow drawl had the ability to dampen her panties. Swallowing heavily, she straightened, crossing her arms over her chest to hide the fact that her nipples poked at the front of her sweater, and shivered against the chill. Touched when Dillon removed his own jacket and draped it around her shoulders, she cuddled into its warmth, her surprise at the way men in Desire cared for women growing with every gesture.

Gathering her courage, she faced Ryder, allowing the word she wanted to say to tumble out before she could stop it and ruin her chance to experience something she may never get the chance to experience again.

"Okay."

Chapter Seven

Not quite sure what she'd expected, she certainly hadn't anticipated being hustled into their truck and driven to the doctor's office.

Sitting out front of the small building, she pulled Dillon's jacket tighter around her and stared at the sign to the doctor's office. "Why are we here? I told you I didn't want to go to the doctor's, and I offered to have sex with you. What's your problem? Decide you didn't want it after all?"

Ryder shocked the hell out of her by sliding a hand over her thigh and leaning close, brushing his lips over her temple, the gesture of affection a sharp contrast to the steel in his tone.

"Oh, I want it all right. Now, behave yourself. You're hurt, and my hand's just itching to connect with that fine ass for all the trouble you caused me. Don't think for one minute I'm not going to get even for your teasing."

Sucking in a breath as Dillon turned toward her, she lifted her face to his, feeling small and fragile against his size and strength. She stared at his lips, her own tingling with anticipation.

"I don't tease."

Her words came out in a strangled whisper, her body stiff as Dillon's eyes held hers and he licked his lips. She held her breath as he moved steadily closer, the warmth of his breath caressing her lips as he spoke.

"Our *problem* is that you were hurt before you even got here, and before we could even find out the extent of *that* injury, you got hurt again. I'm sure as hell not going to take you—"

Alison bit back a groan, as every erogenous zone sprang to life. "Take me?"

God, the way he said it made it sound sexier, more intimate than anything she'd ever heard.

Dillon nodded, rubbing his nose against hers. "Take you. That's what a man does with a woman he wants to possess. Strips away her defenses and draws everything from her—her passion, her fantasies, her softness, her caring—because he wants them, *needs* them from her. I need those things from you, and I'll have them, but not until I know for sure that you can take the lovin' we're going to give you in return. I have a feeling, Alison, that you're going to take us just as thoroughly as we take you."

His lips covered hers, even more demanding and firm than before but with a gentleness that tore through her defenses, some deeply feminine need she'd buried for far too long breaking free and demanding she yield to him.

On a moan, she melted against him, her lips softening and parting beneath his, opening more as his tongue slid against hers, silently coaxing her to follow him.

The underlying demand in his kiss told her more than words ever could that he would accept nothing less than her complete surrender.

A surrender she gave eagerly.

His hands slid around to her back, hot and gentle against her bare skin as he steadily pulled her closer.

She didn't realize she'd wrapped her arms around his neck until she felt the cool strands of his hair slide through her fingers. Her stomach muscles quivered beneath the warm hands that circled her waist and began an upward journey, her breath quickening with each inch they travelled higher. When they reached her breasts, pausing, she sucked in a breath, letting it out in a whimper when his hands closed over them.

Danny's words rang in her head, chilling her as effectively as having cold water thrown on her. Yanking her hands from around his neck, she held them in front of her, pressing her forearms over his arms to push his hands away.

She could practically feel his confusion as he stilled and slowly raised his head, his eyes hooded and glittering as they held hers.

Swallowing heavily, she lowered her eyes. "My breasts aren't firm enough. Please don't look at me there."

The tense silence in the confines of the truck seemed to last forever. She could feel Dillon's gaze on her face, but was too embarrassed to meet it. Remembering Charlene's voluptuous curves, she could only imagine what the other women who went to the men's club looked like and knew she would be found lacking.

Danny thought so, and he wasn't even in the same league as Dillon or Ryder.

She wanted to be mad at Danny for her insecurity, but knew she had only herself to blame, which pissed her off even more.

Gripping her chin, Dillon lifted her face, the look of impatience and anger tightening his own features both surprising and alarming.

"If you weren't hurt, I would prove to you just how wrong you are about that. Your ex has a lot to answer for, and it pisses me off that you let him hurt you even now. As soon as we get you back home, we're going to have a nice little chat."

Alison relaxed when he straightened and lowered her arms. "You mean when we get back to the hotel, right?"

Gripping both of her hands in one of his, he held them against his chest.

"No, I mean when we get back to our place. You're not staying in the hotel alone anymore." With a small smile, he reached for the hem of her sweater.

"You'll find there's no room there anymore."

She gasped when he started to lift her sweater, her heart racing when Ryder turned in his seat and loomed over her from the other side. Confused by the tenderness in his eyes, she loosened her grip. Before she knew it, her sweater had been bunched under her chin.

Fisting her hands against Dillon's chest, she waited breathlessly for the disappointment she knew she would see in their eyes.

Instead, sitting there with the late day sun streaming through the windshield and warming her naked breasts, Alison stilled, her breath catching at the looks of desire in their eyes.

Her nipples, already beaded, tingled under their gazes. Her breasts seemed to warm even more, feeling heavy and swollen.

Although the parking lot was empty, the decadent feeling of being outside with her breasts exposed added a sexual tension that made her feel naughty and extremely feminine.

Ryder's eyes became hooded as he reached out a hand to place it over her breast, widening at her gasp when she cried out. His callused palm slid over her nipple, his soft touch and the tender indulgence in his heated stare easing the sense of vulnerability and filling her with a sense of feminine power she hadn't experienced in a long time.

"Dillon, look at her. Look at how sensitive she is." Clenching his jaw, he lifted his hand, leaving her bereft of his warmth until he touched her nipple with his thumb.

She couldn't hold back her cry, the jolt of pleasure too strong to allow it. Dropping her head back, she swallowed heavily, her breath coming out in whimpered pants as Ryder's rough thumb tenderly caressed back and forth over her nipple.

"She's so delicate. Her nipples are so damned sensitive. Holy shit. I'll bet she's soaking wet. Christ, that has to be the sexiest thing I've ever seen. Give me some room, damn it."

Dillon ignored Ryder's attempt to shove him aside, keeping his eyes on hers as he lowered his head to her other nipple.

She couldn't look away from Ryder's face, fisting his shirt in her hands and pressing her lips together to keep from crying out, a little embarrassed at how easily such a simple touched aroused her.

Used to being grabbed or having her breasts totally ignored, she never would have imagined experiencing such pleasure at having her breasts touched so tenderly, especially by such large and strong hands, hands that could bruise her so easily.

Her breasts had always been so sensitive that Danny's rough caresses eventually made it so she didn't want to be touched there at all. With Ryder and Dillon, it was different. Her fear of being hurt faded, allowing her to enjoy the sensation of Ryder's thumb caressing her there even more. Holding her breath in anticipation of Dillon's mouth on her, she stiffened in the seat, shaking so hard her teeth chattered.

Dillon smiled, a slow, tender smile that sent her heart racing.

"I noticed it the other night in her hotel room. We're going to have to be very careful with her. Easy, honey. I just have to have a little taste. I won't hurt you."

Before she could form a reply, his mouth closed over her pebbled nipple, the jolt of heat to her clit drawing a loud cry from her. Writhing against the seat, she closed her eyes, crying out again and again as each stroke of his tongue over her nipple sent dizzying pleasure through her.

Twisting restlessly, she squeezed her thighs together against throbbing that centered there, the strangest sounds coming from her throat as Ryder teased one nipple and Dillon gently sucked the other. She couldn't stay still. She couldn't stop crying out, pushing against them in alarm when she seemed to lose all control of her body.

When she felt Ryder close a thumb and forefinger over the nipple he'd been teasing, her eyes popped open, scared of what he might do.

The look on his face scared her just a little, his fierce expression creating both trepidation and a shocking arousal.

"Beautiful. You've got the most perfect breasts I've even seen or touched. I can see I'm not going to be able to leave them alone. You realize I'm going to get my hands on them every chance I get, don't you?"

Dillon lifted his head, allowing the cool air to blow over her damp nipple and sending another wave of pleasure through her.

"And our mouths. She tastes so sweet." Smiling, he shook his head. "How you could think you're anything but perfect is a mystery to me."

The ringing of her cell phone broke the spell, a sharp reminder of what she'd escaped. Pushing against Dillon, she looked away, wincing when the phone rang again.

Ryder took his hand from her breast and lifted her chin until she met his searching gaze.

"Are you gonna answer that?"

Alison swallowed heavily and licked her dry lips before answering, keeping her tone cool. "No."

Hoping her brisk answer made it clear she had no intention of discussing it, she met Ryder's gaze squarely.

Taking a deep breath Dillon straightened and nodded before pulling her sweater back down to cover her.

"We're gonna talk about this, Alison, and as soon as Doc okays you…hell, I'm hard as a rock."

Still trembling when they got out of the truck and Dillon reached back in for her, she placed her hand in his, searching his face and Ryder's as they patiently waited for her. She'd become used to moving gingerly, and did so now, pleasantly surprised that she felt no pain or tightness at all.

Touched at their tenderness and surprised that the need on their faces brought forth a playfulness in her she hadn't experienced in years, she smiled and drew Dillon's jacket more firmly around her.

"I appreciate you bringing me here, but I don't think it's necessary."

Dillon rubbed her back, urging her along at the same time.

"I'm sure you'll end up getting your way quite a bit with us, but this isn't one of those times."

She tried to stop on the sidewalk, but Ryder reached for her hand and gently, but firmly pulled her along.

Looking up, she realized for the first time that she only came up to his shoulder. Her inability to even slow them down started to anger her.

"Damn it. I'm not taking orders from you! I know when I have to go to the doctor or not, and I don't. Who the hell are you to try to make me go somewhere I don't want to go?"

Dillon opened the door to the doctor's office and ushered her inside.

"Let's get something straight. I'm not *trying* to make you go anywhere. I'm doing it. You're going if I have to carry you."

Ryder came in behind them, patting her ass and bending low to whisper in her ear. "Besides, Ally, as your instructors, we've got to make sure you're in good shape before we start your lessons."

Sliding a nervous glance toward the receptionist to make sure she hadn't overheard, Alison faced Ryder, keeping her tone at a whispered hiss. "Stop it. Sex doesn't take that much effort, and stop calling me Ally."

"Ally suits you." Standing in front of her, he blocked her view of the receptionist and stared down at her breasts, making her even more conscious of her nipples poking against the front of her sweater. His devilish grin made her pussy clench and sent a fresh rush of moisture to dampen her panties.

"And sex is *very* physical, at least when done right."

Reaching out a finger, he traced it over her nipple. "And we do it *very* right. Don't worry, darlin'. We'll do all the work. All you've got to do is spread those legs wide and enjoy."

Thankful that no one else sat in the waiting room, Alison took a hasty step back, so shaken and aroused she probably would have slipped and fallen if Dillon hadn't steadied her.

"Stop it. *I'm* supposed to do everything, remember. You're supposed to show me how to please a man."

Dillon rubbed her ass.

"Letting us play with those pretty nipples was a good place to start. Now behave yourself so I can let Doc know you're here."

* * * *

Twenty minutes later, Alison was sitting on a paper-lined table, wearing what amounted to a paper dress when the doctor came into the room.

Older than she'd imagined, Dr. Hansen had a kind face and twinkling eyes, and she liked him immediately.

"Hello, young lady. I'm sorry I'm late. I hate those fax machines."

Once Dillon explained to the receptionist what had happened and that she'd had a previous injury, she'd asked Alison to sign a paper allowing her doctor back home to release her medical information to Dr. Hansen. She didn't think it would be possible on a Saturday, but since her records were at the hospital, the nurse had faxed them through.

She hadn't really thought it necessary, but figured that if she worked here for a while and needed a refill for her prescription for pain medicine, Dr. Hansen would at least have the information he'd need to write it for her before she left.

"Dr. Hansen. I'm sorry to be so much trouble. I'm not hurt."

Looking up from her chart, he eyed her skeptically.

Blowing out a breath, she couldn't prevent a smile at the kindly looking doctor.

"Really. I swear. But Dillon and Ryder are hardheaded and wouldn't listen. They got all bent out of shape because I took a painkiller and muscle relaxer yesterday."

Closing the folder, he came closer and pulled out the hammer that doctors always used to hit people in the knees with.

"Yeah, Debra's keeping them out there as long as possible. I understand from Hope that they consider you theirs, so they'll be barging through the door any minute. Do you take painkillers and muscle relaxers often?"

Alison blinked, trying to follow. "No. What do you mean, they'll be barging in any minute? Can't you lock the door?"

After checking her reflexes, he stuck the hammer in his pocket and pulled out a little flashlight to shine a light in her eyes before pulling out a blood pressure cuff.

"Wouldn't do any good. Men around here just break doors down when their woman's inside. Got tired of replacing them. You're new here, but you'll get used to them."

Smiling, he slipped the cuff on her arm and grinned. "Here they come. This reading's not going to be worth a darn now."

He started pumping up the cuff just as Dillon came bursting through the door with Ryder close behind.

Coming to her other side, Dillon rubbed her arm. "How is she, Doc?"

Alison shoved at his chest, not moving him at all. "What are you doing in here? This is private."

Ryder stood next to and a little behind the doctor, crossing his arms over his chest. "You won't tell us what's wrong, and I'll be damned if I'm going to hurt you by having sex with you when you're already hurt, but too stubborn to admit it."

Mortified that he would say such a thing in front of the doctor, Alison glared at him, more than a little surprised that the doctor didn't appear at all shocked by Ryder's words. "*I'm* stubborn? I told you I was fine, but you wouldn't believe me. Get out."

Dillon slid a hand over her hair. "No. Doc, what can you tell us?"

Dr. Hansen smiled and shook his head. "I just walked in here. Her blood pressure reading's not worth a darn since you walked in and started arguing with her. Why don't you wait outside and let me check her over?"

Ryder was already shaking his head. "No. We want to know what's wrong with her."

Alison had had enough. She'd already learned that butting heads with them wouldn't get them anywhere, so she tried another tactic. The tenderness in Dillon's eyes hadn't wavered at all since he'd touched her in the truck, so she appealed to him.

Touching his arm, she looked up at him through her lashes. "Please, Dillon. I'm very embarrassed to have you and Ryder in here. I'll let the doctor look me over if you'll just wait out in the waiting room."

Dillon's eyes flared. Bending close, he whispered to her, touching her hand. "I like the way you say my name."

Straightening, he narrowed his eyes and regarded her steadily. "And you'll tell Doc everything—even what happened when your ex-boyfriend threw you down the stairs?"

Dr. Hansen's brows went up, his kind eyes sharpening. "Well now."

With a sigh, Alison found herself smiling at the doctor. "I'm fine. I promise to tell you everything."

Ryder came to stand in front of the table and placed in hands on her knees, sending a delicious warmth through her, and waiting until she met his gaze before speaking.

"And then tonight you're going to answer our questions about it?"

Bristling, Alison crossed her arms over her chest and frowned. "I really don't think—"

Using a booted foot, Ryder snagged the doctor's stool and sat.

Grinning, he slid his hands under the paper to rub her knees. "Then I guess we'll be staying."

Fisting her hands on her lap to quell the sudden urge to smack him, Alison took a deep breath and involuntarily leaned into the hand Dillon used to caress her back, comforted by his touch.

Without knowing quite why she did it, and letting instinct rule her, she reached out to cup Ryder's strong jaw, thrilling at the rough stubble beneath her hand.

"Please, Ryder. I'd like to be alone with the doctor. Will you do this for me? Please?"

* * * *

Ryder froze, his smile falling. The combination of Ally's soft touch, the fact that she'd reached out to him and the plea in her eyes hit him like a jolt to his system, bringing protective instincts he hadn't known existed inside him to the surface with a strength that knocked the breath out of him.

The breathless way she'd said his name would have knocked his legs out from under him if he'd been standing, the soft plea in her tone going straight to his cock with a force that made it actually hurt. His cock pressed against his zipper so painfully, he winced, wanting her with a desperation he hadn't felt since the first time he and Dillon took a woman together.

Afraid she would move her hand away if he turned his head, he slid his gaze to Dillon, unsurprised to find his best friend and partner staring down at Alison with a look Ryder had never before seen on his face and rubbing her back as if he couldn't stop touching her.

Her naïveté when it came to sex already had Ryder close to climbing the walls. Used to taking submissives, he still liked a little backbone in a woman, and Ally appeared to be a little too tame for him. She'd been stubborn, but still almost meek.

So why the hell did he want her so badly?

Of course, having a boyfriend who threw her down a flight of stairs and apparently got away with it might have something to do with it. The fact that she'd left showed strength, but still…

The surprise and feminine interest he saw in her eyes now only made him want her more. She seemed so delicate, so…soft, a far cry from the type of woman he usually went for.

Looking up into those big doe eyes of hers, he knew right then and there he was a goner.

He sighed, already knowing what he was going to do, but hesitated, not wanting to break contact with her. Promising himself he'd make up for it later, he held her gaze as he turned his lips against her soft palm and kissed her there.

The shocked heat in her eyes made his cock throb, and he tightened his hands on her knees, his cock jumping again when she gasped, making one of those little breathless sounds she made when pleasure hit her. Each time she made that sound, as she had in the truck, a strong surge of lust burst forth inside him, and he knew he would easily be able to rip down a wall to get to her.

Barely resisting the urge to run his hands higher up her thigh and separating her folds to bury his face between them, he sighed again and straightened, immediately missing the warm softness of her hand against his face. Looking at Dillon, he grimaced.

"I'm in trouble here."

Dillon nodded and smiled faintly before kissing Ally on the head.

"We'll be in the waiting room."

Ryder stood just as her cell phone rang again, and seeing the panic and anger on her face, he reacted instinctively and grabbed it from where she'd placed it in the chair nearby.

"I'll take care of this."

He admitted to himself that answering her phone would be invading her privacy, something that he had no right to do, but right now he didn't care. She seemed upset at the phone calls she'd been getting, and with this unfamiliar protectiveness creating havoc in his system, he acted on impulse.

"No!"

Lifting a brow, he hid his amusement. After how easily he'd given in to her just a minute or two ago, he was determined to get the upper hand back as quickly as possible.

Realizing he'd never really had it with her, he frowned, more determined than ever.

"I'm taking it. I'm getting rid of whoever keeps calling and upsetting you. Now behave yourself and let the doctor look at you, or I'll come back in here and rip that paper off of you, and we'll all take a look at you."

Satisfied that he'd had the last word and buoyed by the look of shock on her face, he left the examination room, not allowing a smile until he'd closed the door firmly behind him.

His grin fell when the phone rang again and the wave of protective possessiveness surged again. Scowling, he took the call.

"Yeah."

"Who's this?"

The arrogance in the masculine voice suited Ryder's mood, and he looked forward to this confrontation immensely. When Dillon looked up from his seat in the waiting room, raising a brow, Ryder grinned and spoke into the phone.

"Who's this?"

"Shit."

When the phone clicked in his ear, he frowned and disconnected.

"He probably thinks he has a wrong number."

A muscle worked in Dillon's jaw. "So it *is* a man? Is it Daniel Peller?"

Ryder smiled when the phone in his hand rang again. "That's what the caller ID showed."

Taking the call, he glanced back toward the closed door of the examination room, thinking about Ally's panic-stricken look. "Yeah."

"Who the fuck is this?"

Pleased at the anger in the other man's voice, Ryder strolled around the empty waiting room, keeping his tone light. "You called me, remember?"

"I called Alison. Where is she? Put her on the fucking phone."

Imagining this asshole using the same angry tone with Ally infuriated Ryder. "No, Daniel, or do they call you Danny? Ally's busy right now. She'll be busy later, too. Don't call again."

"What? Ally? You call her Ally? Wait a minute! Who the hell is this? How do you know my name? How do you know Alison?"

Ryder chuckled coldly. "I can read a police report."

An angry string of curses followed. "Listen, I don't care what that bitch says. She can't prove a thing. It was all her fault anyway. Now put her on the phone. I want to talk to her."

Arguing with the other man didn't give him the satisfaction beating the hell out of him would have, so Ryder didn't intend to waste any more time playing with him.

"No, you're not talking to her. She's under my protection now, and if you call her again, you'll get me on the phone. Don't try to find her. You'll have to go through me to get to her."

"Listen, she's my woman and—"

"Is that why she left you?"

"It was a misunderstanding, and it's none of your fucking business. If you're so tough, why don't you tell me your name and where to find you?"

Ryder grinned. "Ah, now that's *much* better. My name's Ryder Hayes, and you can find me at the garage in Desire. I'm looking forward to meeting you."

He kept his tone cold on the phone, but the second he disconnected, his temper flared, and he flung the phone against the wall, filled with satisfaction when it shattered into several pieces.

Sitting back, Dillon crossed one booted foot over the other. "And there he is. I wondered how long it would take you. So, you tell him where you are, which also tells him where Alison is. Did he sound like he'll come after her?"

Ryder smiled reassuringly at the startled receptionist and walked over to the broken phone, kneeling to pick up the pieces. "He sounded possessive—and not the good kind. Yeah, he'll come for her."

Dillon inclined his head and sighed. "We'll be waiting."

Rising, Ryder walked over to the garbage can and dropped the pieces of the broken cell phone inside, staring down at them. He wished he could erase the rest of the unpleasantness from her life with the same ease, but knew it would take much more. Remembering the shyness, the insecurity, the passion on her face in the truck, the plea in her eyes when she'd touched his face, he knew he would do whatever he could to make her happy and wipe all the unpleasantness away.

He didn't understand it, but he wanted her. And not just for sex.

Looking back up as the door to the examination room opened, he smiled at the annoyance on her face, vowing to get under her prickly defenses to the seductress he would bet loomed inside.

Under his breath, he repeated Dillon's words. "We'll be waiting."

Chapter Eight

"Damn it, I can't believe you broke my phone! Stop looking at me like that. You heard the doctor. I'm fine."

Sitting between them in the front seat of their truck, Alison looked back and forth from one to the other, a little unsettled at their stony expressions. They'd been that way ever since they left the doctor's office, and she didn't know either one of them well enough to know what it meant.

She could literally feel her back tighten muscle by muscle at the tense silence and wondered if they'd changed their minds about her.

After all, she carried a lot more baggage than the women they were used to.

Dillon turned toward her, wrapping an arm around her to rest it on the back of her seat, his eyes narrowing when she jumped. Frowning, he rubbed her shoulder.

"Why the hell are you so jumpy? You didn't think I was going to hit you, did you? Oh, hell. You would be jumpy after what happened to you."

Ryder whipped around to look at her, dividing his attention between her and pulling into the parking lot of the hotel.

"Just because we're pissed off, doesn't mean we're mad at you. And even if we get mad at you, we're sure as hell not going to hit you." He pulled the truck into a parking space near the entrance, slammed it in park, and cut the engine before turning toward her, smiling at her while his eyes narrowed in concern.

"Now, I can't promise I won't paddle your ass if I think you've earned it, but then you'll suffer a different kind of pain. Your clit will ache so bad you'd do anything to get me to relieve it."

Alison couldn't hold back a gasp, her clit tingling at the threat.

Dillon lifted her gently, settling her on his lap. Gripping her chin, he turned her face to his.

"We're mad as hell, but not with you. How the hell are we supposed to feel when we learn that your ex-boyfriend not only threw you down the stairs and broke your hip, but left you there at the bottom of the stairs in agony while he stormed out to get drunk with his other girlfriend? How long did you lie there before your neighbor heard you and called an ambulance?"

Remembering that day always made her tense, which knotted the muscles in her back even more.

Dillon somehow seemed aware of it, his jaw clenching as he rubbed the spot that had begun to hurt.

"A couple of hours. Look, I don't want to think about it. It was a small break. They put a pin in it, and it healed completely. It doesn't even hurt anymore. My back just tightens up now when I do something like drive too long on bad shocks. I'm fine. I promise you. I'm not a fucking invalid. Yeah, I have an ugly scar and there are times when my back hurts, but that doesn't make me fucking useless. Let me out. I want to go to my room."

When their expressions became even colder, Alison realized she'd given away too much. Taking a deep breath, she let it out slowly and attempted to backtrack.

"Look, I'm sorry. In the last two days I've left the only home I've ever known, had my truck break down, arrived in a new town, been bombed and poked, prodded, and questioned by a doctor I don't even know, and grilled by two strangers, who, in a weak moment that I'm still regretting, I've asked to teach me about pleasing a man. I've lost my mind. I'm tired. I'm hungry. I'm broke. I'm sore, and I just want to go to my hotel room, get the smell of smoke off of me, see if I can get my purse, which is where my pain pills are, take one, and go to sleep. When I wake up, I have to decide what I'm going to do next. I appreciate all your help, but I really just want to be alone."

Ryder pursed his lips and nodded. "Nice speech. But we're not leaving you alone. Forget it. Let's get your stuff together."

"You two are fucking hardheaded."

The tenderness in Dillon's smile reflected in his eyes as he opened the door and got out of the truck with her in his arms, surprising her with his show of strength.

"You're right about that. Look, you've been through a lot. Why don't you let us take care of everything tonight, and we'll talk in the morning?"

Watching Ryder circle the front of the truck and come toward them, she struggled to remain stiff in Dillon's arms, fighting the urge to slump against him and just relax for a little while.

"This is probably the wrong time to ask, but is the job offer still open, or were you kidding about that?" She didn't know what she'd do about money if she couldn't earn some soon. If they weren't serious, she'd get up early and go look around town to see if there was a job available that she could walk to.

Dillon bent and kissed her forehead as he started toward the entrance, the affectionate gesture once again unsettling her.

"Of course. We'll talk about it tomorrow."

Self-conscious that he still carried her, she looked around the lobby, her cheeks warming when the man who'd been in the restaurant the night before smiled and came forward.

Brandon strode toward them, his eyes full of concern, not looking the least bit surprised that Dillon carried her. He stopped short when Ryder stepped between them.

"Is she hurt? I heard what happened at the women's club. Everyone's over there now cleaning up. Did you take her to see Doc? Do you want me to call him?"

Ryder sighed and stepped to the side, gesturing toward her. "We just came from there. She's fine, but sore. We're taking her back to our place as soon as we get her things and get something to eat before she takes another one of those pain pills."

He ran his hand over her thigh, making it tingle. "We don't want her to be alone when she takes it this time. Put her bill on my card."

Shaking her head, Alison pushed against Dillon's chest in an unsuccessful effort to get down. "I can pay my own bill. Put me down, damn it. And stop talking about me as if I'm not here."

Ryder leaned over her, blocking Brandon's view and slid a hand over her ass, the warning in his glittering green eyes clear. "She's a little cranky. Be quiet, Ally. I'll dock your pay, okay?"

Brandon grinned as Ryder turned back. "At least she's got some color now. By the way, Charity came over and dropped off her jacket and her purse. Jesse sent some things over, too. They're behind the front desk."

He gestured toward the woman working there, calling out for her to bring them over, and handing a plastic bag to Ryder, smiling at Alison's attempts to get Dillon to put her down, attempts he blatantly ignored. "It was nice meeting you, Alison. I'm sure I'll see you around town again."

Alison liked looking at a gorgeous man just as much as any red-blooded female, and she couldn't look away from Brandon's fine ass as he walked away. Without his jacket, she could see his tight butt much better than she could earlier and took full advantage of the view until Dillon turned away, still carrying her.

"Stop staring at other men's asses, or I'll beat yours."

The matter of fact way he issued the threat scared and excited her more than the threat itself. Looking up at him through her lashes, she could see he was dead serious. The wave of lust that raced through her at the thought of being draped naked over his lap alarmed her even more.

Crossing her arms over her chest, she did her best to glare up at him, ignoring Ryder's chuckle. She couldn't believe all their talk of spanking her did crazy things to her system, but she sure as hell couldn't let them know that.

"I can't help it. He's got a nice butt. Don't you look at other women's butts?"

Ryder opened his mouth and snapped it shut again. His eyes narrowed, the look of frustration on his face making her smile. "That's different. You definitely need to be spanked."

"I don't know why you think threatening me with beating me is going to endear you to me."

Ryder slipped his hand into her back pocket to retrieve her key card, sliding his other hand over her breast as he did it.

"Because you know we won't hurt you. You're nipples are hard, and I'll bet anything your panties are soaked. You trust us whether you want to or not because you know damned well we wouldn't hurt you." He flicked her nipple with his rough thumb before turning to stick the keycard in the lock.

Still reeling from his almost casual touch, Alison crossed her arms over her chest again, hiding her pebbled nipples. "Trust is earned, and my panties are *not* soaked."

Ryder pushed the door open and stood aside so Dillon could carry her in, his laser-sharp focus on her face making her tremble.

"I guess now is as good a time as any to see if we can trust you."

As soon as Dillon set her on her feet, she took a hurried step back, hitting the backs of her knees on the edge of the bed.

"What are you talking about?"

Dillon reached for her as Ryder shut the door with a decisive click.

Grabbing the hem of her sweater, Dillon lifted it over her head and tossed it aside. "You wanted a shower, didn't you? We're going to see if those panties are wet or if you're lying to us."

Being naked from the waist up made her feel far too defenseless, and in a panic, she turned to run.

Dillon caught her easily. "No, we're not going to let you hurt yourself."

Lowering her onto the bed, he reached for the fastening of her jeans. "Now let's see about those panties."

Alison opened her mouth to object, but nothing came out except a moan as Ryder took his place on the bed beside her and reached for her breast, watching her face as he lightly circled her nipple.

When Dillon started to pull her jeans down, she tried to kick at him, stilling with a gasp when Ryder switched his attention to her other breast and tugged at her nipple.

Dillon paused. "Easy, honey. I don't want you to hurt yourself." He removed her shoes and socks with a gentleness she wouldn't have believed a man capable of, especially not one his size.

Trying to suck enough air into her lungs, Alison gripped Ryder's hand with the intention of pulling it away, the jolts of electricity from her nipples to her clit and pussy so strong she couldn't even think. Instead, she ended up holding on to the back of his hand, alarmed and excited when her jeans came off and she heard the material hit the floor.

"Oh, God."

Dillon tugged her panties down her legs and off before spreading her thighs and moving to stand between them, using his strong legs to push them wide.

Holding up her panties, he smiled, lifting a brow. "These feel pretty wet to me. How are we supposed to establish any kind of trust between us if you're going to lie to us?"

Nerves and excitement at being naked and having her thighs spread wide made her tremble, her arousal for Dillon and Ryder soaring. Alison shivered, trying hard not to rock her hips, but she couldn't remain still. She *ached* there so much, and with Dillon's rock-hard thighs pressing against the inside of hers and holding them spread, she couldn't get any kind of friction against her clit. It tingled more and more with each stroke of Ryder's thumb over her nipple, sending a barrage of hot sizzles racing everywhere.

She'd felt need before, but never anything like this.

Before she could come to grips with it, Dillon leaned over her, bracing his weight on one hand while separating her folds with the other, exposing her completely.

"You're wet, sweetheart, so I know you've got to trust us, at least a little. Let's see if we can earn a little more. A little more trust. A little more of your juices."

A whimper escaped, her breath coming out in harsh pants. "I…oh…it's just—"

Ryder grinned and rolled toward her, somehow managing to keep his weight off of her.

"Yes, it is."

Brushing his lips over hers, he used sharp teeth to nibble at her bottom lip. "Don't ever lie to us again. There's no need for lies and certainly no room for them."

He pressed his soft, firm lips on hers, forcing her mouth open and stroking her tongue with his. His long hair fell forward, moving like silk against her cheeks. Tangling his tongue with hers, he sank his fingers into her hair, his other hand warm on her breast.

The finger tracing her inner folds moved slowly and with a deliberate precision that stole her breath and left her in no doubt of Dillon's experience and patience.

She'd been braced for fumbling like Danny's and a finger plunging deep, not this decadent teasing that had every muscle in her body drawn up tight like a bow. She couldn't stay still, writhing and bucking her hips in an effort to get his finger inside her, to get him to touch her clit, anything.

Dillon seemed to anticipate every move she made and continued to tease her, making it clear that he was firmly in control.

Expecting him to deny her, she bit her lip and squeezed her eyes closed in an effort to rein in an arousal unlike anything she'd ever known.

She couldn't believe she lay in bed with not one, but *two* men.

And they weren't just any two men.

Dillon and Ryder each brought something irresistible to their lovemaking, so amazingly incredible she had no defense against it.

She couldn't get over Dillon's tenderness, so surprising in such a masculine man. The strength she'd witnessed so far alarmed her at first, but the gentle way he touched her made her feel safe and secure with him. He obviously knew his own strength and had the strength of will to control it, but not knowing how long that control would last kept her on edge, adding a dangerous element to the intimacy she'd long ago learned not to trust.

Ryder, on the other hand, had to be the sexiest man she'd ever met. His long hair, his earring, his many tattoos just added to the image of a wild bad boy, but even without them, that image would have been clear.

It shone in his amazing green eyes even now as he lifted his head and stared down at her, the knowledge that he knew just how to please her, his decadent grin telling her that she was in for a wild ride.

As Ryder rolled back to the side, running his hands over her body, his eyes on hers, she realized they both had one thing in common, perhaps the most irresistible thing of all.

Both men appeared to be completely focused on her, their low murmurs of encouragement and immediate reaction to everything she did unbelievably arousing.

Dillon grinned, his eyes dancing with heat and amusement.

"She's trying her best to get my finger inside her."

Bending, he touched his lips to hers, sweeping his tongue inside before lifting his head again.

Licking her lips, she savored the combined taste of both of them, drawing a shuddering breath when Dillon poised his finger at her pussy entrance and held it there, unmoving.

"Hold her still. I don't want her to hurt herself."

Alison groaned, her temper flaring. She'd forgotten all about any pain, feeling nothing but desire.

She gritted her teeth, opening her eyes to meet Dillon's watchful gaze. "I don't hurt anywhere. Stop babying me."

Dillon raised a brow. "No. I like babying you. Something about you just brings out all my protective instincts. I guess you'll just have to get used to it."

She fisted her hands in the bedding to keep from reaching for Ryder again, her breath catching when he flattened his hand on her belly and Dillon slid the tip of his finger inside her pussy. Tilting her hips, she took him a little deeper, biting her lip to keep from moaning. Unable to meet his gaze, she squeezed her eyes closed again, rocking her hips and waiting breathlessly for him to slide his finger deep.

"Do you think either one of us is going to let you close us out?"

The steel in Dillon's soft tone had her eyes popping open, the surge of heat filling her laced with trepidation.

"I'm not. I don't know what you want." Oh, God. Even with a brief affair she was a failure when it came to sex.

She lifted her gaze, forcing herself to meet his. "I'm sorry. Tell me what you want me to do."

She didn't understand the look Dillon and Ryder exchanged before staring back down at her, but it made her wary.

Ryder skimmed his hand over her belly, his eyes intent as he stared down at her, unsmiling. "I'm going to make you forget about every other man who's ever touched you."

Dillon snarled. "Look at me."

Alison cried out as he slid his finger deep and began stroking. Wanting more, she spread her legs even wider, crying out again when he focused on a sensitive spot inside her.

He massaged it, pressing against it on each stroke with an accuracy that turned her into a mindless puddle of need and had her lifting her hips to give him better access.

She couldn't stop moaning, the desperate sounds interspersed with cries she couldn't hold back. Her cries got even louder and more pitiful when Ryder slid his hand lower and began to toy with her clit.

Dillon straightened, standing between her legs again, running his free hand over her thigh and hip, pausing at her scar.

"Unbelievable. She's all worked up over this little thing. Christ, she's tight."

Her pussy had a mind of its own and gripped his finger no matter how hard she tried not to. Her clit burned under Ryder's rough finger, the bundle of nerves tingling so badly it almost hurt. She kept climbing, her entire body suffused with heat and sizzling everywhere all at once.

Ryder pinched her clit. "Open your eyes, damn it."

Immediately obeying him, she nearly came at the sight of both of them staring down at her. Not even in her wildest erotic dreams had she ever thought about having two men touching her at the same time, her body spread out before them.

Her legs tightened on Dillon's muscular thighs, wrapping around them as need swept through her.

Dillon grinned and leaned over her again. "You're not closing against me. Yeah, that's it. You're going to come for us, and we're going to watch you do it."

Alison twisted her head from side to side, teetering at the edge, but the hand caressing her scar reminded her of ugliness and pain and kept her from going over.

"Please. Please. Please. I can't. Oh, God. Don't look at my hip."

Her entire body shook with incredible pleasure, a pleasure so strong, it took what little breath she had left. She hadn't come in such a long time, and her body was hungry for it, starving to experience it once again.

To her amazement, Dillon knelt between her legs, and with Ryder's help, draped her thighs over his wide shoulders. He removed his hand at her scar, replacing it with his lips at the same time he added a finger, his two fingers stretching her pussy as he stroked deep.

Ryder's slow caresses of her clit became harder, more determined.

"Oh, you're going to come, darlin'. You might as well learn right from the beginning that I won't let you hold back from me."

Completely open with her pussy and clit being manipulated so expertly, she didn't have a chance of holding back. The tongue sliding over her scar added an intimacy that disconcerted her, but nothing could stop the rush of pleasure.

She came with a startled cry, and then another as the pleasure soared. Her entire body sizzled from within, suffused with heat as she came hard, the smooth slide of Dillon's fingers telling her she'd drenched them with her juices.

Ryder leaned over her, holding his fingers over her clit, letting them slide over it just enough to keep the pleasure rolling inside her.

"You're blushing all over. Damn, that's hot. If you weren't so worn out, I'd make you come again."

He flicked her clit one last time, smiling when she gasped. "You are so sensitive everywhere. Next time, baby, you're getting fucked good. If you're so sensitive here, I can only imagine what your ass is like. Have you ever been fucked in the ass?"

Alison shivered, involuntarily clenching her butt cheeks together, which also tightened her pussy on Dillon's fingers. Still struggling to catch her breath, she didn't have the energy to move, but the awareness of where they still touched her kept her on edge.

Dillon grinned and slowly withdrew his fingers, sliding them lower to touch her bottom hole, making her pussy clench again in response.

"She likes having her ass touched. Scared, but she responds well to it." He wrapped a hand around her thigh when she attempted to close them, holding it high and wide, increasing her awareness of her vulnerability. Dillon watched her face as he circled her puckered opening, his fingers slick with her juices.

"She's got her ass clenched tight like she thinks that'll keep me out."

She sucked in a breath and tensed, her insides quivering. She'd never heard such an erotic and terrifying threat in her life.

Ryder gripped her other thigh and lifted it against his chest, spreading her even wider until she could feel the air blowing over her wet folds. He settled his fingers over her sensitized clit again, moving them lightly over it, but with expert precision.

"Answer me. Have you ever been fucked in the ass, Ally?"

Shaking her head, she pushed against their hold and tried to sit up. "No. He tried. It hurt so bad. Don't touch me there. Don't hurt me."

The firm fingers stroking her clit distracted her, building her arousal again even as she tightened her bottom as much as she could to prevent Dillon from entering her there.

Dillon leaned over her, keeping his finger poised at her puckered opening.

"Alison, I want you to trust me. I wouldn't hurt you for the world. I just want to show you something. You did tell us to teach you everything, didn't you?"

Alison arched as he bent and took a nipple into his mouth, his hot tongue swirling over it and sending more jolts of pleasure to her clit, where

Ryder moved his fingers faster. Oh, God, she was going to come again, her body so hungry for pleasure she couldn't seem to stop.

"I'm s–scared."

When Dillon lifted his head again and nuzzled her jaw, hitting a particularly sensitive spot, she arched automatically to give him better access. His warm breath tickled her ear as he gathered more of her juices and began to circle her bottom hole again.

"I won't hurt you. I promise. Tell me you trust me not to hurt you."

Ryder bent to her other breast, swiping his tongue over it, and then grinning as he lifted his head just enough to blow on her wet nipple.

"Wait until you see how hard you come, darlin', when Dillon slides his finger into your tight ass. You're going to have to trust both of us if you want us to teach you."

He bent again and took her nipple into his mouth, his attention on her clit becoming more focused, zeroing in on the exact place she needed it.

Moaning, she concentrated on not rocking her hips, the threat of Dillon's finger breaching her bottom keeping her still.

"You're supposed to be teach–teaching m–me how I can p–please you."

She stilled as the warning tingles began, her body stiffening in anticipation. When Dillon and Ryder both lifted their heads to stare down at her and Ryder's fingers stopped their slippery caress, she kicked her legs, lifting against Ryder's fingers and whimpering when he avoided her.

"Damn it. Put it back. I was going to come."

Dillon smiled tenderly. "And you think we didn't know that. We're paying attention to every move, every sound you make, Alison. In time, we'll know your body as well as you do. You want to please me? Let me show you this."

He pressed his finger at her forbidden opening, his tone sharpening when she turned away.

"Look at me, Alison."

His slow smile seemed strained as he slid the tip of his finger inside her, setting off a barrage of shivers at the foreign and too-intimate sensation.

"And now, honey, you can come."

Both of them watched her intently as Ryder began manipulating her clit again. Just as the first warning tingles began, Dillon slid his finger deep inside her bottom.

Stunned at the decadent fullness, Alison tightened on him, crying out as her orgasm slammed into her.

Dillon moved his finger inside her, awakening nerve endings in a place she'd always considered forbidden. "Damn, she's tight. That's it, Alison. That's a girl. Oh, hell, I'm close to coming in my pants."

Ryder bent low and wrapped an arm around the top of her head, running his lips over one cheek, while caressing the other. Slowing his strokes, he dragged out her orgasm, each small movement of his finger making her cry and shake helplessly.

"See? I told you. You like having your ass played with, don't you, Ally?"

Dillon moved his fingers, making her gasp before she could answer. "You lie again like you did about your panties, and I'm spanking you."

Ryder grinned. "Lie, Ally. Please lie."

His naughty grin left her speechless. She couldn't believe they were actually talking to her while Dillon had his finger pressed deep inside her bottom. Her face burned, and she looked away, wishing she had the experience to know how to get out of this situation gracefully.

Dillon's finger in her ass held her attention as nothing on earth ever could have. It had to be the naughtiest, most decadent thing she could imagine, and the knowledge of the kind of pleasure she got from it made her wonder what other naughty pleasures she would be able to explore with them.

Dillon chuckled and slid his finger free. "I'll have pity on you this time, but next time you'll be expected to answer me. Come on, honey. Take a shower to get the smell of smoke off of you, and we'll go to dinner. You'll feel much better after you've showered and eaten."

Relieved, Alison accepted the hand Dillon offered, grabbing her shirt from the corner of the bed to cover herself as she rose.

"Wait."

Ryder gripped her shoulder and turned her until her scarred side faced him and leaned closer. Running his finger down the length of the scar marring her hip, he looked up at her with raised brows.

"*This* is the hideously ugly scar you were talking about? Hell, you sounded as if your leg had almost been sawed off. This is nothing."

Alison stiffened. "It's ugly. Don't try to pretend it's not. I have eyes, you know. And Danny said—ow!"

Ryder scowled, rubbing her bottom where he'd slapped her. "I don't give a flying fuck what Danny says. He sounds like a real asshole, and if you compare me to him, I'm turning you over my lap, shoving a butt plug in that gorgeous ass, and spanking you until you beg me to let you come. I have eyes, too. And a cock, one that doesn't give a shit about your little scar."

To her surprise, the heat from his slap spread to her already sensitized slit, adding to the warm tingling still there. Not wanting them to know how it had affected her, she squeezed her thighs closed against a fresh flood of moisture, stiffening when Ryder touched his lips to her scar.

Dillon bent to nuzzle her neck from behind. "Go take your shower, honey, so we can eat and go home."

She nodded, too shaken to speak, and walked carefully to the bathroom on rubbery legs, grabbing her robe on the way. Not until she closed the door behind her and locked it did she rub her warm buttock. Turning, she stared at her reflection in the mirror, marveling at the look of stunned delight on her face.

Home.

She'd liked the sound of that too much and blamed it on the intimacy they'd just shared.

No one would have to know that while she showered alone, she fantasized about having a home with two of the most fascinating men she'd ever met.

It would be her little secret.

Hearing the door open, she stiffened, covering herself with the washcloth and jolting when the shower curtain jerked opened and Dillon stuck his head inside.

"I just came in to wash my hands. I checked out that bag Jesse sent. It's a bunch of that lotion and stuff. I put it on the counter." With a grin, he reached out and tugged at the washcloth. "You look good wet, honey."

Chuckling, he turned away, and a moment later she heard the water in the sink running.

"Damn it. I locked that door."

Ryder wrapped an arm around her from the other side, chuckling at her yelp, steadying her when she might have fallen.

"I picked it. Don't tell Ethan or Brandon." Running his hand down her body, he slid his fingers through her slick folds, at the same time running his teeth over her shoulder. "Feel good wet, too. Especially that pretty little pussy. Hurry up. I'm starving. After dinner, we'll take you home, and I can have my dessert."

He tapped her clit, leaving her in no doubt of his intentions.

Accepting the bottle he held out to her, she turned to look at him over her shoulder, surprised to see that he met her gaze squarely instead of looking at her nakedness.

Bending, he dropped a kiss on her lips before he released her.

"Don't worry so much. We'll take care of everything."

With a smile, he patted her ass again before disappearing, yelling from the other side. "If we hadn't just come from the doctor's, I'd be in there with you."

Looking down at the bottle in her hand, she traced the label, marveling at Jesse's generosity and still a little amazed that neither Dillon nor Ryder had made any attempt to have sex with her.

Angry at herself for not reaching out for their cocks and doing her best to please them, she listened as they both washed up, their voices so low, that with the shower running, she couldn't understand what they were saying.

She'd been so caught up in what they'd done to her, she hadn't been able to keep up.

Vowing to do better next time, if there *was* a next time, she soaped herself with the bodywash Jesse had sent and gathered her courage, waiting until she heard Ryder leave so she could talk to Dillon alone.

"I'm sorry I didn't—"

Damn it, Alison. Didn't what? What could she say? Sorry I didn't jerk you off? Sorry I didn't give you a blow job?

The water from the sink shut off, and Alison could hear Dillon moving around.

Dillon poked his head in again, smiling faintly, his eyes full of concern. "What did you say, honey?"

Mortified and feeling like a failure, Alison hoped he would think her burning cheeks came from the hot shower. With a shrug, she struggled not to cover herself and end up looking even more unsophisticated.

"I'm sorry I didn't, um, participate more. I was supposed to be learning how to please you, and I, well...didn't."

Surprised when Dillon reached for her, pulling her against him despite the fact that she was soaking wet, she dropped the bottle, the loud clatter obviously also getting Ryder's attention.

He rushed in from the other room just as Dillon threaded his fingers through her wet hair and tilted her head back.

"Hey, what's going on?"

Dillon's gaze never left her face. "Alison's apologizing because she didn't *participate*."

With Dillon's shoulders blocking her view of Ryder, she leaned closer, whispering furiously. "You didn't have to tell him that. I was talking to you."

Dillon slid a hand down to her bottom and rubbed.

"When it comes to you, Ryder and I have no secrets. You pleased us just fine."

"Stop patronizing me!" At their almost identical looks of surprise, she took a deep breath and blew it out slowly. Placing a hand on Dillon's chest, she looked up at him through her lashes. "I'm sorry, but you're supposed to be teaching me how to please you. Remember? This is supposed to be about your pleasure. Not mine."

Coming to stand behind Dillon, Ryder eyed her thoughtfully. "We'll teach you all you want to know. Tonight we just wanted to learn a little more about you."

Without thinking, she pushed at Dillon, ashamed of herself that she'd allowed them to use her own body against her, the pleasure she'd had weakening her against them. "Damn it. That wasn't the agreement."

Dillon grinned and tweaked her nipple. "Can't quite hold that temper in, can you? Good, you're starting to trust us."

Left alone in the shower, Alison stood under the spray, staring at the spot where they'd stood, stunned as the impact of Dillon's claim sank in.

She hardly knew them. How could she trust them?

Could it be true? She'd thought herself incapable of ever trusting again, but already felt the beginning of the return of her old self.

The Alison she'd been before she met Danny.

It seemed like so long ago, but it had only been a little over a year since she'd started to fade away, becoming scared and needy and insecure.

No matter what, she had to leave soon anyway, so she could just have fun with them and keep as much of herself private as she could. She would just have fun. She deserved it.

With a grin, she squeezed out a large dollop of the scented gel and washed herself, loving the feel of her hands on her still sensitized body. She felt as though a huge weight had been lifted from her shoulders, so happy she wanted to dance.

Yes, she could have a lot of fun with Dillon and Ryder before she left town, and she was determined to make the most of it.

Who knew when she'd ever have a chance to have fun again?

Grateful to them for making her see what a wimp she'd become, she planned ways of paying them back. She'd have them teach her every way they knew to please them, and she'd do each and every one.

Being a source of pleasure for Dillon and Ryder certainly wouldn't be a hardship. They had to be the sexiest men she'd ever had the pleasure of knowing, and she would use her time here in this amazing town to the fullest. She'd get her self-confidence back, and when she went back home, Danny wouldn't know what hit him.

After shutting the water off, she snapped back the curtain, grinning at her reflection in the mirror.

Alison Bennett was back!

Chapter Nine

Dillon's lips twitched, his eyes dancing with amusement as he watched her slather butter on her roll and take a big bite.

"Why do I have the feeling that the woman who came out of the shower is not the one who went in there?"

Ryder, in the process of buttering his own roll, looked up. "I thought you didn't eat bread or butter."

Determined to enjoy herself, Alison slowly licked the butter from her lips, hiding a smile when both men stilled, stopping what they were doing to watch her.

"I've been dieting for so long, it became a habit. I'm not doing it anymore. I'm going back to the old me."

Dillon's eyes narrowed. "The Alison Bennett sitting here with me now intrigues me already. I'd love to help draw you out of the shell you've built around you and get to the woman you were before you got hurt."

Ryder frowned. "Dieting? Why?" Shaking his head, he held up his hand. "Don't tell me. If you say his name, I'm liable to get violent. You sure as hell don't need to diet. Hell, why do you women think men want to fuck toothpicks?"

Laughing, Alison accepted the buttered roll Ryder offered. "I'll never be that, but I weighed forty pounds more than I do now. My butt got too big." Amazed that she had no problem admitting that, she bit into the roll. "If I eat like this, it's going to get big again."

Ryder leaned closer, his eyes glittering the way they did when he'd first met her. "Not many things I like more than a nice rounded butt. I'd love to give yours a nice, slow spanking, pull those cheeks apart, lube you real slow, and play with you until you beg for me to finish you."

Alison choked on the roll and reached for her water, slapping Dillon's hand away when he jumped to his feet and started to pat her back. Before she met Danny, she'd been a flirt and loved teasing and being teased, but none of the men she'd ever met flirted the way Ryder did.

Ryder flirted with more intensity than some men used for sex, making her wonder, not for the first time, what having sex with him would be like.

She would never forgive herself if she didn't find out.

It would be one of those naughty pleasures every woman should have, something to bring a smile to her face every time she looked back on it.

Looking around to make sure no one could overhear them, she kept her voice low and reached for her iced tea, attempting for nonchalance while shifting in her seat. "Like Dillon did earlier?"

Dillon chuckled and took his seat again, clearly enjoying their banter.

Ryder shot a look at his friend and turned back to her with that slow, devious grin that made her stomach feel funny.

"That was nothing, darlin'. Dillon was real gentle with you because you're new to anal sex and because of what you've been through today. When you're feeling better, I'm going to give your ass a real workout. Once I've lubed and stretched you a little, I'm going to work my cock into that tight little hole and fuck you slow and deep."

Alison's butt cheeks clenched in response, still sensitive there from Dillon's earlier play. After Danny's fumbled and painful attempt at taking her there, she'd been nervous, but Dillon's tender touch made her yearn to explore that aspect of sex.

She didn't know about letting Ryder touching her there, though, and tried to change the subject.

"I thought I was supposed to learn how to please you."

Settling back, he reached for his beer. "Darlin', you takin' my cock up your ass will please me just fine."

Cursing the fact that her cheeks burned, Alison dug deep for the spirit she'd had in the past and tried again to get the upper hand. Leaning close, she ran her hand over his, her nipples tightening at the way his eyes narrowed. Hoping to shock him, she smiled.

"But Ryder, I want to take your cock into my mouth. I want to suck it, run my tongue over it, and make you feel so good." Fluttering her lashes, she licked her lips, her own arousal growing when he followed the movement.

Thinking about the kind of things he probably enjoyed at the men's club, she attempted again to shock him. Running a finger through the butter on her roll, she stuck it into her mouth, hiding a smile when he followed the movement and licked his lips.

"Wouldn't you like that? Wouldn't you like me to get on my knees in front of you? Would you like to force me? Would you like to pretend that I'm your slave and make me do all kinds of naughty things to you?"

Brandon approached the table, grinning at her before looking over at Ryder as he choked on his beer. "Well, Alison, you certainly look better. I guess Dillon and Ryder are taking good care of you, and if you said something that can shake Ryder, I guess we'll be seeing a lot more of you."

His smile fell as his gaze went to Dillon. "Did you hear that Ace caught the guy? It was one of the Doms in training from the club, one that Blade's been trying to deal with for months. He liked to hurt women and wanted to use the guise of being a Dom to do it."

Dillon scowled. "You're kidding. I remember that guy. He was a real piece of work. King almost beat the hell out of him more than once."

Brandon nodded. "Yeah, that's the one. I don't remember him, but I remember them talking about him. Blade even flew out to meet with him once, thinking he could get through to him if he met the guy on his own turf, but it didn't work. Royce and King tried to reason with him, but he wouldn't listen. Blade contacted every club he knew of around the guy's hometown, trying to get him banned before he hurt someone."

Ryder's jaw clenched, but his touch on Alison's hand remained gentle. "I'm just glad they finally caught him. He's caused enough trouble around here."

"Isn't that the truth? Everyone's been on edge, and Ace is livid, especially since the guy's already out on bail. He blames himself for everything and now with Hope's club in shambles...Everyone's helping with the clean up, and Ace is hiring Boone, Chase, and the Madisons to work on it." Brandon paused, smiling at her. "At least no one got seriously hurt. I'm real glad to see you're all right."

Dillon touched her arm. "Once we get Alison settled tonight, I'll be over to help with the clean up while Ryder stays with her. I don't want to leave her alone."

"What?" Alison turned to Dillon, blinking in stunned amazement.

Brandon nodded in agreement, surprising her even more.

"Of course not. You can't leave her alone, especially since she's been hurt. Enjoy your dinner."

Brandon turned and started to walk away, turning back almost immediately and snapping his fingers. "Oh, Miss Bennett, I almost forgot. Charity told me to tell you that she'll be returning your money for the seminar. She apologizes and says that if you ever want to reschedule, you'll probably be getting the Desire discount anyway. She tried to call you but couldn't get through."

At the mention of her getting her money back, both Dillon and Ryder stiffened and glared at Brandon, which made no sense at all.

Sliding her hand out from under Ryder's, she met his scowl and sat back, crossing her arms over her chest and smiled up at Brandon.

"She's going to have a hard time getting in touch with me. *Someone* broke my phone."

All eyes turned to Ryder, who shrugged.

"I told you I'd buy you a new one. I'll make sure Hope has your new number."

"New number?" Alison blinked. "I can get the same number. I just need to get—"

"No."

Brandon sighed. "Ryder, one of these days that temper of yours is going to get you into trouble." Flashing a smile at Alison that sent her pulse tripping, he nodded. "Don't let him scare you. He's only a menace to us when we get him riled. Enjoy your dinner."

Dillon spoke up, calling Brandon back. "Brandon, can you reserve a privacy booth for Saturday night?"

Brandon grinned and waved a hand, his attention diverted when one of the waitresses called to him. "Will do."

Alison waited until Brandon left and was out of earshot. "It sounds like you have a reputation for having a bad temper. You're not like that guy the sheriff arrested, are you? Go to the men's club and have sex with the subs as an excuse to hit them? Is that why you keep talking about spanking me?"

Slapping his hands on the table, he clenched his jaw. "Damn it, Alison! I would never hit a woman."

Blinking at the outrage on Ryder's face, she automatically leaned closer to Dillon. "And yet you keep threatening to do that to me."

Dillon held up a hand when Ryder shot to his feet, cutting off whatever Ryder had been about to say. Waiting until Ryder blew out a breath and dropped into his seat again, Dillon leaned closer to her, wrapping his hand around hers.

"Ryder wouldn't hit a woman any more than any man in this town would. He's got a hair trigger, but it's almost always in defense of someone else. Sure, he's the first to jump into a bar fight, but he would never do it maliciously."

"But—"

"Let me finish." The steel in Dillon's tone brooked no argument. "Since you've never had an erotic spanking, it's only natural that you would misunderstand. We use spankings in Desire to keep our women in line. Don't give me that look. The men in Desire protect their women by any means necessary. You live here, you accept that."

Ryder moved his own chair closer to hers. "The rules in this town are explained very clearly to everyone before they move here. People who don't agree with them are free to leave."

Alison reached for her iced tea, taking a sip to ease the sudden dryness in her mouth. "Well, since I won't be living here, those rules don't apply to me."

Ryder grinned. "Oh, but they do. You'll be living here until you get your truck fixed and save some money, and you've already put yourself in our hands for the time you're here. Until you leave, those rules apply to you, too."

Dillon squeezed her hand to get her attention focused back on him. "What you don't know is that once they've been subjected to an erotic spanking, women in Desire will go out of their way to earn another. I think they feel more secure knowing their men have the upper hand."

Remembering the conversation she'd had with the women in Lady Desire, Alison swallowed heavily and carefully set down her iced tea, hiding a smile.

The men thought they used spankings to keep their women in line, while the women purposely initiated them in order to control their husbands.

Interesting.

Ryder sat forward, his eyes glittering as they held hers. "You'll understand once you've had one."

Dillon pushed her hair back, leaning closer. "If a woman wants to play, we're more than happy to oblige, but if she does something that puts her at risk, we're not so indulgent. The spanking she gets then will make her think twice about doing anything dangerous again."

Sitting back, Alison crossed her arms over her chest again, her nipples beaded at the thought of play in the bedroom, play she couldn't wait to experience. The other, however, gave her pause.

"So you beat a woman's ass until it hurts so bad she'll never do it again? That's archaic!" She didn't bother to hide her disgust at such treatment, or disappointment in them.

Dillon's slow smile sent a shiver through her.

"We don't use pain, at least the kind you're talking about, to get our point across." He gripped her chin, forcing her to face him, and ran his thumb back and forth over her bottom lip.

"If you did something like seeing your ex-boyfriend come into town and didn't tell us about it, I'd strip you and put you over my knees. I'd paddle your ass enough to warm it up good and then get the lube out. I'd work one finger into your ass, and then two, and then three. I'd spank you in between to keep your ass nice and warm."

Alarmed at the rush of pleasure that raced through her, Alison clenched her butt cheeks against the tingle of awareness at the memory of his earlier ministrations there.

Dillon tightened his hold on her chin when she tried to turn away, holding her gaze with his.

"Then I'd get your biggest butt plug, oh, yes, don't look so surprised. You'll have quite a few of them. I'd work it into you until it filled you completely and you were squirming on my lap, so aroused that your thighs were coated with your juices. Then, I'd spank you some more, slow, deliberate slaps that sent the heat to your pussy."

His low, deep tone enthralled her, making it impossible to look away, the steel in it sharpening with every word.

"You'd be mad, but you'd be so aroused you'd do anything for relief, squirming on my lap and making my cock so hard it ached. Now at this point, if we were playing, I would make you come as many times as you wanted. I'd fuck you. I'd bury my face between those creamy thighs and give you all the pleasure you could take. But, for a punishment spanking, I'd play with your pussy, but I wouldn't touch your clit at all. I'd keep you right on the edge for so long, it would be almost painful. Only when you admitted your mistake would you be allowed to come. You'd be mad as hell, but you would remember it. And you'd do your best to avoid the punishment spankings in the future."

Stunned, aroused, speechless, Alison could only stare at him, transfixed by the light of anticipation in his eyes and the sharp awareness making her slit leak moisture and throb with the need for Dillon and Ryder's attention.

She would never have believed that she could be turned on by such blatant chauvinism, and fought not to be, but the underlying respect for women and determination to protect them made it impossible to work up any outrage.

Damn it.

When Dillon released her chin, she turned to Ryder, hardly daring to breathe.

His eyes sharpened with the same anticipation as he reached under the table and rubbed her thigh, sending a wave of heat to her slit.

"So, now that you know what to expect if we continue from here, do you accept our terms or not?"

She reached for her iced tea again, unsurprised that her hand shook so badly she almost spilled it. She couldn't even get past the idea of them having a collection of butt plugs to use on her. It appeared that these men could teach her a lot more than Hope's seminar could have, and even through her trepidation, she couldn't deny the excitement and anticipation at the chance to experience sex with not one, but two men, men who didn't appear to have any boundaries in that department and had the experience to make it something spectacular.

Despite their archaic attitudes regarding women, they displayed a respect and genuine affection for them that she'd never seen before.

She'd never forgive herself for walking away from such an opportunity.

Butterflies took flight in her stomach as she met each of their gazes. Taking a deep breath, she smiled. "And you're going to teach me what you promised?"

Dillon inclined his head, his eyes laser sharp on hers. "We will."

She took a sip of iced tea and placed her glass back in its spot with more care than the action deserved, trembling so hard she was afraid she would spill it.

Looking from one to the other, she clasped her hands together to keep them from shaking. "Okay. I accept."

Chapter Ten

Alison woke aroused, restless, and lighthearted in a way she hadn't been in too long to remember.

Savoring the delicious feeling, she kept her eyes closed, as it slowly dawned on her that she'd kicked the covers off, leaving her completely naked.

She never slept naked.

Frowning, she tried to remember why she'd taken off her clothes. She remembered putting on her nightgown the previous night before she'd crawled into bed. She also had a fleeting memory of waking up to find herself cuddled warm and toasty against Ryder.

She didn't remember anything after that.

Slowly she became aware that fleeting touches, like those of a butterfly's wings, seemed to be everywhere all at once, sensitizing every inch of her skin.

A firmer caress touched her hip, just as the bed dipped near her feet. Her eyes shot open, widening at the erotic sight in front of her.

At first she thought she was dreaming, until Ryder chuckled.

"Good morning."

Still blinking, she sat up, drinking in the sight of him. If she'd ever seen anything sexier than Ryder—tall, dark, lean, and tattooed, wearing nothing but a towel wrapped around his waist—she sure as hell didn't remember it.

She gulped, her eyes following the line of the large tattoo that went from his chest over his shoulder on one side and another on his bicep on the other side.

That and the look in his eyes, his long hair damp and slicked back, screamed *bad boy*, the kind of man she'd sworn never to get involved with again, but one who proved to be irresistible.

Leaning forward from where he knelt between her legs, he brushed his lips over hers, bringing with him the scent of warm, clean male.

"What a nice present to unwrap."

Tasting mint and coffee on Ryder's breath, she leaned into his kiss, his warm, soft lips teasing hers between playful nips to her bottom lip.

The bed dipped on her left side, the touch of denim against her naked thigh a sharp reminder that she had more than one man to satisfy.

Since Ryder's hands settled on her thighs, the other hands that slid over her had to be Dillon's.

The large hand on her belly kept her in place while the one at her back massaged gently. "How's your back this morning? Do you want another back rub?" Dillon's soft rumble tickled her senses, his warm, caressing hands adding to the delightful feel.

Suddenly she remembered how she'd ended up naked.

He'd given her a massage last night with some of the peach-scented massage oil Jesse had sent, and she'd fallen asleep under his hands.

Fisting her hand in the sheet, she surreptitiously pulled it up to cover her hip as she kissed Ryder back, before turning to smile at Dillon, arching into his caress.

"No, thank you. My back feels great. I told you it didn't hurt last night, but this morning it feels wonderful. Why did you take off my nightgown? I didn't have to be naked to get a massage."

Dillon, already dressed in jeans and a white T-shirt that stretched over his magnificent chest, slid the hand at her back into her hair and tilted her head back. Covering her breast with the other hand, he loomed over her, his lips just a breath from hers.

"You're naked because I want you that way, and I'm going to get you naked every chance I get. Trying to hide your scar with the sheet won't work. We've already seen it, touched it, kissed it. We won't let you hide from us, Alison."

Pressing his lips against hers, he forced her mouth open, tugging her nipple when she tried to resist and drawing a gasp from her.

Dillon took advantage of her parted lips, plundering deep, his kiss tasting of possession and need, the hand at her breast tender, but just as possessive.

Alison melted, slumping against him and lifting her arms to tangle her fingers into his still damp hair. Raising her arms exposed her breasts even more, making them more sensitive to Dillon's callused palm sliding back and forth over her nipple.

When the hands on her thighs began to work their way upward, she stiffened, whimpering in her throat when Dillon lowered her to the bed and leaned over her. He slid his hands up her arms, igniting every nerve ending along the way, until he reached her hands. Threading his fingers through hers, he interlaced their fingers and pressed the back of her hands into the mattress, his warm body also pressing hers into the soft bedding.

His mouth moved over hers with hunger and increasing passion, driving her own growing need even higher. Dillon held her easily, swallowing her moan when Ryder hooked her thighs over his shoulders and parted her folds.

Except for kicking her feet, Alison couldn't move. Her thighs, held spread wide by Ryder's shoulders, trembled when she felt his warm breath on her clit. Struggling to get her hands free, she dug her heels into Ryder's back, involuntarily lifting herself to his mouth and crying out against Dillon's mouth at the first swipe of Ryder's tongue on her clit.

Ryder's hot mouth worked magic at her center, licking and sucking his way around her clit and pussy until she shook everywhere. His long, damp hair felt cool on her inner thighs, a sharp contrast to the heat of his tongue stabbing repeatedly into her pussy.

Dillon swallowed her cries, kissing her with a hunger that left her breathless, his big body hot against hers as he transferred both of her wrists into one of his strong hands above her head, lifting his head to stare down at her as he rolled slightly to the side and slid his other hand to her breast.

"She responds so beautifully and almost immediately, even though she appears to be trying to fight it. I told you that she would if we got her before she could get her defenses up again."

Ryder swiped his tongue over her clit, making her cry out and jolt, at the same time sliding a finger into her.

With a soft chuckle, Ryder stroked her pussy, pressing insistently at the spot inside her Dillon had focused on the night before. He chuckled again when she pumped her hips and cried out, and bent to swipe his tongue across her clit again. "She's trying so hard not to lift up to me, but she can't help it. Christ, I could spend all day in bed just exploring every inch of her."

His hot mouth closed over her clit again, sucking gently and making the tender nub burn.

Kicking against Ryder's back, she cried out, cries that Dillon swallowed with his kisses. She instinctively fought against his hold, thrilled at the strength of it.

Dillon lifted his head, staring down at her, his eyes searching hers before he smiled, a smile that lit his eyes and turned them a sparkling blue.

"No, baby, you're not scared at all, are you. You like having pleasure forced on you, and you're not afraid of us." He brushed his lips over hers, his eyes flaring when she cried out again, Ryder's attention to her pussy and clit making it impossible to remain quiet.

Each cry became louder and more desperate than the last, something Dillon appeared to enjoy.

"I knew there was fire inside you. We won't let you hide it, Alison. We want it all."

Alison whimpered, arching against Dillon.

"I need to come. Oh, God. I'm so close."

Unable to help herself, she pumped her hips, fucking herself harder on Ryder's finger, nearly mindless with pleasure now. As Dillon's fingers closed harder on her nipple, he watched her intently as though gauging her reaction, his eyes narrowing when she bowed against him and cried out hoarsely.

"You like that, don't you? I thought you might. I'm certainly going to have a good time exploring all of you, Alison."

The pressure building inside her became unbearable, the sizzles racing through her growing hotter with every stroke, every touch, every erotic promise.

"I want to touch you. I want to touch you. Oh, God! I...aaahhhh!"

Stiffening, she came hard, her pussy tightening on Ryder's finger and soaking it with her juices. Each stroke of his tongue over her clit made her jolt, the sensation too strong to bear. Sliding his hands under her thighs and up to rest on her stomach, he held her down, his shoulders under her thighs keeping her hips tilted upward to a position that left her wide open to him and completely defenseless.

She whimpered. She cried. She fought against their holds, the entire time coming like she never had before. She couldn't believe herself capable of such delicious and mind-blowing pleasure, the kind that made every inch of her body sing with delight.

Easing his touch, Ryder lapped at her clit, the light, slow strokes drawing the delicious sensation out, making her wish it could last forever.

Caught up in it, she heard Dillon's voice as though from a distance, but couldn't make sense of what he said.

His tone, however, gritty and harsh with need, sent a wave of erotic tension through her, sharpening her pleasure until it crested, making even her fingers and toes tingle. Overwhelmed, she couldn't take any more.

"Please. It's too much." Closing her thighs on Ryder's head, she thrilled at the soft, cool silkiness of his hair over her inner thighs, the decadent sensation a sharp reminder that she couldn't close her legs against his erotic assault until he allowed it.

Her helplessness added another layer to her excitement, an added enticement she never dreamed she would welcome.

He didn't stop, at least not until he'd drained every last ounce of pleasure from her and her cries had become whimpers and then nothing but soft, weary moans.

By the time he lifted his head, every nerve ending in her body tingled in delight and her limbs felt like wet noodles.

To her surprise, Ryder slid out from under her thighs and rolled her to her side, dropping a tender kiss on her scarred hip before rising.

Little pinpricks of pleasure raced over her hip as he knelt at the foot of the bed and leaned over her.

"Good morning."

A giggle escaped before she could prevent it, and shaking her head, she sat up with Dillon's strong arms supporting her. Still trembling, she slumped against Dillon, nearly melting under his caresses. Looking up through her lashes into his indulgent smile, she moaned.

"What a way to start the day! You know that you're supposed to be teaching me how to please you, well, how to please men in general—not making me come every chance you get."

With a low growl, Dillon lifted her onto his lap, draping her back over his arm. Nuzzling her lips with his, he ran his hand down her body and slipped his fingers through her slick folds.

"We're the teachers here, not you."

A little surprised at the teasing glint in his eyes, and excited by the bulge that pressed against her hip, she slid a glance at Ryder as he moved around to the other side of the bed. Her breath caught when she saw the tenting of his towel over his cock, and she automatically reached for his outstretched hand when he dropped onto the bed beside her.

He licked his lips as though savoring the taste of her, running his hand over her breast.

"You're in Desire now, babe. Just relax and enjoy it."

Dillon teased her already sensitive clit, tapping his fingers over it. Grabbing a fistful of her hair, he tilted her head back. With his face just inches from hers, he pinched her clit, his eyes flaring at her cry. His indulgent smile touched an inner softness she hadn't been aware of and accentuated his strong masculinity.

"That means that it's our responsibility to learn how to please you. Before long we'll know every sensitive spot on your body and just how and where you like to be touched. The men in Desire learn to please their women well and train them to crave their touch."

Caught up in his eyes and the feel of his fingers teasing her clit, it took a few moments before Alison could make sense of what he'd said. Bristling with outrage, Alison tried to close her legs against him, but only managed to trap his hand there. Struggling to hide her response to his fingers teasing her clit and Ryder's fingers rolling her nipple, she fisted a hand on Dillon's back and gripped Ryder's forearm.

"Damn it. You can't train women."

"Sure you can." Dillon slid a finger into her pussy and pressed at that spot they both seemed to find with remarkable ease.

"You're getting mad at me right now, but you still want the pleasure. If I arouse you and make you come no matter how I touch you, how hard, how soft, how intimately, your body will crave it and be programmed to expect it. Now, don't look so mad. Think of all the pleasure you'll get out of it."

Amazed to find her arousal building again, she opened her mouth to snap at him and then thought better of it. He'd only reinforced what she'd known all along. But that's how Danny controlled her for the longest time, and she'd already promised herself she would never allow another man that kind of control over her.

She'd come to this town to learn how to turn the tables, and that's exactly what she'd do.

Running her hand over his chest, she smiled up at him, swallowing a laugh when he narrowed his eyes and regarded her warily.

"Every time you touch me, it feels so good, but I want to please you, too." Pouting, she stared up at him through her lashes. "You promised."

She lowered her eyes to hide her amusement at the heat mixed with wariness that flared in his, then snapped her head up again in shock at their reactions.

The bulge beneath Dillon's zipper jumped against her hip. Ryder cursed and threw off the towel, fisting his hand around his long, thick cock and began to slide it up and down its length from base to tip and back again.

Dillon lowered her head back onto the pillow and stood, his hands going to the fastening of his jeans. "You want to learn how to please us? Come here. Damn it, that fucking pout drives me nuts."

Pleased with herself, Alison hurried to her knees, unable to take her eyes away from the sight of Dillon's cock as he slid his pants to his knees and freed it, wrapping his hand around it to stroke it. Ryder's cock looked longer, but Dillon's appeared to be thicker, and she couldn't wait to experience each of them.

Mesmerized by the pearly fluid at the tip of Dillon's cock, she reached for him, stopping abruptly when he caught her hand. Looking up at him expectantly, her eyes widened when he closed his eyes and drew a deep breath before opening them again.

"Take it into your mouth."

His sign of weakness at something as insignificant as a pout had her struggling to remember everything she'd learned at the women's club. Leaning toward him, she had to open her mouth wide to take the large head of his cock inside, swirling her tongue around it as she did and licking off the creamy white bead at the tip.

Knowing that both he and Ryder watched her, she closed her eyes and gripped his hips to steady herself, taking his cock into her mouth as far as she could.

"Slowly, Alison. Make me crazy."

His rough, grating tone told her she didn't have far to go.

Caught up in pleasing him, she started to suck him, careful not to touch his cock with her teeth.

The deep groan that rumbled from somewhere deep in his chest seemed to vibrate over her skin, increasing her awareness of her nudity and sending little prickles through her. His groan and the way his hands tightened in her hair stimulated every erogenous zone, his lapse in control spurring her on.

"That's it, Alison. Use your tongue. I want to feel your tongue all over my cock."

The tone of his voice had deepened, sending another surge of lust through her. Her pussy clenched, hungry to be filled, making her shift restlessly and clamp her thighs together.

She didn't know where Ryder had gone, didn't know if he still watched them, but she found herself listening for any sound that would tell her his whereabouts.

With the intention of making Dillon as mindless as they both made her, she began to slowly bob her head over his cock, using her tongue to learn every bump and ridge, playing close attention to what pleased him. She soon became immersed in the thrill of earning one of Dillon's groans, a thrill going through her when his hips jerked or his cock jumped in her mouth. Delighting in his taste she brushed her tongue along the underside, smiling around his cock when he groaned and his cock jumped again.

With the hand wrapped in her hair, Dillon pulled her head back.

"Look at me. Lick my cock while you're looking at me."

The steel in his hoarse tone sent another wave of need through her, and she shifted her position, kneeling with her slit over her ankle to provide friction against her clit. She hid a smile when his hips trembled beneath her hands, more proof that what she did pleased him.

Excited that she could have this kind of power over him, she couldn't hold back a smile. The inner glow that filled her gave her a confidence she hadn't had in a long time, the confidence of a woman who knew she had her man's undivided attention and made him lose a bit of that hard edge of control.

She'd almost forgotten what it felt like, this soft, womanly power that flowed through her, a reaffirmation that she did still possess feminine wiles.

Her growing confidence ignited a playfulness inside her, one that aroused her even more and made her want to drive Dillon out of his mind with need for her.

Sticking out her tongue, she licked the head of his cock and stilled. Sucking in a breath, she dug her nails into his hips, taken aback at the intimacy of looking into his indulgent, but watchful gaze while taking him into her mouth.

Closing her eyes, she ran her tongue all around the head of his cock. Concentrating on Dillon's reaction, she worked her tongue from base to tip, paying particular attention to the sensitive underside right below the head. She tried to remember what she'd learned at the club as she took him into her mouth again, taking him deeper the way she had the chocolate cock she'd practiced on.

"Oh, no, you don't."

Dillon's tug on her hair pulled her away from his cock and had her eyes popping open, meeting his hooded ones.

Cupping her face, Dillon ran his thumb back and forth over her moist bottom lip, his tight expression and the grittiness in his voice telling her just how much her play affected him. "Don't you dare try to close me out."

"I'm not." Wondering what she'd done wrong, Alison involuntarily touched her tongue to his thumb, snapping her mouth closed when she realized what she'd done.

With a smile, Dillon pressed against her bottom lip. "You're concentrating too hard. Nothing you can do is wrong. Just don't use your teeth. If you do, I'll turn you over my knee."

Ryder grinned, reaching down to cup her breast. "You've never learned to have fun with sex, have you, darlin'? Well, you're in luck. We're just the men to teach you."

Flashing a grin that sent a jolt of lust through her, he slid a hand down to pat her ass before straightening.

"And we're *all* going to have a hell of a lot of fun."

The soft caress of his work-roughened hand over her bottom made her breath catch, the promise in his touch filling her with anticipation.

She watched as he circled the foot of the bed again, his eyes holding the same promise, but she found herself brought up short when Dillon tightened his hand in her hair.

Keeping her facing him and preventing her from seeing Ryder, Dillon held her gaze with his own and caressed her jaw.

"I want to feel that hot mouth on my cock, Alison, and while you're pleasuring me, I don't want you thinking about any damned lessons you learned at a seminar."

Alison moaned at the possessive firmness of the hand that moved over her back, a moan cut short by a gasp when Dillon's cock touched her cheek. Turning toward it, she took him into her mouth again, this time staring straight into his eyes.

"On your knees, Ally. Stop trying to rub your clit. Get that ass up and those legs spread wide."

Startled when Ryder lifted her to her knees, she held on to Dillon, whose eyes flicked back and forth between hers and her ass.

Watching him, feeling Ryder's hands on her, and listening for any clue as to what he planned to do, she realized she'd become so distracted, she hadn't been paying attention to pleasing Dillon.

Cursing herself for her lapse, she sucked harder, determined to regain some sort of control.

Dillon slid his hands through her hair, his voice like shattered glass.

"Just feel, Alison. Do whatever comes naturally. Don't try so hard. You don't need to. You captivated us just the way you are."

A little startled by his words, she couldn't deny they wrapped her in a warm, fuzzy feeling and made her feel desired and ultra-feminine. Circling the head of his cock with her tongue, she thrilled when another of those deep moans rumbled in his throat. Every movement of her tongue, every bob of her head made him stiffen as he seemed to be scrambling for control.

Nothing could have excited her more.

At least that's what she thought until Ryder flattened a hand on her back and slid a thick finger into her pussy, her slick juices easing his way. Letting her eyes flutter closed, she clamped down on his finger and pushed back against him and in her excitement sucked Dillon harder.

The sexual tension mounted when Dillon held her face between his hands and began to slowly fill her mouth with his cock and just as slowly withdraw almost all the way. He did it again and again, each slow thrust measured and deliberate, his hands tightening with the effort it must have cost him.

Each time he withdrew, she swirled her tongue around the head, or teased the tip of his cock with it, alternating her rhythm to surprise him. When the finger in her pussy began to move, she bucked restlessly, and without thinking, she sucked hard, drawing Dillon's cock all the way to her throat.

"Jesus!" Dillon's hands moved over her hair, his movements jerky and uncontrolled.

Determined to shake that calm control even more, Alison tried to concentrate on giving him even more pleasure, but Ryder's strokes to her pussy distracted her and made her clumsy. Frustrated that she kept letting Dillon's cock slip from her mouth, but excited by the low curses pouring from him, she closed her lips around the head of his cock again, and sucked, hungry for his taste and more of those erotic and deep sounds of pleasure that rumbled from him.

Ryder withdrew his fingers, teasing her pussy entrance and chuckling softly when she thrust back against him.

"Patience, darlin'. Let me get a condom so I get my cock inside you."

She shuddered, craving the feeling of finally having her pussy filled. She wanted to be taken, to be the object of their desire, but more than that, she needed the orgasm that loomed closer with every second that passed.

Holding on to Dillon and on her knees with her legs spread wide, she waited breathlessly for Ryder to possess her. Every inch of her body sizzled with heat, each touch of their hands stoking the fire inside her until she burned everywhere.

Her nipples demanded attention, so tight and so achy she would have used her own hands on them if she could have. Her clit felt swollen and heavy, and her pussy clenched of its own volition, leaking moisture to trickle down her thighs.

Even her bottom tingled, the remembered threats of what they wanted to do to her there making her aware of that part of her, disconcerting her because she'd never experienced that kind of awareness before.

Dillon ran a hand down her face, his thumb tracing her lips that stretched over his cock.

"That's better. You're not thinking about anything else now except Ryder and me, are you, baby?"

The endearment settled over her skin like a warm blanket, the tenderness in it making her feel special and cherished.

Ryder's powerful thighs brushed against the backs of her legs as he used them to push hers farther apart.

"She's not going to be thinking about anything else for quite a while."

Forced to release her hold on Dillon's thighs and flatten her hands on the bed, Alison moaned around Dillon's cock at the caress of air over her damp folds, shaking uncontrollably when she heard a drawer open and close, followed almost immediately by the rip of foil.

She moaned again when Dillon bent forward and cupped her breasts, his gentle hands tugging at her nipples. The answering surge of heat shot straight to her clit, but Ryder's thighs held hers apart, not allowing her to press them together to get some relief.

When the head of Ryder's cock pressed against her drenched pussy, she stilled, only then realizing that she'd been rocking back and forth on her knees. Pushing back against him in the need to be filled, she whimpered in her throat when he denied her.

Ryder slid a hand around her to tap her clit, laughing when she bucked and took the head of his cock inside her.

"That's it, Ally. Damn, you're tight. I want to feel that pussy clench on me and milk me real good."

Frantic now, Alison rocked her hips, trying to get more friction on her clit, crying out around Dillon's cock when Ryder slid deep, filling her with thick heat.

Filled at both ends, she tried to concentrate on making both of them come, but each caress of their hands or stroke of their cocks made her forget everything except the pleasure. Relying on instinct, she struggled to keep up with them.

She sucked harder at Dillon, starving for his taste. Each groan or tightening of his hands thrilled her, the knowledge that she could shake his control giving her more confidence.

Dillon's hands left her breasts to cup her face again, holding her still for his smooth strokes into her mouth.

"Taken from both ends, Alison." His calm tone had her redoubling her efforts. "That soft mouth feels so good. I like how that tongue feels sliding over my cock. Easy, Ryder."

"Easy, my ass. She wants it rough, don't you, Ally?"

In answer, Alison pushed back against him, moaning in her throat when he groaned and rubbed his hands over her back.

Ryder plunged deep, his hands flat on her back, holding her in place for his thrusts.

She reveled in each bump and ridge of his cock sliding over her inner flesh, fisting her hands in the covers to steady herself. Trembling everywhere, she couldn't stop moaning around Dillon's cock, her breath catching each time Ryder's sac created friction against her clit. Focusing on pleasing Dillon got harder and harder, her attempts to lick and suck him getting clumsier as the need to come blocked out everything else.

She couldn't stop gripping Ryder's cock, his words of encouragement rendering her senseless.

"That's it, Ally. Fuck. Your pussy's so damned tight. Slick. Soft. Christ, I could fuck you forever."

Dillon's hands slid into her hair again, guiding her movements. "Her mouth's incredible. Not thinking about chocolate now, are you, baby? Her tongue's like fucking velvet."

His hiss was like music to her ears.

"Damn. She forgets to suck while I'm fucking her mouth, and then she remembers again. It gets me every fucking time."

She sucked on him eagerly, addicted to his taste and the deep groans that poured from him. Struggling to concentrate on what he said, she sucked in a breath when one of Ryder's hands slid around to cover her abdomen and moved lower.

Her clit burned, but Ryder merely held her folds spread, not giving her the touch she needed.

Dillon groaned again. "That's it, baby. Damn, that mouth feels good. Not too far. Yeah, honey, just like that."

Ryder chuckled from behind her, his low laugh ending abruptly when she clenched on him. "Damn, darlin', you feel so fucking good. I know you want me to touch your clit, darlin'. You're just going to have to wait for it."

Dillon's thrusts into her mouth came faster, but his hold on her kept his cock from going too far. "Give it to her then. She needs to come."

"No way. Not yet. Look at her buck. If she bucks like this now, can you imagine what she's gonna be like when we take her ass?"

Alison whimpered at the wave of shivers that raced through her and somehow zeroed in on every one of her erogenous zones. Since she'd never been with two men at the same time and Danny hadn't spoken during sex, she'd never had the decadent experience of having two men not only speak to her during sex, but talk about her to each other.

Shifting her weight to one side, she held herself up with one hand and reached down with the other, trying to keep her balance as she placed her fingers over her clit.

Ryder slapped her ass, a sharp slap that stunned her. Even now he avoided her injured side, slapping her again on the other before forcefully jerking her hand from her clit.

"No, you don't."

He thrust faster, each word bit out between clenched teeth on each deep stroke.

"No. No. No. I. Make. You. Come."

Frustrated that he wouldn't give her clit the attention she needed, she pushed back against him and lost her balance.

Dillon caught her, dropping his knees on the bed and using his thighs to support her, rubbing his hands over her shoulders. "Easy, honey. I've got you. Hell, I'm gonna come. If you don't want to swallow, baby, let go—oh, hell."

The jolt of fire that hit her when Ryder pinched her clit had her whimpering in her throat and sucking Dillon harder.

Dillon cursed, holding her steady with his hands in her hair and pulsed his release into her mouth. The muscles in his thigh became rock hard and trembled beneath her hands as he groaned and slowed his strokes.

Awestruck that she could draw such a response from him, she eagerly swallowed every drop, crying out from the strokes to her clit, each one like a live wire touching her and sending sharp sizzles racing through her.

She couldn't stay still, rocking her hips no matter how hard she tried not to, afraid that she would dislodge Ryder's finger from where he held it over her clit.

Withdrawing from her mouth, Dillon knelt on the floor in front of her and held her against his shoulder, pushing her hair back from her face and smiling down at her. Cupping a breast, he used his thumb to caress her nipple just as the pleasure at her slit seemed to explode.

Arching her back, she lifted her bottom higher into Ryder's deep thrusts, crying out as he plunged deep and came, his cock jumping inside her. Her pussy milked him as the waves of bliss continued to race through her, the slowing drag of his fingers back and forth over her slippery clit keeping her on the razor-sharp edge of release for so long she screamed, a pinch of her clit sending her the rest of the way over.

Holding on to Dillon and pressing her face against his soft T-shirt, she breathed in his clean scent, wishing this moment could last forever.

"Fucking incredible. Christ, she's milking my cock so hard it's killing me." Ryder slid his hands to her bottom and with long, firm strokes, caressed her from the cheeks of her ass to her shoulders and back again.

The muscles beneath her cheek shifted. "Her back!" Dillon gently lowered her shoulders to the bed, easing the arch in her back, his hands joining Ryder's to slide over her damp body. Bending, he ran a hand over her hair.

"Are you okay, Alison?"

Closing her eyes, she moaned as Ryder withdrew from her and dropped on the bed beside her. Facing Dillon, she opened one eye.

"I'm not fragile, and if you start treating me that way, I'm going back to the hotel."

Ryder reached around her and slid a hand over her scar.

"Hotel's completely booked. No rooms available."

"Bullshit."

Chuckling, Ryder rolled her to her back and covered the top half of her body with his own.

"That's exactly what they'll tell you if you try to check in." His eyes followed the movement of his hand down her body.

"I told you, we all stick together in Desire."

Shivering, she flicked a glance toward Dillon, watching him pull up his jeans again and fasten them. Caught up in the intimacy of watching him dress seemed a little stupid under the circumstances, and she hadn't realized until just now how much she missed all the little things that made up a relationship.

Reminding herself that this couldn't last past next week, she turned back to see Ryder eyeing her thoughtfully, his gaze laced with concern.

"Did I hurt you?"

Smiling, she stretched. "Of course not. I'm mushy, though."

Ryder's brows went up, a faint smile teasing the corners of his sexy mouth. "Mushy?"

Dillon finished dressing and bent, dropping a quick kiss on her lips.

"I like you mushy. Get showered and dressed. We eat breakfast at the diner."

Too worn out to move, Alison reached for the covers. "You go ahead. I'll meet you at the garage in a little while."

"No." Slipping his hands under her shoulders, Dillon lifted her from the bed. He set her on her feet just long enough to change his grip and lifted her high against his chest before striding into the bathroom.

Ryder laughed and followed.

"Most people in town gather at the diner for breakfast. I think Dillon wants to show you off."

Dillon set her on her feet and turned on the light. "I can speak for myself Ryder." Running a hand over her hair, he searched her features. "Don't tell me you're one of those people who don't eat breakfast."

Shrugging, she turned away to start the shower, eager now to get away from their prying eyes. She knew she still needed to lose several pounds, and now that the sex was over, she felt very self-conscious about being naked in front of them. "I usually have just a glass of juice."

Ryder's grin fell. "Not anymore. You've got to keep your energy up because I plan to fuck you every chance I get. You try to diet, and I'm spanking your ass."

Dillon cursed under his breath and caught her as she started to step into the shower. With a smile, he tapped her nose. "You're not fat, and you need to eat breakfast."

He ran his hand down her back to her bottom and squeezed. "I happen to love curves. Wear something comfortable and your boots."

Standing next to him completely naked made her feel even smaller than she had before and more feminine, exposed, but in a good way. Even when Dillon turned her and ran a hand over her scar, she didn't flinch.

It hit her hard that she trusted them more than she'd trusted anyone in a long time, even though she'd sworn to keep her emotional distance.

Ryder, comfortable enough to rid himself of the condom in her presence, even grinned at her when he caught her staring at his gorgeous body.

"Like what you see, babe?"

His dancing eyes invited her to play.

Turning to hide her scarred hip, she cocked the other at him. "I seem to have developed a recent fondness to tattoos."

He took a step closer and wrapped an arm around her back, sliding the other down the front of her body to cover her mound.

"Once we get you waxed, we should get you your own tattoo. Right here."

"Over my dead body!" Dillon's steely tone made her jump.

Ryder nuzzled her jaw. "Don't worry about him. He's no fun. He'll love it, I promise."

Straightening, he slid a hand over her ass, his grin pure sin. "And you're not kidding anyone. It wasn't my tattoos you were looking at."

Chapter Eleven

Hours later, Alison grimaced at the rumbling of her stomach, which seemed to grow louder by the minute. She looked up at the now shiny clock, surprised to realize how long it had been since breakfast. She'd been so immersed in cleaning up the office she hadn't realized so much time had gone by.

No wonder she was hungry. Dillon and Ryder would be starving by now.

She smiled in amusement when she thought about their breakfast that morning.

Dillon and Ryder had hearty appetites, and apparently thought she should eat as much as they did. The diner had been full, and it seemed to her every person in there stopped by their table for an introduction.

Between visits, Alison leaned closer to Ryder.

"Do you know *everyone* in here?"

To her surprise, Ryder took her rhetorical question seriously and lifted his head, scanning the interior of the diner. "Yep." He took another sip of his coffee and grinned, giving her a slow wink.

"And now they know you."

Dillon looked down at the food on her plate and frowned. "If you have any trouble, you can go to any one of them. Eat your damned breakfast."

It took quite a while to convince them she'd had enough, a wonderful contrast to being criticized for every bite of food she put in her mouth.

By the time they'd left the diner, she was so full she could barely walk.

But that had been hours ago, and she wouldn't admit she was hungry until either Dillon or Ryder came in. If she did, they would pester her to eat even more the next time.

Used to ignoring her hunger, she sat down with the stack of papers she'd retrieved from every available surface in the office and started to put them in some kind of order. Neither Dillon nor Ryder appeared to like paperwork of any kind, and they had no filing system at all.

Bills, invoices, and paperwork dealing with parts had all been thrown in whatever drawer happened to be handy. After that, they'd started using the surface of the desk, the chair, the floor. Hell, even the window sill had papers on it.

She'd gathered them all while she'd cleaned, and now they sat in a big box on one corner of the desk.

Wondering if she could talk them into computerizing their system, she sighed, her smile falling.

Judging by the amount of greasy fingerprints she'd found everywhere, a computer wouldn't last long in this environment. If they didn't like sticking a piece of paper in a filing cabinet, she doubted they'd take the time to enter the information into the computer.

Maybe if she explained to them how easy it would make their lives, she could talk them into it, but then they would have to hire someone to handle the computer. She could have done it, but she would be gone by then and they would have to hire someone else.

Not about to let thoughts of leaving creep in and depress her, she set the papers aside and got up, going out to the garage to see what they were doing. A giggle escaped at the string of curses that poured out of Ryder. Curious, she moved closer, her brows going up at some of the more inventive cursing.

"Look at this thing. It's a wonder she made it here at all."

Alison paused, enjoying the view. Both men appeared to be preoccupied with tearing her truck into as many pieces as humanly possible, so many that she worried that it might not be ready in time for her to leave next week.

This looked as though it could get very expensive.

Ryder had the hood open and leaned inside, his jeans stretched over his tight ass and showing it off to perfection. His every movement sent a wave of longing through her and brought back the image of how his naked ass had looked this morning.

Dillon's deep voice, as calm as always, came from under the truck, where he lay on one of those boards with wheels.

"She made it here. That's all that matters."

Working her way around another car sitting in the garage, she rubbed her arms, chilled now from the cool breeze blowing through the garage. They'd left one of the large doors open, but she didn't bother looking outside, drawn to the sight of Dillon's body, from the waist down, sticking out from under the truck.

Remembering the feel and taste of the thick cock, now hidden behind washed out denim, along with the rock hard thighs that had trembled beneath her hands made her shiver again as she took another step closer.

Apparently, Ryder didn't feel the cold. He'd stripped out of his jacket, wearing only a black T-shirt that left the tattoos on his arms exposed and didn't quite cover the large one that ran from his back over his shoulder to end part of the way down his arm. Even though she already knew what the bold lines of it looked like, she wanted to rip away his shirt to see the rest of it.

Wondering what he would do if she walked up to him and slid her hands over his ass, she stepped off to the side to watch the show. Listening as they talked about car parts, some she'd never even heard of before, she let her gaze slide from Ryder's ass to Dillon's belly and thighs, becoming more aroused by the minute.

Amused at herself, she continued to watch, smiling when their curses continued.

Ryder stilled. "Fuck me." Tossing a wrench aside, he hung his head. "Someone tried to fix the damned engine with duct tape."

"Here, too." Dillon slid out from under the truck, pausing when he saw her. With a smile, he stood and used the rag from his pocket to wipe his hands. "Finished already?"

His once-pristine shirt now had streaks of grease and dirt all over it, somehow only emphasizing his masculine good looks.

Her breath caught when Ryder lifted his head and turned toward her, wiping a spot on his cheek and inadvertently smearing the spot of grease that was there. He'd tied his hair back, reminding her of the way he looked when he'd combed it back fresh out of the shower.

Remembering how gorgeous he'd looked wearing nothing but a towel made her nipples tighten, becoming drawn and needy for attention.

She couldn't wait until tonight.

The knowledge that she would leave again soon—that she would be leaving such warm and welcoming people to face cruel and malicious ones—increased the cloud of anxiety hanging over her, and the ever-present knot in her stomach tightened again.

"Are you kidding? I cleaned what you call an office, and now I can start filing everything away. I wanted to know if you could tell me where I can buy a new cell phone around here. I wanted to take my lunch hour and—"

Dillon approached slowly, his smile growing when her stomach growled again. "Don't overdo it. I don't want you hurting your back or hip again. And since Ryder's the one who broke your phone, he can go out tonight to get you a new one. In the meantime, we're going to get some lunch."

In the end, she finally talked them into letting her go to the diner to get lunch, insisting that she wanted to get outside a little after being inside all morning and that she really wanted to see a little more of the town.

After sharing a look, they'd both nodded and given her their lunch orders.

After retrieving her jacket, she enjoyed the brisk walk to the diner, taking in several of the stores she hadn't noticed when she'd walked before. She'd been too upset from Danny's phone call to pay much attention.

Delicious smells drew her the closer she got to the diner, and with her stomach rumbling, she hurried inside. The number of people in the diner didn't surprise her. She'd grown up in a small town, after all.

The number of people who called out her name in greeting, however, did.

Gracie, the older woman who owned the place with her *three* husbands, wiped her hands on the apron tied around her plump waist, smiling broadly. "Alison, it's good to see you again. Three lunch specials?"

The mouthwatering smells coming from the kitchen had Alison's stomach growling with renewed vigor. Looking around at the other diners' plates, she could see that most of them had ordered the lunch special.

Meatloaf.

The plates also held fluffy mashed potatoes drowned in brown gravy and a huge helping of buttery corn.

Thinking of the large breakfast she'd eaten that morning, Alison looked away from the enticing food and met Gracie's eyes again, shaking her head with regret. "Dillon and Ryder each want the lunch special, but I'll just have a salad."

One of Gracie's husbands, Garrett, stuck his head out from the kitchen, his eyes narrowed in displeasure. "Just a salad? Dillon won't like that."

Defensive now, Alison snapped back. "I don't care if Dillon likes it or not."

She would have laughed at the look of shock on Garrett's face if she hadn't been so embarrassed at her rudeness.

Gracie *did* laugh, turning to wag her finger at her husband. "Dillon and Ryder are going to learn they're not in charge, just like every other man in this town."

Garrett grumbled something under his breath about women being spanked more often and went back into the kitchen, leaving Gracie grinning at Alison.

"They all like to think they're in charge and hate to be reminded when they're not." Leaning on the counter, Gracie nodded and waved a hand to acknowledge an order for pie, never taking her eyes from Alison.

"You don't like my husbands' cooking?"

Scared of offending the sweet, older woman, Alison grinned. "I love your husbands' cooking, but if I keep eating it, I'm going to be even heavier than I am. I just lost some weight, and I don't want it back."

Straightening, Gracie put her hands on her hips, her eyes hardening. "Did either one of them say you should go on a diet?"

Gracie's anger on her behalf gave her a warm fuzzy, making her smile.

"No, if anything, it's the opposite. They're always trying to get me to eat more."

Lowering her voice to a whisper, she leaned over the counter closer to the older woman. "I'm tired of being told what to eat and what not to eat. I want a salad, and that's what I'm having. If they give me a hard time about it, I just won't eat with them anymore."

Shrugging, she straightened, the blanket of depression weighing her down again. "I won't be around long enough for it to matter one way or another."

Gracie refilled iced-tea glasses and cut pie before retrieving the coffeepot. Starting at one end, she made her way down the counter refilling coffee.

"You don't like our town?"

The scrape of forks on plates and noises coming from the kitchen suddenly seemed much louder as all conversation in the diner stopped.

Shrugging, Alison pulled a napkin from one of the dispensers on the counter for something to do with her hands.

"I have to leave again next week. I have some things to take care of before I can start a new life somewhere."

Used to small town living, Alison wasn't surprised at all when one of the other diners chimed in from the end of the counter.

Clay Erickson, one of Jesse's husbands, set his coffee down and turned on his stool, leaning back against the wall.

"Do Dillon and Ryder know about this?"

Lifting her chin, she met his dark eyes. "Yes."

"They know you're leaving?"

"Of course."

"Didn't you just start working at the garage?"

Alison sighed, wishing she could tell him to mind his own business, but didn't want to offend Dillon and Ryder's friend after snapping at Gracie's husband. "Yes, but they know it's only temporary."

"Do they know why you have to leave town?"

Looking down, Alison grimaced when she saw she'd ripped the napkin to shreds. Gathering the pieces, she straightened, backing away from the counter, hoping he would take the hint.

"It's none of anyone's business."

His brother, and Jesse's other husband, Rio, grinned and looked over at Clay. "When Jesse came to town, she was only staying for a week, too."

Uncomfortable with where this conversation was going, Alison smiled gratefully when Garrett placed the bag of food on the counter.

"Tell Dillon I put it on his tab."

A man she didn't recognize smiled faintly into his coffee. "If anyone's got problems with their vehicles, I suggest you get 'em fixed now. Looks like Dillon and Ryder are gonna be busy for awhile."

Gracie flashed a mischievous grin, but her eyes remained laced with understanding and concern. "Just you wait, Hunter. One day some woman is gonna turn your world upside down, just like the rest of them."

Thanking Gracie, Alison turned away, crossing the restaurant and opening the door before she heard him reply.

"Never."

The bitterness in his tone made her pause. She almost turned around, but realized that she had no business meddling in other people's affairs, especially since she didn't want to answer any questions about herself.

Closing the door behind her, she started back to the garage, wondering, not for the first time, if she would have stayed in this town if she'd had the chance to do so.

Mentally shrugging, she continued on her way, glancing across the street in time to see Erin coming out of Preston Furniture.

Happy to see someone she knew, she waved, smiling when Erin enthusiastically waved back.

When Erin dropped her arm, her smile falling, Alison realized Erin must have thought she was somebody else.

Feeling stupid, Alison dropped her arm and turned away, intent on getting back to the garage. Staring straight ahead, she tried not to be hurt, but memories of the way she'd been treated in her own hometown haunted her and made it impossible.

She blinked back tears, determined not to let either Dillon or Ryder see them.

Without any warning, someone grabbed her arm on the other side, pulling her so hard that the bag of food fell to the ground. She cried out, struggling to remain on her feet as she was pulled around to the side of the building.

"You fucking bitch."

Danny.

Gathering her wits, she pulled back, wincing when it pulled the muscles in her back. She thought she heard a scream but couldn't be sure, too intent on fighting Danny off.

"Danny? What the hell are you doing here? Let. Go. Of. Me!"

She kicked at him, trying to break free, crying out again when he backhanded her. If not for the hold he had on her arm, she would have gone flying.

Instead, he held her, grabbing her other arm and lifting her to her toes. He started shaking her, and she grabbed onto him, automatically trying to lessen the pull to her back.

What she once thought of as handsome features contorted in rage as he shook her. "You even think about showing up and testifying against me, I'm going to kill you, you hear me? I'm not going to jail because of you."

His strength surprised her, his rage making him stronger than she'd remembered. His dark eyes that she'd used to love so much shone nearly black with anger.

She still found it hard to believe that a man who claimed to love her, who'd held her in his arms, could ever do something like this to her. Her shock cost her several precious seconds, seconds he used to get a better hold.

With his hand in her hair, he pulled her head back painfully, the sharp tug and backbreaking position bringing tears to her eyes.

"This is all your fault, remember? Why don't you stay here fucking the two men who've taken pity on you and stay the fuck out of my life? I've got a paper with me that says that everything you said is a lie. You're gonna sign it right now, you understand me?"

He shook her again, sending a searing across her lower back.

"You understand me, you bitch?"

He shoved a paper in her face. "You sign this right now, bitch, or I swear I'll break your fucking neck."

In a move so fast she didn't see it, an arm shot out, a large hand circling Danny's neck and using it to pin him against the brick wall behind him.

Alison slid her gaze sideways, recognizing Erin's husband, Jared, from outside the club after the fire.

Jared kept his attention on Danny, his eyes glittering like ice.

"I don't think so, hotshot. Let go of her right now or I'll break *your* neck."

Seeing the fury on Danny's face, she choked back sobs as the hand in her hair tightened, pulling her head back even further. The pain in her scalp was nothing compared to the pain in her back, both bringing tears to her eyes.

Feeling a hard body press against her back, she whimpered again, crying out when Danny's hold went slack and she folded, her legs unable to support her.

Caught from behind, she closed her eyes, having no choice but to let whoever stood behind her take her weight.

Picking her up, he carried her out from between the two buildings and lowered her to a set of nearby stairs. "You're okay, honey. Just be still for a minute. He can't hurt you anymore."

Alison opened her eyes to find a man she'd never seen before crouched in front of her and Erin sitting next to her on the step. She winced at the sound of fists pounding flesh and tried to turn to look, but her back protested.

Erin touched her arm. "Are you okay? Who is that man? Do you know him? Where are you hurt? Reese, do something."

The man in front of her shook his head, smiling indulgently. "Honey, give her a chance to talk, and don't you even think about getting up. Jared's got him. Call Ace, then call Dillon and Ryder."

As Erin spoke into the phone beside her, Alison looked up into Reese's face. "Thank you. I don't know what he's doing here. He surprised me. I dropped the food. He wanted me to sign a paper."

Reese nodded, smiling tenderly. "I know, honey. Erin saw the whole thing and yelled for us. Jared and I had just run out of the store when we saw him backhand you."

He pushed her hair back, wincing. "Looks like you're going to have a shiner. Mom, can you get me a cold towel, please?"

A voice filled with feminine outrage came from behind her. "Of course. I hope Jared beats the hell out of him. He really hit her? Son of a bitch. Oh, hell, your fathers are going over there. Erin, you'd better get Ace in a hurry. I'll be right back with that cloth."

Erin disconnected from the call. "Linc will be here in a few minutes. What's the number of the garage?"

As Reese rattled it off, Erin punched in numbers again, standing and moving away from them.

Alison shook her head. "I wish you didn't have to call Dillon and Ryder, but I'm afraid I'm going to need their help." Now that the adrenaline had started to ease, the pain in her back made itself known with a vengeance.

Holding on to the smooth wooden spindle on the railing she leaned against, Alison held herself as still as possible.

"I'm in front of the market. Your family owns this?"

Reese frowned, running his hands over her arms and turning her face from side to side, staring intently into her eyes. "Yes. Alison, do you know who that man is?"

"Danny Peller, my ex-boyfriend." Frowning, she glanced up as Erin returned. "I don't know how he found me."

She jolted as a police car screeched to a halt on the street in front of her, gasping at the pain that shot through her back.

A tall man with short, blond hair and dressed in the same kind of khaki uniform the sheriff wore strode straight toward her. "Is she okay?"

Reese nodded, glancing toward where Danny stood cursing at Jared. "I think she's just shaken and sore. I've got her while you deal with *him*."

The deputy nodded and moved away, just as the sound of running feet came closer and closer.

Reese stood and reached for her, wrapping his hands around her upper arms and attempting to lift her. "Come on, honey. I'll help you—"

"No!" Alison closed her eyes against the pain, gripping the railing tighter. "Please don't touch me. Don't move me. Don't move me. I need Dillon. Please, I need Dillon. Don't move me. Please, don't move me."

"I'm here, baby."

She opened her eyes to find Dillon crouching down in front of her, his eyes filled with anguish. "I'm here. Thanks, Isabel."

Dillon's eyes flared with rage, but his touch was gentle as he placed the cold cloth on her cheek. "Thanks, Reese. Thanks, Erin, for calling. Christ, I never should have let her come alone. Just stay still, baby. I know where it hurts. Just relax, lean against me and let me help you."

A sob broke free at the enormous sense of relief she experienced now that Dillon was here. Carefully lowering her upper body against his, she slumped, holding on to his shoulders and trapping the wet cloth between them as his fingers began to knead the exact spot that had knotted up and kept her in such pain.

"Oh, Dillon. I'm sorry to be so much trouble. I don't know how he found me."

* * * *

In his entire life, Ryder had never experienced the white-hot fury he did in that moment.

Or the gut-wrenching hurt.

I need Dillon.

He'd been only a step or two behind Dillon when he'd heard her pain-filled plea. Seeing that she didn't need him right them, he kept walking, avoiding the pity in Erin's eyes, and concentrated on the furious and obviously disheveled man Linc led toward his car.

Curses poured out of the other man.

"I'm not going to jail for that bitch!"

Linc nodded once. "Oh, yeah, buddy. You are."

"She attacked me! It was self-defense!"

Ryder knew, without a doubt, the identity of this man. He also knew, with as much conviction, that this was all his fault.

He knew damned well how he found her. Ryder had let his temper get the better of him and told him exactly where she was.

Clenching his fists at his sides, he strode to stand toe-to-toe with Danny Peller.

Shaking off Jared's attempts to restrain him, Ryder got right in Danny's face. "You were supposed to come after me, you son of a bitch. Not her. Take the cuffs off of him, Linc."

Linc shook his head and moved to put his body between them.

"No, Ryder. If you hit him, I swear to God I'm going to lock you up. I don't want him beating this wrap because of your fucking temper."

Danny puffed his chest out. "You think you could take me, grease monkey? Not a chance."

Ryder could see Dillon tending to Alison, holding her against his chest as he rubbed the tight knots from her back. No, he wouldn't let his temper get the best of him and let this guy go free. But it cost him, dearly, not to swing.

Shaking off Jared's hand again, he didn't bother to hide his anger.

"You telling me that she attacked you?"

"Damned right she did!"

Ryder didn't like the way Danny kept glancing in Alison's direction and moved to block his view of her.

"So a little thing like that can scare you enough that you had to hit her to get away? Hell, no wonder you didn't come after me if little Ally could take you. Why did you come here then?"

Danny fought against Linc's hold. "You piece of shit. I could take you anytime I wanted to. I came here because she's got to tell the truth. She lied and is going to testify against me for hitting her. It was self-defense and she's going to admit it!"

Ryder started laughing, a cold laugh, calculated to infuriate the other man. "Oh, hell. This is priceless. So she beat the hell out of you before? I'm surprised you didn't come with a posse. So, you're scared of Ally, huh? No wonder you had to confront her in broad daylight. You chickenshit. You're not worth her time. Or mine."

Ryder started to turn away, counting on Danny's anger to get the best of him.

Like his had.

Danny kicked out at him, almost falling from the force of it. "You fucking bastard. You don't know anything about it. She came at me with a knife! Now they're going to try to send me to jail. She's gonna tell the truth. I've got witnesses."

Ryder didn't believe for one minute that Alison went after this guy with a knife, and without jeopardizing Linc's case against him, he couldn't beat the truth out of him. Having had a bad temper his entire life, he knew how the other man thought and was determined to use the other man's temper against him.

He met Jared's eyes briefly. Having been in more than his fair share of bar fights around his friend, he knew Jared had braced himself to stop him if he threw a punch. A look of understanding, one born of long friendship, passed between them, and Jared nodded once, the look on his face never changing.

Turning back to Danny, Ryder folded his arms over his chest. "Yeah, well, you're going to lose. Ally's temper isn't to be trifled with. She's tough, isn't she?"

Danny lifted his chin. "She ain't so tough. Maybe *you* think she is because you can't handle her. Yeah, that's right. I saw that both you and your friend over there have the hots for her. Can't handle her on your own, can you?"

Aware that Jared tensed beside him and Reese came up to stand at his other side, Ryder shrugged. "Like I said, she's a hell of a woman."

"She ain't nothin'. She *used* to be a hell of a woman until she started gettin' all needy and clingy. Tryin' to tell me not to fuck other women. Who the fuck does she think she is? I fuck who I want to fuck."

Ryder forced himself to laugh when all he wanted to do was plow a fist into this guy's face and rush to Ally.

"Apparently not. She scared you, didn't she? I read the police report. It said you weren't there when the ambulance got there. What did you do, run and hide afterward?"

As expected, Danny fought Linc's hold again. "You fucking asshole. If I wasn't in cuffs, I'd kick your ass. I don't run and hide from nobody."

Linc cursed a blue streak. "Ryder, you're paying for this later."

Ryder grinned and leaned back against the police car. "You're so full of shit. You're scared of her. What did you do, follow her around town and hide around the side of the building, waiting for her to come out?"

"Fucking bastard! I don't need to hide from anybody. I hurt her before, and I'll do it again. I wish she'd died when I threw her down those stairs!"

Ryder hadn't thought it possible to get any madder, but his anger grew to outrageous proportions and turned ice cold.

"You really are scared of her. Tell me, chickenshit, how scared were you when you threw her down the stairs? Tell the truth. You were more scared of her than you were of going to jail. Scared of a woman." He turned to Jared. "Can you believe that? Do you know any man in Desire scared of his woman?"

Jared shot a glance at Erin, who dealt with the crowd gathered around with the brass and efficiency of a general. Amusement flashed in his eyes when he met Ryder's gaze, but it disappeared before he faced Danny.

"Nope. Can't say that I do."

Danny struggled furiously against Linc's hold. "I ain't scared of her. I ain't scared of no woman. I wasn't scared when I threw her down the fucking stairs. I was mad. Fucking bitch tryin' to tell me who I can fuck in my own bed." Danny sneered, looking in Ally's direction. "I'm not like you.

I can handle a woman by myself. I don't need no help. Get these fucking cuffs off me right now!"

Linc had obviously had enough of playing with this guy. Firming his hold, he lifted Danny until he practically had to stand on his toes. When Jared opened the car door, Linc muscled a still-cursing Danny inside and shut the door.

"I take it you got what you wanted?"

Ryder nodded. "Yeah. Thanks. I owe you one."

Linc shook his head and smiled. "I don't think he realizes that police cars have cameras that record video *and* audio. Ace just got them installed, too, not six months ago. After this, he'll consider it money well spent."

Jared scrubbed a hand over his face and eyed Ryder. "I would have bet big money that you would have hit him."

Taking a deep breath, Ryder let it out slowly. "My temper's what got her into this. If he hadn't been in cuffs, I would have hit him and probably wouldn't have stopped." He nodded in Ally's direction. "She got hurt because I told him where she was. I wanted him to come after me."

Linc opened the front door of the car and took out a clipboard. "I need Alison's statement."

Holding his hands out in front of him, Ryder fisted and straightened his hands, working the kinks out of them from being tightened into fists for so long.

"Talk to Dillon."

"Don't."

Reese moved to stand in front of him. "I heard her. She wanted Dillon. Don't let that cause distance between you. I've learned that Erin depends on each of us in different ways. It's all part of sharing, Ryder. As much as we're surrounded by it, and as much as we think we know about it, you learn when you start sharing a woman that you didn't understand half of it. Go to her. She needs you, too, and if you avoid her now because you're hurt, it's going to hurt her, too, and it's going to be a tough bridge to cross later."

Jared touched his arm, nodding encouragingly.

Ryder nodded back, not convinced, but separated himself from the others and headed toward where Ally sat on the steps of the market with Dillon's arms around her. With each slow step, he worked to brace himself for her rejection.

Of course she would want Dillon when she was hurt. Dillon had been the one to massage her back for over an hour getting the kinks worked out. Dillon had shown her tenderness. Dillon had proven himself to be levelheaded and someone she could rely on.

Besides sex, what the hell did Ryder have to offer?

He smiled faintly at Erin when she stood, making room for him to sit beside Ally. Meeting the rage in Dillon's eyes, he touched Ally's arm. "How bad is she hurt?"

To his surprise, Ally lifted her head, lowering the cloth she'd been holding there.

"Ryder! Did you beat the hell out of him?"

Hiding a grimace that he'd disappointed her, he shook his head, determined that she know the whole truth. "No. Ally, I'm sorry. He came here because when I answered the phone in the doctor's office, I told him where to find me—and therefore, where to find you. I wanted him to come after me so I *could* beat the hell out of him. I'm sorry, babe. My temper got the best of me. This was all my fault."

Taking his hand, Alison smiled. "It's okay. I know you didn't mean for him to find me. Will he go to jail?"

Bringing her hand to his lips, he kissed her fingers. "Oh, yeah. As a matter of fact, Linc's waiting to ask you some questions."

He looked over to see Erin talking animatedly with the deputy, pointing her finger repeatedly at Danny, who still yelled obscenities from the back of the police car. Jared and Reese stood protectively on either side of Erin, rubbing her shoulders when she got worked up.

"Looks like Erin's giving her statement now. Got a good head of steam on her, too."

Turning back to Ally, he frowned. "How's your back?"

Alison touched Dillon's cheek, smiling up at him. "It's feeling better. Dillon's been rubbing it for me."

Ryder bit back jealousy when Dillon smiled back and nuzzled her jaw.

Still rubbing her back, he removed the cloth so Ryder could see her reddened cheek. "As soon as we get home, I'll give you a real good rubdown."

Ryder had never felt so out of place before and had started to wonder if he had what it took to have a relationship with someone like Ally. He cared about her, wanted her like he'd never wanted another woman, but what could he really offer?

Gently tilting her face so he could get a good look at where Danny had obviously hit her, he grimaced. "Got you good, didn't he? By the way, we're going to have a talk while you're getting that rubdown. Apparently you didn't want to tell us that the reason you have to leave town is because you have to testify against this asshole. Did you know he was going to use self-defense as his reason for throwing you down the stairs?"

Dillon straightened, leaning back to see Ally's face. "Self-defense? You're kidding, right?"

"Nope. Seems he was going to say Ally came after him with a knife."

Ally grabbed Ryder's arm. "I didn't! I swear. But his distant cousin is the judge."

"You knew about this? And you didn't say anything?" Ryder felt his temper rise again and forcefully clamped it down.

Alison shrugged, her wince telling him that her back still hurt, despite her claim to the contrary. "He's been calling me, threatening me so I wouldn't testify against him. But if he tells the judge, his cousin, that I came after him with a knife, they might put me in jail instead."

Ryder sighed. "And you kept all of this from us?"

Ally looked away, frustrating him. "It's not your problem. Do you realize we just met? I didn't want you involved in my problems. I just wanted to have some fun. I wanted to forget for a little while. I wanted to feel like a woman again."

She looked up at him through her lashes. "Isn't that what you wanted? Some fun?"

Dillon stiffened beside him.

"Fun?" He scrubbed a hand over his face, his expression bland. "I guess we can't really fault you for thinking that way. I thought we were building something here, Alison, but you already had one foot out the door the entire time. You told us, but I guess I didn't listen."

The defeat in Dillon's eyes shook Ryder. Carefully gathering Ally in his arms, he smiled.

"I don't think you have to worry about going to jail anymore. I got Danny to admit that he threw you down the stairs because he was pissed because he felt that he could fuck anyone he wanted to and you had no right to tell him differently."

Alison jerked upright, wincing again. "You did? He admitted that?"

She slumped again. "It'll be his word against yours and the judge—"

Ryder tightened his arms around her, loving the feel of her leaning against him. "—is his distant cousin. I know. But he said it in front of Linc, Jared, and Reese, too, and the entire conversation was recorded by the recorder in Linc's car. He admitted it, plain as day. Bragged about it, even. Linc's coming over. You can ask him about it. As soon as you give your statement, we can go over to Doc's—"

Sitting up, she was already shaking her head. "No. No more doctors. I'd just like to go back to your place."

Aware that she hadn't used the word *home*, Ryder bit back his frustration and nodded. "Fine. We'll go back to our place."

Listening to her answer Linc's questions, Ryder would swear he could feel his blood boil. While she explained the details to Linc, Ryder leaned closer to Dillon, keeping his voice at a whisper.

"If the trial's next Friday, we've only got about a week and a half with her."

Dillon nodded soberly. "We'll just have to make the most of it. By then, the two of you should know what you want."

"What about you?"

"I already know what I want. I want Alison to stay. Linc's finishing up. Let's get her home."

Chapter Twelve

In his no-nonsense way, Dillon sent her into the bedroom as soon as they got back to their apartment, telling her to get out of her clothes and lie down on the bed while he cleaned up.

She watched him walk away with a sigh. He'd brooded all the way home, not speaking. Her comments earned her a grunt or a look, but not much more.

Moving carefully, she started undressing, grimacing at the grease stains on her clothing.

It struck her that she'd never seen either one of them with dirty hands before, or grease under their nails. Today, though, they'd obviously run out of the garage in a hurry.

"I guess when you hang out with grease monkeys, you're going to get dirty."

Turning at the sound of Ryder's voice, Alison smiled. Now that she knew him a little better, she recognized the insecurity behind the anger. Thinking back to the incident in the parking lot when they'd first met, she took a step closer.

"You look a little dirty yourself." Moving toward him, she met his beautiful eyes, caught up in the wariness she'd seen there ever since he'd reached for her on the market steps.

Ryder, whose confidence regarding sex blew her away, appeared to have self-doubts in other areas. He shrugged, his eyes narrowing at her approach. "I have to work for a living. Being with me, you're bound to get dirty."

His vulnerability pulled at her, and she wanted to see the self-confidence light up his eyes again.

Taking slow, careful steps, she approached him, not stopping until they stood toe-to-toe. Flattening her hands on his chest, she looked up at him through her lashes, attempting a coy smile she hadn't used in years.

"How dirty are you going to make me?"

Elated at the flicker of surprised delight in his eyes, she nearly melted under his teasing smile.

Lifting her chin, he pursed his lips as though considering his answer, making her want to pull his head down to smash her lips against his erotically full ones.

"I would say, very dirty, especially since you mentioned submitting to me not too long ago. Something about you being on your knees and being forced to suck my cock, if I remember right."

Scowling, he released her, dragging a rag out of his pocket to wipe her chin. "Hell, Ally. I can't even touch you. I'm getting grease all over you."

Kicking off her shoes, Alison reached for the hem of her sweater. "I guess you'll have to clean me up, then." She sucked in a sharp breath when the muscles in her back protested at her attempt to pull her sweater over her head, and she ended up with her sweater covering her face, unable to raise or lower it.

"Here, darlin', let me help you."

He gently worked the sweater over her head and tossed it aside, eyeing her in concern. "We need to get you rubbed down."

Alison turned and moved away, her face burning. "So much for my attempt at seduction."

"Honey, Christ, I can't touch you until I get this grease washed off. Ally, look at me."

She turned again to find him right in front of her, his eyes full of understanding.

Smiling faintly, he bent low and kissed her forehead, the promise in his eyes when he straightened urging her closer. "As soon as you feel better, you can seduce me all you want."

"You aren't undressed yet?"

Alison turned to see Dillon coming into the room, wearing a fresh pair of faded denims and clean T-shirt, his wet blond hair slicked back. Carrying a towel and the bottle of oil Jesse had sent, he got right to work, spreading the towel on the bed before reaching for her.

"Come on, Alison. Let's get that back taken care of."

Ryder reached out to touch her cheek, stopping at the last second and grimacing. "Damn it. I'm going to go take a shower. I'll be right back. I want to get my hands on you."

As he left, Dillon whipped off her bra and tossed it to land on top of her sweater before reaching for the fastening of her jeans. "I'll have you feeling better in no time. Just stand still and hold on to my shoulders."

She obeyed him, holding on to his massive shoulders as she lifted one leg after the other so he could remove her jeans.

"I'm sorry to be so much trouble. If I just take one of those pills and lie down awhile, it'll loosen up. I'm sure of it."

Dillon slid her cotton panties down and off before standing and helping her to lie on her stomach on the towel.

"Let's see if we can get rid of those knots without any pain medicine or muscle relaxers. If you still need them when I'm done, I'll get them for you, okay?"

Lying on the bed with Dillon's big, strong hands sliding over her skin, Alison fisted her hands on the pillow. She tried not to think about how vulnerable she felt at being naked while he was fully dressed, a little taken aback at how it excited her.

"Dillon, that feels so good."

His hands worked their magic, the firm pressure of his strong fingers forcing the muscles to loosen a little more with each stroke. Each minute that went by, she could feel herself melting, the muscles in her back going slack while the rest of her became tighter, stiffening with awareness in every erogenous zone.

A little embarrassed that she'd become so needy for pleasure that even a healing massage could arouse her, she squeezed her thighs closed against the ache that started to make itself known.

Damn Ryder for getting her worked up.

Dillon's strokes became more fluid and lengthened, soon covering her entire back.

"It's supposed to feel good. Now that I know where you tighten up, it's getting easier and easier to work you loose again. No, stay still. Let me work on you a bit more."

Alison fought against the waves of decadent pleasure that raced through her, finding it increasingly difficult to lie there naked with Dillon's slippery hands moving over her skin. She moaned into the pillow as his hands slid down the middle of her back, fisting her fingers into the soft bedding when his fingers brushed along the sides of her breasts.

Each time his hands moved lower over her back, she held her breath in anticipation, the need to have them slide over her bottom and between her damp thighs growing steadily. Curling her toes against the bedding, she parted her knees, her pussy clenching in desperation to be filled and her clit tingling with the need to be stroked.

As his hands began another upward journey, she lifted the upper half of her body slightly and turned to her side, moaning when she got what she needed and his fingers brushed her nipples.

His low chuckle danced over her skin, building the awareness and making it nearly impossible to stay still. She wanted the Dillon from the hotel to emerge, the one who touched her so possessively.

"You must be feeling better."

Alison spread her thighs a little farther apart, using her knees to push her ass in the air as his hands moved lower again, hoping to entice him. "Damn it, Dillon. You're making me crazy. My back feels better."

She tried to turn over, stiffening when her back protested.

Dillon gently pushed her back down again, running his hand over her bottom in a caress that felt more like a threat.

"No, you're still stiff. Behave yourself and let me get the kinks worked out."

"What's going on?"

Alison lifted her head at Ryder's question and tried to turn, but Dillon merely sighed and pushed her back down again.

"I've almost got the kinks worked out, but she won't stay still. She's aroused and doing her best to get me to touch her. She's fidgeting all over, and she's going to make it worse."

Alison turned her head toward him, and would almost swear she could feel Ryder's gaze skimming over her nakedness. Once again, being with both of them and naked created quite a few erotic images in her mind, images she'd love to explore.

"Well, what do you expect? You're teasing me. Come on, Dillon. I'll lie here real still and you can take me."

Chuckling again, Dillon ran his hand over her bottom. "I'm not teasing you. I'm massaging your back. You're not supposed to get aroused. I thought you were in pain."

Alison felt the bed shift on the other side as Ryder sat next to her, dropping her forehead onto the pillow.

"I was. I'm not anymore."

Dillon ran a slick hand over her bottom. "Bullshit. Every time you move, you wince, and the muscles in your back knot again. I'll make a deal with you, though."

Wary now, Alison lifted her head and looked over her shoulder, trying to hide her wince when her back tightened at the movement.

"What kind of deal?"

Ryder ran a hand over her leg, sending a barrage of sizzles to her clit. "Yeah, what kind of deal. I might want to get in on this."

Bending, Dillon touched his lips to her shoulder. "If you behave yourself and let me finish getting the knots out, I'll make you come."

Oh, God. She wanted to come. Needed to come. Would give just about anything to come. But damn it, she wanted more.

"What about you? Damn it, Dillon. This is not part of our deal. You're supposed to—"

She gasped when a slick finger slid down the crease of her ass and pressed at her puckered opening.

Dillon scraped his teeth over her shoulder, sending shivers down her spine, shivers that seemed to rush to where his finger pressed threateningly.

"You're in Desire, remember? Behave yourself or I'll turn you over my knee, well, as soon as you feel better. You don't tell me what I'm supposed to do. You put yourself in our hands, remember?"

The tenderness mixed with steel undid her every damned time. More of her juices escaped to coat her thighs, her pussy clenching almost incessantly now.

Ryder laughed softly at her low moan, smoothing her hair out of the way. "Remember that fantasy you have about being our slave? You have to lie there and let us do whatever we want with you. We can arouse you for hours and not let you come. Is that what you want?"

Alison buried her face in the pillow. "I never said I fantasized about that."

She hadn't thought about that fantasy in years, but as soon as she met Ryder, she couldn't stop thinking about it. After the incident with Dillon at the hotel, she'd become almost obsessed with it, but she didn't feel as comfortable talking about it with him near.

Of course, Dillon wouldn't let it pass. Circling her bottom hole and making it tingle, he seemed to enjoy the fact that she kept clenching her bottom cheeks and, to her surprise, teased her there mercilessly. His voice dropped, reminding her of the time they'd been alone in her hotel room.

"But you do get excited at the idea of submitting. You want to let us have you however we want, don't you?"

Concentrating on not clenching her bottom, Alison kept her burning face hidden but lifted her upper body several inches to allow Dillon and Ryder's searching hands to each close over a breast.

"That wasn't the deal."

Ryder tugged her nipple. "The deal was that we teach you how to please us. We love having you soft and pliant. While Dillon's loosening up that back, I'm going to loosen up that ass."

"Oh, God."

She didn't even think of objecting, the lure of even more pleasure and the promise of relief from this decadent torment too strong to deny. The chance to visit one of her forbidden fantasies was now within her grasp, and she couldn't resist reaching out for it.

Stilling at the sound of the nightstand drawer opening on Ryder's side, she lifted her head, sucking in a breath in surprise to find his face only inches away.

His eyes flashed with heat, his slow grin a mixture of sin and seduction, as he tugged and released a nipple. "Now, darlin', you're just going to have to lie here and take what we give you."

The hands on her back moved to her shoulders, holding her down when she would have lifted.

"Stay put, Alison."

Dropping back to the pillow, Alison moaned, melting under Dillon's firm, skilled hands. She wanted those hands on her breasts and lower, and could only imagine what it would feel like to feel those same talented hands intent on arousing her instead of easing her pain.

Knowing instinctively that they would move with the same kind of purpose, she found she couldn't wait any longer.

"Dillon, let me turn over. Oh, God. I want your hands on me."

Another drizzle of the scented oil followed her moaned plea, down her spine and lower to trickle between her bottom cheeks.

Since Dillon's hands hadn't left her body, it had to be Ryder pouring the oil. He said something low to Dillon, too low for her to hear, but the low rumble in it set off a series of shivers.

Trying to keep track of four hands heightened her senses, as did trying to focus on their low conversation, listening for any clue of their intentions.

The bed shifted by her legs at the same time Ryder's callused hands slid from her ankles to her knees, parting her legs wider and making room for himself between them.

Whimpering in frustration when rubbing her nipples against the towel didn't give her what she needed, she dug her knees into the mattress, arching upward when Ryder's lips followed his hands and moved higher.

Dillon's fingers brushed the outer curve of her breasts on every stroke to her back, making her nipples burn with the need for attention. On an upward stroke, he bent over her, brushing his lips over her shoulder while sliding his hands around to cup her breasts, finally giving them the attention she craved. Smoothing the oil from his hands over them, he toyed with her nipples, sending a barrage of shimmering heat to her slit, her pussy clenching in anticipation as Ryder's touch got closer.

Dillon licked her shoulder. "Hmm. I heard that the scented oils were edible. Creates some interesting possibilities, don't you think?"

She'd become so relaxed and pliant under Dillon's hands that her reflexes were slow, which made their decadent seduction even more overwhelming. Moaning her pleasure, she trembled helplessly, every inch of her skin quivering in expectation.

Ryder's hands slid over her hips as he worked his way higher. The touch of his lips over the backs of her thighs as he licked and nibbled his way up to her buttocks left a trail of heat that made the tingling clit begin to burn.

"*Very* interesting possibilities."

Dillon released her breasts to snag a pillow from beside her, lifting her with an ease that amazed her and settled the pillow under her belly.

"That feel better? Stop arching, baby. You're going to hurt your back. You'll get what you need. We're going to have to teach you patience. Don't be in such a hurry. Let us enjoy discovering all of your secrets."

Wrapping his arms around her again, he cupped her breasts, teasing the outer shell of her ear with his lips.

"Remember, I can move you and get to any part of you I want to. This position will protect your back but lifts that gorgeous bottom up for more attention."

The vulnerability that hit her when she realized the truth of those words sent her arousal higher, and she began to rock her hips, unable to keep them still any longer.

Dillon massaged her breasts, *this* massage designed to arouse instead of relax. His clever hands worked the slick oil all around them, his slick fingers using slow, tender tugs to her nipples to make her nearly mindless with need.

Her toes curled as Ryder's lips moved over her bottom, digging into the mattress when something touched her puckered opening. She tried to tighten against it, but her legs had been spread too wide, her body too relaxed from Dillon's massage and Ryder's erotic kisses to put up much of a struggle.

Her clit burned, and she rocked to get some kind of friction against it, but with her belly raised, she couldn't.

"What is that? Ryder, it doesn't feel like your finger. Oh, God."

Each word came out on panted breaths, the feel of something pushing at her forbidden opening almost more than she could stand.

Ryder came to his knees between hers. "It's your butt plug. Christ, Dillon. You're gonna want to watch this."

Slipping his hands out from under her, Dillon fisted a hand in her hair and turned her face to the side, his eyes more possessive than ever.

"Be still, baby. It's a small one. We just want to give you pleasure. Once I work the knots out of your back and you come, you'll sleep like a baby without any fucking pills."

Alison groaned as Dillon released her and turned on the bed, in a position now to watch Ryder push the plug into her.

Dillon laid a hand on each of her bottom cheeks and parted them. "Go slow. Easy. Is she lubed up enough?"

Ryder continued to caress the back of her thigh as though to calm her, an impossible task when something was being inserted into her anus.

"I didn't just fall off the turnip truck, Dillon. I know what I'm doing. I am going slow. Look at her. Ally, you've got the greatest ass."

Ally sucked in a breath as the plug pushed deeper, filling her bottom a little more with the hard rubber cone. Chills went up and down her spine as he applied pressure to push it in a little more and withdrew about an inch before pushing it back into her again, the friction of the plug moving on her sensitive inner walls drawing a whimper from her and then stealing her breath.

Digging her toes into the mattress, she tried to lift higher, needing more of the erotic feeling, a frustrated moan escaping when she found Dillon's hold wouldn't allow it. Cursing, she buried her face in the pillow again and gave up the fight to keep still.

The hand Dillon slid to her lower back massaged but also kept her from lifting up again. "Yeah, baby. We know. That clit needs some attention. Do it, Ryder. I'll keep her from bucking. The more she comes with something in her ass, the more she's going to want it."

Alison gasped and lifted her head as Dillon rubbed his hand soothingly over her bottom.

"I can hear you, you know?"

Ryder slid the hand from her thigh to her clit, still using the other to stroke her ass with the plug, his shallow thrusts going deeper and deeper, stroking her sensitive inner walls, and somehow forced her anus to clench on the plug.

"It's all right if you hear us. It's not like you're not going to find out anyway. Hmm. Nice and wet and open. See, darlin'. In this position, I can do whatever I want to your pussy, your clit, and your ass, and there's not a damned thing you can do about it. Just in case you're wondering, this is a position you're going to find yourself in quite a bit."

Alison cried out at the first swipe of his fingers over her clit, sucking in a breath when Dillon's hand slid lower and with no warning, he pushed two fingers into her pussy.

In no position to stop them, her arousal soared. She couldn't hold back her cry, one of surprise and pleasure as her pussy gripped Dillon's two fingers in a desperate attempt to keep them inside her.

She cried out again as Ryder applied more pressure to the plug, stretching her bottom hole as the plug got wider and making it burn. Dillon's fingers in her pussy made the plug in her ass feel even fuller, just as the plug in her ass made the fingers in her pussy feel even larger.

When the plug narrowed sharply, her puckered opening closed tightly over the firm rubber, the full sensation making her cry out again. The plug, now held securely inside her, felt huge as it stretched her and shifted with the tiniest movement.

Struggling for air, she reached a hand back. "I want to touch both of you. Don't make me come yet. I want you to take me."

Ryder moved his fingers in a circular motion over her clit, the almost constant friction making it tingle in a way that already had her close to coming.

"Your back's too sore for that. That's a girl." He pressed against the base of the plug, smoothing his hand over her ass when she cried out again. "Come for us, babe."

Dillon slid his fingers deep. "That's it. Clench on my fingers. You like having your ass and pussy filled, huh, baby? As soon as your back's feeling better, Ryder and I are going to take you together. One of us in your ass and the other in your pussy. That's it. She's coming."

Alison stiffened as the shimmering waves running through her body seemed to all gather at her slit and explode, the additional stimulation of her bottom being filled making her come harder than ever. The intensity of it stole her breath, making it impossible to even cry out.

Ryder slowed his strokes. "That's it, babe. Yeah, just let it go. Damn, you're a hot little thing. Dillon, she's soaked. We've got to shave her. If she's this sensitive now, can you imagine what she'll be like once she's shaved?"

She didn't know if she'd ever get used to hearing them talk to each other about her during sex, but she knew that for the rest of her life, she would miss it.

Coming down from her orgasm, Alison melted into a quivering mass, moaning when Ryder removed his fingers and ran a hand over her bottom.

The tension in his low groan skittered over her skin, making her pussy clench on Dillon's fingers and the plug still filling her bottom.

"Just sleep now, babe. You've had a lot of excitement today."

Stiffening as Dillon slid his fingers from her pussy and the plug was worked from her, Alison lifted her head, gripping the pillow tightly. Her body clamped down, taking every last bit of pleasure as both slid free.

Between Dillon's massage and coming so hard, she didn't have the energy to hold her head up for long and dropped it back on the pillow.

"Any more excitement right now might kill me."

Alarmed at the tense silence that followed, she turned slightly and lifted her head again.

Ryder stared down at her bottom, patting it before standing.

"That's what I'm afraid of."

He stood and left the room, leaving her staring dumbfounded at Dillon.

"Dillon, did I do something wrong?"

Dillon helped her struggle to a sitting position, removing the pillow from under her belly and tossing it toward the headboard.

"Of course not. What could you have done wrong? Your eyes are drooping. Get some sleep, and when you wake up, we'll eat."

Feeling guilty, Alison grabbed his arm when he stood.

"Dillon, why didn't you take me? Why didn't Ryder take me?"

Dillon sighed, running a hand through his hair. "We weren't even going to make you come. My only intention was loosening up your back. You got aroused, so—"

Insulted, Alison yanked the sheet around her. "I guess that's what happens when you touch me. Pity it doesn't work the other way around. If you'll excuse me, I'd like to get dressed."

Dillon's cold smile filled her with trepidation. "You think you're going to dismiss me? Do you really think I'm going to allow you to hide yourself from me?"

Alison gasped as he ripped the sheet out of her hand and bent over her, easing her back down to the mattress again. Unable to look away from the possessive intent in his eyes, she shifted restlessly, arching into the hand he ran over her.

Swallowing heavily, she bit back a moan as his hand closed over her breast.

"Look, you son of a bitch, I don't need any fucking pity from you. If you don't want me, just have the balls to say so."

His eyes darkened, filled with cold anger.

"You think I don't want you?" He moved, and before she knew it, she found herself spread wide by his muscular thighs, his impressive bulge pressed insistently against her slit.

She bit back a moan as he lowered himself over her, pressing her into the mattress, careful even now to keep most of his weight off of her.

Loving the feel of him on her, she wrapped her legs around him, surprised and delighted that her back didn't bother her at all. Flattening her hands on his chest, she looked up at him through her lashes, trying to hide the thrill of having his rock hard body on hers. Responding to the evidence of his arousal pressing against her sensitive clit, she arched against him, thrilled at the flare of heat that came and went in his eyes.

"If you wanted me, you'd take me. You obviously don't, so get the hell off of me."

The sudden stiffening of his body as his cock jumped against her slit told her the dare hit its mark.

Excitement raced through her when his eyes widened and narrowed again.

"Do you remember that conversation we had at the hotel room when I told you what would happen to you if you were mine?"

Alison attempted to look bored, hiding the fact that her pulse raced out of control.

"Vaguely. It doesn't really matter, though, since I'm not yours."

A muscle worked in Dillon's jaw, his eyes alight with challenge. "Vaguely, huh? You gave yourself to me, remember? I accepted. In Desire, that means you've been claimed, lady. Maybe it's time you learned just what that means."

Reaching over to the nightstand, he rummaged inside, producing a condom, which he tossed onto the bed next to her hip. Coming up to his knees, he threw off his shirt, baring his gorgeous chest.

Unable to resist, she reached up to run her hands over his hard stomach and started to sit up to reach his magnificent chest.

"Don't you fucking move."

Tired of not being the one to give any pleasure, she ignored him, gripping his hips to lift herself. Smiling against his stomach when he cursed, she ran her lips over every inch she could reach, lifting her hands to run them over his chest as he fumbled with his belt.

"How am I supposed to make you feel good if I don't move? You know, you've got the most amazing chest."

Dillon yanked his pants and tight boxers to his knees and tugged her head back, running his free hand over her breast.

"And you've got the most amazing breasts. Right now, though, I want to get into that tight pussy." Releasing her with a smile, he reached for the condom and slipped it out of the foil, stilling when she cupped his sac.

"What do you think you're doing?"

Alison ran her fingers over the sensitive skin and licked the pearly drop from the tip of his cock. "If you have to ask, maybe I'm not doing it right."

Dillon growled and grabbed her hair again, fisting his hand and pulling her head back. "You're doing just fine. Still doubt that I want you?"

Alison shrugged, sliding her hand up and down the length of his cock, marveling at its thick heat. With her legs still spread wide and the air moving over her moist slit, making her clit throb with reawakened need, she leaned against him, brushing her nipples over his hair-roughened thighs.

"You promised to teach me how to please a man, but you just keep making me come and walking away. At least Ryder fucked me. So, am I doing this right?"

Dillon cursed under his breath and gritted his teeth. "You're doing fine. Damn it, Alison, you're not listening to me."

The frustration in his voice made her smile. Thrilling at his response to her touch and the surge of power that went though her, she couldn't help but tease him. Taking the condom from his hand, she rolled it on.

"Of course, I'm listening to you. You said that since I'd given myself to you, I was *claimed*, and you were going to show me what that meant. Since you're not teaching me what you said you would and you insist that you've claimed me but you haven't even fucked me, I'm starting to think you don't know what the hell you want."

The look on his face told her she'd finally managed to push him over the edge. Instead of being scared, her body raced with excitement, her pussy clenching in anticipation of being filled with the hard cock filling her hands.

Dillon lowered her back to the bed, his touch firm, but still gentle. "Excuse me?"

Wrapping her legs around him again, she lifted herself, groaning in frustration when she couldn't get his cock inside her.

"Damn you, Dillon. Take me, or get off. Oh!"

With one powerful thrust, Dillon's cock slid to the hilt inside her. "I'll take you. I'll take what's mine."

Even with her juices easing his way, her body struggled to adjust to his thickness. Surrounded by him, his massive body pressing hers into the mattress, she clung to him, blinking back tears.

It had been so long since she felt so close to anyone, so amazingly sheltered in a man's arms that she wanted to cry.

His cock, so hard and huge, stretched her deliciously as he held himself deep, unmoving.

Wrapping one hand around to flatten between her shoulder blades, he used the other to wrap in her hair, bracing himself on his elbows as he lifted his head.

"How you can think I don't want you when I've spent—hey! Baby, what's wrong? Oh hell, I'm hurting you." He started to push himself off of her, withdrawing slightly before she could tighten her legs around him again.

Meeting the concern in his eyes, she blinked back tears. "No. Oh, Dillon. It feels so good. *You* feel so good. Hold me again. Tighter. Don't leave."

Touching her cheek, he smiled, stealing her heart as he wiped away a tear. "Tell me, baby. Why are you crying?"

Shaking her head, she grabbed his shoulders tighter and buried her face in his strong neck.

"I know it's only supposed to be sex. I know we agreed that you would teach me things, but it feels so good to be held this way. It's been so long since I felt so safe. Please, hold me. Take me, just this once, like I'm really your woman."

She moaned when he thrust deep again, her entire body trembling with need and emotion. She didn't want to care about him, didn't want to leave her heart behind when she left Desire, but right here, right now, she wanted to belong to him.

Just this once, she wanted to forget all about erotic pleasure and just embrace the mysteries of man and woman taking and giving of each other.

Embarrassed at feeling so needy, she kept her face hidden, wishing she'd kept her mouth shut.

Dillon didn't let her stay hidden for long, lifting his own head and using his body to force her back down to the pillow again. With a hand on either side of her face, he used both thumbs to lift her chin.

"Where's this coming from, baby? You don't just want sex, no matter how much you claim that's all you want from us. You need more. And after the day you had—God, you're so sweet."

Wrapping his arms around her and gathering her against him, he took her mouth with his in a kiss so consuming and sweet, tears leaked from the corners of her eyes.

At the same time, he withdrew several inches, sinking into her again so slowly it left her breathless and allowed her to savor the feel of every inch of his cock against her inner flesh.

Her pussy tightened on his cock as desperately as she held on to his shoulders. She never wanted this to end. She wanted to feel this passion, this connection she felt with him now, more than she wanted her next breath.

Man to woman. His strength against her softness. His strong arms holding her and making her feel cherished and all woman.

His heat, his strength touched her everywhere, inside and out. His gentle caring combined with the possessiveness she felt in his hold filled a need in her, an empty place inside her that she hadn't expected to ever have filled.

Each slide of his lips over hers, each stroke of his tongue led her deeper into a magical journey she never wanted to end.

Dillon's strokes lengthened, each slow thrust going deep, the friction from his cock over sensitive nerve endings making her gasp and writhe in his arms.

Feeling small and defenseless, overwhelmed by his strength and her uninhibited response to him, Alison could do nothing but hold on as he increased the speed of his thrusts, each one driving her relentlessly closer to the edge.

Dillon lifted his head, staring down at her, his gaze hooded as he laced his fingers with hers and pressed her hands to the mattress on either side of her head.

"You need this. You need what I can give you every bit as much as I need to give it to you. Stay here with us, Alison."

Digging her heels into his tight butt, Alison squeezed his hands with hers, loving the feel of being taken with such power.

"Dillon, I can't believe how this feels. I can't believe how you take me."

Dillon moved faster, his cock digging ruthlessly at the place that brought her so much pleasure.

"You'll be taken often and in many ways if you stay. I swear, baby, I could just eat you alive. Don't leave."

Alison didn't want to think about anything past this. This was real, and now. She'd never experienced anything like this before, and she wanted to savor it, not think about the ugliness ahead. Her body gathered, becoming so tight she didn't think she would survive the impending explosion.

The sizzles grew stronger, her pussy clenching desperately at the cock thrusting deep into her body with a force and deliberation that stunned her.

The tingling heat gathered there burst into thousands of pinpricks of unbelievable pleasure, travelling with lightning speed all over her body. Shaking with the force of it, she screamed, unable to process the indescribable pleasure that consumed her.

Dillon's hoarse groan mingled with her cries, the sound of it setting off another surge of pleasure to layer over the last.

It felt like coming home.

* * * *

Dillon emptied himself into her, for the first time in his life hating the fact that he wore a condom. He wanted to fill her with his seed and feel nothing between his cock and her velvety softness.

Her cry echoed in his ears, followed by the soft whimpers that tore at his heart and excited him at the same time.

He'd never experienced anything like it before, but now that he had, he craved it and promised himself he'd do everything he could to hear it as often as possible.

Releasing her hands, he used what little strength he had left and lifted himself to his elbows so he didn't crush her. Spent like he'd never felt spent before, and with every muscle in his body quivering as though he'd just had his first lay, he drew the sweet scent of Alison into his lungs, a scent that felt like home.

Staring down at her, he brushed her bangs back from her forehead, marveling at the exquisite creature that had come into his life.

The scar he revealed sent a surge of anger through him, the scar she'd gotten when she'd been pushed down a flight of stairs.

When another tear slipped from the corner of her eye, he caught it with his thumb, staring at the glistening drop of moisture while biting back a groan as her tight pussy continued to milk him dry.

The tingling in his groin signaled a renewed awakening, and he knew if he stayed inside her much longer, he'd take her again. Already angry at himself for taking her when he should have been caring for her, he started to withdraw, stiffening when she tightened her legs around him and opened her eyes.

The drowsy warmth in them made his cock pulse again, his wanting of her seemingly never ending.

"Don't go."

Two little words somehow managed to cement his possessiveness of her, the sweet huskiness in her voice rallying all of his protective instincts to the forefront.

In that moment, he knew he would fight with everything he had to keep her.

Fighting to keep the fierce emotions racing through him from showing in his expression, knowing if what he felt now showed it would scare her to death, he smiled tenderly. He had to swallow before speaking, keeping his voice low and calm while fighting the urge to scream that she was his.

"I have some things to do, and you need to rest a while." Bending to kiss her cheek, he tasted her tears, gathering her to him again when she wrapped her arms around his neck.

Nothing he'd experienced in his life had ever felt any better.

He hadn't known himself capable of both dominance and such gentleness while taking a woman, had never even considered that the two would meld, but they had, and in a way that had ripped open doors for him that he wanted to explore to the fullest.

He had to get her to stay.

Lifting his head, he stared down at her, waiting until she opened her eyes again before speaking. Gripping her chin so she couldn't look away, he held her gaze, his heart beating nearly out of his chest.

"I want you to stay."

His stomach knotted when she closed her eyes and sighed, frustration and anger surging to the surface again.

She opened her eyes slowly, and in them he now saw a sadness and wariness that scared the hell out of him.

"Dillon, I have to go back. You know that. I have to testify."

Not wanting to scare her, he bit back his temper and forced a smile. "I know that, but afterward—"

"I don't want to think about it. Please. Let's just deal with one day at a time."

She smiled impishly, making his hand itch to turn her over his knee.

"You still have a lot to teach me, don't you?"

That he did. He'd teach her about her own body and the kind of pleasure only he and Ryder could give her. He'd train her body to respond to every touch until he controlled her so completely she'd never think of leaving him.

Hiding his impatience, he smiled. "Of course."

Withdrawing, he lay beside her and gathered her against him, pillowing her head on his shoulder as he rubbed her back, pushing aside the numerous chores waiting for him, including the garage. Right now, he had another responsibility—the responsibility of a man to his woman.

Taking a deep breath, he let it out slowly, smiling at the ceiling.

He rubbed her back and shoulders, listening as her breathing evened out and she slumped against him, and a hundred scenarios played through his head.

Yes, he would teach her. He would teach her how much she needed him. And he hoped that where her body led, her heart would follow.

* * * *

Dillon forced himself to look away from Alison's sleeping form, only the knowledge that he had things to see to in order to protect her making it possible to leave.

Assuming Ryder had gone back down to the garage, he came up short as he entered the kitchen, surprised to see Ryder staring out the kitchen window, apparently deep in thought.

With the intention of leaving so he could get back to Alison, Dillon started for the door.

"Alison's asleep. Stay with her in case she wakes up. I put a cold cloth on her eye. It's still a little red where he hit her. I hope like hell she doesn't get a black eye. I'm going down to close up the shop, and then I'm going to go talk to Linc."

The loud crash had him spinning on his heel, turning back toward the kitchen.

Used to living with Ryder and his temper for several years, it still surprised him to see that Ryder had kicked in the door of the cabinet under the kitchen sink.

Lifting a brow, he grimaced at the mess. "Feel better?"

Ryder sighed and turned, his hands clenched in fists at his sides. "Not much."

Yanking the refrigerator door open with enough force to make the bottles in the door clang together, Ryder reached inside and snagged two bottles of beer. Tossing one to Dillon, he twisted the cap off of the other and tossed it in the direction of the sink before taking a healthy swallow. Grimacing, he slammed the bottle to the counter.

Dillon had known Ryder long enough to wait him out. As he expected, Ryder had become wound up so tight it didn't take long at all for him to spit it out.

Hanging his head, Ryder sighed.

"I'm the one who told that asshole where to find her. I was supposed to protect her. He was supposed to come after me. Then I had to stand there and get him to admit what he did to her without plowing my fist in his face the way I wanted to."

Dillon set his beer on the table unopened, not wanting to lose the sweet taste of Alison's kisses.

"I know you wanted him to come after you, but you're pissed at yourself because he didn't do what you wanted. That's on him, not you. Now she's got proof, though, of what he did and a confession that he threw her down the stairs in anger, not self-defense. Christ, can you believe he was actually going to say that? You didn't mean for him to come after her, and Alison knows that."

Ryder lifted his beer again. "Yeah, but it would have been a hell of a lot more satisfying if I could have hit him."

Dillon allowed a smile. "Undoubtedly. I know it would make me feel better. You never know. We still may get a chance. In the meantime, I'm going to go talk to Linc and see what's on the video. Erin saw the whole thing. I want to talk to her. After that, we need to talk to whoever the hell's prosecuting this case and see about getting a lawyer for Alison."

Ryder, in the middle of taking another sip of beer, swallowed hurriedly and set the bottle aside. "Do you really think she'll need one?"

Shrugging, Dillon moved to the back door. "I don't know, but it couldn't hurt. I want to make sure we have all the cards we need to win this hand. If she wakes up, tell her to call the prosecutor and give him our numbers so he can contact her here. I want to know everything that's going on."

Dillon headed down the steps, his head swimming with thoughts of Alison, pausing when Ryder called down to him from the top.

Gripping the rail, Ryder appeared really shaken.

"Dillon, if they believed she attacked him with a knife, she just might end up in jail."

Dillon nodded and turned away. "We're just going to have to make sure that doesn't happen."

Chapter Thirteen

"Well, I finished up the last of the filing. I don't know how either one of you ever found anything in that mess."

Smiling, she started to wash out the coffeepot and straighten up the small table she'd commandeered to keep the coffeemaker and the supplies.

Dillon watched her like a hawk as he locked up, so much so that she could almost hear the lecture forming in his mind. Once he'd finished, he went to wash his hands and arms in the huge sink on the far wall, eyeing her critically as he soaped himself.

Watching him scrub the grease from his arms and hands proved to be no hardship. Something about the way soap and water looked streaming off of his muscles just fascinated her every time.

Her hands itched to touch the slippery soap covering his arms, each swipe of his hand over them making his muscles bunch and flex, tantalizing her as always. Circling him to get to the door, she eyed the way his jeans hugged his gorgeous ass as he stood bent over the sink, her imagination running wild with visions of the night ahead.

She couldn't take her eyes from him as she moved to his other side, aware that his own gaze followed her, eyeing her in much the same way she eyed him.

Lifting her gaze to his, she inwardly cursed.

Damn it. His eyes had darkened with concern, not the need she wanted to see in them.

Dillon smiled, but it didn't reach his eyes.

"Look at you. I can't believe you didn't even get a shiner. We'll stay in tonight. I'll have Ryder pick up something to eat. You're sore, and you didn't eat enough for lunch." He kept his tone low, intimate even, but the ever-present hint of steel came through loud and clear, telling her the subject was closed for discussion.

Gritting her teeth, she threw on her jacket, grabbed her purse, and slung it over her shoulder. Striding toward the back door with the intention of going upstairs, she avoided his eyes, scared he would see more than she wanted him to.

"I'm fine, Dillon. Don't try to baby me. I'm a woman. I'm not a fucking invalid. If you two are just going to sit at home, maybe I'll go to the bar."

"Excuse me?"

Ignoring him, she flung open the door and went outside, coming face-to-face with Ryder.

Fresh from the shower, he'd combed his still-damp hair back, but she knew that as soon as it dried, it would be like silk through her fingers. Even though the jacket he wore covered his tattoos, the wildness inside him couldn't be contained.

It shone in his eyes.

Glittering green eyes that held promise and the knowledge that he could make every one of her erotic fantasies a reality.

God, she wanted him. She wanted both of them with a hunger that seemed to grow every day.

His eyes raked her body as he strolled toward her, his long-legged stride drawing attention to his slim hips and the fascinating bulge between them.

She'd spent the entire day thinking about tonight, and with Dillon treating her like she was injured, it didn't look like she would be getting any satisfaction from him.

Ryder would give it to her.

Running toward him, she jumped and threw herself in his arms, confident that he'd catch her. When he did, she wrapped her legs around his waist and rubbed herself against him. Threading her hands in his hair, she closed her teeth on his earlobe, inwardly smiling when he shuddered and tightened his hand holding her ass.

"Ryder, I'm horny. Let's go upstairs."

He stilled, clearly surprised, but it didn't last. Leaning back, he met her eyes and smiled while sliding a hand under her sweater to cup her breast. "I'm glad you don't wear a bra. I've been looking forward to getting my hands on you all day. And my mouth. I'm stopping at Beau's and buying a bigger butt plug for you. When I get back, I'm gonna slide it right up that cute ass and bury my face in your pussy."

With arms and legs, she gripped him tighter, caught up in a wave of longing that dampened her panties and made her stomach tighten. Using her legs, she rubbed her slit against him, moaning softly as his hand moved over her breast and he bent to touch his lips to hers.

He swallowed her moan, his mouth moving over hers in the demanding way she'd come to love so much. His hand slid lower, pressing against her bottom between her cheeks, so close to her forbidden opening, she whimpered and wiggled against him. Holding her in place, he ravaged her mouth, his kiss unlike any she'd ever experienced as he worked his strong fingers at her slit, wakening every nerve ending along the way.

Alison's legs shook, and she had to hold on to him for support, a whimper escaping when he closed his fingers over her nipple and tugged gently.

When he lifted his head to stare down at her, she nearly melted at the passion swirling in his eyes. The promise behind it was unmistakable, telling her without words that he could satisfy every hunger he stirred to life with incredible ease.

How could any woman resist such confidence in a man or his determination to give her pleasure?

She wanted nothing more than to open herself completely to him, put herself entirely in his hands, and let him take her on a journey she knew she would never forget.

"Ryder. Oh, God, what are you doing to me?" Fisting her hand in his leather jacket, she tightened her legs around him, cursing the fact that their clothes kept her from feeling his bare skin on hers. "Teach me. Teach me how to please you. I want to make you want me as much as I want you."

His hooded gaze just made him appear more dangerous. Tugging her nipple once more, he slid his hand free and up to circle her neck, the danger and wildness surrounding him only making her want him more.

"I already want you so much I can't sleep. I watch you sleep and want to stick my cock inside you and fill you all night long. I fantasize about all the things I want to do to you, and it keeps me hard all fucking day. When I get back, I'm gonna show you what I was thinking about today."

Alison rained kisses over his jaw, breathing in his fresh, clean scent. "I can't wait. Hurry back. No, better yet, don't go. Dillon doesn't want me. He's treating me like a baby. You want me. Let him go run your errands."

"She's sore, Ryder. She needs a rubdown. Pick up some oil from Jesse while you're out. Tell her you want the peach stuff she sent before."

Stiffening, Alison slowly turned in Ryder's arms, eyeing Dillon over her shoulder. She appreciated his tenderness when she was hurting, but damn it, there were times when a woman just wanted her man to see her as a desirable woman.

It pissed her off that right now he didn't, and she couldn't let him get away with it.

"Kiss my ass. I'm fucking Ryder. He wants me. You can watch if you want to."

Ryder's brows went up. "You really want to lead with that temper? If so, I'm gonna stick around so I can watch Dillon paddle your ass."

"He keeps threatening that, but he'll never do it. He's too scared of hurting me even when I tell him I feel fine. He wants a doll, not a woman. Hey, does that store you're talking about sell blow-up dolls? We can get one for Dillon to fuck while you're taking me."

Dillon took her hand and pulled her with his usual tenderness out of Ryder's arms, scaring her just a little because he showed no emotion at all. Bending, he lifted her, gathering her against his chest.

"In Desire, when a woman issues a challenge like that, her men are obligated, and more than willing, to take her up on it, something I'm sure you'll become well used to."

Ryder slid his hand under her sweater again and cupped a breast. "You're trying to goad us into losing our tempers. That's another form of control, Ally. You're testing us. Trying to see how far you can push. Be prepared, darlin'. When you reach the limit, you're gonna get a spankin' you'll never forget."

Alison sucked in a breath, realizing the truth of his words. She hadn't even realized she'd been testing them, trying to provoke them into losing their tempers. Knowing she didn't have a future with them, and scared of getting too close, she'd been subconsciously pushing them away.

Ryder ran a hand over her hair. "Go with Dillon. He knows how to make you feel better."

Recognizing the defeat in his tone, she reached for him, but he'd already walked away. Staring after him, she promised that as soon as he got back, she'd get to the bottom of whatever the hell was bothering him.

After what they'd already done for her, she owed him that. Even more, though, she found she couldn't stand to see him hurting.

Dillon turned her toward the stairs. "You're sore, Alison, otherwise I'd turn you over my knee right now. You're going to go upstairs and lie down until Ryder gets home."

Pushing at his chest, she struggled to get down, but he only cursed and tightened his hold on her and started up the wooden stairs.

"Damn it, Dillon. I'm tired of being told what to do. First by Danny and now by you. Why do men think that just because they fuck you, they have the right to boss you around? Put me down, damn it!"

Ignoring her struggles with an ease that both irritated and impressed her, he kept climbing the stairs. "No. Stop struggling before you fall."

As soon as they entered the small apartment, Dillon set her on her feet. "Go take a shower. Just put on your robe when you're done so I can give you a rubdown."

She appreciated that he cared when her back bothered her, but his annoying habit of ignoring her claims that she felt fine would be something they'd have to work on.

Resigned to the fact that he wouldn't be taking her anytime soon, she turned away and started toward the bedroom, only to have Dillon grip her arm to stop her. Wrapping an arm around her from behind, he bent low, sending a shiver through her when he nipped her earlobe.

"I'm not Danny. Don't ever compare me to him again."

The icy coldness of his tone hit her like a brisk wind, sending a chill through her entire body and leaving her frozen in place.

Sliding his hands up to cover her breasts, he ran his lips over her neck. "As soon as I take my shower, Ryder should be back with the food. After we eat, I'll give you a rubdown."

* * * *

Dillon had purposely gentled his tone, not wanting to scare her any more than he already had. In time, she would trust that he wouldn't hurt her, and her wariness would diminish.

Hiding a smile at the thought of the things he wanted to do to her, he cuddled her closer. He wanted to have the ability to make her nervous when the situation called for it, knowing her trepidation would heighten her senses and make punishing her that much more enjoyable for both of them.

Comparing him to her ex-boyfriend had him seeing red, and it had taken a hell of a lot of willpower not to turn her over his knee and redden that irresistible round ass of hers.

Reminding himself that she was sore and very fragile, he patted the rounded softness now and sent her on her way to the shower, barely restraining the urge to join her.

Once he heard the shower running, he started to gather a clean change of clothes and paused, standing in the middle of the room. Closing his eyes, he imagined the scented bubbles from the stuff Jesse had given her running down her body.

He knew Alison thought she was fat. Hell, most women did. He also knew that after being on the receiving end of criticism about her weight, she wouldn't believe how sexy and fascinating he found her lush curves.

Telling her wouldn't do any good. He would have to show her, but he'd be damned if he'd take advantage of her when she was sore.

Fisting his hands at his sides, he tried to convince his cock to behave itself but didn't have much luck. Hell, he wanted her.

Badly.

All the fucking time.

He was a grown man, for God's sake, and he spent most of his time either remembering what it felt like to be inside her or planning the next time.

Fate must have been having a good laugh at his expense.

His entire adult life had been spent suppressing his possessive instincts, which had become easier to do when he and Ryder had started sharing women. He'd been raised by a frail mother and learned early in life that, although women had an inner strength that never failed to astound him, they needed to be cared for and protected.

Sharing with Ryder had made it easier to fight the possessiveness. Sex was sex. He took it when he wanted with women who wanted nothing more than fun and pleasure.

He knew Ryder appreciated not having the sole responsibility of day to day problems in a relationship, more interested in pleasure than having to show up on time for dates or, God forbid, listening to a woman ask him about his feelings.

He loved that together they could drive a woman wild, and women who received that kind of pleasure usually came back begging for more.

Through it all, though, they'd never had a woman who *belonged* to them. They'd never met anyone they could see in that role.

Until now.

Thinking about the sorts of problems they would have to deal with if they lived anywhere else, he appreciated the town he lived in more than ever.

They'd learned of Desire, Oklahoma, through a chance click on the Internet and had been curious enough to come for a visit.

Dillon, intrigued by the old-fashioned values regarding the way men here treated their women, decided to move here almost immediately. He loved that women were protected by each and every man in town and had enjoyed looking out for them.

It added a sense of community he'd never experienced before, one he embraced with an enthusiasm that had surprised him.

Ryder loved the fact that they could live the way they wanted openly, and within a month they'd bought this property and opened their own garage.

They'd lived here a little over eight years and had no desire to ever leave.

The women at the club provided enough enjoyment that they'd both been happy. He could take advantage of the fantasies of the women there to release some of the need to completely dominate a woman, to possess her, if even for a short time.

Ryder could indulge in his wildest fantasies, spurred on by women who wanted everything he had to offer.

They lived the best of both worlds, and it had been enough for a while.

Until he'd started yearning for a woman of their own.

Hearing a sound coming from the bathroom, Dillon automatically turned, smiling when he realized Alison was singing.

Now he had one, as soon as he could convince her. He winced when she hit a high note, grinning.

She probably had the worst singing voice he'd ever heard, but the happiness in it loosened some of the knots inside him.

He heard a bump and the sound of the bottle hitting the floor and started to rush in there, pausing when she cursed under her breath and started singing again.

To hell with it. He was going in.

He knocked, but didn't give her the chance to answer before barging through the door, his cock leading the way.

"Alison, are you all right?"

He could see only the faint outline of her body through the shower curtain and promised himself that as soon as possible, he would buy a clear one. His hands itched to run over her sleek, wet body, and hold her slippery form against him.

Remembering his promise of a massage, he smiled in anticipation. He couldn't wait to get his hands on her nakedness again.

To his regret, Alison stopped singing.

His cock jumped to attention when she pulled the curtain aside and gave him a glimpse of wet shoulder as she poked her head out.

"Dillon! How'd you get in here? I locked the door."

Without meaning to, he took a step closer, breathing in the tantalizing scent of peaches and biting back a groan when his cock demanded attention.

"Lock's broken."

Inwardly wincing at the low growl in his voice, he automatically searched her features for any kind of fear or anger, stilling when he found desire instead.

She pushed her slick hair back and grinned. Still holding the plastic curtain, she straightened, inadvertently giving him a glimpse of wet thigh.

"You're a mechanic. You can't fix it?"

His cock jumped beneath her gaze, lengthening as though reaching out for her. Through the curtain, he could just make out the dark hair covering her mound, an enticing shadow that had him taking another step closer.

"No point. I work on cars, not bathroom doors. Are you all right? I heard a noise."

Hell, he'd been with a lot of women over the years, fucking them in the club with and without an audience, and here he was standing in his own bathroom sneaking glances of a wet woman through a shower curtain and fighting not to whip the shower curtain away and take what he wanted.

Fuck. She was probably in pain, despite her insistence that she wasn't, but he couldn't stop thinking about getting inside her.

Disgusted with himself, he clenched his jaw. "Are you hurt?"

Her smile fell, her eyes flashing sparks at him. "I'm *fine*, damn it!"

Christ, he wanted to turn her over his lap. Her temper excited him, challenging him to take her in hand. He could have sworn he saw the dare to do so in her eyes, but decided he must have been mistaken.

In an effort to rein his lust in, he turned his back to her, meeting her eyes in the mirror over the sink.

"Do you mind if I shave while you're showering?"

Her smile fell briefly and then widened in a way he didn't trust at all. "Nope. Go ahead. I'll be out in a minute."

* * * *

Alison closed the curtain and stuck her head under the water to rinse her hair one last time. Standing there with the water pouring over her, she kept sneaking glances toward where she knew Dillon stood, waiting expectantly for him to remove his shirt and reveal that gorgeous chest and muscular back.

Sharing a bathroom had always been too intimate for her, but she had to admit she liked having Dillon there now. She wanted a chance to spend some time alone with him before Ryder got back, hoping to break through portions of that wall he kept between them.

He seemed to be walking on eggshells around her, and she didn't like it one bit.

Whenever she got angry with him, raised her voice, gave him dirty looks, got smart with him, whatever, his eyes came alive with emotion, his cock tenting his pants while he clenched his hands into fists at his side.

Each time, she held her breath, excitement coursing through her veins as she waited expectantly.

Each time, his eyes became shuttered and that tender smile would appear again, one that made her heart trip, but that left her feeling like she'd been shut out.

He carefully avoided looking at her nakedness, even though she'd tried to entice him with peeks of bare skin.

She'd been offended at first, until she saw the tenting at the front of his pants and the way a muscle worked in his jaw while he stared at a point somewhere behind her. She wanted him, and she'd be damned if she let him ignore her because he stubbornly refused to believe her when she said she was okay.

Evidently, she was not cut out to be a femme fatale.

Right now, however, she felt good and wanted Dillon.

Not knowing how much he could see, but imagining him seeing her when he cleared the fogged mirror to shave, she stretched, lifting her hands over her head and arching back as far as the muscles in her lower back would allow. Delighted that it felt so good, she did it again, the warm water running over her making the muscles in her back even looser.

Dillon's deep growl could be heard easily over the running water, followed by a clatter that sounded as though he'd dropped the razor in the sink.

Hiding a smile, she adopted a look of innocent concern and pulled the edge of the curtain aside, carefully allowing a breast to show. Her abdomen tightened, her nipples beading with awareness when she saw that he'd removed his shirt.

Standing at the sink wearing only a pair of jeans and with streaks of shaving cream on his face, he had to be one of the sexiest things she'd ever seen.

And for now, at least, he was all hers.

Blinking innocently, she frowned. "Dillon, are you all right? I thought I heard—"

"I'm fine, damn it." He sighed, his eyes meeting hers in the mirror as he smiled tenderly, his harsh features softening before her eyes. "Are you almost done in there, honey? I want to get cleaned up before Ryder gets back with the food."

Damn it, he'd done it again.

Smiling, she nodded, not about to let him get away with it, the idea that had been forming in her mind too irresistible and naughty to ignore.

"I'm done now. While you're taking a shower, do you mind if I borrow your shaving cream?" She held up her razor for his inspection. "My razor has one of those strips, but I don't think it'll be enough to shave my mound."

To her delight, Dillon stilled, his eyes going wide for several seconds before he recovered. "Uh, what did you say?"

Keeping a straight face, she swallowed a giggle before it could escape. "Dillon, would it be all right if I used your cream? It's probably better. I've never done this before, and I don't want to cut myself."

To her surprise, Dillon bowed his head over the sink, and in the mirror she could see that he'd closed his eyes, his jaw clenching. His hands tightened into fists on either side of the sink, and he mumbled something under his breath, something that sounded a lot like curses.

Blowing out a breath, he straightened, opened his eyes, and turned, his jaw still tight and his hands still fisted. "Why do you want to shave your pussy now?"

Alison shrugged, purposely allowing a nipple to show. "Ryder said something about it, and I've been thinking about it ever since. Since I seem to be having a wild affair with two men, why not go all the way?"

Blowing out a breath, he smiled, his smile not as tender as before and hard with tension.

"Why not, indeed? Turn the water off."

Alison blinked as he came closer and hurried to do his bidding. As soon as the water had been turned off, he shoved the shower curtain aside and reached for her, a dry towel flung over his shoulder.

"Dillon, what are you doing?"

He wrapped the towel around her and grabbed another from the shelf over the toilet and started to pat her dry.

"I'll shave you. You've never done it before, and you'll only end up cutting yourself."

Alison stood still as he towel dried her with brisk movements that somehow didn't jar her at all. She couldn't remember ever being towel dried by a man before and had to admit to herself that she liked it.

Eagerly surrendering to his ministrations, she stared down at him as he dried her legs, holding on to his shoulder and lifting each foot at his command so he could dry them. She automatically reached out to touch him as he stood, towering over her.

That possessive gleam in his eye told her she had his full attention now. Holding out a hand, he reached for the towel she held around her, his eyes narrowing when she held tight.

"Let go, Alison, so I can finish drying you."

Self-conscious now, she gripped the towel tighter.

"Dillon, I feel better if I'm covered up. You can still part the towel there without uncovering all of me. I know I'm not as thin as—damn it, Dillon!"

He'd whipped the towel away with an ease that made her wonder why she ever bothered to defy him and started drying her, paying more attention than necessary to her breasts. His light caress of the towel over her tender nipples sensitized them even more and sent sharp jolts of pleasure to her slit.

"I'm getting a little tired of hearing that you're fat. I love your curves, and if you weren't hurting, I'd turn you over my knee and paddle that round ass that gets me hard every time I see it."

Holding on to his shoulders as he dried her came naturally, and she did it without thinking. It helped steady her when her knees turned rubbery, and he seemed to expect it. Taken in by the vulnerability of having him care for this way, she let go to stand on her own, only to be swooped up into his arms with the towel wrapped around her again.

"Dillon, where are we going? Why are you carrying me?"

Dillon grabbed the razor and shaving cream on the way out of the bathroom, making his way to the room she'd slept in the previous night.

"We're going to the bedroom where I can spread you out and do this without cutting you, and I'm carrying you because I want to. You feel good in my arms."

Not knowing what to say to something like that, Alison looked away from his tender expression, yearning for the man who'd dried her in the bathroom.

"Why do you do that?"

Dillon paused at the side of the bed and lowered her onto the covers with her feet touching the floor, spreading the towel under her hips.

"Do what?"

If not for the intensity in his narrowed gaze and the muscle working in his jaw, she would have thought him completely unaffected by the sight of her lying naked on his bed.

"Why do you always get this look on your face like you want to throw me over your shoulder and drag me off to your cave, and then smile at me like I'm a little girl you're offering a lollipop to?"

Dillon bent low to brush his lips against hers, his muscular, denim-clad thighs nudging hers wide.

"When I put something in your mouth for you to suck on, it sure as hell won't be a lollipop."

Alison reached for him, unable to resist exploring the hard lines and ridges of the gorgeous male specimen in front of her. Smiling up at him, she touched a finger to a male nipple, rewarded with his sharp intake of breath.

Touching her lips to his cheek, she breathed in the scent of shaving cream and male, and wrapped her arms around his shoulders to press her nipples against him. "I know. You had that look on your face when I was sucking your cock, too. Why don't you want me to see how much you want me? I want you, too, you know?"

She pushed against him, needing to see his face. "Or is it anger? No, you don't have any reason to be mad at me. Disgust? Why? Because of my scar? Because sometimes my back hurts, and I can't have sex? Because I have a temper?"

Annoyed that he showed no emotion and frustrated that she couldn't seem to get through to him, she shoved against his chest.

"Get off of me. I'm going back to the hotel."

Pitting her strength against his proved futile, of course, especially when he won the fight simply by lying on top of her and pressing her into the mattress.

Even then, and with his own eyes flashing with an anger she welcomed, he kept most of his weight off of her. "Be still before you hurt yourself."

He waited until she stopped struggling before lifting his face, threading his hands through her hair. "You're right."

Stunned, she froze, eyeing him warily, not sure what he meant. "Right about what? What are you saying?"

His faint smile disappeared almost immediately, and that hard look that excited her so much came back into his eyes.

"Do you know why some men want their woman's pussy bare?"

Alison shrugged, wondering what having her pussy shaved had to do with anything. "I hadn't really thought about it. It's sexy, right?"

Please don't let her sound stupid or naïve.

Dillon inclined his head. "Very. Not only does it make a woman's pussy more sensitive, but it exposes her completely. Nothing is hidden from the man who takes her."

Running a hand down her body, he pressed his cock against her center.

"And if he's the one who shaves her, he's claiming possession of her. Her body becomes his."

Fascinated by the flash of possessiveness in his eyes and the low, hypnotic cadence of his tone, Alison could only stare up at his face as his hand moved down her body to cup her mound. She couldn't hold back a low cry as his fingers parted her folds and moved over her slit, her juices easing the way.

The faint light from the sunset shone through the window, making his chest and shoulders gleam like gold. Running her hands over him, she thrilled at the hard, sleek muscle and pressed her fingers into it.

"Is that why you want to be the one to shave me? Do you want my body to belong to you...while I'm here?"

Her voice trembled at the end, the thought of leaving here and facing Danny again almost unbearable.

She gasped as Dillon's finger slid deep inside her pussy, bringing her back to him and the present and making her forget all about everything else but him.

She reached for him, instinctively seeking reassurance, her breath catching at the flash of predatory intent, one that had her heart racing. "Dillon, tell me what you want from me. Tell me how to please you."

Despite her attempt to close her thighs on his hand, Dillon kept them spread wide, pressing against the spot inside her that had her entire body bowing.

Sliding lower, he knelt between her thighs, the hot hand he placed over her abdomen, effectively holding her in place. Holding her gaze with his fierce one, he pressed against that spot again.

"You have no idea what you're asking, Alison. Just leave it alone."

"No." It came out as a distressed whimper when he withdrew from her, leaving her clenching at emptiness. She made a frantic grab for him when he started to stand, taking his hand in hers and holding it over her breast.

"Damn it, Dillon. I won't leave it alone. Stop playing games with me. I can't give you what you want if I don't know what it is. You promised to teach me."

Dillon sighed. "I promised to teach you how to please a man." The muscle worked in his jaw again, his eyes becoming shuttered once again. "Although why you think you need any lessons is beyond me. You're very passionate. Very giving. Very sweet. You don't need to learn a thing."

He made it sound as though it was over.

Obviously the thought of her belonging to him in that way proved to be more than he'd wanted from her.

The chill that went though her had her gripping him tighter and then reluctantly releasing him. Gathering the towel around her to cover herself and ward off the chill, she averted her gaze. "I see. I guess I should be going then. I'll stay at the hotel. Do I still have a job?"

Dillon gripped her chin and lifted her face to his, his eyes hard as they searched hers. "I thought we'd gotten past that."

Threading his fingers through her still-damp hair, he pushed it back from her face. "Haven't we gone past that?"

At that moment she felt closer to him than she'd ever felt with any man before and yet somehow a million miles away.

Not looking away from him, she shrugged, shaking her head. "I don't know. It's all very new. With Ryder, I know where I stand, but with you, I'm never quite sure. When Ryder wants to avoid me, he does it. At least it's honest."

Lowering her back to the bed, he separated the ends of the towel, exposing her again to his gaze.

"You have no idea what's in Ryder's head. He thinks he can't take care of you and he wants to. As you said, it's all a little new. Why don't we forget all about lessons and concentrate on pleasure. Things will work out. Now, lay back so I can shave you."

Alison lay back, thrilling at the feel of his hands on her inner thighs as he spread her wide again, and fought to stay still.

With a hand on her mound, he met her gaze. "Be still while I get some warm cloths."

Alison nodded, still wondering what she could do about Ryder. The last thing she wanted to do was to make someone feel as worthless as Danny always made her feel. Remembering how she called out for Dillon while on the market steps, she winced.

Up until then he'd been all arrogance. Damn it. She had to fix it somehow.

When Dillon came back, his eyes met and held hers again, a demand in them she didn't understand. "I need you to trust me. You need to stay perfectly still for me, okay?"

"Okay. I can't wait to see what it feels like."

She never took her eyes from Dillon's face, following his movements as he turned on the lamp next to the bed and then as he slowly and methodically lathered her mound. Fascinated by the way the muscle kept clenching in his jaw, she wished she could see his eyes, but they remained downcast, hidden from her.

"Dillon, if you don't want to—"

"Do you know anything about dominance and submission?"

Blinking at the unexpected question, she started trembling with excitement and a little bit of fear, wondering if he meant to do any of the things he did at the men's club with her. Her nipples and clit tingled at the deep rasp in his gentle tone as he asked the question, but she didn't understand the underlying tension in it.

"I've heard about it, of course. I know that's what you find at the men's club, but Danny wanted me to be subservient to him, and I hated it. I think it would be different with you. Do you want me to submit to you?"

Dillon lifted his gaze and set the can of shaving cream aside.

"The thought's occurred to me once or twice."

His tone made it sound as though he'd thought about it a hell of a lot more than once or twice. Intrigued at the thought that maybe that's why he got that look on his face, she lifted up to her elbows.

"I only think it's fair to tell you, though, that if you're talking about whips and chains, I would hate it. You and Ryder talk about spanking me like it would be fun, but I've heard that some people like to draw blood. That's just scary." She didn't even bother trying to hide her shudder.

After wiping his fingers free of the shaving cream, he rubbed her stomach as if in understanding, which didn't surprise her a bit.

Dillon seemed to notice everything.

"Most dominant men don't want to draw blood. They want to possess. Protect."

"Possess? You mean own?" Fisting her hands at her sides, she fought to remain still when Dillon began to shave her, the backs of his fingers brushing her clit making it nearly impossible.

He lifted a shoulder, his matter-of-fact tone not fooling her for a minute. "To a certain degree."

"It doesn't sound like much fun for the woman."

He smiled, glancing up at her. "Oh, it can be. How do you suppose a man would keep a woman in line, a woman he considered his? We told you, even a spanking can give a lot of pleasure to a woman. And to the man administering it, for that matter. What if a woman gave herself over to a man because she trusted him not to hurt her and knew the pleasure he had in store for her? It takes a strong woman to be submissive. It also takes an attentive man to be a dominant, a good one anyway. He would have to know his woman so completely that he could anticipate her."

Alison bit her lip, her abdomen tightening each time her pussy clenched and released more of her juices. Falling back to the bed, she struggled to remain motionless as he wiped the top of her mound and squirted more of the shaving cream into his hand.

She held her breath when he parted her wide and began smoothing the cream over her folds, letting it out on a moan when his fingers brushed over her clit.

He seemed to brush his fingers over her clit far more than necessary, but she would have been crazy to complain.

Pressing her thighs against Dillon in an automatic attempt to close them to ease the ache there, Alison jolted when he touched her clit again, fisting her hands in the bedding.

"You haven't answered me."

It took her a minute to remember what they'd been talking about, her mind so focused on her clit she had a hard time trying to focus.

"I think, oh, God, I think a woman who trusts a man that much needs to get her head examined." It came out in harsh pants, the muscles in her thighs and abdomen trembling with the struggle to remain still.

Kneeling on the floor between her legs, Dillon ran the razor carefully over her folds, his face a mask of concentration.

Wiping the blade on the towel, he looked up.

"And yet here you are, allowing me to use a sharp razor on the most delicate part of your body because you trust me not to hurt you, and you know how good it's going to feel afterward."

Without waiting for an answer, he ran the razor over her again.

"And part of the reason you're doing this is because you know it'll please both Ryder and me. Curiosity's another. The same way you're curious now about a spanking. And having your ass taken."

She couldn't deny any of it. He was right. She did trust him not to hurt her, and she did it knowing that all three of them would get pleasure from it. Their teasing, their threats intrigued her more than scared her.

The knowledge floored her.

Frowning, she looked up at the ceiling as he ran the blade over her tender skin again, not even attempting to lie. Dillon would probably know anyway. "I am curious, but that doesn't mean I'm not nervous." She looked down in time to see him nod.

Wiping the blade again, he met her eyes briefly before resuming his task. "And you'll be curious about more things and want to try them, and when you get pleasure from them, you'll be willing to try something else. Your trepidation won't stop you. Ryder and I would learn your body so well that we'd be able to give you enormous pleasure. Would you like to know what a dominant man would be thinking while shaving a woman's pussy, a woman who's already given herself to him?"

Intrigued, she smiled, a fresh flood of moisture escaping at the inner reflection in his tone, as though his thoughts about it surprised him. "What?"

Shaking his head as though amused at something, he wiped the last of the shaving cream from her with a warm, damp cloth, smiling when she rocked her hips. When he removed the towel covering the rest of her body, she sucked in a breath, amazed at the naked feeling between her legs. Even the air moving over her bare flesh felt too intimate. She wouldn't have believed such a small thing would add to the vulnerability of having her pussy spread, but it felt bared now as it never had before. Shaken, she tried to close her legs, disconcerted to have him looking there now.

Coming to his feet, he kept her thighs parted and bent over her. Bracing himself with a hand next to her waist, he ran his fingers over her mound and folds, his eyes dark and intense as they held hers. Sharper now, his eyes held possession and an unmistakable command for her full attention as his hand covered her mound, his thumb brushing back and forth over her clit.

"With every swipe of the blade, he's thinking, that he wants this pussy to belong to him. He wants to care for it, to have the right to possess it and the beautiful woman beneath him more than he's ever wanted anything in his life. He wants her to belong to him in ways she's never belonged to another man. His to care for. To pleasure. To control. To punish. To protect."

Sucking in a breath at the too-sharp sensation of having her bare pussy caressed, she fisted her hands at her sides, trembling harder than ever. "Dillon. Oh, God, that feels incredible. Dillon, what are you saying?"

Dillon's smile held a hint of sadness. "You know what I'm saying, Alison. You're very fragile right now, physically and emotionally. You're asking for something from me that you're not ready for, and it's getting to the point that I won't be able to hold it back anymore. I'll pleasure you and teach you what you want to know, but don't ask for the rest unless you're prepared to give it all."

Alison sat up, grabbing him when he started to walk away.

"Damn it, Dillon. Don't do this." Reaching out, she placed her hand over the huge bulge at the front of his jeans, smiling when he closed his eyes, the muscle in his jaw working again.

"I want you. You want me. Take me, Dillon." She squeezed, running her other hand over his magnificent chest.

Dillon's eyes popped open, the combination of fury and heat in them stunning her. Grabbing both of her hands in one of his, he bent over her, sliding his hand under her wet hair to hold her face lifted to his. His voice remained harsh, his jaw as tight as the rest of his body.

"I want you. Yes. God help me, I want you. But with you, Alison, I want more. Do you really think if you belonged to me that I would allow you to keep secrets from me? That I would allow you to try to pit Ryder and me against each other? That I would put up with your lying when you insist you're not in pain and I can see it in your eyes? Do you think I would allow you to criticize yourself the way you do? To hide parts of yourself you think are undesirable?"

His tight smile sent a wave of alarm through her. "No. I wouldn't. I'd want it all, Alison, not just the bits and pieces you choose to give me. Until then, we'll enjoy each other in the time you have here. God help me, I can't give that up. But don't expect something from me you're not willing to give in return."

Releasing her, he wiped a hand over his face, his frustration apparent. "I'm going to go shower. Wrap up in your robe so you don't get cold, and I'll give you a rubdown after dinner. Ryder should be back soon."

Staring at his back, Alison lifted the blanket to cover herself to ward off the sudden chill.

Damn it to hell, he was right. She hated that he was right about everything.

How could she expect more from him than she could give?

The pain that flashed in Dillon's eyes before he turned and walked away hurt her more than anything Danny had ever done.

Sitting there on the bed, she pulled the covers around her, staring at the empty doorway.

The knot in her stomach grew, turning cold and heavy. Taking a deep breath, she let it out slowly as the realization hit her.

She loved him.

She'd actually fallen in love with him.

And there wasn't a damned thing she could do about it.

Hearing the door to the apartment open and close again, she stilled. She heard the rustle of bags and Ryder's footsteps, curling her toes into the carpet when he appeared in the doorway.

Grinning from ear to ear, he came toward her, swinging a small bag in front of him.

"Hey, darlin'. I got dinner and a little something else to use on you while I have my dessert."

Dropping the bag on the bed, he knelt between her thighs, bending to kiss one of her bare shoulders.

"Now this is nice to come home to, a warm, scented woman just waiting for me to unwrap her. Hell, I'll never be able to smell a peach again without getting hard. I can't wait for my dessert. I want it now."

He straightened and reached for the ends of the blanket and paused, his smile falling.

"What is it, darlin'? What's wrong?" Releasing the ends of the blanket, Ryder slid his hands into her wet hair and tilted her face toward his.

Swallowing the lump in her throat, Alison forced a smile.

"I think I'd better go. I can't stay here this way anymore."

Chapter Fourteen

The tenderness in Ryder's eyes undid her, and with a sigh, she slumped against him, blinking back tears.

"Dillon's mad at me, and I don't blame him. It was just supposed to be sex, damn it, but I did something stupid. Dillon keeps holding back from me, and when I got mad at him for it, he told me that I had no right to demand something I couldn't give in return."

Lifting her head, she smiled tremulously. "He's right. I'm so stupid. I should never have gotten involved with either one of you. I knew from the beginning that I should have stayed away, but I just couldn't help myself."

Ryder rubbed a hand over her back. "If it makes you feel any better, I felt the same way, but I couldn't stay away from you any more than you could stay away from us. Now we just have to figure out what to do about it."

With another sigh, Alison sat up. "I can't do anything about it. Danny says he's going to claim self-defense and say that I attacked him. He's going to do whatever he can to get out of going to jail, even lying to send me there."

His eyes hardened. "You won't go to jail, especially after the court hears the tape."

Shaking her head, Alison pushed away from him. "You don't even know if they'll hear it. Danny's very popular in Muskogee. Hell, his second or third cousin, once or twice removed is the judge. His mother even had an affair with the sheriff."

Ryder gathered her hands in his. "You should have gotten out of that relationship a long time ago."

Still kicking herself for not doing so, Alison snapped at him.

"Don't you think I don't know that? I was stupid. But, he'd never hit me before. He kept having affairs, and I thought it was all my fault. I'm too fat.

I don't know what the hell I'm doing in bed, and I'm plain. His family is the most popular in town, and has the most influence. Everybody loves Danny. They all think he's a great guy and couldn't figure out why he'd fallen for me."

She tried to pull away from him, only managing to let the covers fall. "Neither could I."

Ryder ignored her attempts to dislodge his hands, effectively keeping her trapped where she was and kneeling between her parted thighs.

"It's not your fault he couldn't keep his dick in his pants."

He released her hands to slide his up and over her breasts, teasing the underside and tapping her nipple. "You're not fat. You're lush and curvy and so fucking sexy I can't keep my hands off of you. Sometimes it pisses me off. You're not plain, and if you satisfied me anymore, my head would explode."

Dillon walked into the room, dressed in unsnapped jeans and towel drying his hair. "I've already been in touch with the prosecutor and an attorney. You're not going in there defenseless, Alison. Everything is going to work out just fine. Your new phone's on the kitchen table, but with a new number. The prosecutor has our numbers if he wants to get in touch. It's already dealt with."

Feeling closed in and finding it hard to breathe, Alison pushed Ryder's hands away and stood, reaching for her robe at the end of the bed. Wrapping it around herself, she ignored Dillon's narrowed gaze and went to the window, staring down at the empty street.

"I even thought about running, but then I'd spend the rest of my life looking over my shoulder. I want him to pay for what he did, but the entire town loves him and wanted to blame me for it. They'll testify on his behalf, character witnesses, I think the prosecutor called it. They'll make me look unstable and jealous, and the judge and jury will believe him."

Dillon stood and came to her, pulling her close and wrapping his arms around her.

"You're not running anywhere, and you sure as hell aren't doing this alone."

"Dillon, I—"

"No."

Dropping her head to his chest, she sighed, turning to meet Ryder's eyes. "I have to leave. I'll leave now and go back to the hotel and look for another job in the morning."

Ryder shook his head before she'd even finished. "No."

After sharing a long look with Dillon, he turned back to her and smiled.

"You have no reason to leave. You want it to be about sex? Fine. It's all about sex."

Alison looked up at Dillon, nervous about the look in his hooded gaze. She didn't want to leave, unwilling to give up one minute of the time they had together, and didn't want to stay alone in the hotel room and brood about the trial.

But she didn't want to spend the time with them arguing about something she had no control over.

"And we won't talk about the other stuff?"

Dillon inclined his head, his jaw tightening.

"For now. If it's just sex you want, that's what you'll get. Strip out of that robe and show Ryder your shaved pussy."

Shocked by the sudden change in his attitude, she glanced at Ryder uncertainly. "What?"

Moving to stand behind her, Dillon slipped his hands around her waist and untied her robe, letting the belt fall. Slipping his fingers inside, he parted the robe as he slid them upward, smoothing the backs of his fingers over her skin along the way.

When he got to her breasts, he paused, rubbing his knuckles back and forth over her nipples.

"I told you to show Ryder your bare pussy. You gave yourself to us. That means that pussy is just as much his as it is mine. Don't you think he has a right to see what belongs to him?"

Holding on to his forearms, Alison moaned as his fingers continued to dance over her nipples, the sharp pinpricks of need shooting like arrows to her clit.

One minute they'd been arguing, but Dillon's demeanor changed in a heartbeat, becoming once again the cool, controlling, and very sexual man she'd first seen in the hotel room.

A man she'd so far been unable to resist, finding the low, seductive cadence in his voice mesmerizing.

"Dillon, I, oh, God. I don't know how—"

"That's what we're here for. To teach you. You said that's what you wanted. You don't want any talk about the future. You want here and now and sex. We're giving you exactly what you asked for. But it comes with conditions. You're ours. You put yourself in our hands to do whatever we want with you. We'll give you more pleasure than you ever dreamed. That's what you want from us, isn't it?"

Alison swallowed heavily and nodded, unable to speak. A whimper escaped when Dillon began to toy with her nipples, rolling each of them between a callused thumb and forefinger.

"Good. In return, we want something from you. In the time you have left here, you belong to us. Until you leave, you're ours. Yes or no, Alison? Right here. Right now."

Oh, God. It was like something out of her wildest fantasies.

Only better.

It was Dillon and Ryder.

No fantasy she'd ever had could compete with the reality of being with them.

Ryder moved closer, dropping his weight onto the bed and reaching down to remove his boots. Tossing them aside, he waited, his eyes moving up and down every inch of her body as Dillon exposed her completely, widening when they stopped at her mound.

Dillon released her nipples and cupped the underside of her breasts. "Well, Alison? Yes or no?"

She didn't even have to think about it.

"Yes."

The atmosphere in the room changed almost immediately, becoming heavy with sexual tension. Ryder's eyes took on a cool possessiveness she'd never seen in them before, the light of anticipation making his green eyes glitter like emeralds.

"Lose the robe, darlin'."

Dillon whipped off her robe and tossed it aside before cupping her breasts again, running his work-roughened thumbs over her nipples.

"I like you naked, as often as possible."

A fresh wave of longing went through her at the seductive steel in his tone, a tone much like the one he'd used that night in the hotel. Willing to do anything in order to be able to enjoy this time with them, she leaned back against him, lifting her hands to wrap them around his neck.

"Yes."

Only when his fingers traced patterns over her breasts did she realize how much she'd opened herself to him, her breasts lifted high and unprotected. When his fingers brushed her nipples, she sucked in a breath at the jolt of heat to her slit, shocked to find how ultrasensitive they'd become in this position.

Rubbing against the bulge pressing at her lower back, she started to lower her arms, sliding her hands across Dillon's broad shoulders and down over his amazing biceps. Watching Ryder's eyes follow the movement of Dillon's hands over her breasts added to the sexual tension, as though Dillon were putting on a show with her body for Ryder's enjoyment.

Enjoying the tickle of the hair from Dillon's forearms against her palms, she gasped at the sudden sharp pinch to her nipples, throwing her head back against him.

Dillon bent low and scraped his teeth over her shoulder.

"Put your hands right back where they were."

Coming to her toes in an automatic gesture to relieve the pressure, Alison hurriedly raised her arms again, breathing a sigh of relief when he loosened his hold.

He hadn't pinched them hard, just hard enough to get her attention, even now treating her sensitive nipples with care.

Dillon ran his fingers over the vulnerable underside of her breasts, teasing them when she squirmed as the blood rushed back to her nipples, making them tingle. His warm breath against her neck made her shiver all over, and he responded by wrapping his arms more tightly around her.

"I like having your arms around my neck, Alison. I like having you open to me this way. I like knowing that this is mine to touch as I want, and I like having you wide open and ready for whatever we want to do to you."

His gentle caress of her breast sent a shock of heat through her tender nipples.

"You like it, too. Your nipples are extremely sensitive, so tender that even the lightest tug gets a strong response from you. Do you have any idea how much that turns both of us on?"

Ryder ran a hand over her belly, his eyes full of dark intent.

"She responds to whatever we do to her. Every time we touch her, she melts. I don't think she realizes, though, that her touch has the same effect on us."

Dillon tugged her nipples again, bringing her to her toes.

"Open those thighs and ask Ryder to inspect you."

Alison froze, not expecting anything like that at all. Once again, she felt out of her element regarding sex, feeling clumsy and naïve.

"Dillon, please. I don't know what to do. I thought you were going to just take what you wanted. Can't you just do whatever you want to do to me?"

Ryder's eyes gentled, but the wicked gleam in them made her nervous.

"Of course we're going to do what we want to do to you. Right now Dillon wants you to show yourself to me. Are you going to keep your word or not?"

Gulping, she turned away to look up over her shoulder at Dillon, indignant that he would put her in a situation like this.

"Damn it, Dillon. I told you I don't know how—"

"Quiet."

His fingers closed over her nipples, the threat unmistakable.

"I'm going to help you. You swear at me again, and I'm turning you over my lap and spanking your ass. Now, look at Ryder."

Bristling at his tone, Alison nevertheless obeyed him. Meeting Ryder's eyes, she felt her face burn as he crossed his arms over his chest, grinning at her predicament.

"Yes, Ally. Look at me, or Dillon's gonna spank that gorgeous ass, and I'm going to watch."

He licked his lips, his eyes going hot as they moved lower and quickly moved back up again.

"Did you look away? Dillon, if she looks away, are you going to spank her?" His eyes danced with anticipation, his grin pure sin.

Dillon's voice lowered to velvet-coated steel, rumbling against her ear. "Yes, I will."

Excited at their play, but with her hand itching to smack Ryder, she shook her head, the fingers Dillon closed over her nipples making her nervous.

"I didn't, Dillon, I swear. I'm looking at him." She glared at Ryder, knowing Dillon wouldn't be able to see it.

Ryder, the tattletale, sold her out. Clearly enjoying this, he smiled, an erotic and playful smile that made her pulse trip.

"Dillon, Ally just gave me a dirty look." Clicking his tongue, he shook his head. "I know it's more your thing than mine, but I don't think a sex slave should be showing that kind of disrespect to her master."

Dillon's solid arm went around her middle, holding her firmly while the other hand went around her, caressing the scar on her hip before going to her bottom cheek.

"No, she shouldn't. Alison, did you give Ryder a dirty look?"

Not wanting Ryder to witness the spanking he seemed to be looking forward to Dillon administering, Alison turned, looking up at Dillon through her lashes and adopting the most innocent expression she could muster.

"No, Dillon. I'm doing everything you tell me to. Please don't let Ryder get me into trouble. I'm really trying."

The wariness in his eyes told her she needed to try harder.

Pouting, she blinked, sucking in a deep breath as though holding back tears.

"I'm sorry. I knew I would never be able to be good at this. Danny was right about me."

Dropping her head as though in defeat, she bit her lip to hold back a moan when Dillon's hand moved over her bottom. The sudden sharp slap shocked her, and she lifted her head again in alarm, sucking in another breath when the arm around her tightened and Dillon's hand covered a breast, toying with her nipple.

"You ever put yourself down again, or mention that man's name to me again in the bedroom, and you're going to get an ass-fucking you'll never forget."

Alison struggled to stay still as the heat from the slap spread, alarmed that it heated her slit and more moisture leaked onto her thighs.

Dillon cupped her breasts, using his thumbs and forefingers to lightly roll her nipples, the threat that he could tighten them at any moment making her tremble.

"Repeat after me. Ryder, please examine my pussy."

Alison gritted her teeth when Ryder's brow went up. She wanted to smack that cocky look off of his face when he smiled and waited expectantly.

He could have easily adopted the same expression he'd worn with her before, and she would have done it readily, but Ryder had decided to tease her and make it a game, a battle of wills he knew he would win.

"Well, Ally? I'm waiting."

She wished she had the nerve to stick her tongue out at him, but Dillon's eyes had sharpened as he watched over her shoulder.

It all came out in a breathless rush. "Ryder, pleaseexaminemypussy."

Ryder, of course, had to make things more difficult.

"What? I'm sorry, Ally. I didn't understand you."

Embarrassed that she'd become soaking wet at their play and afraid that the lightest touch on her clit would send her over, adding to Ryder's amusement, she took a deep breath, willing her body to settle.

Standing here naked between them, their eyes on her body like caresses and Dillon's fingers closing over her too sensitive nipples, Alison knew she didn't have a chance of faking indifference. Drawing a shuddering breath, she fought to get the words out.

"Ryder. Pl–Please examine m–my pussy."

Ryder grinned. "With pleasure."

He laid a hot hand over her mound, his eyes flaring when she shook even harder and whimpered.

"Very smooth. I like it shaved. I want to keep it that way. Any objections?"

His eyes dared her to object.

"N—"

"None at all. I like her this way, too." Dillon slid a hand over her mound, his work-roughened fingers creating the most amazing friction against what had become a really sensitized area. "Alison, you didn't think he was talking to you, did you? You have no say in what's done with this pussy, remember?"

Ryder grinned.

The stinker.

His wicked grin flashed, his eyes hooded as he waited expectantly, knowing damned well she would have no choice but to answer with Dillon watching her every move.

Looking over her shoulder, she gave Dillon a tremulous smile, fluttering her lashes and pushing her bottom lip out just a little, not wanting to overdo it. "I'm sorry. I'm really trying very hard to please you."

Dillon gave her an indulgent smile, running his fingers over her jaw. "I know you are, Alison."

He bent, touching his lips to hers briefly before releasing her again.

The lack of endearment unsettled her, more so when he took her hands in his and lowered her arms to her sides. Fearing she'd disappointed him somehow, she grabbed his thighs, scared he would walk away.

"Dillon, what's wrong? Did I do something wrong?"

Frowning down at her, he patted her butt. "Of course not. I'll tell you when you do. Spread your legs and part your folds for Ryder so he can finish examining you."

His brow went up when she hesitated.

"If you're going to be ours, we have to know exactly what you're offering, Alison."

Her legs shook so hard she feared she would have fallen if not for Dillon supporting her from behind.

"What?"

"Do it."

She jumped at Dillon's voice, like an icy whip.

Not daring to defy him, she looked down to see Ryder watching her, his eyes gleaming with unholy delight as he sat there on the bed in front of her. Vowing to get even with him for this, she did as Dillon commanded.

Spreading her thighs several inches apart, she started to reach for her slit when Ryder clicked his tongue and shook his head.

"No. Wider. Spread those thighs for me, Alison. Hmm, I see they're already covered in your juices. You like playing the slave, don't you, Ally? You like being forced to do something, even when you think you don't want to do it. Now spread those fucking thighs."

Alarmed at the abrupt change in him, Alison hurried to obey him, parting her legs until her feet were about two feet apart.

Ryder nodded, apparently satisfied, and looked back up at her.

"Well, are you going to spread that pussy or not? I'd love to see that ass spanked before I get to it."

Alison gulped, her legs shaking so hard she didn't know how much longer they would support her.

"G–Get to it?"

Ryder's cold grin scared the hell out of her, a sharp contrast to the heat swirling in his eyes.

"I went out and got you a bigger butt plug, remember. I've got to see if it fits. Well, actually, I have to *make* it fit."

Reaching behind him, he retrieved the bag he'd tossed there earlier. He reached inside and pulled out an object still in its wrapping. He ripped the package open, holding the plug up for her inspection.

Her bottom clenched in response, her puckered opening pulsing as she looked over the black plug. Unable to believe he would try to stick something that large inside her bottom, she began trembling, her eyes flying to his.

"It's too big. Ryder, please. That'll never fit. I'll do anything."

Ryder's slow smile made her knees rubbery.

"Oh, you'll do anything, all right. And this isn't as big as my cock or Dillon's. Our cocks are going up that ass, Alison. Not tonight. But soon. You might as well get used to it. What do you think happens after a spanking, darlin'? Your ass gets fucked."

Dillon reached out and took the plug from him, nodding in satisfaction.

"This is perfect. I'll go wash it up while you finish checking out Alison's pussy." He slid a hand over Alison's ass and pointed toward the bathroom only feet away.

"I'll be watching the entire time. Do everything Ryder tells you to do." He turned and walked toward the bathroom. Seconds later, she heard water running and turned back to meet Ryder's cool eyes.

"Now reach down, part those folds, and show me your clit."

With shaking hands, Alison did it, sucking in a breath at the sensation of air blowing over her damp folds.

"Stick it out toward me. I want to see it good."

Biting her lip, Alison closed her eyes and pushed her hips forward.

The touch of a callused finger on her clit made her cry out, her knees buckling at the too-strong sensation. Throwing her hands out to Ryder's thighs to catch herself, she struggled to breathe.

Her clit had become so sensitized that his touch brought her close to coming, the bundle of nerves at her center too swollen and needy to withstand any friction.

To her surprise, Ryder gathered her against his chest.

"Poor darlin'. Would you like some help?"

Relieved and grateful for his offer, Alison wrapped her arms around his neck and cuddled against him.

"Please, Ryder. Help me." She didn't care about the need and submission on her voice. Only relief from this torment mattered.

* * * *

Dillon glanced over his shoulder, smiling at the sight of Ryder holding Alison.

His cock, hard as stone, demanded attention. The knowledge that he could walk into the other room and have Alison suck him to pleasure or that he could sink into that tight pussy didn't help.

She and Ryder needed some time alone to establish a closeness that would ease both of them.

He knew how much it hurt Ryder to hear her call for him and knew, also, that favoritism had no place in the relationship they wanted with Alison.

Stripping, he got into the shower, turning the water to lukewarm. Without hesitation, he took himself in hand to get the edge off, knowing damned well that as soon as he got back to Alison, his cock would come to attention again.

It infuriated him that Alison wouldn't talk about the future, wouldn't talk about whether or not she planned to come back to Desire when the trial had finished.

She filled the emptiness inside him like no woman ever had, and the thought that she wanted to keep him and Ryder at a distance pissed him off.

Picturing the way she'd looked when he'd left her, he groaned and stroked faster.

Now he understood how his friends felt. It was hard as hell, and more challenging than he would have ever imagined, for a man who needed to be in control in the bedroom to be brought to his knees by a fucking pout.

He'd almost given in to her right then and there, but that's not what either of them needed. He wanted to start as he meant to go on, but it proved to be hard as hell to resist that look of innocence in her eyes.

He'd used sex, used her innocence, to lure her into experimenting, and done it in a way that ensured that she wouldn't go elsewhere. She would live with them, and hopefully, through sex, he and Ryder could form a bond with her, one that would make her want to come back after the trial.

Sex brought closeness, and he would make damned sure to use it and every other weapon in his arsenal to form a strong bond with Alison before she had to face testifying against that asshole.

Bracing a hand against the wall, he stroked himself to completion, not finding half the satisfaction fucking Alison gave him.

Christ, he wanted her. All the fucking time. He woke up hard and went to sleep hard. He spent all fucking day hard because of her, and it had really started to grate on his nerves that he didn't have the freedom with her he needed.

He dried off and wrapped a towel around himself, grabbing the plug before going back into the bedroom just in time to hear Alison cry out, a cry of pleasure, a cry of need.

His cock twitched again, already stirring.

If Alison Bennett thought she was going to get away from him easily, she'd better think again.

* * * *

Wrapped in Ryder's arms, Alison looked up at him through her lashes, struck by the change in his expression, from teasing and daring to affectionate and full of lust.

"I'm sorry, Ryder. I can't stand it. I need to come. If you touch me there again, I'm going to come. I can't help it. I want to do this, but I can't. I'm not good at this. I'm sorry."

With a finger under her chin, Ryder lifted her face to his, which kept her from seeing the hand he slid to her breast. Smiling at her shocked cry at the unexpected caress, he stood, lifting her effortlessly. With a knee on the mattress, he lowered her to the center of the bed, batting her hands away when she would have reached for her clit.

Sitting on his heels between her legs, he ran a hand over her belly, his eyes now dark and mysterious. "Do you have any idea how much it excites me that you're so close to coming and I've barely touched you? I'll help you by letting you lie back this time instead of trying to stand, but I'm not finished with you. Part those folds and let me see that clit."

Crossing his arms over his chest, he lifted his shirt over his head, tossing it aside and revealing all those tattoos she found sexy as hell. He kept her thighs parted wide with his own, the denim against her inner thighs a sharp reminder of her complete nudity.

It wasn't enough for Ryder. Not only did he want her pussy bare, he wanted her to spread herself, allowing nothing to be hidden from his eyes and exposed for him to explore.

Reaching down, she parted her folds, sucking in a breath at the sensation of being so completely exposed.

The heat from his gaze made her clit throb as he traced a finger lightly over her folds and circled her pussy opening.

"Not long ago, I was at an auction. The woman on stage reminded me a lot of you. You'd rejected me, and I was pissed off."

Knowing what night he spoke of, she bit back jealousy that he'd been at the club. Almost immediately, an image formed, one of her being naked and auctioned off, meeting his eyes across the room as he bid on her.

His eyes lifted to hers now, the look in them just like the one she'd imagined. "I wanted to do to you what they did to that woman. My cock was so hard it hurt when I was watching them spread her and explore her because I imagined it was you. You're going to give me what I wanted that night."

Alison cried out when he touched the tip of his finger to her clit, writhing to get friction, but he removed it too fast, his eyes even harder than before.

Narrowing his gaze, he clenched his jaw. "I'll have it from you, Alison. You're going to give me what I wanted that night—what I went through agony for, trying not to be jealous because those men touched a woman who looked so much like you."

She'd never seen this side of Ryder before. The cold calculation in his voice sent waves of fear through her, but the heat in his eyes kept her from running, the knowledge that he wanted her as much as she wanted him.

"Ryder. Please. Make me come. I'm too close to play."

His gaze swept over her, hooded and darkly possessive.

"That night, I imagined it was you. Tonight I've got the real thing, but not in a room full of other men. When they auction off a woman in the club, she must submit to being examined and explored by any man who wants to."

Alison gulped, very conscious of the finger hovering over her clit. She could hardly imagine such a thing. To think that Ryder wanted to do something like that to her...

"Submit? Examined?"

"I'd be interested in seeing this."

Whipping her head to the side, Alison watched Dillon approach.

He didn't stop until he reached the foot of the bed. Wearing nothing but a towel wrapped around his waist, revealing the thick muscle over his arms, chest, and shoulders, he stood with his hands crossed over his chest. Although his eyes remained flat and cold, the towel he wore tented at the front, telling her that he wasn't as unaffected as he tried to appear.

Glancing at Ryder, he smiled, a cold smile filled with lust.

"Since neither one of us has had the chance to fully explore her, I think this is the perfect opportunity. Have you checked out her breasts yet?"

Ryder shook his head, staring at her slit, running a hand over her trembling fingers. "Just that day in the truck, and we were rushed. She couldn't stay on her feet while I inspected her pussy, so I allowed her to lie down."

Dillon nodded thoughtfully. "We'll have to work on that."

Alison sucked in a breath, hardly able to believe that they were talking this way in front of her. She was being treated as an object, but the way they spoke and the need in their eyes made her feel treasured, almost like a prized possession.

How could that excite her so much?

Ryder turned back to her. "Keep that pussy spread. Dillon and I need to inspect you thoroughly."

Both sets of eyes narrowed as Dillon and Ryder stared at the place between her legs.

Ryder touched his finger to her clit, making her jolt.

"She's very excited, so I can't really play with her clit. I think we should get one of those clit clips for her. She can wear it Saturday night when we go out."

Dillon inclined his head. "I'll order one from Jake tomorrow. She's very wet, isn't she? I think our Alison likes being explored. We're going to have to do this more often."

Alison swallowed heavily, so close to coming she could taste it. "We're g–going out Saturday?"

Ryder flicked a glance in her direction. "Quiet or I'll gag you." Pushing a strong finger into her pussy, he began to stroke right away, moving it around inside her and making her inner walls quiver and grip him.

"God, she's like velvet. Hot and tight and incredibly wet. You should feel for yourself."

Dillon whipped his towel off and tossed it aside, apparently very comfortable with his nakedness.

Alison's eyes flew immediately to his cock, her breath catching to see him hard and thick and ready for her. Her pussy clenched in remembered pleasure, drawing a chuckle from Ryder.

"Check out her pussy while I get undressed. My cock's so hard it's going to break my fucking zipper."

Dillon lowered himself to the bed next to her, not touching her anywhere.

"Keep those thighs spread while Ryder gets undressed and keep that pussy held open for me. Would you like me to feel your pussy, Alison?"

Why didn't he call her baby anymore?

"Dillon, are you mad at me?"

His tender smile should have felt out of place right now, but he seemed to know just how much she'd needed it. Knowing he could read her so easily still made her a little uneasy sometimes, but it comforted her somehow. "Of course not."

Shaking, she had trouble keeping her legs parted, crying out when a thick finger plunged into her.

"Be still."

Be still?

How the hell could she even hope to be still when he had a finger inside her, using it to stroke and stretch her tender inner flesh?

"Tighten on my finger."

"Oh, God." Alison did it without even trying, her pussy obeying him and gripping his finger before she even made a conscious thought to do so. It was as if her body had a mind of its own, clenching on him as he withdrew as though trying to keep him inside.

Dillon looked up as Ryder came back and sat on the other side of her, pressing his finger against her inner walls and holding her down when she dug her heels into the mattress and tried to lift up. "Very tight and wet. She loves being stroked. Her G-spot is really sensitive, and she goes nuts when I press against the walls of her pussy."

Her slick juices made it difficult to keep herself open, and her fingers kept slipping. Her clit felt so swollen and heavy it bordered on agony, and each time she had to readjust her fingers, she brushed against it, making the throbbing burn even worse.

Looking up when she moaned, Dillon kept moving his finger in and out of her pussy, lifting a brow and pressing down on her abdomen when she tried to lift into his thrusts.

"I'm also going to have to teach you to be still while I'm playing with you. I'll be exploring your ass the same way."

Her anus clenched, the threat of having Dillon's finger inside her, doing what he did now to such a private place, making her bottom tingle in reaction.

The look in his eyes and the conviction in his tone convinced her that he wasn't kidding and had every intention of exploring her bottom in the same way.

She'd never survive it.

Ryder looked up at something Dillon said under his breath and nodded.

"Yeah, it's a shame we can't use the vibrator I bought on her now. One touch of that and I'm afraid she'll come before we've finished."

Dillon withdrew his finger and to her astonishment, licked it clean of her juices. "We've got time." Wrapping his hand around her knee, he lowered her leg while Ryder did the same with the other.

"Time to get up, Alison, so we can explore you a little more."

She had no coordination left at all, her movements clumsy as she sat up and worked her way to the edge of the bed. Taking her time, she eyed Ryder's lean body, the hunger in her growing at the beautiful sight in front of her.

He didn't have a spare ounce of fat anywhere, his body whipcord lean, hard, tattooed, and completely naked. His cock stood out at attention, reaching for his flat belly, the head large and purple with a bead of creamy essence at the tip. Licking her lips, she smiled when his cock jumped and raised her gaze to his face.

His cold look didn't fool her for a minute now. He was as hot and hungry for her as she was for him.

Struggling to lock her rubbery knees, she came to her feet, alarmed when Dillon took both of her wrists in his and raised her arms over her head. "Her nipples are already tender, so be careful."

Ryder studied her breasts as though deciding on whether or not to buy her, reminding her of his determination to treat her as a woman being auctioned.

The combination of seriousness and play from both of them kept her guessing and turned her on big time.

Reaching out one devious finger, Ryder tapped a nipple, shooting sharp need to her clit and pussy.

"Very nice. I love that her nipples are so sensitive. She hardly ever wears a bra. I was thinking we can get her a few from the lingerie store, you know, the ones where the nipples are cut out? I'll take her tomorrow. I like your plan to dress her. I think we can have a hell of a lot of fun with that. She'll have to model her clothes for us."

Standing as still as she could, Alison couldn't take her eyes from Ryder's hand as it closed in on her breast. Still, the tug at her nipple shocked her and had her crying out and rising to her toes.

"Why are those legs together?"

Her gaze flew to his, glaring at him as he tugged her nipple again and another jolt of lightning shot to her clit. Giving him a dirty look, she gritted her teeth, her frustration at being on the verge of coming for so long spiking her anger.

"You didn't tell me to keep them apart, you jerk."

She didn't even see Dillon move before a sharp slap landed on her right buttock. At the same time, Ryder pinched her nipple, sending dual arrows of heat to her slit.

Dillon held his hand over where he'd slapped her, holding the heat in.

"You have a temper when aroused for so long. I'd hoped you would. I like temper and attitude in a woman I'm dominating. It adds quite a bit of spice, and it's very satisfying to overcome it."

He lifted his hand, leaving her bereft, and almost immediately slapped the other cheek.

"I guess I'll have to do my best to keep you aroused as long as possible. No coming yet, Alison. Let's see how long it is before you realize who's in charge and are begging to come."

Ryder lifted a brow, his eyes dancing. "I think she's going to have to suck my cock before I let her come. Now, spread those legs and let me finish playing with these cute nipples."

Spreading her legs about a foot apart, she sucked in a breath and waited. Her clit throbbed incessantly now, so swollen and heavy she wanted to cry in frustration.

Ryder's grin should have warned her that he would tease her mercilessly, but she hadn't been prepared for how much.

Lowering his head, he ran his tongue all around her breast, not touching her nipple. To make matters worse, he blew on the damp skin, making her shiver at the cold and accentuating the fact that he paid no attention to her nipple at all. He moved to her other breast and did the same thing, chuckling when she fought Dillon's hold.

"Poor thing. Do your nipples need some attention?"

"Bastard!" The cool air around her nipples made them bead even tighter, something she hadn't thought possible. They ached so badly she'd give anything to have some friction on them to relieve her torment, and without thinking, she reached for them.

Another sharp slap landed on her bottom as Ryder's brows went up, his eyes full of mischief. She jumped, and only Dillon's hard arm wrapped around her waist and holding her arms down kept her from falling.

"Easy, Alison. I don't want you hurting yourself."

With her hands now at her sides, she curved them around Dillon's arm. "Ryder's being mean."

Nuzzling her hair, Dillon laughed softly. "No, he's trying to give you pleasure, but you're very impatient and are proving to be a very belligerent little sub. I couldn't have imagined a woman better suited to me. Don't you dare reach for those breasts again."

Releasing her arms, he wrapped his around her waist again and nuzzled her neck.

Smiling at the affection in his tone, she leaned back against him and lifted her arms around his neck, loving the feel of having her breasts unprotected and available to them. Wiggling her ass against his cock, she couldn't resist teasing him.

"I guess you'll have to take me in hand."

Dillon slid his arms around her, cupping both breasts and tapping her erect nipples with his thumbs.

"I'm going to take you in both hands."

Dillon and Ryder seemed to enjoy, hell, revel, in every response from her and appeared to love the challenge of her moods. Nothing seemed to put them off, or confuse or disappoint them. Their focus kept them one step ahead of her, something she found arousing, and her playfulness broke free, filling her with a determination to try to surprise them.

How could a woman not respond to a man, or men, who met every challenge she issued and dealt with every mood with such patience and competence?

Pulling on his neck to lower his head, she kissed Dillon's jaw.

"Thank you for being so patient with me. I know I'm awkward with this, but I'll get better."

A finger slid through her slit, gathering her juices before circling over her clit.

Crying out, Alison released Dillon's neck and would have doubled over if not for the hands covering her breasts keeping her upright. Her clit burned, and her legs shook from the fast-approaching orgasm, but Ryder withdrew his finger before she could go over.

Swearing at him and struggling to catch her breath, she slumped, eyeing him as he moved to the side.

"I hate you. I swear I'm going to get even with you somehow."

Ryder's slow grin gave her a moment's pause, especially when he held up the butt plug, twirling it between his fingers.

"I wouldn't issue threats to the man who's about to shove this up your ass. Bend over, baby, and spread those cheeks for me."

"Oh, God."

Dillon massaged her breasts one last time before sliding his hands to her shoulders and down her arms to her hands, placing them on the edge of the bed. Getting on the bed next to her, he reclined beside her, pulling her hands to the center of the bed, not stopping until her mound touched the edge of the mattress.

Knowing their intentions, she couldn't stop clenching her bottom cheeks, the awareness around the tight ring of muscle at her forbidden entrance scaring her and at the same time filling her with anticipation.

Oh, God. They were going to push that big plug inside her!

Each time she thought her vulnerability couldn't get any stronger, they did something else, keeping her on edge and always guessing.

Ryder slid an arm under her hips, lifting them and shoving pillows beneath them, lifting her bottom and leaving her even more defenseless. Once he had her settled, he stood between her thighs, using his strong legs to spread them wider.

Alison shivered, knowing what would happen next and so close to coming, she actually felt the first wave of shattering tingles racing through her. She rocked her hips, but Ryder had placed her over the pillows in a way that she couldn't get any friction on her clit to send her the rest of the way over, the small orgasm not even coming close to satisfying her. Her ass, her pussy, and her clit, hung over the edge, totally open to him, all sizzled with heat and throbbed with sharp awareness.

Dillon released her wrists and ran a hand over her hair, the sensation of his warm fingers even stronger than ever before.

"Turn toward me, Alison."

With a whimper and a shudder, Alison turned her head on the soft bedding, meeting his brilliant blue eyes. Trembling beneath the hand he ran down her back, she moaned as a hard hand settled over her buttocks, simultaneously lifting and separating them to expose her bottom hole completely.

At the first touch of a cold, lubed finger touching her puckered opening, she closed her eyes on a harsh moan, sucking in a sharp breath. Fisting her hands in the bedding as Ryder traced circles around the delicate tissue, she waited in breathless anticipation, knowing that the finger circling there would soon be plunging inside.

Ryder pressed his finger against the tight ring of muscle, forcing it to open no matter how tightly she clenched her bottom.

"That's it, Ally. Much easier. Your body's learning how good it's going to feel. As soon as I get you lubed up, I'll fill your ass with the plug and fuck your pussy."

She shivered and cried out as he sank his finger inside her, moaning helplessly when he moved it around and coated her inner walls with the lube.

Unable to get enough air in her lungs, she couldn't stop the flow of whimpers that poured out of her. The decadent sensation of having her bottom breached was something she knew she'd never get used to.

It was too private, too naughty, too intimate.

"Dillon, she's ready for you."

A thumb traced over her bottom lip, and she opened her eyes to find Dillon watching her intently.

"I told you I was going to explore your ass, too. You didn't think I forgot, did you?"

Alison groaned as he slid from the bed and stood next to her left hip. She clamped down on Ryder's finger, curling her toes as the need to come became too overwhelming.

"I can't. Oh, God. I need to come so bad." A sob escaped when a barrage of those sizzles hit her again, and her body began to tighten.

Out of the corner of her eye she saw Dillon squeeze a generous amount of lube onto his finger before tossing the tube aside.

Ryder withdrew, cutting short the building pressure inside her.

"You fucking bastard!" Screaming, she kicked her legs, her screams cut short a second later when Dillon slid his finger deep into her ass.

"Careful, Alison. That temper's gonna get you into more trouble than you can handle."

Aware that Ryder watched her while he rolled on a condom, Alison closed her eyes, unable to stop the moans that flowed from her. When the finger Dillon held deep inside her began to move, Alison kicked her feet, her toes curling as she fisted her hands in the bedding. Groans and whimpers escaped one after the other until they blended together into sounds she'd never made in her life.

The pressure inside her had moisture running down her thigh, the level of her arousal so strong it scared her, the impending orgasm promising to be stronger than she could stand.

As Dillon worked his finger all around inside her, she lifted into him, wanting the plug now with a desperation she wouldn't dream of admitting.

Dillon withdrew, only to press two thick fingers into her, forcing her puckered opening into stretching wide to take them.

"Very nice. You're ready for the plug, aren't you, Alison?"

He withdrew his fingers with a speed that left her opening grasping at air and reclined again on the bed beside her, wiping his finger clean with the towel he'd dropped earlier.

She gasped at the feel of the plug pushing against her opening and would have turned away from Dillon's searching look, finding it too intimate for him to see her this way, but Dillon's hand in her hair wouldn't allow it.

"No. You stay right where you are. I want to watch your face while Ryder fills your ass with the plug."

Unable to stay still, she kicked at Ryder's legs, tightening her bottom against him. Finding the idea of craving this kind of attention alarming, she fought to get away from it, too scared of how much her body wanted this kind of erotic play.

Ryder firmed his grip when she wiggled.

"I don't care how much you move around. This is going in, Ally."

Chills went up her spine as the tight ring of muscle gave way under the pressure and the plug started to enter her. Every breath came out as a moan as the plug went deeper, forcing her anus to stretch wide to accommodate the relentless invasion.

It felt so foreign, so big, so hard going into her, filling the most private part of her, even more sensitive than before because of their play. The lube eased its way, not allowing her to stop it from going any deeper.

Ryder used the fingers of his other hand to force her cheeks wider, making her bottom hole sting. "Yeah, baby. That's it. You can take it. Do you know how fucking hard I am watching your ass take this plug and imagining my cock inside you?"

Overwhelmed at the sensation of having her ass being slowly, mercilessly filled with the firm rubber plug, Alison pulled at the covers, fisting them in her hands, her eyes never leaving Dillon's watchful ones. Her nervousness only added to the sexual tension, the added fear of the unknown as her bottom was forced to stretch to accommodate the plug, sending her into a world where nothing mattered but pleasure.

"Oh, God. Ryder. It's so big. It's filling me up. Oh, God. It feels too good. It burns, Ryder. Dillon, please. Touch my clit. I have to come. I have to come."

Running his hand over her back, Dillon bent and kissed her shoulder. "Soon. Let Ryder get the plug inside."

His low rumble excited her, and Alison reached for him, closing her hand on the arm he used to brace himself. "I feel so full."

Dillon smiled, his hand firming on her back. "Wait until we both take you together. Easy, now. The plug is going to keep getting wider as it goes into you, and then it's going to get really narrow. When your bottom closes around it, it'll be snug inside that tight ass. Just like the other one, the base will keep it from going in any farther, but it'll stay inside you while we take you."

Moaning at the unrelenting pressure, Alison dug her nails into Dillon's bicep as the muscles in her anus rippled all around the plug. "It's stretching me. Ryder, damn you, do something. Oh, God. How much more? It's too big. I think I'm coming."

Ryder laughed softly and smacked her bottom, startling her so much that the threat of orgasm eased, leaving her hanging there on the edge.

"You asshole! I hate you. I'm not telling you anything again. Oh, God, Ryder! Yes! Push it in."

Ryder pushed the plug in another inch and wiggled it around. With a surprising move, he thrust a finger into her pussy, withdrawing again before she could react.

Teasing her folds, he chuckled when she tried to get friction against her clit.

"Take a deep breath, darlin'. The last of it's going in."

Her slit sizzled from her clit to her bottom, her abdomen tightening each time she clenched.

"I swear. Oh, God. I swear I'll, ah, get even. Yes, Ryder. Oh, God. It's in all the way. Okay. Okay."

Panting, she gripped Dillon's arm tighter, her toes curling as Ryder's hands settled on her hips.

To her shocked delight, he bent and kissed the scar on her hip, the gesture so unexpected, she stilled. Moaning as he readjusted his grip, she gasped when he thrust into her.

Thankful for Dillon's touch, she cried out, struggling to pull him closer as the waves of sizzling heat exploded from her center and started to wash over her.

"So full. Oh, God. I'm coming."

Ryder cursed, his hands tightening on her hips as he began to thrust fast and deep.

"Holy hell! I'm not gonna last. Too fucking tight. Milking me too hard. Fuck. That's a girl, Ally. Keep comin', darlin'."

Alison didn't have much choice, her body no longer under her control. Every muscle went tight as she came, the sharp tingles racing through her again and again, the pressure inside her almost unbearable.

She noted, almost as though from a distance, that even now, Ryder kept a hand on her lower back, lessening how much she could move.

Beside her, Dillon flew into action, ripping the foil packet with his teeth and hastily rolling on a condom. As soon as he finished, he, too, placed a hot hand on her back, massaging firmly and keeping her held down.

Loving the feel of their hard, hot hands on her, she cursed that their constrictive holds kept her from moving much at all.

She'd never even imagined this too-full feeling, her bottom clenching tight on the plug, and her pussy tightening on Ryder's cock, stretching her everywhere all at once.

The incredible pleasure seemed to last forever, rolling through her in intense waves that slowly began to lessen.

Ryder sank deep, his cock pulsing inside her, the groan coming from him so deep and long it set off another wave inside her. The hands he held her steady with tightened on her bottom, his fingers digging into her.

With no warning, he withdrew, slipping out of her with a speed that startled her, dropping onto the bed next to her with a groan and curling against her.

Her inner muscles still rippled when Dillon's hands closed over her waist and he surged into her and stilled. Struggling for air and grateful for Ryder's caresses, she couldn't stop clenching on Dillon's cock, her body slumping as the waves slowly subsided.

She couldn't seem to stop rippling around the plug and Dillon's cock, but knew herself well enough to know she would never be able to come again.

"Dillon, I can't. I can't come again."

Dillon gripped the base of the plug and began shifting it inside her, while his other hand came around to rest on her mound, his fingers dancing with expert precision over her clit.

"Wanna bet?"

Alison sucked in a breath at the jolt to her system, the movement in her bottom and the light friction over her already engorged clit making her buck beneath him.

Unable to stop, she worked herself on his cock and his fingers while he kept the plug shifting inside her.

Dillon's quick strokes, strokes that dug mercilessly at that spot inside her, soon had her clenching on him again, her body so lethargic she couldn't even move.

Amazingly, she soon found herself climbing all over again.

The shift of the plug in her bottom felt so much like Dillon's cock, it was as if he fucked her with two cocks at once.

Barely able to catch her breath, she heard Ryder curse from beside her.

"Hell, babe. Don't hurt yourself."

"Fuck you. I want to come."

Her voice sounded thready and weak to her own ears. The breathless whimper in her tone made her curse sound even more pitiful.

Ryder laughed, reaching a hand under her, and closed his fingers over a nipple.

"Do you now? Well, we're just going to see what we can do about that."

Dillon's smooth, quick thrusts, the quick strokes of his fingers over her clit, the pressure of the plug being manipulated in her ass, and Ryder's attention to her nipple all combined and sent her over in a blaze of heat.

Screaming, she stiffened, the waves of pleasure so sharp they bordered on pain as they swelled, battering her already weakened system.

The crest left her breathless, the huge wave that held her in its grip seemingly endless. She thought she screamed again, but couldn't be sure, fisting her hands in the bedding as the surge continued, trying her best to hold on to something solid.

Finally she became aware that Dillon had stopped moving, holding himself deep inside her.

All three of them breathed harshly, Ryder's soft words mingling with her moans of completion.

She didn't know what he said and couldn't focus enough to pay attention. She found herself slipping, some part of her consciousness aware of Dillon withdrawing. A moan slipped out when she felt the plug being removed, the hard rubber stretching her bottom hole again as it slipped out of her, making her puckered opening sting.

As it pulled free, she moaned and sank into the soft bedding, hearing the rustle of movement all around her but unable to open her eyes.

Some time must have passed—she didn't know how long and didn't care—before a warm, soft cloth wiped her clean. She kicked out a leg in protest, grumbling when her legs were held and Dillon chuckled softly.

She didn't even open her eyes as she was lifted and placed on the soft sheets and the blankets were pulled over her.

Groaning at the low conversation that kept disturbing her when she wanted to sleep, she rolled to her side, burying her face into the pillow.

The next thing she knew, it was morning.

Chapter Fifteen

Half sitting, with one foot on the floor and the other on the rung of the stool, Ryder dragged the rag from his pocket to wipe at a smear of grease on his arm. Giving the task far more attention than it deserved, he glanced toward the office doorway, listening for any sound from Ally, something he did with increasing regularity.

He'd gotten so used to her being around already that he knew that when she left, she would leave a big hole in his life, an emptiness that he'd never really noticed before.

Hearing a noise, he looked up to see Duncan and Erin walk through the garage door.

With a wave in their direction, Erin headed straight into the office to greet Ally.

Hiding a smile at the surprise in Ally's voice to be getting a visitor, and grateful for a distraction, Ryder stood. "Duncan and Erin are here."

Dillon looked up from where pieces of the engine of Ally's truck covered the workbench, turning to greet Duncan, who paused to slide a hand over his wife's ass before joining them.

The mock look of outrage on Erin's face didn't fool anyone at all and only appeared to amuse Duncan, who said something low, making his hard-nosed wife blush a fiery red.

Laughing, Duncan came toward them.

"Hey." Looking around at the piles of parts all over the place, he lifted a brow.

"What the hell are you doing, building a car from scratch?"

Ryder tucked the rag in his pocket and offered his hand. "Hey, Dunc. We're working on Ally's truck which is about the same thing. What are you doing here? Something wrong with one of the cars?"

Duncan gestured toward the office where the two women laughed at something.

"No. Erin wanted to stop in to see Alison. She's been worried about her. Hope and Charity have been trying to get over here, but they've had their hands full with the club, and evidently Alison's cell phone isn't working."

Ryder shrugged. "I threw it against the wall and broke it. She has a new one now with a new number."

Duncan grinned. "You and that temper." His smile fell, and he looked back over his shoulder, keeping his voice low. "Is everything okay now?"

Dillon tossed a part he'd been cleaning aside. "We just have to wait for the trial. Alison's jumpy and doesn't want to talk about it. We want her to come back here afterward, but she won't fucking commit to anything."

After explaining about the charges Ally might be facing, Ryder reached into the small refrigerator and snagged a couple of beers.

Duncan accepted one, twisted off the cap, and tossed it into the nearby trash can.

"So have the two of you decided to keep her?"

Dillon shrugged. "I want her, but I don't think Ryder knows for sure yet."

"Oh?"

Ryder took a sip of his beer to ease his dry throat before answering, not exactly comfortable with all this talk of feelings, but too frustrated to keep everything inside.

"I didn't think it would be so fucking complicated. You guys have all had it pretty easy."

Duncan burst out laughing.

"Where the hell have you been? None of us had it easy." He looked back over his shoulder toward where his wife stood, the love in his eyes obvious. Turning back, he grinned.

"Who the hell ever said it was gonna be easy?"

Ryder shrugged, feeling a little foolish. "I just didn't expect to be tied up in knots like this. I understand what you mean now, when you guys talk about counting on the others to be there for her, too."

Thinking about the way she'd called out for Dillon when she'd been injured still had the power to hurt him, but he'd been relieved that Dillon had been there to help her.

Dillon, of course, couldn't let it go.

"I've been the one to massage Alison's back when her muscles tighten up, so when she got hurt and Reese tried to help her, she begged him not to move her and wanted me."

Duncan nodded in understanding. "And it hurt. That happens sometimes with Erin, but when we first met her, it's one of the things we had to discuss with her to convince her how relationships like ours work. We all have to play to our strengths."

Intrigued, Ryder glanced toward the office to make sure the women couldn't hear them.

"And this happens to you, too?"

Duncan shrugged. "Sure. When she has a problem, she usually goes to Jared first. Jared likes to take charge anyway, and if she comes to Reese or me, he gets involved anyway. When she wants to just talk, she goes to Reese. She says that Jared tries too hard to fix her problems, and she doesn't want advice, she just wants to talk it out. When she wants to argue, or she's in a mood she can't shake, she comes to me."

Dillon blinked. "She comes to you to fight?"

Duncan grinned, proof that it didn't bother him at all. "Jared won't argue with her. He puts his foot down and that's the end of it. Reese tries to reason with her and sometimes she's mad as hell and is looking for a way to vent it. So, she comes to me. Hell, you know me. I'll argue about anything."

Chuckling, he looked over his shoulder. "It always ends good. There's nothing like a good argument to bring out the passion in a woman."

Sobering, he took another sip of beer, his expression thoughtful.

"But that woman knows that each of us love her and there's nothing we wouldn't do, separately or collectively, to make her happy. She loves us. Each of us. It's not always easy for her, but she makes time for each of us. We do things together, and we each spend time alone with her. It's important, and something you're going to have to do yourselves if you want this to work."

He took a step closer to Ryder, keeping his voice low. "Don't make the mistake of thinking she doesn't need you or want you because she called out for Dillon. Find your strength with her and use it to get closer. We've all said, many times, that relationships like ours can't survive with jealousy. If you want a relationship with her, you're going to have to work on it. Separate from Dillon. Make time for her."

Dillon nodded. "Good advice." He glanced at Ryder. "I'll make myself scarce whenever you want, and you can spend some time with her."

Duncan finished his beer and tossed the bottle into the large can. "Another reason Erin wanted to talk to Alison is to make sure she knew that the attorney she told you about is really good and that she has nothing to worry about."

He grinned, his eyes dancing. "Erin didn't think she'd believe you."

Insulted, Ryder snarled. "Why the hell not?"

Duncan shrugged. "She said she wouldn't have believed us. Women. Who the hell can ever figure them out?"

Dropping back onto the stool, Ryder stared toward the office, where he could hear low feminine conversation, and fought the urge to barge in there.

"If we don't figure ours out soon, I'm afraid we're going to lose her."

* * * *

After dinner of soup and sandwiches, Alison attempted to put everything away, laughing as she stepped around yet another of Ryder's teasing attempts to catch her.

He moved fast, grabbing her around the waist, and leaned back against the counter, wrapping his arms around her from behind.

"What do you want to do tonight? I have a few suggestions if you don't have any specific plans."

It sounded so much like a normal conversation a couple might have at the end of the day, making her smile and easing some of the tightness she'd felt in her stomach ever since Erin's visit this afternoon.

Her giggle was cut short, becoming a moan when his hands slid under the hem of her sweater and closed over her breasts. Leaning back against him, she ran her hands down to the sides of his thighs, pressing her breasts out and into his hands.

"Don't try to get on my good side. I'm still mad at you for teasing me last night." Glancing up at him over her shoulder, she smiled. "I don't know about you, but I'm going to the market. I want to thank Isabel for helping me and we really need some groceries."

When Erin came by today, she gave her an envelope with the money Hope and Charity had sent, her refund for the seminar weekend that had been cut short.

Alison didn't care for the fact that she'd had to depend on Dillon and Ryder for each bite of food that went into her mouth and wanted to buy some food and hopefully even be able to make a few meals for them before she left.

From his chair at the table, Dillon sipped his coffee, sharing a long look with Ryder before turning back to her.

"We eat at the diner most of the time. It's easier for us, and we give the diner our business. Edna cleans the apartment for us, too, and for the same reasons."

Alison stiffened in Ryder's arms. "Oh. Okay. I didn't mean to—"

Dillon waved a hand, shaking his head. "Don't be offended. We watch out for each other here, and we don't want to cook."

Ryder lowered his hands to her waist and hugged her, kissing her shoulder, his easy affection a far cry from the sinful tease that had driven her crazy the night before.

"Do you cook, Ally?"

She shrugged, wishing she'd never brought the subject up. "Not much. Danny always said I was a horrible cook."

Dillon set his mug down and sat back in his chair. "I wouldn't put too much store in anything he said."

The hard gleam disappeared, and his eyes danced with amusement. "I'll eat anything you want to cook for me. I'm sure you want to get some girl food, though, don't you?"

Alison blinked. "Girl food?"

Straightening, Ryder ran a hand over her bottom. "Yeah, I've heard about that. I've always wondered what the hell it is. Come on, Ally. We'll go to the market, and you can show me."

Alison found herself hustled out of the house and down to Ryder's truck.

Looking back toward the apartment as they pulled away, she frowned. "What about Dillon?"

Ryder glanced over at her as he turned the corner. "Dillon has a few things to do. What's the matter, scared to spend time alone with me?"

Alison shrugged and stared out the front window.

"I'm just surprised you'd be willing to take me to the market. You don't seem the type."

He turned, frowning. "The type? I don't seem the type to buy food?"

Feeling stupid, she shrugged again. "You don't seem the type to do, I don't know, *normal* things. I picture you in bar fights and at the club having your way with naked women."

"Having my *way* with them?"

Ignoring that, Alison continued. "You want to fuck me, which is fine because that's what we agreed on, but the rest of the time you don't seem to like me very much."

She held up a hand when he would have spoken. "I know. You like me when we're naked, and that's all I should expect from you. That's all I *do* expect from you. You like to tease and play in the bedroom and fight everywhere else. I know you really don't like me, and that's fine. I just don't like it when you try to pretend otherwise. I know what I walked into with you, and I have no regrets, but doing something like this with you just feels strange to me."

Ryder pulled up to the front of the market, slammed the car in park, and turned to her, his eyes shooting sparks.

"What the hell makes you think I don't like you?"

Alison reached for the door handle, only to have Ryder come out of his seat, leaning over her and slapping a hand on her arm to stop her.

"Ally, why would you think I don't like you?"

The dumbfounded look in his eyes made her smile.

Touching his arm, she laughed softly.

"Ryder, you're a lady's man. You're one of those men that women go crazy for. You're gorgeous and sexy as hell, and you've got this wildness in you that's impossible to resist. You could have, and probably have had, any woman you wanted. I understand it would be a challenge for you, and a novelty, to have someone like me to ask you to show me how to please a man, but the novelty would wear off fast."

Cupping his jaw, she touched her lips to his.

"You're exciting and the kind of man women would dream of taming, but you're untamable." Laughing, she ran her hand down his chest. "You're a hell of a lot of fun, but I'm sure you've broken the hearts of dozens of women who wanted to tame you. Come on. Let's go inside so we can get back to Dillon."

She opened the door and jumped to the ground before he could help her and strode straight into the market.

If he had any idea how much she'd come to care for him, or how desperately she wanted the chance to have him as her own personal bad boy, he'd probably laugh at her.

Aware of Ryder's scrutiny as she talked to Isabel, Alison kept glancing at him, sighing at the anger in his eyes. As soon as she walked away from the older woman, Alison got a cart and started down the first aisle, giggling when Ryder placed his hands next to hers on the cart and walked behind her, his body brushing against hers with every step.

"Okay, so now you're mad at me. I thought you wanted the truth. Why do you look so pissed off?"

"I'm not pissed off, damn it. I'm—"

"Pissed off. Look, I'm sorry I made you mad. I'm still mad at you for teasing me so much last night, so I guess we're even. You have to admit, though, you're not exactly the domestic type."

"So you want to tame me?"

Alison shivered at the feel of his lips against her neck.

"Like I said, you're untamable. You're also very devious—like the way you tried to goad Dillon into spanking me."

Ryder slid a hand to her belly, making her nipples tingle with awareness.

"I like to play. You like to play, too, and don't try to pretend that you don't. I saw your eyes. That doesn't mean I don't care for you."

Sharp teeth tugged her earlobe. "Don't you want to play with me?"

Alison laughed softly, looking around to make sure no one could see that he cupped her ass.

"I love to play with you, Ryder. I'm still mad at you, though, for trying to make Dillon spank me."

Ryder pinched her butt, making her yelp.

"Wait until I spank you. Then you'll really have a reason to be pissed at me."

Bending low, he scraped his teeth over her shoulder.

"But when I make you come so hard you scream, you'll forgive me."

* * * *

Alison couldn't believe Dillon and Ryder's fascination with the things she'd bought at the market. It took her much longer than it should have to put things away because they kept taking things out of her hands as soon as she removed them from the bags.

Dillon squinted as he read yet another label.

"They have cereal that has pieces of chocolate candy in it?"

Ryder made a face, holding up a tub for Dillon's inspection. "Look at this. Cottage cheese. Did you know anyone actually ate this stuff? And you should see how much fruit she bought."

Alison elbowed him aside. "You're the one who said we needed more grapes."

Ryder grinned and slid a hand up her sweater.

"Yeah, but that's because I pictured you feeding them to me."

Forcing herself to push his hand away, she reached for another bag.

"Maybe you can feed them to me."

Ryder laughed. "Darlin', you sit on my lap naked and I'll feed you whatever you want."

Alison laughed back, but she couldn't help thinking about what Ryder said in the market.

When I make you come so hard you scream, you'll forgive me.

It sounded so much like Danny, she wanted to cry.

Reminding herself that she wouldn't be here long enough for it to matter, she took the box of cereal from Dillon and put it in the cupboard. Turning, she smiled to see Dillon striding toward her.

"Did you get your errands done?"

Bending, he lifted her into his arms, carried her into the living room, settled her on his lap, and reached for the remote.

"Yep. Bought your nipple clips. You can wear them when we go to the hotel restaurant Saturday night. Did you and Ryder get a chance to talk?"

Blinking at the abrupt change of subject, Alison looked up at the doorway to the kitchen where Ryder had water running.

"What do you mean 'nipple clips'? I thought you weren't going to use them on me."

After tossing the remote aside, Dillon reached under her sweater, closing his hand over a breast.

"They're padded and not tight enough to hurt, just tight enough to keep your attention focused on them. That way, you can wear them a little longer, too. Did you have a nice time with Ryder?"

"Why do you keep asking me about Ryder? I can't go out to a restaurant wearing nipple clips."

"Sure you can. Tell me about your trip to the market."

Alison dropped her head against his shoulder, a moan escaping when he used a callused fingertip on her nipple.

"We just bought groceries. Hmm, Dillon, that feels so good."

He lifted her slightly and removed her sweater altogether, tossing it over the back of the sofa.

"Let's see if we can make it feel even better. Tell me about your time with Ryder."

"What if Ryder doesn't want me to tell you?"

Shaking his head, Dillon danced his fingers to her belly and back up again.

"Ryder and I won't have any secrets regarding you. That's the only way a relationship like this works. We share everything. Now, tell me."

Lying across his lap, she arched into his caress, moaning again when he traced patterns over her breasts and teased her nipples. Everything he said about sharing a woman convinced her more and more that she could never be the woman for them.

It made every moment she spent with them even more special.

"Ryder rubbed my butt and kept trying to sneak a hand up my sweater when he thought no one was watching. It took twice as long to shop as it should have, but it was fun."

Dillon tugged a nipple, smiling down at her when she gasped.

"And you didn't get to talk at all?"

Twisting restlessly, Alison rubbed her thighs together against the heat that had begun to gather there.

"We just talked about him not really liking me. I think he was surprised that I knew. Dillon, let's go to bed."

Closing his fingers around a nipple, Dillon tugged slightly.

"You think Ryder doesn't like you?"

"Dillon, I don't want to talk about this." She tried to lift up, but Dillon wouldn't let her.

Using the forearm resting against her stomach, Dillon held her down and tugged her nipple a little harder.

"Answer me."

Recognizing the icy steel in his tone, Alison shivered with both alarm and arousal. How something that made her so nervous could also arouse her so much, she didn't know, but it did.

"Ryder only wants to have sex. Even if he doesn't like me the rest of the time, he likes me when we're naked, and that's fine. That's the deal we made, and I don't expect anything else."

Wrapping her arms around Dillon's neck, she pulled him down for a kiss, needing to feel close to him again.

To her surprise, he allowed her to lead, remaining still while she brushed his lips with hers.

Nibbling at his firm bottom lip, she smiled. "I missed you while I was at the market."

"Did you?"

"Hmm, mmm. Let's go to bed."

Dillon parted her lips with his, pushing past them with his tongue just as her legs were lifted from the sofa and Ryder sat, pulling her feet onto his lap.

She held Dillon tighter as Ryder removed her shoes and socks and started rubbing her feet, his hands going under her pant legs to rub her calves.

Dillon lifted his head and stared down at her, his eyes dark with possession as he continued to manipulate her nipples.

"Did you tell Ryder that you don't think he likes you?"

Alison slid a glance toward Ryder, not at all surprised that he watched them. "Of course."

She lifted a brow, silently daring him to contradict her and get her in trouble with Dillon.

Inclining his head, Ryder rubbed a hand over her thighs.

"She did. I'm going to have to see what I can do to convince her otherwise." He reached up to unfasten her jeans and tugged them down her hips and off of her with a speed and expertise that never ceased to excite her.

"You don't have to—"

Ryder ripped her panties and tossed the torn scrap of material aside, leaving her totally naked and draped over them.

"Oh, I think I do, and I want to."

Expecting him to spread her legs and play with her pussy, she sucked in a breath when he took her foot in his hand and kissed her ankle, sending shivers of delight up her leg and to her center.

With a hand in her hair, Dillon turned her away from Ryder and toward him and kissed her again, each sweep of his tongue laced with stark possession. The hand he moved over her was filled with confidence and possession.

God, she loved when he touched her as though he owned every part of her, something she never would have admitted out loud.

She shivered with desire when Ryder's lips began to move upward, kissing and nibbling her calf and then the back of her knee, a place that she'd never thought of as an erogenous zone before, but every caress of his lips there sent tongues of flame to her clit.

Twisting restlessly, and aware of the moisture that now coated her thighs, she lifted into the finger Dillon used to circle her nipple.

Ryder parted her legs, moving the one he held to rest on the back of the sofa, spreading her wide for him, the cool air on her exposed slit a sharp contrast to the fire raging at her center.

Running her hands over Dillon's big shoulders, she tried to press her hip into the large bulge against it, only to be thwarted when he adjusted her position, sliding her down until her shoulders lay flat over his thigh.

He smiled down at her, his hands moving over her.

"I don't want to hurt your hip. Just stay put."

Wiggling, she tried to smile up at him, but Ryder chose that moment to press his lips to her inner thigh, startling a cry from her.

"Dillon, I love when you talk to me that way."

Taking her wrists in one of his big hands, he lifted them over her head, lifting her breasts and leaving them defenseless.

He ran his fingers over her belly and lower, tracing them over her smooth mound, his eyes indulgent. "What way?"

She held her breath as Ryder's lips moved higher, letting it out on a frustrated moan when he chuckled and lifted her other foot and started all over again. Her entire leg quivered, the nerves awakened and dancing toward her pussy and making her even wetter.

"You know. All dark and authoritative."

Digging her heels into Ryder's back, she lifted her hips in invitation, silently urging him to hurry. He seemed content to take his time, nibbling at her calf and the back of her knee and sending arrows of sizzling heat to her slit.

"You know I like to play. Be still and let me play."

Keeping her hands over her head, Dillon ran his fingers from her mound to her breasts and back again, stopping to explore along the way and making her body hum.

She held her breath as Ryder moved higher, her stomach muscles quivering as his lips moved over her mound. The skin was smooth there now and so sensitive that the lightest breath blowing over it made her skin tingle and reminded her again that nothing hid her vulnerable slit from his view.

After covering every centimeter, he lifted his head with a groan, his eyes, hooded and dark, moving over her.

"She thinks I just want to play. She doesn't realize I have a hunger for her that no other woman could ever satisfy. One of these days I'm going to lick every drop of juice from her and not stop until she begs for mercy."

Alison let out a shuddering breath, holding it again when he slid his pants and underwear to his knees. Eyeing his cock, she smiled, her stomach tightening when he pulled a condom from his pocket and rolled it on.

Lifting her hips restlessly, she felt a fresh warm rush from her slit. "Is that mine?"

Ryder stilled and turned his head, his eyes cool and assessing.

"That's what I've been trying to show you, but that's not what you want, is it, honey?"

Not quite sure what to say to that, she hesitated, inwardly wincing when Ryder's expression hardened. With a sigh, he dropped back onto the sofa and reached for her.

"Never mind. Come here, honey."

Not knowing what to make of his mood, Alison searched his features, reaching out for him when Dillon helped her up.

"Ryder?"

"Hmm?" Gathering her close, he ran his hot hands up and down her spine, bringing them around to cup her breasts, the brush of his fingers over her nipples making her squirm.

She heard and felt Dillon get up and leave the room, going into the nearby bedroom, but Ryder chose that moment to tug her nipples, and she eagerly turned her attention back to him. She smiled when the cock pressing against her abdomen jumped, desperate to get back to the playful Ryder, the one she understood a hell of a lot more than this one.

Rubbing against him, she smiled. "Are you plannin' to use that, Mister?"

Ryder's naughty grin sent a surge of relief and need through her.

He rolled a nipple between his thumb and forefinger, providing the perfect amount of pleasure to send her pulse racing. "I sure am, ma'am. Why don't you get up on your knees for me?"

Holding on to his shoulders, she got to her knees, straddling him. A moan escaped when his lips closed over the nipple he'd tormented, and then another when his hand slid down to her hip, his thumb unerringly finding her clit. Fisting her hands in his hair, she worked it free of the piece of leather he'd restrained it with and ran her fingers through his dark, silky tresses.

"Ryder!"

His thumb teased her clit, his touch so light she wanted to scream. The suction on her nipple sent pleasure straight to where his thumb teased the sensitive nub, making the heated sizzles even stronger.

The hand holding her unscarred hip held her steady as the head of his cock pressed insistently against her pussy opening.

Releasing her nipple, he dropped his head against the back of the sofa, holding on to both of her hips. "I've been thinking about getting inside you all day." He lifted her and then lowered her onto the head of his cock, teasing her entrance.

"Take me inside you, Ally."

Nervous about being the one doing the taking, the need in his eyes and her determination to please him spurred her on. Fisting her hands on the back of the sofa, Alison sucked in a breath, keeping her eyes on his, and began to lower herself. The muscles in her abdomen quivered, her nerves and raw need making her clumsy, and she appreciated the hands at her hips that guided her.

"That's it, darlin'. Nice and slow. Damn, honey. You're so hot and soft. Nice and wet. You're always wet for me, aren't you?"

Alison threw her head back and pushed downward, taking the thick head of his cock deeper. With each downward tilt of her hips, she took more and more of him, his cock so hard and going so deep, she started to shake.

"Ryder. Oh, God. It feels so good." She tried to smile, but the feel of his cock stretching her and sliding over her inner walls made it impossible. "And you're always hard for me." She lowered herself the rest of the way, gasping at the fullness.

Ryder smiled and pulled her down onto his chest, making the hard heat inside her shift and push impossibly deeper. "A perfect match."

He surprised her by cupping the back of her neck and pulling her closer, his actions more affectionate than the demanding the way he'd been before.

Shocked that his kiss contained none of the playfulness she'd expected, she wrapped her arms around his neck, unable to resist the feeling of being cherished she experienced in his arms. Leaning over him, her hair provided a curtain on both sides, creating a private place for the two of them to enjoy, hiding her expression from him and allowing her to savor the precious moment.

His kiss sent her senses soaring, the slight movement of his large hand rocking her over his cock also moving her clit against him and making it swell.

The combination of erotic heat from someone so dark and playful mingling with caring that she'd never hoped to experience in Ryder's arms had tears stinging her eyes.

As long as she lived, she knew she would never forget this moment.

He explored her mouth with a thoroughness that left her weak and pliable, his kiss coaxing instead of demanding. It lured her deeper, the thrill of having this wild and sexual man kissing her with affection and patience so arousing she went limp, giving herself over to him with an ease she never would have believed herself capable of.

Her pussy clamped down on his cock repeatedly, demanding the satisfaction she knew he could give her, but still he denied her, cradling her against him.

Lifting her head the few inches he allowed, she struggled for air.

"Ryder. Let me move. I want you. I know you want me. I—"

She broke off with a start as another hot hand ran over her bottom, and tried to lift up, but Ryder held her firmly, staring down at her with a look of hunger in his eyes, one so raw with emotion it made her heart trip. "Ryder! Dillon's—"

Ryder smiled and ran his lips over her forehead. "I know."

She shivered at the feel of Dillon's lips against her back. Digging her knees into the sofa, she fought to move, but Ryder tightened his hold, keeping her firmly against him.

She moaned, another shiver going through her when Dillon ran a trail of kisses down her back and to her bottom, the building anticipation of what they were about to do to her both scaring and arousing her. She shook everywhere already, unsure if she could handle it.

Dillon touched a finger, cold with lube against her bottom hole, sending a spike of vulnerability through her and awakening nerve endings in a place that always seemed foreign and decadent no matter how many times they touched her there.

"Hold on to Ryder, Alison."

The huskiness in his deep voice told her the calmness he'd injected into it didn't come easily.

Shaking harder now, she let go of the sofa, more because she needed to hold on to Ryder's strength than because Dillon had told her to. Burying her face in his neck, she sucked in a sharp breath when Dillon started to press a finger into her, letting it out as a harsh moan when Dillon moved it around inside her.

"Ryder. Hold me. Oh, God. I don't think I can do this."

Closing his arms around her, Ryder kissed her hair. "I've got you, babe. Just hold on to me." The tension in his voice made her feel much better.

Dillon withdrew his finger and bent to kiss her back again. "More lube and two fingers this time. Just try to relax this tight ass for me."

Gripping Ryder, she tried to push his T-shirt out of the way, desperate to feel his warm, bare skin against hers. Alarmed at the overwhelming vulnerability of having her bottom so open and accessible left her feeling defenseless and a little scared, and she needed reassurance.

Already aroused and with Ryder's cock deep inside her pussy, she couldn't focus on any one thing, the bombardment to her senses leaving her feeling shattered. Needing something solid and warm to hold on to, she whimpered and tightened her hands on Ryder.

"Ryder. Please. I need to feel you. Please."

The last word came out as a sob as Dillon pushed two fingers into her, forcing her puckered opening to stretch wider, the erotic burning making her cry out.

Ryder's cock jumped inside her, his groan harsh as he buried his face in her hair.

"Hang on to me, darlin'. I've got you. Oh, hell, you turn me inside out like nothing else."

Dillon swept a hand over her back. "Ryder, damn it, can't you hold on to her? She's wiggling all over the place."

With a groan, Ryder moved her on his cock, chuckling softly.

"I like her wiggling. She's moving that hot pussy all over my cock and squeezing the hell out of it."

With his hands in her hair, he lifted her head.

"Aren't you, darlin'? You ready for Dillon's cock?"

Digging her nails into Ryder's shoulders, she tried to rock against him, but he murmured something into her hair and tightened his arms around her, the whipcord strength in his arms not allowing her to move at all.

"Yes. I want it. I want to feel both of you. I want to move. I'm scared, but I want it."

She held on tight, her anus clamping down on Dillon's fingers as he withdrew. Her clit felt as though it had a life of its own, tingling and throbbing to the beat of her heart.

The nerve endings in her bottom came alive like never before, the need to have her anus filled so alarming and foreign, she struggled to fight against it.

The sound of foil ripping from behind her made her pulse jump and sent a chill through her. Her mind ceased to function, her body so overwhelmed with sensation it made it almost impossible to think.

At the first touch of Dillon's cock at her puckered opening, she stilled, digging her knees into the sofa cushion. Her mind screamed that she couldn't do this, but her body craved having both Dillon and Ryder inside her.

She wanted to be taken like never before by the two men she knew would make it good for her and would make it an incredible experience she'd never forget.

Shaken by the fact that the tender inner walls of her bottom tingled with awareness, she cried out as the head of his cock breached her opening, relentlessly pushing through the tight ring of muscle and into her, the raw power of his thrust stealing her breath.

Her bottom stung, the rough curses coming from Dillon making her tighten on him and making the sting even stronger.

She cried out, her knees digging into the soft cushion beneath her, the muscles in her thighs tight and trembling. "Ryder. Oh, God. Help me."

Ryder held strong, his voice like broken glass.

"Easy. I've got you."

Dillon held on to her hips, his voice a low growl.

"Easy. Hold on to Dillon. Fucking tight. Do you know what it feels like to know that no one else has ever had this ass before? Easy, honey. I've got the head in."

His voice had that hard edge she loved so much, but also held a desperation she'd never heard in it before.

"Oh, God. I'm so full." Her slit burned, her pussy clenching repeatedly on Ryder's cock as Dillon's moved his hips, working more and more of his cock into her with each shallow stroke.

Releasing Ryder, she gripped the back of the sofa crying out in pleasure, the emotion welling up inside her like little bubbles racing through her veins.

Feeling as wild as Ryder and deliciously wicked, she threw her head back and cried out again, thrilling at the decadent sensations running through her. Trembling at the chills racing up and down her spine, she called out their names, shocked and thrilled by their responses to her desperate cries.

Dillon stilled for just a moment before sliding a hand into her hair, using the other to hold her hip steady, and growled into her ear.

"Mine, damn it. Mine."

He sank the last few inches into her, his lips pressing hard against her temple when she shuddered and cried out again.

"That's it. Be still. Let your body adjust, baby."

Baby.

That one little word calmed her as nothing else could.

Even though she couldn't see Dillon's eyes, that one word connected them in ways she wouldn't have thought possible.

"And for God's sake, don't move."

Sandwiched between them, their hard bodies pressing against hers, their groans and harsh breathing mingling with her own moans and panting breaths, Alison experienced a surge of sexual power unlike anything she could have imagined.

Having both of them inside her this way had to be the most erotic and wicked thing she'd ever done.

She couldn't believe how amazing it felt to be so incredibly full, to become so focused on pleasure and the two men inside her, two men who possessed more of her than just her body. Every breath they took washed over her.

Holding on to Ryder and moving as little as possible, she pressed her face against his chest, breathing in the scent of male and sex.

So warm and familiar.

Her body adjusted in increments to their possession, the tender inner walls of her pussy and anus rippling all around them, struggling to adjust to the hard cocks filling her.

Dillon slipped his hands around her from behind, lifting her and pinching her nipples between his strong fingers as he slowly withdrew his cock several inches from her bottom.

"You buck and I'll paddle your ass."

Her eyes flew open, meeting Ryder's glittering ones. Whimpering at the feel of the friction of Dillon's cock moving in her bottom, she clamped her knees against Ryder in an effort to be still. She tried to speak, but nothing came out except another moan as Ryder gripped her hips and surged deep.

Almost immediately, Ryder lifted her and tilted his hips, withdrawing several inches just as Dillon thrust deep into her ass again.

They did it again. And again.

The constant friction in her pussy and ass, the tug of her nipples each time Dillon moved, and the rub of her clit each time Ryder lowered her onto his cock made her putty in their hands, stunning her so much that she only moved when they moved her.

Their cocks filled her, stretched her, took her with such force and confidence, *such caring,* that she found herself lost in sensation, trusting them completely.

Fuller than she could have ever imagined, she felt taken as never before, in what had to be the naughtiest and most erotic thing she'd ever done in her life.

But the affection she felt for both men made it more. Much more.

It filled empty spaces inside her she hadn't even known needed to be filled.

She shook so hard she could barely hold on to Ryder, but their firm grips kept her steady and secure. Waves of heat washed over her, the sharp spasms of pleasure making her jolt in their arms.

Ryder kept his eyes on her face the entire time, his jaw tight.

"That's it, darlin'. Clamp that fucking pussy on me. Faster, Dillon. She's gonna come."

"No shit."

Dillon released her breasts to wrap a hard arm around her waist, bracing himself with the other hand on the back of the sofa by Ryder's head.

"She's gonna come in my arms, with my cock deep in her ass."

The need to come became a living, breathing thing, the sharp arrows of pleasure taking her higher and higher but not allowing her to go over.

"Fuck me harder, damn you."

She could almost feel their shock.

She even had a few moments to glory in it before both of them cursed and let loose, as though they'd been holding part of themselves back until then.

Ryder's hands tightened on her hips.

"You wanna be fucked harder, darlin'? You got it."

Dillon took his hand from her waist and fisted her hair, tilting her head back and to the side, his breath hot on her cheek.

"This ass is mine, baby. You're so fucking tight. That's it. Let go. There's no way you can hold back now. Ryder and I own this ass, baby, and don't you ever forget it."

God, she loved when he talked like that. She loved his possessiveness and dominance, a caring dominance.

Gentleness and dominance were two things she'd never imagined would work together, but they did, each making the other more potent and exciting.

Staring down at Ryder, she cried out, the friction and too full feeling overwhelming her. Still, she needed to prove herself strong enough for them and couldn't resist the chance to defy them.

"Only when I, oh God, I'm going to come, only when I give it to you. Aahhh!"

It slammed into her, a wave of pleasure so strong it stunned her. Her almost breathless scream came from deep within, the pleasure mingling with the warm caring of the men wrapped around her in a way that warmed her from within.

"I can't. Stop. Coming. Too full. Burns. Don't stop. Don't stop. Ever."

Her pussy and ass clamped down on them, the fullness so overwhelming she whimpered.

Dillon cursed and surged deep only seconds before Ryder did the same, both of them holding her against them as their cocks pulsed inside her.

The huge swell finally released her from its grip, and like a puppet that has had its strings cut, she collapsed against Ryder.

Still trembling, she struggled to breathe, grateful for the strength surrounding her. She welcomed their warmth, especially when the trembling continued.

She didn't know how long they remained like that, but when Dillon moved, she found herself jerked back to awareness, leaving her wondering if she'd fallen asleep.

Moaning, she automatically held on to Ryder as Dillon began to withdraw.

"Oh, God. Oh, God. Don't move. I can't believe how that feels."

Dillon chuckled and ran a hand over her ass. "As much as I'd like to spend the rest of my life in this ass, I can't. Come on. I'll wash you in the shower."

"No." Snuggling against Ryder, she closed her eyes again. "I can't stand. Just let me stay here."

Dillon turned, frowning. "You moaned. Are you all right? Fuck, we didn't hurt your back, did we?"

Laughing, Alison stretched. "Nope. But my butt is sore."

Running a hand over it, Ryder chuckled. "I'll be glad to massage it for you."

The sound of her cell phone ringing made Alison jump.

"Hell."

She started to get up, but Ryder held her as a still-naked Dillon changed direction and headed for her cell phone.

"Damn it, Dillon."

"Hush." He pressed the button to answer and put the phone to his ear, his expression grim.

"What?"

Surprised at his tone, she exchanged a look with Ryder, grateful for his help in getting to her feet. Watching Dillon's face, a cold chill went through her, and she raced to get dressed.

"Yeah, this is Dillon Tanner."

Ryder rubbed a hand over her shoulder and pulled her close.

"Relax. Dillon can handle whoever's on the phone."

Dillon expression softened as he winked at her.

"That's good news. Yeah, I'll tell her. Thanks."

He hung up and held out a hand to stop her before she could even speak.

"That was Mark Reynolds, your attorney, the one that you obviously called because you didn't trust us to handle it. He said that he's already talked to the prosecutor. The trial is the talk of the town around Muskogee. Danny's keeping quiet until the trial. He's not pressing any charges against you for now. He's waiting until he gets up on the stand, and then he plans to accuse you of attacking him at his house, and then again here. He's going to claim both were self-defense. He thinks if he waits until the trial, it'll cause more of a stir. He's using that time to gather witnesses to support his story."

Alison blinked. "How the hell is that good news? Sure, he's not going to try to have me arrested now, but he will as soon as I go back. Damn it, Dillon, you don't know these people. You guys live in a dream world."

"Excuse me?"

Angry for letting herself get lost in the fantasy, she met his furious look squarely.

"Desire, Oklahoma is not the real world. People don't live this way. Sure, it's fun and exciting having sex with two men, but this kind of fantasy would never survive the real world. Men who share a woman would eventually get jealous of each other and fight. Your rules are crazy. What kind of woman would put up with being spanked if she did something her men didn't like?"

He reached her in three strides, gripping her chin and kissing her hard.

"You would, baby doll—and I'd make damned sure you liked it."

Chapter Sixteen

"I don't want to talk about it!"

Ryder sighed and looked up from where he stood at the garage sink washing his hands in time to see Ally storm past him. Turning at the waist, he watched with a combination of resignation, frustration, and amusement as Ally threw open the back door and stomped out, slamming the door closed behind her.

Her long, dark hair streamed out behind her as she flew past the window, her hurried strides taking her to the stairs leading up to the apartment.

Breathing a sigh of relief, as he had several times already this week, that she hadn't attempted to storm out of their lives, Ryder turned off the water with a flick of his wrist. The silence enabled him to make out Dillon's inventive curses more clearly, and he reached for one of the paper towels from the stack over the sink and turned.

He took his time drying his hands, waiting for Dillon's anger to subside somewhat. Lifting a brow when a wrench went flying into the concrete block wall, he bit back a smile.

"As much stock as we put into keeping our tools in good condition, you must be really pissed to throw one. I'm supposed to be the one with the temper."

Finished, he tossed the towel into the can and gestured toward the window. "And yet I've spent the last several days acting as a buffer between you two."

Dillon threw a dirty rag aside and walked across the room to retrieve the wrench, shooting a glare at Ryder.

"Nobody told you to. I don't need a fucking buffer to deal with Alison."

Leaning back against the sink, Ryder studied his friend.

Dillon had always been the cool one, but this week he'd exploded several times, his frustration with Ally's refusal to talk about the trial, her ex-boyfriend, or anything beyond next Friday growing more every day.

Folding his hands over his chest, Ryder braced himself, not trusting Dillon with the wrench in his hand.

"Somebody needs to with the way the two of you are butting heads this week. Why do you keep harping at her? If she doesn't want to talk about it, let it go."

Dillon hung his head, running his fingers back and forth over the wrench, his voice so low Ryder had to strain to hear him.

"She's not planning to come back. She's gonna leave us."

A cold ball of ice formed in Ryder's stomach. "Bullshit. She's just scared that she's going to jail. She's not. We both know that. We've both told her that her attorney already has his arguments ready, and Danny's gonna end up looking like a fool for even suggesting it. She's just nervous about it. We have a booth tonight. We're just gonna have to take her mind off of it."

Dillon sighed and lifted his head.

"I wish I believed that. No, Alison doesn't believe that we can make things work here. She's halfway out the door already."

* * * *

Alison shot wary glances at both Dillon and Ryder as they walked into the restaurant, not trusting their moods at all.

Ever since they'd come up to the apartment after she'd stormed out of the garage this afternoon, Dillon had been nothing but polite, but in that cool way he had that made her nervous as hell.

Dillon being cool and polite was not to be trusted.

Ryder, on the other hand, kept smiling, an innocent smile that made her even more nervous.

As soon as they walked through the door of the restaurant, Brandon approached, his dark good looks drawing several feminine stares. It irked her even more that some of the women also eyed Dillon and Ryder, even though she stood right between them.

They probably didn't know which one she was with.

She acted before thinking, pulling a surprised Dillon down so she could touch her lips to his.

He reacted immediately, wrapping his arm around her and pulling her closer, slipping his tongue between her lips to tangle with hers. His hand at the back of her head held her still for a kiss she'd begun but he controlled right from the start.

"Can't you wait until you get to the booth?"

Dillon lifted his head, staring down at her as he answered Brandon.

"Every minute counts, doesn't it, Alison?"

Ryder took her hand and pulled her along with him. "Not that I'd mind watching you two fight right here in the middle of the restaurant, but I've already learned that Brandon doesn't like it. Besides, I'm hungry."

Pretending not to notice the looks of amusement from several of the other diners, Alison rushed to keep up with Ryder.

"What's your hurry? I've seen how much you eat, but you can't be that hungry." She had the strangest feeling that something was going on, but couldn't imagine what they could do in a restaurant.

She soon found out.

The table Ryder led her to sat back from the others in what appeared to be a small alcove, with heavy curtains on either side of the entrance.

Under other circumstances, she might have considered it romantic, but because of the way Dillon and Ryder were acting, it gave her a funny feeling in the pit of her stomach.

Seeing the look of wicked anticipation on Ryder's face, she glanced at Dillon.

Dillon must have somehow sensed her attention, because he reached out to stroke her arm as he continued to speak in low tones to Brandon for another minute or two before releasing her.

The fact that he'd felt her attention even while looking the other way gave her another of those warm feelings inside, the kind of feeling she'd started to get more and more around them.

His eyes stayed sharp on her as Ryder helped her take off her jacket and seated her while he finished his hushed conversation with Brandon.

Nodding once, he slid onto the bench seat beside her, dropping his big arm over the back of the seat, his fingers drawing a pattern over her shoulder.

Brandon stepped aside as a trio of waiters came in, each carrying a tray.

They didn't appear to mind the tense silence as they set up food and drinks, not even looking at any of them.

Brandon directed two of them to set their trays on a nearby table while the other set drinks, appetizers, and a basket of fragrant, still-steaming bread on the large table in front of them. As soon as the waiters finished and left, Brandon pointed to a button located on a box at the far side of the table, one she hadn't noticed until now.

"Just press that button when you want the waiter. Until then, you won't be disturbed. Enjoy yourselves." With a faint smile, he stepped back and reached up to close the dark heavy curtain, enclosing the three of them in a private cocoon, separated completely now from the other diners.

Feeling the men's stares, Alison stared at the curtain and swallowed heavily. Pissed off at herself because she had to gather her courage before turning to Dillon, she took a deep breath and turned her head to find him watching her closely, his expression hard and unforgiving. His eyes, however, held possessiveness and, if she wasn't mistaken, a hint of desperation.

"Why aren't we out in the restaurant like we were the last time?"

Reaching out to cup her breast, Dillon bent toward her.

"We wanted privacy, and we wanted to give you a night you won't soon forget. Something to think about when you leave."

Ryder's hands came around her and, with deft fingers, began to unbutton the cotton shirt she'd worn.

"We're gonna make damned sure you don't forget us."

She opened her mouth, but closed it again on a moan as Ryder finished unbuttoning her shirt and worked it down her arms, leaving them trapped behind her. She drew in a shuddering breath when Dillon unfastened her bra and separated the two sides and stared down at her now exposed breasts.

She desperately wanted to tell them that she would never forget either one of them. She desperately wanted to let them know that they made her feel more alive, more womanly, more desired, than she'd ever felt in her life. She wanted to let them know that her feelings for them had become jumbled in her mind because she didn't believe that people could actually live the way they proposed, no matter how badly she wanted to.

But what would be the point?

If Danny had his way, she wouldn't have any say in her future, and she'd be damned if she'd get her hopes up only to have Danny take away her chance of happiness. She wouldn't allow herself to wish for something that could be taken away at a moment's notice and spend the rest of her life missing it.

When she walked away, however, she was determined to take a lifetime of memories with her.

Lifting her eyes, she met Dillon's squarely and smiled, wishing with all her heart she could stay right here in this town with Dillon and Ryder as her lovers.

Reaching out for him, she lifted her breasts in invitation, her arousal at being so exposed making her more aggressive. Determined to tease him out of his strange mood, she smiled seductively.

"Show me."

Dillon's eyes flared at the challenge, his smile somehow calculated and indulgent.

"We'll show you. Just remember that if you scream, the other diners will be able to hear you. I don't want anyone else to hear the sounds you make when you come. Those are for Ryder and me alone."

She ran her hands up Ryder's thighs behind her until she could cup him through his trousers, giggling when he groaned.

"I've learned a thing or two this week. Maybe you'll be the ones who come."

Adopting the sternest expression she could under the circumstances, she eyed Dillon. "You'll have to be quiet. I don't want those women to hear those sounds you two make either. They're very sexy, and those women might get ideas."

Ryder laughed and finished removing her shirt and bra and tossed them aside.

"Sexy, huh?" He ran his hands up her sides, his fingers caressing the outer curves of her breasts. "We don't make much noise at all except for swearing because you're squeezing our cocks. You, on the other hand, make the kind of sounds that make my cock ache."

Dillon ran his fingers over the sensitive underside of her breasts and flicked his thumbs gently over her nipples, smiling when she cried out.

"How about those growly noises you make when you're coming inside me?"

"Growly noises?" Dillon tapped both of her nipples at the same time, smiling smugly when she whimpered.

Ryder groaned.

"That's one of those sounds we love so much. I'll bet we can get you to make even more of them. Hmm, I see shrimp cocktail. Would you like one?"

Sucking in a breath when Dillon caressed her nipples again, she fumbled for Ryder's zipper.

"How can you think about food? I thought you were going to fuck me."

Dillon ran his hands from her breasts, down her sides, and to her thighs.

"Oh, you're getting fucked, but only when you're good and ready."

She could feel the heat from his hands through her pants, the firm strokes up and down her thighs sending a barrage of erotic sizzles to her center.

Being bared from the waist up while the rest of her remained covered made her more aware of her exposed breasts and made her feel naughty and very much a sexual being. She'd never considered herself an exhibitionist, but she had to admit that being exposed this way in a public place turned her on.

As long as only Dillon and Ryder saw her.

Alison struggled to get her fingers to work, but she shook so hard she had no coordination. "I'm ready *now*. Ryder, damn it. I can't get your zipper down."

Ryder chuckled and lifted her hands from his cock.

"No. You don't want the other diners to hear how naughty you are, do you? You'll get my cock when I decide to give it to you."

Dillon took one of the warm slices of bread, broke it in half, and buttered it liberally. "Nice and warm. The butter melts as soon as it touches it. Gives me ideas."

Alison watched in fascination as he brought the bread toward her breast, a shocked cry escaping when he touched the buttered side to her nipple. The warmth on her breast felt incredible, and she arched upward to get more. She rocked her hips, shifting restlessly as Dillon moved it over her nipple, spreading the melted butter all around.

Ryder put his arms over hers, forcing her shoulders back and effectively pushing her breasts out. "Now, about that shrimp."

Apparently satisfied that he'd coated her nipple thoroughly, Dillon lifted the bread and tapped her lips with it.

"Open."

She obeyed him, taking a bite of the warm bread, savoring the buttery taste on her tongue.

She'd never be able to taste butter again without remembering this moment.

She hurried to chew and swallow it, her eyes on Dillon's as he popped the rest of it into his mouth and bent toward her nipple.

"Did I mention how much I like butter?"

Just as his lips closed over the buttery peak and he began to suck, Ryder took the cold shrimp coated with cocktail sauce and began to smear it over her other nipple.

The contrast between warm and cold sent her senses soaring, intensifying both so much that she whimpered and reached for Dillon.

Threading her fingers through his hair, she held him to her breast, biting her lip to keep from crying out as every pull on her nipple created an answering tug to her clit.

He took his time, licking all the butter from her nipple and what had dripped lower, sensitizing her entire breast. When he finished, he lifted his head, his eyes dark with possession.

"You're ours, Alison, and before we leave here tonight, you're going to admit it. Come here."

He settled her on his lap facing Ryder.

"I think Ryder's ready for some of that cocktail sauce with his shrimp."

Dillon kept her face turned toward his while Ryder bent his head and licked her breast clean, the feel of his warm tongue cleaning away the cold of the sauce, making her squirm.

"Don't try to turn away from me. Tonight I won't let you hide anything from me. You won't talk to me about the future, but I'll have everything from you tonight."

Keeping her on his lap, he fed her bites of food, pausing to kiss her and run his hands over her back, her belly, her breasts, everywhere, sensitizing every part of her.

"Beautiful. Be still a minute so I can put your nipple clips on you."

Alison shivered, blinking. "Dillon, I won't be able to stand it. I thought you said—"

"I'm not going to hurt you. These are padded, and I'm just going to tighten them enough to keep your attention. You really didn't think you would get away with avoiding my attempts to get some answers from you this week, did you?"

Ryder tugged off her shoes and socks before reaching into his pocket and pulling out a box. "Here they are. I'll put them on her."

Nervous now, Alison automatically put her hands over her breasts. "Is it going to hurt?"

Dillon took both of her wrists and pulled them gently, but firmly, behind her back, holding them in one hand. His eyes flashed with displeasure, sending a chill through her and making her yearn to please him.

"Since you don't trust that we're not going to let you go to jail, it would be a waste of my time to try to convince you we won't hurt you. I guess you'll just have to wait and figure it out for yourself."

Ashamed of herself for doubting him and hurting his feelings, she nodded and turned to Ryder as he took one of the rings from the box and placed the box on the table.

Dillon tapped a nipple. "Arch your back and thrust those nipples out to Ryder. Show him how much you want those clips."

Nodding again, she did it, her pussy clenching as he parted her legs to move closer.

Ryder grinned. "I've been looking forward to this all week. You're going to be my little harem girl, sitting next to me naked and feeding me my dinner."

Unable to resist, she flashed him a coy smile. "What makes you think I'm going to feed you?"

Ryder tapped her nipple, his eyes flashing wickedly when she cried out.

"Because, darlin', we're going to make sure you enjoy every minute of it."

Holding her breath, she watched Ryder place the padded clamp over her nipple, letting it out on a sigh of relief when he released it and it didn't hurt at all.

"Tighten it."

She whipped her head up at Dillon's deep command, but bit back her protest when he lifted a brow, swallowing her protest.

Ryder smiled again. "Absolutely. It's too loose, Ally. It'll fall off. We can't have that, can we, darlin'? We gotta keep these nipples tight and responsive." His big fingers closed over the small wheel at the side and began to turn it.

Dillon released her hands and bent her back over his arm, covering her mouth with his and swallowing the cry that escaped when the pressure on her nipple increased. With an arm around Dillon's back, she gripped his shirt, grabbing onto Ryder's forearm with the other.

The pressure on her nipple sent sharp pinpricks of pleasure to her slit, and she twisted restlessly to try to relieve it. With her legs spread and Ryder between them, she had no way to close them and ended up rocking her hips in frustration.

Dillon lifted his head, meeting her eyes before running his hand over the breast with the clip and tugging at the small chain dangling from it.

The dark possession in his eyes seemed more intense than ever, as though a shutter had been lifted and she saw a part of him he'd kept hidden until now.

"Perfect. Go ahead and put the other one on. I want to see them on her."

As nonchalantly as though she weren't lying across his lap naked from the waist up with clips being placed on her nipples, Dillon reached across her for a shrimp, dipped it in cocktail sauce, and tapped her lips with it.

"Open."

The shock of a clip being placed on her other nipple had her turning her head away.

"I can't. Dillon, my nipple."

Ryder started tightening the clamp. "You'd better learn to focus on more than one thing at a time, or you're going to be in real trouble later on."

Alison soon learned what he meant.

Sitting between them, she struggled to keep up with their totally random questions while trying not to focus on the clips attached to her nipples that seemed to become heavier with each passing minute.

When she stretched out her arm to reach a stuffed mushroom, Ryder took the opportunity to run a hand over her breast.

"What's your favorite color?"

Alison stilled, the mushroom forgotten as she leaned toward him, moaning when he tugged on the small chain dangling from it. The vulnerability of being partially bared while both Dillon and Ryder remained fully clothed sent an unexpected surge of lust through her.

Sitting between them this way, she really did feel as though she was an object for their pleasure, but at the same time, cherished.

She just couldn't resist it.

She had their undivided attention, both of them always touching her and seeming to respond to every shift of her body, every sound she made. Even when she leaned against Ryder, he turned his chest toward her, his arm going around her.

Looking up at him through her lashes, she pressed her breast more fully into his hand, feeling aroused, playful, and wanton.

"I'm never going to be able to eat like this."

She didn't want to think about food right now. She was starving for something a lot more satisfying.

With a hand sliding up her back to her neck, Dillon reached over and plucked one of the mushrooms from the nearby plate. He held it to her lips, waiting until she opened her mouth and took it before tugging the chain on her other breast.

"Imagine the trouble you're going to have when we finish the appetizers and we strip your pants and panties off of you. If you belonged to us, we'd pick them out for you. Lace ones. See-through ones."

Ryder tipped her head back and played with the chain on her nipple, making her entire breast feel swollen and heavy and her nipples so sensitive that the slightest touch seemed too intense.

"And some of those bras that have the opening for her nipples. I'd love to see her in one of those. Those thigh-high stocking with the garters and no panties. Darlin', I'd love to see that pussy surrounded with silk and lace."

Tapping her nipple, he grinned at her low moan. "But then again, I love to see that naked pussy any way I can."

Dillon unfastened her slacks and pulled her facedown over his lap, the underside of her breast brushing against his hard thigh, her nipples touching the cool leather seat. "There's no point in waiting. I want her naked now."

The steel in his tone sent a thrill through her, but being facedown made her nervous.

"Dillon, let me stand up. I'll take off—"

"No." Dillon ran a hand over her naked ass, which Ryder had exposed so fast it had to be some sort of a record. "We'll undress you. We want you to understand that you have no say in what we do to you tonight. If you stayed here with us, you could expect a lot of nights like this."

The silky promise in his voice flowed over her, made even more potent as Ryder pulled her pants and panties the rest of the way down her legs, leaving her naked over their laps.

Her nipples tingled as they brushed over the leather seat, much like the rest of her as both men continued to caress her. Not being able to see them, she never knew where they would touch her next, which added another layer of excitement and tension.

Ryder ran his hands up the back of her thighs, parting them and bending her left leg to touch the back of the seat, holding it there with his body. With the other hanging off the edge of the seat, it spread her thighs and kept her from closing them again.

Once again, the shock of air moving over her bared pussy sent her pulse racing, but she couldn't rub her thighs together the way she wanted to.

"You always spread me this way, damn it."

Her clit came alive, swelling and tingling with the need for attention, the tingling becoming sharper when Ryder stroked up her thighs again, his thumbs running up her inner thighs and moving closer and closer to her slit.

"We like you spread. Your thighs are wet, darlin'. Just as I thought. You like having this ass in the air. Don't try to convince me you aren't curious about being spanked. You're hot for it, baby."

Alison gasped as he slapped her ass, not hard, but with enough sting to heat her vulnerable buttock. Knowing that diners sat several feet away on the other side of the curtain, she bit her lip to hold back her cry. In an effort to relieve the throbbing of her clit, she rubbed herself against Ryder's thigh. Not until he chuckled softly did she realize she'd been wiggling her ass at him.

Using her arms for leverage, she lifted her head to look over her shoulder, sucking in a breath when Dillon took advantage of her position to caress her breast, sending another shock of delight through her. The sharp possessiveness in his eyes softened.

"Don't curve your back that way. You'll hurt it."

Bracing herself on one hand, she lifted the other to his chest and toyed with the top button of his shirt, smiling when he sucked in a breath.

Thrilled that he reacted so strongly to her touch and totally taken in by the possessive gentleness, she twisted to rub up against him.

"I guess then you'll have to give me another one of your massages."

Dillon's eyes narrowed. "You flirtin' with me?"

Shrugging a bare shoulder, she shot a glance at a smiling Ryder.

"Maybe. What are you going to do about it?"

Ryder ran a hand up her thigh to her hip.

"Well, we're gonna take you up on it, of course."

Dillon lifted her, settling her on his lap facing him, her knees on either side of his hips.

"Fuck those appetizers. I want this appetizer."

With his hands at her waist, Dillon lifted her to her knees and began to nibble at the delicate underside of her breasts.

Wrapping her arms around his head, she threw her head back, moaning at the contrast of Dillon's sharp teeth on her tender flesh and Ryder's warm hand running down her back to her bottom and lingering.

Ryder's hooded gaze sent another surge of lust through her.

"I think I like eating this way. Having you naked to play with makes dinner a hell of a lot more fun. My little slave girl to play with." His hand went lower to her thigh and up again. His fingers inching closer and closer to her slit.

"Hmm, nice and wet. I want you on my cock. How about it, darling? You wanna sit on my cock while we're having dinner?"

"God, yes!"

Sticking her butt out, she gasped when he slid a thick finger into her, her pussy clenching at it in desperation.

"Ryder, take me." She lifted and lowered herself on his finger, threading her fingers through Dillon's hair. She cried out at the scrape of Dillon's teeth over her nipple, moving faster on Ryder's finger.

Bending her head, she breathed in the male fresh scent of Dillon. "Give me more."

Ryder chuckled and withdrew his finger, pausing to tap her clit and laughing softly when she bucked.

"Oh, you're gonna get more, darlin'. I want a nice hot pussy hugging my cock while I have my dinner." He threw off his clothes, pausing to dig a condom out of his pocket and rolling it on before he shoved the appetizers aside to make room for the other covered plates.

After putting his on the table in front of him, he slid back on to the bench and reached for her.

"Come here."

Dillon stopped nibbling and lifted his head, moving her back several inches and staring into her eyes.

"Just a minute. I want to lube her ass first."

Ryder grinned. "Definitely." He bent and dug through his pockets again, producing a small tube.

After lowering her to his lap, Dillon accepted it, not breaking eye contact with her.

"Ryder's gonna have his dinner while he's in your pussy. Guess where my cock's gonna be while *I'm* having my dessert."

Alison's breath hitched when Dillon slid his hands to her bottom cheeks, his expression cool and determined. She searched his features, looking for the tenderness he'd shown earlier, her heart skipping a beat when she found it in his eyes.

Sparkling and darkened, they stayed on hers as he squeezed lube onto his finger and recapped the tube, narrowed slightly as though searching for something.

Her bottom clenched, already addicted to the anticipation of being breached. When the cool lube touched her puckered opening, she hissed, her body bowing at the touch that, as always, felt more intense than she'd been ready for.

Out of the corner of her eye, she saw Ryder fisting his cock, his own excitement a tangible thing. It shone in his eyes, the clenching of his jaw, and the tightening of his body. His stillness, she'd already learned, could end in a flash. At any moment he would strike, his body a flurry of motion, and he would be inside her before she could do more than draw a breath.

"Hurry up, then. I want to sink my cock into that sweet pussy. My cock's aching for her."

Dillon shook his head, lifting a brow in that superior way that irritated her as much as it turned her on.

"No. It affects Alison more when I take her ass nice and slow. It satisfies her need to submit to me more than if I just take it. Plus, she likes it easy and knows damned well if she fights me, I'm taking it anyway, but it'll be a hell of a lot rougher." Dillon applied pressure, his other hand lifting to slide his fingers through her hair and keep her face turned to his.

"She's got just that hint of fear in her eyes every time we touch her ass. She knows what to expect now, and the vulnerability that hits her excites her even more. I think she'd respond very well to being tied up, her ass taken over and over. Yeah, there's that excitement. She's afraid, but she wants it. It gives it an edge, doesn't it, Alison? Sharpens the excitement. It surprises you, doesn't it, baby? You stick around and we're going to teach you things about yourself you never knew."

Alison trembled helplessly, shaken that he saw what she hadn't thought anyone else would ever be able to see. Feeling even more vulnerable than ever, she closed her eyes, only to snap them open again when Ryder slapped her ass.

Patting it, he grinned.

"Don't close your eyes, darlin'. We want to see that look in them. Damn, I can't wait to feel that pussy clamping down on me."

Dillon pressed his finger into her ass, moving it around as though to reinforce the fact that she was helpless against whatever he chose to do to her, the firm press of his finger against her delicate inner walls making her shiver everywhere. Cupping her face, he ran a thumb back and forth over her cheek, smiling when she leaned into his hand and rubbed against it.

"She's almost purring. I don't even think she realizes how much passion is inside her."

She moaned softly as he slid his finger the rest of the way into her, the stark invasion of her most private place once again creating an intimacy and sense of belonging to him. It grew as he worked the lube all around inside her, pressing against her inner walls with sure strokes, almost as though he owned her.

It always stunned her and left her confused. The thought of being his property, something he could use at will, sounded great in fantasy, but the reality should have insulted her. Somehow, Dillon made the reality a fantasy, treated her like he owned her, but with a gentleness and caring that tugged at her emotions and heightened her awareness of her own femininity.

"I can't believe the things you make me feel. When Danny tried, it hurt and—"

Ryder slapped her ass. Hard.

"I don't want to hear his name."

Dillon slid his hand from her hair to her nipple and pinched, the combination of pleasure and pain making her clench on his finger, the feeling of fullness exciting her even more.

"We have no desire to see you hurt, just pleasured. Pain like this brings you pleasure, doesn't it, Alison?"

Rocking against him, she moved on his finger, unable to deny it.

Bending, he swallowed another moan as he worked his finger in her ass, his strong finger forging a path for what was to come.

Crying out at the erotic burn of her bottom around his finger and the friction of her clit against him, she fisted her hands in his shirt as the tingling sharpened. She couldn't look away from his eyes, now narrowed and darkened with a look that sent a thrill through her.

The raw desire and possessiveness burning in his eyes now pulled at her as much as the tenderness that had shown in them before. At that moment, she belonged to him like she'd never belonged to anyone else, the need to be more to him than any other woman ever had almost overwhelming.

Arching her back, she pushed her bottom out even more, opening herself to him completely, her heart racing when he smiled and pushed his finger deeper, moving it around inside her with a strength and purpose that had her whimpering against him.

His eyes raked over her body, flickering when she moaned.

"That's my girl. I knew you could do it. You're ours, aren't you, baby?" His eyes hardened briefly. "At least for now."

Eager to please him, she laid her head on his chest and curled against him.

"Yours."

Withdrawing his finger, he patted her bottom and kissed her hair.

"Good. Go to Ryder. I'll be right back."

Ryder reached for her and settled her astride him, his jaw clenched with tension as he lowered her onto his cock.

Her bottom, awakened now from Dillon's attention, clenched with the need to be filled. His abrupt departure left her shaken, and she grabbed for Ryder, needing assurance.

Sliding her fingers through the cool strands of his long, silky hair, Alison moaned her pleasure as he filled her inch by incredible inch, each ridge of his cock caressing her inner walls.

With his strong hands around her waist, he lowered her to his lap, filling her completely.

"You feel so fucking good, darlin'. I think I could stay inside you forever."

His hands covered her breasts, his touch light as he moved his palms over her nipples.

Ryder grinned when she started to move. "In a hurry, darlin'? I like having your pussy all soft and wet around my cock. Be still. I'm starving."

Alison moaned again when he sat forward to reach for a bite of food, the action pushing his cock deeper.

"Ryder, oh, God. You can't really expect to eat like this."

Sitting back, he teased her lips with a bite of juicy steak. "Oh, yes, I do. I've never eaten with a naked woman on my lap, and especially not while my cock was inside her." He waited until she took the bite of meat before lifting her by the waist and lowering her again so slowly she wanted to scream.

She hurriedly chewed and swallowed her food, not even tasting it. Digging her fingers into him, she stared at the tattoo on his shoulder.

"Ryder!"

"You're too damned impatient. Christ, I am, too. One of these days I swear I'm going to take you so slow that you're begging, but tonight I can't." Gripping her hips, he raised and lowered her again, chuckling when she whimpered and used her knees to move faster.

Once she started, she couldn't stop, digging her knees into the padded leather seat and moving on Ryder's cock.

"Ryder, it's so good. Oh, God."

Each movement made the chains on her nipples swing, tugging at them and increasing her pleasure even more.

He groaned, his jaw tightening. "Yeah, darlin'. It sure as hell is." He guided her movements, keeping her steady and helping her move faster and faster.

"That tight little pussy's hungry for it, huh, Ally? Come on, darlin'. Fuck me. Move that pussy on my cock. That's it. Oh, yeah. Fuck, honey. Damn, I love being inside you."

Alison's whimpers grew even more desperate, her body tightening against his. Leaning against him, she turned her head, kissing the tattoo that never failed to excite her.

"Ryder, I'm gonna come. These things on my nipples are making me crazy."

With a hand beneath her hair, he bent her back over his arm and tugged at one of the chains.

"They're supposed to." He surged deep again and again, his thrusts coming faster and more shallow, digging at that spot inside her that he seemed to find with such incredible ease.

Ryder surged deep, the hand at the nape of her neck holding her against the edge of the table, and leaned over her, his eyes narrowed and darker than ever. His hand covered her breast, his devious fingers tugging at the chain and sending another wave of heat to her slit.

"You planning on taking all this fire to someone else? You really think I'm gonna sit by and let another man fuck you like this?"

Taken aback at his intensity, at the raw desire blazing from his eyes, Alison couldn't hold back a sob at the barrage of pleasure to her system.

Those warning tingles kept getting stronger, making her entire body shake with the need to come. The pressure kept mounting, the reality that she was naked in a restaurant and being taken by the most dangerous and sexual man she'd ever met making this seem like more of a fantasy.

"Ryder, please! I don't, oh, God!" The cock in her pussy jumped, each movement of the solid heat inside her sending her closer and closer to the edge.

Unable to stand the torment anymore, she reached down to stroke her clit, her eyes flying open when he slapped her hand away.

"Oh, no. You're not getting the easy way out of this."

His hair had come loose from the band he usually kept it in, giving him a wild, untamed look that never failed to send her heart racing. Although the wild hunger in his eyes remained as strong as ever, the emotion swirling with it now drew her in, demanding she submit to whatever he desired.

He lifted her and turned, and the next thing she knew, her back was pressed against the seat where Dillon had sat, her ass in Ryder's firm grip and held several inches above the seat.

On his knees between her legs, he thrust into her several times in rapid succession, not even letting her catch her breath. His expression, all hard lines and angles, gave him an even wilder, more primitive look, scaring her just a little.

Propping her thighs on his, he ran a hand from her abdomen to her breasts and back again, his strokes strong and sure as they moved over her.

"This body knows what it wants even if you don't. Yeah, squeeze my cock with that pussy." His slow, deliberate strokes came faster now, his eyes filled with a wild hunger she hadn't seen in them before. They flashed with anger and lust, a combination that sent her pulse racing and made him look even more untamed than before.

Unable to stand the torment anymore, she kicked her legs and reached for her clit, only to be thwarted when the bench seat dipped above her and Dillon took both of her hands in one of his.

"No, damn you! Let go of me."

She tried to pull her hand away, her clit already burning with the first warning sizzles of orgasm.

"Let go of me, you son of a bitch! I need to come. Oh!"

Ryder's slap to her clit alarmed her into stilling, fear and excitement vying for supremacy at the sharp pain. The pain didn't last, but the burn of it did, making her clit feel ten times its normal size.

It took her a second or two to realize that she was coming, the sensation this time so foreign and overwhelming that her brain didn't immediately process it.

Still holding her hands, Dillon covered her mouth with his just as she exploded, swallowing her cries of release. The feel of his hand on her breast, his fingers tugging the chains on her nipple, had her struggling against him. Flattening his hand on her belly, he held her down as Ryder increased his strokes, digging at that spot inside her.

She screamed into Dillon's mouth as the wave of ecstasy crested, her entire body awash in sensation.

Her inner muscles rippled around the hard cock inside her, prolonging her pleasure until she thought she would die of it.

Ryder groaned, a hoarse sound that delighted her, just seconds before he surged deep, his hands hard on her hips and holding her upward.

"Fuck, yeah. Ally, you feel so fucking good."

Wrapping her legs around him, she rocked her hips on his cock, the depth of his cock startling another cry from her and another of those deep groans from him.

Both remained frozen as the waves washed over her, his muscular body trembling against hers.

After what seemed an eternity, Dillon lifted his head, pushing her bangs back from her forehead, and stared down at her.

"What do you think of being shared by two men now?"

Struggling to draw enough air into her lungs, Alison licked her lips.

"Oh, God. Why doesn't it feel strange to have both of you touching me?" She shook her head, hardly able to believe how natural and right it felt to be the center of their erotic attention. "It should feel strange, shouldn't it? I've never done anything like this before."

Each seemed very comfortable with the other there and made love to her with the smoothness of a well-oiled machine.

Trying to bite back her jealousy of the implication of how they got so experienced at making love to a woman together, she looked first at Dillon and then at Ryder, amazed at the tenderness in Ryder's eyes and the dark need in Dillon's.

The unexpected change sent her pulse tripping, and only then did she realize she'd automatically reached for Dillon for comfort.

Surprised at herself because she'd long since stopped expecting to be held by Danny after sex, she started to lower her hands, only to have them caught by Ryder.

"And you won't with anyone else. Come here, Ally."

Dillon released her, the hunger in his eyes flaring as Ryder caught her up in his arms.

With his cock still deep inside her, Ryder readjusted his position until she sat astride him, the hands caressing her back and shoulders gentle now, so tender and surprising it brought tears to her eyes.

Still trembling and held against Ryder, she accepted bites of food from both of them, settling while they all picked at the delectable assortment of foods in front of them. Their low conversation seemed more intimate now, even though none of them spoke of anything important.

The sexual tension emanating from Dillon kept her on edge, desire flaring again when he stood and started to undress.

Ryder fed her another bite and ran a hand down her back, seemingly unconcerned that Dillon held her rapt attention.

"So what's your favorite color, honey?"

The shift of muscle in Dillon's arms and chest fascinated her as he reached across the table for his beer, but couldn't compete with the sight of his long, thick cock rising majestically from his lap.

She stared at the purplish head, as large and almost as dark as a plum, and shivered. Soon it would be deep inside her bottom, the hard heat of his cock stretching her and filling her in the most intimate way a man could take a woman.

Her bottom clenched with awareness, already sensitized from his attention there earlier. She found it hard to believe that in the short time she'd been with Dillon and Ryder that she could consider her bottom an erogenous zone, especially since it had been off limits her entire life.

Even more surprising, once the nerve endings around her puckered opening had been awakened, she *needed* attention there. She needed the pinch and burn, the overwhelming stretch, and their determined demands for entrance. Even though the vulnerability of being taken there still filled her with trepidation, the anticipation of having her bottom filled with Dillon's thick cock had her pussy leaking moisture and her arousal simmering once again.

Dillon tapped his finger beneath her chin, lifting her gaze to his. The knowledge of what she was thinking was there in his eyes as one masculine brow went up.

"It's going in your ass soon enough. Answer Ryder's question."

Alison blinked. "Question?"

With a chuckle, Ryder nudged her back and ran his hands up and down over her chest, lingering on her nipples.

"I asked you what your favorite color is. I'm learning your body, and with any luck, I'll have the chance to know it as well as I know my own. I know you're shy, even though you think you're brazen. You're very passionate and, as Dillon proved, submissive in bed, but you really don't believe either one is true. You're as sweet as pie except when you lose your temper, and then you're downright adorable."

He tugged at the chain on her nipple and grinned when she cried out, grabbing her hand before she could cover her breast with it to relieve the sting.

His grin turned sinful when she growled at him in frustration. "And, darlin', the madder you get, the harder my cock gets."

Alison swallowed heavily and glanced at Dillon, at a total loss for words. She couldn't believe he'd so easily gotten the reaction he wanted from her, and with very little effort at all.

Dillon smiled sardonically. "You didn't think we saw all those things in you? You're not dealing with children here, Alison, despite what you think. We're grown men who know what the hell we want and have been waiting for a woman like you to come into our lives. It's very important to us to get to know you. We've learned some, but we want more."

Leaning her back over his arm, Ryder cupped her jaw.

"If you think either one of us is going to make it easy for you to leave us, you're sadly mistaken. Favorite color?"

Crying out when he tugged the chain again, Alison grabbed at his shoulders, thrusting her breasts out in front of her to ease the sharp pull. "Red!"

She found herself transferred to Dillon's lap, a strong arm around her waist holding her back against his chest. Feeling the head of his cock pressing against her puckered opening, Alison stilled, shivering, the helplessness she always experienced when either one of them touched her bottom coming back in full force.

Dillon tightened the arm around her waist and lifted her several inches.

"My cock's so fucking hard it hurts, and it's going in that tight ass right now."

He lowered her, positioning the head of his cock at her puckered opening.

"Red means stop. You don't want me to stop, do you, baby?"

"No. Oh, God." Her bottom clenched, but she had no chance of closing against the head of Dillon's cock pushing insistently against her puckered opening. Her bottom gave way under the pressure, burning as it stretched around the thick head of Dillon's cock.

Breathing heavily, Alison groaned, each clench of her bottom on his cock making it sting and burn. Her stomach muscles tightened. Her thighs trembled, but the sharp invasion and the fact that the slightest movement caused an overwhelming sting in her bottom kept her frozen in place. Just the thought of dropping all at once onto Dillon's cock scared her and kept her focused on her ass.

The touch of Ryder's finger on her clit made her yelp in surprise and jolt, and then whimper as it moved her on Dillon's cock, making her opening burn.

Dillon kissed her shoulder.

"Easy, Alison. Nice and slow."

His hands shook, his breathing harsh as he lowered her inch by inch over his cock, invading her most intimate opening with his thick heat, stretching her inner walls as he forged his way inside her. His lips caressed her shoulders and then her neck, sending delightful shivers through her, while his words of encouragement and praise warmed her all over.

"Yes, that's my girl. Yes, you can take me, baby. Relax those muscles so I can shove my cock up that ass. We've done this before. You know it fits. You know how good it feels. Every time Ryder touches that clit, you clamp down on me. You're squeezing the hell out of my cock."

Sitting naked beside them, Ryder bent to lick a nipple, tapping her clit with a work-roughened finger at the same time.

Each time he touched her, she tightened on Dillon, making him groan, making her burn, and making both of them tremble a little harder. Inch by hard, thick inch, Dillon worked his cock into her, each shallow thrust drawing a groan from him and a whimpered moan from her.

By the time she'd taken all of him, a fine sheen of perspiration covered her and her movements had become shaky and uncoordinated.

Hard and tense behind her, beneath her, Dillon kept his movements slow and measured, the tiniest shift in his position sending chills and sparks of awareness through her.

Lifting his head, Ryder smiled at her cries, his fingers putting the chains on her nipples in motion.

"You're so damned soft and so fucking responsive that it makes it almost impossible to be around you without wanting to rip your panties off and sink into you."

She hoped she never got used to the way they talked, their words adding to the eroticism of every moment and making it more sexual and unbelievably intimate.

Making each moment uniquely theirs.

"Oh, God. I can't believe this is happening to me. I can't believe I'm with you." She closed her eyes, her entire body trembling so hard her fingers didn't even work. She tried repeatedly to grab at Dillon's hands, needing something to hold on to, but couldn't quite catch them.

Dillon slid both hands around her and covered her breasts, moving her over his cock and pulling her back until her head rested against his shoulder.

"You're ours, Alison. Get used to it."

"I have to leave. Don't make me make a promise I can't keep." She gasped when he raised her slightly and plunged into her at the same time Ryder tapped her clit again, her body too highly sensitized to withstand the storm raging inside her.

Dillon knocked Ryder's hand away and covered her mound, letting a callused finger rest against her clit.

"I don't make promises I can't keep either. I promise you this. Tonight will be a night you'll never forget."

He lifted her and inch by inch, lowered her again.

So full it overwhelmed her, Alison fought to remember that other diners sat only feet away and bit her lip to hold back her cries. Her bottom burned, the pinch each time Dillon moved her just as strong and mind numbing as the last.

The tingling of her clit had her desperately trying to move against the finger poised over it, but each time she tried, the sharp shift of Dillon's cock inside her ass elicited a whimper from her despite her best efforts to remain quiet.

Ryder straightened her legs out in front of her, leaving her effectively impaled on Dillon's cock and spread wide.

She'd never felt anything quite so amazing. Her breasts, pussy, and clit lay wide open for them while Dillon's cock filled her ass and kept her from moving at all.

Dillon kissed her temple, his slow drawl rough with tension.

"Damn, woman, you shake my control like nothing else."

A thrill went through her at his admission, tightening her on his cock, making it feel even thicker, hard and unyielding inside her. It excited her and filled her with the need to challenge him, to shake his control even more.

"Is that what you want? Control?"

Dillon chuckled against her ear, his big hands moving over her breasts and lower to caress her abdomen before settling over her spread thighs.

"I think I'm going to have a little trouble staying in charge with you, but when it comes to sex, you betcha. Don't bitch about it. You like it too much to put up much of an argument."

Alison held her breath as the hands at her thighs shifted, still holding her thighs spread as he parted her folds. A second later, a sharp slap to her clit made her cry out and buck against him, inadvertently moving her on the cock lodged deep inside her ass.

Reacting instinctively, she reached for her clit, whimpering at the combination of pain and pleasure that made it swell and tingle.

"You touch that clit and I'm slapping it again."

Shaking, she grabbed Dillon's forearms, tightening on his cock again, the sensation so strong she stilled.

"It tingles. I'm so close to coming. Oh, God. So full. Dillon, please! I can't take any more."

She could literally feel the moisture trickling from her pussy. The shimmers racing through her warned her that she teetered on the edge of an approaching orgasm, but Dillon did nothing to push her over and thwarted each attempt she made to touch her clit and relieve this unbelievable pressure.

He and Ryder both caressed her, avoiding her clit and breasts with a purposefulness that had her kicking and writhing on Dillon's cock, making the shivers and tingling stronger, keeping her so close to the edge of coming, she wanted to scream.

Ryder studied her, his eyes darkening with erotic intent.

"Let's settle her down a little and bring her back up again. I don't want her to forget tonight anytime soon."

Aghast that they wouldn't give her the relief she needed, she glared at Ryder.

"Go away. Leave us alone. Dillon, you'll let me come, won't you?"

She sucked in a breath when Ryder lowered himself to kneel between her legs, not trusting him a bit.

Holding her gaze, Ryder lowered his head, his grin flashing before he began to blow on her clit.

The cold air on her clit and folds made her squirm on Dillon's lap, crying out at the hard cock shifting inside her.

Frustrated that Dillon's strong hold stopped her movements, Alison used her inner muscles to squeeze his cock in the hopes of tormenting him as much as they both tormented her.

"You bastards! Sons of bitches! I swear I'll get even with you for this."

Ryder chuckled and lifted his head, tapping her clit, and grinned when she jolted. "Of that I have no doubt."

Dillon patted her thighs, stilling her.

"Just remember that when you do things to get even, it won't be long before you find yourself in a situation like this again. I'm getting even for your hardheadedness in not talking about the future. Think about that the next time you tell me you don't want to talk about it."

The cock in her ass seemed to swell, filling her bottom with hardness and heat she continuously had to struggle to adjust to. The rings on her nipples seemed to get tighter and tighter, and her clit felt so swollen and heavy, so alive with awareness that it throbbed with a heartbeat all its own.

She'd give anything to make this fantasy a reality, but just couldn't allow herself to believe it would ever be possible.

"Please. You know, oh, God, you know I might, oh, oh, oh, not be able to come back. Oh, please stop torturing me. Let me come. Please. Please. Please. Just sex. Just this. Oh, God. I never knew I could feel like this."

Dillon kissed her hair and moved her on his cock again. "This is only the beginning, baby. Look at Ryder. Ask him real nice if he'll lick that clit for you."

Her pulse leapt at Ryder's expectant grin, but as much as she wanted it and as forward as she considered herself, she couldn't say the words. She moved on Dillon, hoping the movement of his cock on her bottom would send her over, but as devastating to her senses as it felt, the tingling of her clit couldn't be denied.

Dillon chuckled softly against her ear when she shook her head, moving her on his cock again before tapping her clit.

"Don't you want to feel Ryder's tongue here? I understand he's very good with that tongue, almost as good as I am."

Ryder smiled and raised a brow. "Almost? You're full of shit. I'm well known for how good I am at eating pussy." Running his hands up and down her thighs, he licked his lips.

"I can't wait to get my mouth on that swollen clit. It's all red and shiny with your juices."

Alison whimpered and could almost feel his mouth there. "Please, Ryder. Please!" She closed her eyes, throwing her head back when Dillon withdrew and started thrusting into her ass with steady precision, his thick fullness going deep with every thrust.

Ryder tapped her exposed clit, not even looking up when she sobbed. "It looks like a little berry, and I know already just how sweet it is. I'd love to lick all that juice and take it into my mouth. I would suck on it and maybe nibble a little until I got every drop."

"Oh, God!" Her clit tingled with the need to have his mouth there, each word like an invisible stroke to the throbbing bundle of nerves that seemed to grow with every thrust of Dillon's cock. Shaking hard and grateful for Dillon's firm hold, she sobbed, so overcome with need that tears ran down her cheeks.

Languid with desire, she couldn't even get her muscles to obey her enough to move, while inside her heart raced and the sizzles raging through her grew with every breath she took. Past the point of embarrassment, she held on to Dillon the best she could, taking a gulping breath before she could speak.

"Ryder, do it. Suck my clit. Please. I can't take any more."

Ryder's hands tightened on her thighs, his warm breath the only warning before he swiped her clit with his tongue.

Dillon surged deep once again.

"See, baby? All you had to do was ask."

Sliding his hands back around her, he cupped her bottom and lifted and lowered her with increasing speed onto his cock.

"Now, come so I can feel this tight ass clamp down on me while I'm fucking it."

Ryder sucked her clit into his mouth, giving her no choice at all.

The expert movement of the warm lips and tongue on her clit sent her reeling. Her clit seemed to explode in his mouth, her entire body stiffening with the force of her orgasm.

She started to cry out, only to have Dillon release her bottom and wrap one arm around her, the other going to her hair and turning her face up for his kiss before she could utter a sound.

Tangling his hand in her hair, he thrust deep inside her, his own low groan mingling with her pitiful whimpers as his mouth moved over hers with that possessive hunger she loved so much.

Unable to stand such pleasure, she wept, her body jerking in spasms. Overcome with sensation, she whimpered, moaning when they eased their torment and her body went limp.

Dillon lifted his head, his breath warm on her face as he gathered her against him and began to soothe her with long, slow caresses.

"I swear nothing will happen to you. I won't let it. Trust us to take care of everything. Can you do that?"

Alison opened her eyes, shocked at the emotion in Dillon's.

It pulled at her, and on impulse, she reached up to touch his face, surprised when he turned his strong jaw into her palm. "I don't know, Dillon. I want to, but I don't know if I can. It's like a dream, and you and Ryder will break my heart if I try to convince myself that this could last."

Ryder bent forward to kiss her belly.

"I guess it's up to us to convince you otherwise."

Chapter Seventeen

"Are you sure you don't want any help? I'm a hell of a back scrubber."

Moaning at the feel of Ryder's hand sliding over her bubble-covered breast, Alison opened one eye.

"That's not my back."

The hand slid lower beneath the surface of the water, and seconds later, devious fingers delved between her delicate folds.

"I also massage clits. You just lie there and relax while I take care of it. Just ignore me. Pretend I'm not even here."

"Fat chance of that. Oh, Ryder!"

With her clit still sensitized from his attention at the restaurant, it didn't take long for him to take her to the edge and fling her over.

Still trembling and struggling to stay above the bubbles, she moved lethargically as he finished washing her, his touch as gentle as Dillon's.

She realized with a start that no matter who touched her or how, she'd come to recognize the feel of their hands, their unique scents, and could tell one from the other without even opening her eyes.

"Is she finished?"

Alison looked up to see Dillon standing in the doorway, a towel in his hand.

She opened her mouth to speak, but Ryder beat her to it.

"Yeah, she came again and I bathed her." He lifted her out of the tub and waited for Dillon to wrap the towel around her before lifting her against his chest again.

"Time for bed, darlin'."

* * * *

Hours later she woke to find herself nestled against Dillon's chest, her leg hooked over his, with Ryder pressed against her back.

Not wanting to wake either one of them, she remained perfectly still, surprised to realize that it was the first time since she'd started sleeping with them that she'd awakened in the middle of the night.

It made her realize how soundly she slept between them.

Listening to Dillon's steady heartbeat, she lay there in the darkness and smiled. Surrounded by warm, hard male, she closed her eyes again and just absorbed the feeling of being nestled between them.

In the quiet of the night, she simply savored the sensation of being warm, safe, and wanted.

Dillon and Ryder would be fierce protectors. Remembering the looks on their faces when Danny had attacked her, she smiled again. They'd been like furious warriors who'd appeared, ready and willing to fight, only to realize the battle had already been won.

Amused at her fanciful thoughts, she shifted slightly to a more comfortable position, enjoying the feel of their warm skin against her nakedness. Her body still tingled deliciously from their attention earlier, every movement she made a fresh reminder of how completely they'd taken her. Her nipples still stood erect with awareness even though the clamps they'd put on them earlier had been removed long ago.

Ryder moved behind her, making her aware of the hard cock pressed against her bottom.

"You okay?"

The rough timbre of his sleepy tone sent a shiver of delight through her. His hand ran down her side and over her hip, unerringly finding the scar there and began to caress it at the same time his lips touched her shoulder.

"You hurtin', Ally?"

Arching her neck to give him better access, she snuggled closer.

"No. It's nice sleeping like this. I'm nice and warm." She enjoyed the intimacy of their hushed conversation as Dillon slept on beside her and vowed to try to wake up in the middle of the night more often.

Ryder turned her toward him, nestling her face against his shoulder. "You sleep like this every night, darlin'." He yawned and curved an arm around her. "Dillon and I take turns holding you, and you never wake up. Something bothering you tonight?"

Dillon turned on his side and snuggled against her, rubbing her back in the exact spot her muscles often tightened up.

"Stop worrying. Nothing's going to happen to you. It's all taken care of. Go back to sleep."

In the darkness, Alison blinked back tears and closed her eyes again.

She shouldn't have been at all surprised that both men had woken when she did. Dillon and Ryder always seemed so aware of everything about her, but it amazed her that even in sleep, they'd somehow known she'd awakened and needed them.

How would she ever be able to sleep without them?

How would she be able to walk away, to live her life without the only two people in the world who seemed to understand her completely and somehow fulfill all of her needs?

Swallowing her tears, she forced herself to slump against Ryder.

And realized she'd fallen in love.

* * * *

Dillon stared into the darkness and listened as Alison's breathing finally evened out, wondering why it had taken so long for her to fall back to sleep. His frustration at her refusal to fall into his plans kept him awake as much as the need to bury his cock inside her again.

He'd never come as hard as he had while fucking her ass in the restaurant, the strength of his orgasm stunning the hell out of him. It seemed that every time he touched her, he wanted her more.

All day at the garage, he listened for her, his gaze going often toward the office in the hopes of catching a glimpse of her.

Lying beside her every night had to be the sweetest kind of heaven he could imagine. Breathing in her scent, he held her close, enjoying the feel of her soft skin against his.

In moments like this, he didn't have to hide his emotions and pretend it was only sex between them. In his bed in the middle of the night, he could hold her the way he wanted to without worrying about scaring her.

Bending his head, he brushed his lips across her soft shoulder before covering it with the blanket against the cool morning chill. He stilled when she murmured in her sleep, hardly breathing as he waited for her to settle again. He smiled at the restless movement of her legs, knowing she wouldn't completely settle until she had a foot sticking out of the covers.

Damned adorable.

Loving the way her soft curves fit so perfectly against him, he wrapped his arm around her until his palm covered her abdomen. A wave of longing washed over him as he imagined her heavy with their child, a little foot kicking against his hand.

He found it hard to believe that he'd known her only a short time, but it appeared his heart and body had already decided his fate. Picturing the house they would build on the empty lot he and Ryder owned next to the garage, he couldn't hold back a smile.

Despite her belief to the contrary, Alison would fit in well here. She'd already made friends, and he knew the women would welcome her with open arms.

It would take time to get over her doubts about taking two men on as husbands, but once she saw how happy he and Ryder could make her and that their unique relationship would be accepted here, she would settle down and be fine.

In the meantime, he would do whatever he could to convince her that what they had went deeper than just physical, but in a way that didn't scare her off.

"She's going to bolt, isn't she?"

Since Dillon had been aware that Ryder had been awake the entire time, especially since they'd both learned to be wary of her knee when she stuck her foot out, it didn't surprise him when his best friend spoke.

Keeping his voice low so as not to wake Alison, Dillon flexed his hand against her soft belly, as though keeping the baby he imagined there safe.

"If we don't finish the truck, she'll have no way to leave." It infuriated him that he couldn't get through to her. He'd tried many times to talk to her, but each time, she'd walked away. She trusted him with her body, but that appeared to be as far as her trust went.

She didn't trust them to keep her from being arrested, and she sure as hell didn't trust them when they tried to convince her that relationships like the one they wanted with her *could* work in Desire.

He was scared to death he would run out of time before they managed to convince her.

Ryder sighed. "She's scared. I get that. But, damn it, Dillon, how the hell are we supposed to make her believe everything'll work out if she won't even listen? She won't talk about it at all."

Grimacing as the knot in his belly tightened, Dillon rolled to his back.

"We're just going to have to keep trying."

After a long silence Ryder spoke again, his voice barely a whisper.

"You know, I never really believed it."

Jarred out of his thoughts, Dillon lifted his head, turning it in Ryder's direction.

"Believed what?"

Ryder shifted slightly, readjusting his hold on Alison when she moved.

"Any of it. I never really believed that two men could marry the same woman and live happily. But you just have to look at the way Clay and Rio look at Jesse, or the way Jared, Duncan, and Reese are with Erin, or the way Boone and Chase hover over Rachel. Sure, I've seen the older Prestons with Isabel and Gracie with her men, and I always thought it was something older people could handle when sex didn't cloud the issue. Christ, it turns me on to watch you with her. It's like I see things about her I would have missed if I was the one taking her, things that I never really noticed with other women."

Dillon smiled in the darkness. "Like the surprise on her face when she starts to come? It always shocks her."

"Exactly. Or the way she arches her back and rubs against you to get closer. Hell, even the little frown she makes when she's trying to concentrate on sucking cock. It makes me want to distract the hell out of her. Christ, you should have seen her eyes when you slapped her pussy. I almost came right then and there."

"I plan to watch the next time." Rolling to stare back up at the ceiling, Dillon sighed. "You love her, too, don't you?"

After a long pause, Ryder sighed again. "And that's the thing that I have trouble believing the most. I didn't ever really think I would fall in love. Hell, you know how much I like variety. When I think about how many women we've taken over the years...fuck. Do you know I have trouble even remembering their faces now? It never mattered to me if they went to someone else afterward. I had my fun. They had theirs, and that was it."

The tension emanating from Ryder now was almost a tangible thing, so strong that even Alison made a sound of distress in her sleep.

"I think I could easily kill any man who touched Ally now."

Running his hand over Alison until she settled once again, Dillon blew out a breath.

"I don't even want to think about it."

After a long silence, Ryder spoke again.

"That lawyer has everything he needs?"

"And then some. Ace saw some of the tapes himself. Said no jury in the world would convict her and that the district attorney would look like a fool if he even attempted to charge her."

"Good. Then she'll be coming back."

The knot in Dillon's belly started to burn.

"Even if I have to drag her kicking and screaming all the way."

* * * *

Alison looked up as Ryder walked into the office, grimacing when she saw his hands.

"Don't you dare touch anything! I finally got everything clean in here. Tell me what you want and I'll get it for you."

Recognizing the look in Ryder's eyes, she narrowed hers and stood.

"What do you want?"

Green eyes raked over her body, leaving a trail of heat in their wake. Crossing his arms over his chest, he leaned against the doorway, smiling in a way she knew meant trouble.

And pleasure.

"I came in here to check on an order, but now I think there's something else that needs my attention more. What do I want? I want you to pull those tight jeans and those adorable blue panties down to your knees and spread that pussy so I can suck on your clit."

Taking a step to the side and putting the desk between them, Alison swallowed heavily, pressing her thighs together against her body's immediate reaction to his demand. Her nipples beaded, and her clit came to attention in a heartbeat, swelling and throbbing at the promised feel of his skilled mouth on it.

Struggling for a nonchalance she never seemed to manage with either of them, she waved her hand dismissively.

"Stop your damned teasing. What order did you want to check on?" Wondering if he could hear her heart pounding, she crossed her arms over her chest to hide the evidence of her arousal.

A dark brow went up. "I told you what I want. Pants and panties to your knees and those soft folds spread so I can have that clit."

His tone told her he meant it.

The small office felt even smaller, shrinking even more when Dillon appeared behind Ryder.

"What's going on?"

Taking a step toward her, Ryder smiled when she took an answering step back, his eyes alight with challenge.

"Ally's gonna show me that pussy."

Dillon's brows went up. "I sure as hell wouldn't want to miss this." Moving into the room, he hitched a thigh over the corner of her desk and crossed his arms over his chest, watching her expectantly.

"Well?"

Sliding her gaze from one to the other, she shifted her feet, not quite able to hold back a smile. "You can't be serious. We're at the garage, for God's sake!"

Reaching back to shut and lock the door, Ryder started toward her.

"And you think I don't want you because we're at the garage? You've been wiggling that ass at me all day. What did you expect?"

"I have not!"

Well, yeah, she had, but she sure as hell wouldn't admit it. Once again they'd surprised her by noticing.

Memories of Saturday night had kept her arousal simmering all day, and she'd found excuses to go out to the garage more often than usual, basking under their attention. She'd stretched, arching her back to thrust her breasts out, murmuring something about her back getting stiff.

She felt Ryder's stare on her bottom when she'd leaned over the car Dillon had been working on and stayed in that position longer than necessary.

Dillon smiled faintly. "Yes, you have, along with everything else. This is Desire, Alison, and we men take our woman's satisfaction very seriously.

If you're needy, it's our responsibility, and privilege, to make sure your needs are taken care of."

A little stunned and more than a little aroused at the prospect of having Dillon and Ryder at her sexual disposal, at least for the rest of the week, she lowered her gaze to hide her excitement and looked up at Ryder through her lashes.

"Later."

Ryder shook his head. "Now."

Eyeing the closed and locked door, she bit her lip.

"Someone could come in."

Ryder shrugged. "If they do, Dillon will take care of them while I'm taking care of you. We can do this the easy way or the hard way, Ally. Either way, those pants are coming down, and my mouth is going on that clit."

Holding his greasy hands out in front of him, he showed his palms. "If we do it the hard way, you're going to end up with greasy fingerprints all over you." Shrugging, he took a step closer and reached for her. "But if that's the way you want it."

A giggle bubbled from her as she raced around the desk. "Damn it, Ryder." She came up short when Dillon stood, and she saw that he'd already washed his hands.

The desire to have those firm hands on her made her shiver with excitement, but it appeared he was perfectly willing to stand back and let Ryder run the show.

Crossing his arms over his chest, he raised a brow, tall and imposing as he blocked her escape.

Ryder caught up with her and reached out to grab her arm, but she pulled it away before he could get her sweater dirty.

Laughing, she shook her head. "No. No. No. I'll do it, damn it."

Ryder went to his knees in front of her and gestured toward her slit. "Do it, then."

Shaking her head, she reached for the fastening of her jeans.

"I can't believe the things the two of you do to me."

Ryder nodded once. "That's because you don't understand the way things are in Desire yet, darlin', but you'll learn. Hurry up with that zipper. I'll bet your panties are soaked, aren't they?"

Alison unfastened her jeans and pulled down the zipper with shaking hands. The look on Ryder's face as he watched made her tremble, her clit throbbing with anticipation. With a glance at Dillon, whose ominous stare made her nervous as he moved in behind her, she started to lower her jeans and panties, swallowing heavily when Ryder licked his lips.

"All the way to your knees. Come on. Hurry up and stop teasing me or you'll have to scrub my handprints off your ass after I turn you over my knee."

"You wouldn't dare!"

The repeated threatened spankings made her hunger for a taste of one, something she wouldn't have admitted to in a million years.

"If he doesn't, I will." Dillon's hands came around her to her waist, sliding up to her breasts and taking her sweater up to her chin. "You're desperately in need of one, and soon. I want to know what your plans are after the trial and you won't talk. Maybe a red ass will loosen that tongue."

Ryder scowled. "Speaking of loose tongues, mine's waiting. Get those fucking jeans and panties to your knees right now, Ally, and spread yourself. Show me that clit."

Alison's body came alive, her breathing ragged as she shoved her jeans and panties the rest of the way and straightened, leaning back against Dillon as he massaged her breasts and tugged at her nipples. Moisture already coated her thighs. Her pussy and anus clenched with the need to be filled, and her clit burned for attention.

Ryder nipped her thigh with his sharp teeth. "Spread yourself, Ally. Now."

With a whimper, she reached down and parted her folds, crying out when she accidentally brushed a finger over her clit.

Ryder chuckled. "Yeah, that little red berry looks like it needs some attention, and I know just how sweet it is to suck on."

The first touch of Ryder's tongue on her burning clit buckled her knees, so intense and hot it scorched her.

Dillon caught her against him with a speed and ease that told her he'd anticipated it.

"Don't you dare let go. Keep yourself open for Ryder. You let go and I'm paddling your ass until you open again. You're going to have to learn to focus."

The threat sent her pulse racing, her clit on fire as Ryder licked her, long, sweeping strokes of his tongue from her pussy to her clit. Struggling to lock her knees and keep her shaking hands from slipping, Alison closed her eyes and dropped her head back against Dillon's shoulder, her breath coming out in short pants of excitement.

Ryder shortened his strokes, zeroing in on her clit, the light, rapid flicks of his tongue over her throbbing nub too intense to last. The tingling became stronger and spread, suffusing her entire body with shimmering heat.

Her legs buckled again, and she automatically grabbed Ryder's shoulders for support, crying in protest when his mouth lifted. A split second later, one of Dillon's hands left her breast, and a sharp slap landed hard on her right bottom cheek.

Her cry of surprise echoed off the office walls, the sharp sting rapidly fading to a delicious heat. Digging her nails into Ryder's shoulders, she sobbed, pulling at him in a desperate attempt to get his mouth on her clit again.

When another slap landed on her other bottom cheek, she started cursing, alarmed when the heat from Dillon's slaps ignited sharp, tingling need in her pussy and, to her chagrin and embarrassment, her ass.

She shuffled her feet in place, going from one to the other, doing anything to try to ease the torment.

Dillon pinched her nipple just as he slapped her right bottom cheek again. It made her sting in two places now, the sting rapidly ignited a fire that spread.

"Concentrate, Alison. What do you have to do to get what you need?"

The unmistakable steel in his silky tone grounded her somehow, the underlying threat in it sending a shiver up her spine.

She stopped stamping her feet, but another slap landed before she could steady herself, and meeting Ryder's glittering green eyes, she hurriedly leaned back and braced herself against Dillon's chest, reached down with trembling fingers to part her folds again.

Frustrated that the combination of her shaking hands and the slipperiness caused by her juices kept making her fingers slide away, she whimpered in her throat.

Dillon's hand came down on her bottom again as she struggled for composure, the heat building with each slap making her pussy and ass clench as the warmth spread to them.

Tightening her bottom muscles, she finally managed to steady herself enough to part her folds, but by this time, her clit nearly sizzled.

"Please. Please. Please. I did it. I need to come."

Dillon ran a hand over her bottom. "Yes, you did. I'm very proud of you."

She sucked in a breath, unable to answer him when Ryder took her clit into his mouth and began to suck. Almost immediately, she started coming, her thighs shaking with the effort to hold her up. Afraid that she would lose her grip again, she pressed hard against her folds, keeping them spread wide for Ryder's talented mouth, determined to get every drop of pleasure she could.

She knew if she allowed her fingers to slip, he would stop, cutting her orgasm short, something she wouldn't be able to stand.

Her breath came in huge gulps, her cries filling the room as her orgasm went on and on. Thankful for the strong arm that wrapped around her waist, she slumped against Dillon, her entire being centered on her clit and the incredible pleasure Ryder gave her.

Her body jerked as the waves of bliss washed over her, her cries becoming hoarse and more primitive, and through it all, she was conscious of Dillon and Ryder's strong presence all around her. Trusting Dillon's strength, she let herself go limp against him when her knees gave out, not at all worried that he wouldn't catch her.

And he did.

Holding her to him, he murmured something in her ear, something she didn't understand, but the admiration and caring in his tone slipped through the fog surrounding her to wrap her in a blanket of warmth she'd never experienced with any other man.

Ryder didn't stop sucking her clit, however, even when the pleasure had crested and become too sharp to bear.

"Let go, baby."

Dillon's command came through loud and clear, and she dropped her hands, drawing a shuddering breath when Ryder lifted his head.

He came to his feet in front of her and bent to kiss her, letting her taste herself on his lips.

"Anytime you want to come, darlin', I'm happy to oblige."

She wanted to laugh at the confidence in his tone, but didn't have the energy. As Dillon righted her clothing, she realized that both he and Dillon had every right to be confident. Both proved to be marvelous lovers, ones that any woman in her right mind would love to have.

Dillon sat in the chair at her desk and settled her across his lap, running his hands up and down her arms and back.

"Feel better?"

Cuddling against his chest, Alison closed her eyes. "I always feel better when I'm with you two."

Dillon stilled, the tension coming from him making her realize what she'd just said.

She opened her eyes to see that Ryder stood on the other side of the desk, his shocked gaze dropping from Dillon's to hers.

Holding her against him when she would have sat up, Dillon started rubbing her back again.

"Imagine that." He touched his finger to her lips when she would have spoken. "We'll eat at the diner tonight. Gracie's fried chicken is the best in the world."

* * * *

Still a little embarrassed, and more than a little stunned at her earlier admission, Alison picked at her dinner.

Sitting in the booth by the window, she shifted restlessly under Ryder's scrutiny from where he sat beside her.

Dillon sat across from her and each time she looked up, she found herself caught in his searching stare.

She had no idea what he was looking for, but the knowledge that he saw way too much kept her from meeting his eyes.

"You don't start eating, I'm going to feed you myself."

She looked up at that, glaring at Dillon.

"I had a boyfriend who tried to tell me what I should eat and shouldn't eat. I don't need another."

Dillon's eyes narrowed. "You're getting dangerously close to being turned over my knee."

"You're getting dangerously close to being kicked in the balls."

Ryder stilled beside her and, without a word, slid from the bench seat.

Alison looked up in alarm when Dillon stood and reached for her, sliding her across the seat. "Dillon, what are you—Oh!"

He had a broad shoulder in her belly before she could react and, with effortless ease, straightened with her dangling over his shoulder.

Aware of the amusement of the other diners, Alison pounded at his back.

"Put me down, you Neanderthal! You're embarrassing me."

The sight of Ryder's denim-clad legs and leather boots following close behind filled her with alarm.

"Gracie, we'll be right back. Can you keep our food warm for us, please?"

She heard a few masculine "uh-ohs" but couldn't tell where they came from. Her face burned at the thought that the men Dillon and Ryder had introduced her to knew that she was about to get a spanking.

Cursing the fact that she'd chosen to wear a skirt tonight, she was thankful that Dillon kept her skirt down with a firm hand over her thighs as he strode out of the diner. The denim jacket she wore fell partially over her head, blocking her view of the other diners as Dillon stormed past them, but she could hear the shuffle as several moved out of his way as they headed for the door.

Her nipples burned against his back, despite her outrage.

"Damn it, Dillon, if you spank me, I'm going back to the hotel."

Ryder ran a hand over the back of her knee.

"You're not going anywhere. It's about time you learned other aspects of belonging to men in Desire. Dillon and I have had enough of being compared to that asshole you used to date. Everything we tell you to do is for your own good."

"You're not my father!"

"Thank God."

Dillon ran a threatening hand over her ass. "This is not gonna be a fatherly spanking, baby. You brought this on yourself. Buck up and take it like a woman."

Kicking her feet did no good as Dillon approached their truck and opened the door, hurriedly slipping inside and positioning her across his lap with an ease that astounded her.

She didn't know how he did it, but he'd somehow managed to maneuver the upper half of her body under the steering wheel so she couldn't lift up. Hearing the door close, she realized that Ryder must have been standing right outside it. The truck started briefly, long enough for the window by her feet to be opened and then shut off again.

Ryder chuckled at her struggles, filling her with foreboding.

"Can't complain about the view."

Dillon lifted her skirt, working it completely out of the way, and ripped her panties from her.

"Now I really can't complain about the view."

Dillon didn't say a word, delivering a half dozen sharp slaps to her exposed bottom, three on each side.

Alison cried out, cursing and screaming at him as he heated her bottom with sharp stinging slaps, but no matter how hard she struggled, she couldn't get away from them.

"You fucking asshole! Ouch! Don't you dare—damn it, Dillon. It hurts. Don't you fucking—oh!"

Her bottom burned, the sharp slaps delivered in such a way that the heat covered both buttocks.

"Enough!"

Dillon's barked command made her jump.

Hearing the glove compartment open, she tried to turn to see what he was doing, but he slammed it closed again before she could.

"Give it to me."

Feeling movement behind her, she cursed the fact that the steering wheel kept her from looking back. Not knowing what either of them would do added another layer of trepidation, the unknown threat increasing her arousal.

"What are you doing?" She knew that neither man would miss the husky need in her voice, the breathless quality giving her away. The heat from his spankings spread, and it mortified her to realize her thighs had become soaked.

Ryder laughed softly, his laugh filled with an erotic tension that she'd learned not to take lightly.

"Since meeting you, we're always prepared, darlin', something you'll come to appreciate in the future. I know I'm sure as hell gonna appreciate it right now." Two strong hands came to rest slightly above her knees and parted her legs wide.

With a large hand over her bottom, Dillon lifted and parted her bottom cheeks, exposing her puckered opening to the cool air blowing in through the window.

Alison shivered, embarrassed that the combination of her spanking, being exposed, and Dillon and Ryder's unwavering dominance already had her so aroused that her body leaked moisture. Biting her lip to control the clenching of her pussy and ass, she fisted her hands under her and closed her eyes, filled with fear and anticipation.

"I hate you. Oh, God!"

A plug, coated with lube, pressed at her puckered opening, Dillon's unrelenting pressure forcing the tight muscle to give way.

Alison cried out as the plug was pushed into her, several inches of thick, hard rubber forcing her anus to stretch wide to accept it.

Stunned at the first warning tingles, she remained perfectly still, her breath coming out in sharp pants as she struggled to accept the decadent invasion. Groaning as the plug widened, she nevertheless lifted her hips in an involuntary attempt to take more.

When it narrowed sharply again and the base of the plug pressed against her, she started to pump her hips, moaning in frustration. She wanted, *needed,* to feel it move in and out of her, stroking her inner flesh in the way Dillon and Ryder had taught her to crave.

"Dillon, oh, God. Dillon. Move it. I can't stand it. Fuck me with it."

Ryder's hands slid upward until his thumbs caressed her folds.

"Christ, she's soaked. Fuck. I want to open this door and sink my cock into that tight pussy."

"No." Another sharp slap landed on her ass, followed quickly by several more.

No longer caring about anything but coming, Alison lifted into his slaps, pumping her hips in a desperate attempt to fuck herself on the rubber filling her ass and get more of the erotic heat caused by Dillon's spanking.

"Yes! More! Fuck me! Take my ass. Do something."

She froze as one final slap landed between her legs, the palm of Dillon's hand hitting the plug while his fingers hit her clit, the force of it jarring the plug inside her and making her pussy burn.

The beginning sizzles of coming hit her just as Dillon took his hand away.

"No! Put it back."

Her head spun as Dillon lifted her and settled her on his lap, her thighs spread wide as she straddled him. To her frustration, he slid her back so that her clit touched nothing but air, and watched her with narrowed eyes as she beat at him and pumped her hips.

"No, you bastard! Finish it. Don't leave me like this."

Gathering her close, Dillon ran a hand over her hair.

"Settle down, Alison. Accept your punishment. If you're a good girl, when we get home, Ryder and I will make you come as many times as you want to."

Lifting her face, she blinked back tears of frustration.

"I want to come now." She realized she sounded like a little girl whining for a treat, but she didn't care. She wanted to come. She *needed* to come. Shocked that a spanking could bring her to the edge of coming so quickly, she whimpered and turned to Ryder.

"Please. Make me come. I'll do anything."

Ryder clenched his jaw, his eyes darker than she'd ever seen them.

"If this is the way you react to a spanking, you can plan to be spanked every fucking day. No. You can't come now and don't try my fucking patience. Seeing the way you react to a spanking and having your ass filled has me close to coming in my pants."

He opened the truck door and reached for her, pulling her out to stand beside him with a gentleness that belied the harshness in his tone.

"Let's go."

* * * *

Aware of the attention of the other diners, Alison squirmed in her seat, biting back a moan at the feel of the plug shifting inside her and the stiff leather of the seat on her naked bottom.

"I swear I'm getting even with both of you for this." Keeping her voice low so she wouldn't be overheard, she glanced up at Dillon. "Especially you."

Dillon tore off a piece of chicken and held it to her lips. "Lookin' forward to it. That'll give me a reason to put you over my knee again. Open those lips for me, Alison. Right now."

His tone and the look in his eyes told her that he was thinking about sliding something besides chicken into her mouth.

She opened without thinking, inwardly wincing at the possessive satisfaction that shone in his eyes.

Aroused and angry at herself and both of them, she shot him a dirty look as she swallowed.

"I used to think you were very gentle."

Dillon's brow went up. "I've never been anything but gentle with you."

She shifted in her seat, gasping as the plug moved inside her. The lingering heat from his spanking seemed to envelop her entire slit, warming her erotically.

"After what you just did to me, I'm surprised you can say that with a straight face."

Ryder slid a hand under her skirt from her knee to her thigh and higher, rubbing a finger over her clit.

"I think Dillon showed remarkable restraint. You're not going to try to tell me that spanking hurt, are you? He was even real careful to keep your back straight so you didn't get hurt. He never touched your hip."

Smiling at her gasp at the friction of his finger on her swollen clit, he redoubled his efforts until her breath caught, and she grabbed at his arm, fighting not to come in front of all the other diners.

"I sure as hell wouldn't have been as gentle with that plug. I would have shoved it right up your ass and not given you any time to get used to it."

Squirming under his touch moved the plug in her ass, the erotic tingles racing through her warning her that she would come any second. Looking around in alarm, she buried her face against him.

"Please don't make me come here."

Ryder had already moved his hand, rubbing her knee under the table.

"Not a chance. No one else gets to see that look on your face or hear those cries but us."

Trying to get herself under control, she took several gulping breaths and reached for her lemonade.

"I'll bet you liked making the women in the club scream. Did everyone get to hear them?"

Dillon glared at her.

"We don't talk about that, especially not with you. Eat your dinner so I can have my dessert."

The look in his eyes left her in no doubt as to his plans for dessert.

She looked down, drawing a shaky breath before looking up at him through her lashes.

"Are you as good with your mouth as Ryder is with his?"

As soon as the words left her mouth, she wished she could call them back, but she'd become so aroused and needy, she'd said the first thing that popped to mind.

Dillon's eyes gleamed with challenge. Ignoring Ryder's laugh, he leaned forward.

"You're about to find out."

They rushed her through her dinner and out to the truck with a speed and purposefulness that excited her even more.

On the short ride back to the apartment over the garage, Dillon settled her on his lap, his hand going up her shirt with a possessiveness and familiarity that made it impossible to sit still. His kiss echoed the sentiment, taking her mouth as though to brand her as his.

Each time she moved, the plug shifted inside her, a sharp reminder of how completely they'd taken her over. No part of her had been left unexplored, and both seemed fascinated by her responses to their every touch, studying her face often as they caressed her.

It was heady stuff, but knowing how much pride they had in their sexual prowess, she didn't make the mistake of assuming it to be any more than that.

For the next few days, however, they belonged to her, and she wouldn't waste a minute of it.

Wiggling against Dillon's cock, she slid her hand through his hair, smiling inwardly at his deep moan.

Lifting his head, he caught the hand she ran up his thigh before it could reach its destination.

"What are you doing?"

Disappointed because he'd removed his hand from her breast, she turned into him, rubbing her nipples against his chest.

"I want to touch you. How come you never let me touch you?"

Still driving, Ryder reached out a hand and slid it up her thigh to her pussy, sinking a finger deep.

"Because every time you touch us, we lose our fucking minds. That soft, shy little touch of yours does it to me every fucking time."

He thrust into her several times, digging at that spot inside her that had her writhing on Dillon's lap. The forcefulness in his touch and the hard look on his face told her he didn't much care for how strongly she affected him, but she couldn't deny that it gave her a surge of confidence.

Clamping down on his finger also tightened her ass on the plug, making both openings feel even fuller.

She whimpered as her body continued to gather, gripping Dillon's forearm and leaning into him for support.

"Dillon, why won't you let me play? I want to suck your cock the way you showed me. I love it when you get all masterful and put your hands in my hair."

Hiding a smile at his sharp intake of breath, she ran a hand up to his shoulder.

"I love that deep voice you use when you tell me what to do." Closing her legs to slow Ryder's strokes, she struggled to keep her voice steady.

Leaning back to look up into Dillon's eyes, she touched her lips to his in a soft kiss and slid her hands into his hair, pressing against him. Thrilling at the way his body stiffened and the flare of heat in his eyes, she smiled flirtatiously, loving her feminine power over them.

"It's very sexy." She swallowed back a moan when Ryder withdrew from her, circling her clit with his thumb before straightening.

Dillon's eyes narrowed. "Is that a fact?"

Ryder brought the truck to a stop at the bottom of the stairs and threw it into park before turning off the ignition and reaching under her skirt again. "What about me? You think I'm not sexy because I went all soft on you, right? Well, little girl, don't make the mistake of thinking I can't give you a fucking you won't soon forget."

The vehemence in his tone made her laugh, her laughter being cut short when Dillon opened the truck door and slid out with her, wrapping her legs around his hips before striding up the stairs to the apartment.

Looking over his shoulder at Ryder, she grinned, sucking in a breath when Dillon's hand settled on her bottom, pushing against the plug.

Every step he took rubbed her clit against his flat belly and moved the plug inside her. Hell, just going up the stairs had her teetering on the edge.

"Oh, God. I'm going to come."

Dillon's strides never slowed as he carried her through the door and straight to the bedroom. "That you are. And then I'm gonna feel that smart mouth on my cock while Ryder fucks you senseless."

Before she could blink, she found herself flat on her back on the bed, her skirt pushed high out of the way, and Dillon's face buried between her thighs.

With his hands beneath her bottom, he lifted her to his mouth, using his thumbs to press against the plug that seemed to swell inside her.

His firm grip kept her in place for the most incredible onslaught, one that stole her breath with its erotic torment. He used his lips and tongue on her without mercy, taking her to the brink and throwing her over with speed and efficiency that left her stunned.

She kicked and tried to close her legs against him, the raw pleasure he forced on her too intense to bear. "Holy hell! Dillon, oh, God. Oh, my God. Oh, my God!"

Ryder sat beside her, already naked.

"Stop showing off. I like to play with her a little. I gotta admit, though, I like those sounds she makes."

Dillon didn't even slow down, flinging her over the edge and leaving her scrambling to hold on to something solid as the waves inside her tossed her over and over.

Her cries eventually became whimpers, and it wasn't long before she realized the futility of struggling, and she stopped fighting him altogether, giving herself over to whatever he wanted to do to her. She no longer had the energy anyway.

Raising his head, he pushed at the plug, sending another jolt of searing pleasure through her and forcing another whimpered cry from her, one so weak and pathetic it didn't even sound like her.

In contrast, Dillon's voice sounded deeper and more authoritative than ever. "And sometimes she needs to learn who's in charge."

Alison trembled helplessly, so lethargic she reached for Ryder and missed. "Oh, God. I can't move."

Ryder slid off the bed and stood between her thighs, his eyes glittering with promise as he rolled on a condom.

"You will, darlin'. You will."

He thrust deep inside her and stilled, his big hands holding her hips steady.

Dillon moved to the other side of the bed and leaned over her, touching the head of his cock to her lips.

"Open those lips for me, Alison. Right now."

He used the same tone he'd used in the diner, and she reacted in the same way, obeying his command and opening her mouth immediately.

Reveling in his taste, she raised her arms to grip his hips, digging her fingers into his thighs so they didn't fall. She thrilled at the feel of the hard muscles in his thighs, lifting her breasts in invitation while clenching on Ryder's cock.

Ryder's groan was followed by a small chuckle.

"That pussy's clamping down on me already. Don't worry, darlin'. I'm gonna fuck you hard. Watching you suck Dillon's cock and feeling this wet pussy all around me is driving me wild. That plug in your ass is making you even tighter. Damn, Dillon. Fuck her mouth good. She's been a brat tonight."

He slowly withdrew and thrust into her again, filling her with his heat and making the plug in her ass shift.

"Yeah, that plug moves when I do, doesn't it, Ally? Feels like you're taking two cocks at once."

"Three." Dillon put his hands over her breasts, rolling her nipples between his thumbs and forefingers. "Suck, Alison. Let's put that smart mouth to good use. Let's see how loud you can scream with your mouth full of cock."

Filled in every opening, Alison dug her nails into Dillon's thighs and hung on, her body quivering under their hands. Weakened from her orgasm, she whimpered every time Ryder's thrust caused any kind of friction on her too-sensitized clit.

Their arrogance got to her, and she wanted to do whatever she could to shake some of that control.

With Dillon over her, she couldn't use her tongue on the underside of his cock the way she wanted to, and the lack of ability to tease him frustrated her. She did the only thing she could. She sucked harder, taking him as far as he would allow, his slow, shallow strokes into her mouth making it impossible to take him as deep as she wanted to.

Her mouth stretched wide to accommodate him, and still she couldn't take much more than the head of his cock inside.

Ryder began thrusting in earnest, the friction of his cock over the sensitive inner walls and the movement of the plug in her ass dominating her senses.

Without realizing it, she'd stopped sucking Dillon, holding his cock in her mouth, the waves of pleasure from being fucked by Ryder making her forget everything else.

Dillon's fingers tightened on her nipples, sending amazing arrows of heat to her slit, and made her already aching clit throb.

"Spank her clit."

She froze at the threat, her body stiffening a split second before a sharp slap landed on the delicate bundle of nerves. The slap sent her senses reeling, the sharp sting lasting only a second or two before giving way to a sizzling heat that made her clit swell, the tingling so intense, she wondered briefly if she was coming.

Her clit tingled so much, she just couldn't tell anymore.

Ryder laughed softly. "Oh, yeah. I can't wait to watch her come just from having her pussy spanked."

Dillon released her nipple, the blood rushing back into it causing another thrilling surge. "Don't you dare stop sucking. I don't give a damn what Ryder does, you keep that mouth moving."

Shivering at that deep, dominant tone she loved so much, Alison wanted desperately to submit without hesitation, but something inside her demanded that she push both of them past the point of their control.

She started sucking Dillon harder, hoping to wrest some of that control from him, while clenching on Ryder's cock that thrust with smooth precision into her.

Neither worked out quite the way she'd planned.

The harder she sucked Dillon, the more dominating his demeanor became.

"That's a good girl. Open those lips wide. No, you don't. Keep those hands where they are."

Ryder readjusted his hold, allowing him to push at the base of the plug and slide a thumb over her clit with every stroke.

"She's trying to play with your balls, and she's fucking clamping down on me so hard, I'm about to explode. If I go, darlin', I'm taking you with me."

Caught up in the passion, Alison worked her mouth over Dillon's cock, lifting herself against him as the pleasure in her slit burst free.

Her pussy, ass, and clit all seemed to catch fire at once as the immense pressure burst. Wave after wave of absolute bliss washed over her, her body bowing and going stiff at the enormous pleasure.

Through it and their unwavering dominance, their affection and tenderness never faltered.

With a curse, Dillon withdrew from her mouth and moved to the bed beside her, running his hands up and down her body and crooning to her.

"That's my girl. Look how beautiful you are. No, baby. Don't move that way."

A strong hand settled on her belly, keeping her from lifting higher into Ryder's thrusts.

Her eyes popped open, a long, pitiful cry escaping from her when Ryder thrust his cock deep and held it there, at the same time gripping the base of the plug and pulling it from her ass.

Astounded at the rush of sensation, she stared into Dillon's watchful eyes, whimpering as she came, a slow rush of heat on her already battered system. The finger he placed over her clit kept the massive waves of pleasure going on and on until her vision blurred and her body went limp, the mewing sounds that escaped coming out ragged and weak.

Struggling to draw enough breath in her lungs, she heard Ryder saying something to Dillon, something she couldn't make out, and Dillon's rough tone as he answered.

"I know."

Reaching up, she touched his cheek, moaning as Ryder's cock slid free.

"Holy hell."

Dillon smiled indulgently. "We'll take that as a compliment."

She slid her hands through Ryder's hair as he bent to kiss her belly, frowning and trying to keep her eyes open.

"But you didn't come."

Dillon's smile broadened. "You owe me one." Bending, he kissed her softly. Lifting his head, he searched her features.

"Ryder and I can take care of you, Alison, in every way. Never doubt that. If you belonged to us, we'd spend the rest of our lives keeping you safe and happy. I don't know how else to prove it to you."

She glanced at Ryder as he slid up to lie on her other side, nearly purring at the soft caresses from both men.

"You spanked me."

Dillon nodded once. "And I'm sure I will again. It's all part of the package. We'll do whatever it takes to make you happy, but we'll also do whatever it takes to keep you safe and to make this relationship work. It won't always be easy, but I've seen the results. It's worth it."

Alison looked away. "But the trial—"

Dillon sighed and stood.

"I'll be glad when this fucking trial is over. I'm sick and tired of it hanging over our heads. Until it's over, I won't even know if I'm wasting my time or not."

Alison jumped when he went out the door, slamming it behind him, and turned to meet Ryder's searching look.

"Are you mad at me, too? You know I might go to jail. How the hell do you expect me to make plans for the future when I don't even know if I have one?"

Gathering her close, Ryder kissed the top of her head.

"We've already told you it'll work out. Your attorney has everything he needs to make sure nothing happens. Ace and the others..."

Alison sat up. "Ace and the others what?"

Ryder stood and gathered his clothes.

"All we're asking for is a sign of a little trust, Ally. We've pretty much laid our cards on the table, but you keep yours hidden. We know your past and have tried to show you we're nothing like that bastard. We know you like the sex, but you won't give anything else."

He laughed humorlessly. "Christ, I'm a sap just like the others. Go take your bath, Ally. Until you're ready to give us some answers, there doesn't seem to be anything left to say."

Chapter Eighteen

The darkness had always been his friend, but never more so than now.

But for a different reason.

Ryder lifted his head, waiting breathlessly as Alison turned toward him and snuggled against his side before he wrapped his arm around her and pulled her even closer. He waited, smiling when she worked her foot across his leg and, as he did each night, lifted the edge of the blanket so she could put her foot out.

The first couple of times, she'd kneed him in the groin in her sleep while attempting to free her foot, and he'd learned to lift the edge of the blanket to make it easier for her. He waited for her to settle, which she did almost immediately, before dropping his head back to the pillow.

He'd always loved the rhythm of the night. The erotic hungers in him always seemed more appropriate for the darkness.

Wicked pleasures he fantasized about during the day, a part of him since he'd sunk his cock into his first woman, seemed better suited to the veil of darkness.

Living in Desire and being a frequent visitor to the men's club afforded him opportunities to give full rein to his desires, opportunities he'd taken full advantage of and had no plans to ever give up.

He smiled as Alison moved her leg over his and cuddled closer. If anyone had told him a month ago that he'd gladly give all of that up for a woman, *one* woman to cuddle against him at night, he would have told them that they were nuts.

And yet here he was, using the darkness to hide his feelings from the one woman who could break his heart in two.

She was so shy in some ways, brazen and forthright in others. Her curiosity about the town, about ménage relationships, about sex amused and delighted him. She asked questions, but in a careful way so as not to hurt anyone's feelings, while the look in her eyes said she thought they all had a screw loose.

He couldn't blame her, especially since, at one time, he'd thought the same thing.

Until he'd seen it with his own eyes.

Those who'd found their women appeared to be happier than he'd ever seen them. Not once had he seen or heard of any of them coming into the club to get laid anymore, or to complain about being tied down.

No, whenever they came to the club, they mostly stared out the window, waiting for the women to emerge from the women's club.

Instead of that, he'd been staring through a hole in the back wall.

Sap.

Taking a deep breath, he inadvertently tightened his hold on Ally, loosening it when she moaned in her sleep.

If he and Dillon hadn't been there with Ace that day...no, he didn't want to think about that tonight. He'd spent enough time reliving the horror of not knowing where she was or if she'd been hurt.

Those had been the longest minutes of his life.

Seeing her in Beau's arms had filled him with a violent rage he hadn't felt in a long time, and he knew then and there, Ally would play a big part in his life.

Of course, as luck would have it, not only had he found a woman he wanted to spend the rest of his life with, a woman who seem to revel in every erotic demand they made of her, but other than sex, she kept her distance, not even wanting to talk about a future.

As though reading his thoughts, Dillon sighed beside her and spoke in a whispered tone.

"What if we take the sex out of the equation?"

Ryder lifted his head and turned, careful not to jar Ally. "What do you mean?"

He could almost hear Dillon's jaw clench.

"She's probably convinced herself that it's only sex between us. If we take that out, she's gonna have no choice but to see the rest."

"Fuck."

Knowing his friend was right, Ryder dropped back on the pillow, resigned to spending the next several days with a woman who turned him inside out and unable to touch her.

"You're right. There's no other way."

Fate sure as hell had to be a woman.

* * * *

The first sign that something had changed hit Alison as soon as she came out of the shower.

Since moving in, every time she'd come out of the shower, one of them had been waiting for her. Sometimes they'd been in the middle of shaving, sometimes brushing their teeth, sometimes just leaning against the wall waiting for her to come out so they could dry her.

This time when she flung the shower curtain aside, it was to find the bathroom empty.

Reaching for the towel, she listened for any sound, smiling in anticipation. Hurriedly drying herself, she raced to the bedroom, expecting to see one or both of them lying in wait for her.

The bedroom stood empty.

The only sounds came from the kitchen.

Hiding her disappointment, she rushed to get dressed and ran out to the kitchen, surprised to see Dillon scrambling eggs and Ryder sitting at the table sipping coffee.

Confused, she stepped into the small room, looking from one to the other. "Good morning."

Dillon, who'd turned from the stove when she came in, smiled. "Good morning, Alison. Come here and give me a kiss. Your eggs are ready."

Relieved, she cuddled against him, lifting her face for his kiss.

With a hand in her hair, he brushed his lips against hers and handed her a plate, ignoring her frown. "Sit down and I'll get you some juice and coffee."

Ryder stood. "I'll get it."

Pushing her eggs around on her plate, she watched both men as they moved around the kitchen, unable to stop admiring them even while wondering what the hell was going on.

Each moved with a gracefulness, every movement smooth and controlled, much like the way they both moved during sex.

She couldn't look at their hands without remembering just how good they felt on her body, or look at their lips without thinking about how good they felt on hers.

When Ryder came up behind her, bringing his arms around her as he set coffee and juice in front of her, she automatically leaned back against him, breathing in the clean, fresh scent of him as she pressed against the bulge at her back.

"Hmm, peaches and soft woman. You smell delicious."

The kiss he placed on the top of her still damp hair did nothing to satisfy her.

"I was thinking the same thing about both of you. Danny used to wear a lot of cologne, so much it nearly gagged me."

Realizing she'd once again brought up her old boyfriend, she snapped her mouth shut and waited, unable to deny the excitement racing through her at the thought of her erotic punishment. Ignoring the niggling voice inside her that said she'd done it on purpose, she looked from one to the other, lifting her chin belligerently, silently daring them to react.

Dillon clenched his jaw and said nothing, but she caught the look of dark intent in his eyes before he forcefully suppressed it and turned away.

Ryder looked like he was about to pounce, coiled tight, his body tense. With a promise of retribution in his eyes, he sighed and moved stiffly to the coffeepot to refill his cup.

"Finish your breakfast. I'm going to go ahead down to the shop. We've got a lot of work to do on your truck today."

Thinking he'd decided to leave her punishment for Dillon, she watched him go out the door before turning to Dillon. Shifting restlessly under his knowing stare, she lowered her eyes.

"Sorry about that."

Nodding once, Dillon finished his coffee and set the cup in the sink.

"No problem. Take your time with your breakfast."

Watching him go out the door, she winced at the loud footsteps as he ran down the stairs, nothing at all like the gracefulness he normally exhibited.

Staring at the back door, she sighed and looked down at her now-cold food.

"What the hell did I do?"

* * * *

She used every opportunity during the day to brush up against them, flirt with them and basically make a nuisance of herself, determined to figure out what the hell had changed. Other than a quick brush of lips on the top of her head, a warm hand running over her back or shoulder, and vague smiles, she got no response at all from either of them.

Wondering if they'd tired of her, she sat in her office, staring out the door to catch a glimpse of them as they worked.

They couldn't be tired of her. She'd never yet known a man who tired of sex. She'd been very careful not to treat what they had as a relationship, no matter how much they insisted that's what they wanted.

She didn't know what game they were playing, but she was determined to find out.

It took her a few minutes of throwing out ideas until one of them struck. A giggle escaped as she reached under her shirt and unhooked her bra, wondering why she'd decided to wear one today and, in a move that seemed to baffle men, worked it out of her sleeve.

They'd put a space heater in her office, which kept it several degrees warmer than the garage, but her nipples beaded anyway when she removed her cardigan. Looking around for an excuse to go out there, she jumped when the phone rang.

Lifting the receiver, she glanced toward the doorway, her breath catching when she saw Ryder leaning over the front of a car. Admiring his tight ass, she put the phone to her ear.

"Tanner and Hayes Garage. Can I help you?"

"Hi, Alison. This is Remington Ross. I don't know if you remember me. We met in the diner."

Alison gulped when Ryder straightened and looked her way, her nipples tingling under his blatant stare.

"Yes, Remington. I remember you." She had a vague memory of being introduced to both him and his equally intimidating brother, but after being spanked and having a butt plug shoved up her ass, she didn't even remember if they'd spoken to her.

Aware of Ryder's eavesdropping, she leaned back in her chair and adopted the most seductive tone she could manage.

"What can I do for you?"

After a brief pause, he chuckled.

"Looking to get turned over someone's knee, are you? Can I talk to Dillon?"

A little taken aback, Alison frowned. "Of course. Hold on just a minute and I'll get him."

Glad for the excuse, she went out into the garage, ignoring Ryder's glare.

Spotting Dillon at the workbench, she approached him, eyeing the various little pieces spread out all over that he appeared to be in the process of cleaning and putting back together.

"Remington is on the phone for you. What's that?"

"A carburetor. Don't touch anything, or I'll tan—" He scrubbed a hand over his face. "Don't touch anything."

She barely felt the kiss on her forehead before he walked away, disappearing through her office door.

"Where's your bra?"

Not at all surprised that he'd noticed, Alison turned to Ryder.

"It was starting to dig into me. Look."

Raising her shirt to her chin, she lifted her breasts to show the faint marks the bra had left under them.

"See?"

Ryder reached for her, the flash of heat in his eyes making her pulse leap. Just as quickly, he dropped his hands, and his expression changed as though a shutter had come down over his features.

"Hmm, I'm going to have to get something for that. Let me call the drugstore and see what they recommend."

She stared, openmouthed, as he pulled out his cell phone and started dialing.

"Ryder! I don't need anything for—"

He held up a hand to cut her off and strode toward the bathroom, leaving her feeling like a fool and scrambling to cover herself. Still talking on the phone, he came back with a tube in his hand just as Dillon came back out of the office.

"Thanks. I'll let you know if I need something else." Ryder disconnected and went to the sink to wash his hands, looking up at Dillon. "What's going on?"

Dillon eyed her warily, his gaze lingering on her nipples poking at the front of her turtleneck. "Rem needs some help with one of the tractors. What's going on out here?"

"Ally has some redness from her bra. I'm gonna put some of this on it."

"Let me see." Dillon came forward and lifted her shirt. "Where?"

Shooting a glare at Ryder, Alison focused her flirting on Dillon. Lifting her breasts, she smiled coyly. "There. See?" She arched her back, lifting her breasts in invitation, her nipples tight and needy.

His eyes glittered with amusement as he reached out and ran a finger over the slight redness.

"I see. Ryder, you'd better get that on her. We'll take her to the lingerie shop and let Erin give her some help picking out some bras that fit her while we head out to the Rosses'. Keep your breasts that way so Ryder can get the cream on real good."

Ryder's grin told her he knew exactly what he was doing to her, taking his time with smoothing on the cream on the underside of her breasts and making her nipples bead tight and become achy. Once he finished, he recapped the tube.

"There. All better. I'll check later to see if you need any more."

Feeling like an idiot, and furious that her efforts to seduce them had been unsuccessful, Alison lowered her top, mumbling her thanks before turning away and heading back toward her office.

"Son of a bitch. What the hell are they up to?"

Ryder's deep voice held more than a hint of laughter as he yelled after her.

"Did you say something, darlin'?"

She didn't even pause. "No."

They wanted her. Even she could tell that, but for some reason, they'd decided to avoid her in any sexual way.

Well, she'd already decided to find out what it took to please a man. Now, she had to figure out how to seduce two of them who seemed determined to resist her.

* * * *

"Are you sure this will work?"

Alison eyed the nightgown Erin held out to her dubiously. Instead of the silk and lace creation she'd expected, this pale blue gown screamed demure. Made of the softest cotton, it had thin straps that left her shoulders bare, about a six inch row of tiny pearl buttons at the neckline, and would fall just slightly past her knees.

Tiny white flowers imprinted sporadically all over the material and the pearl buttons were the only embellishments.

She would have called it a comfort gown, one of those nightgowns she slipped on when she didn't feel well or had had a bad day.

Unable to resist caressing the soft material, Alison shrugged. "I love it, of course. It's beautiful, but not exactly the seductive gown I was looking for. I want to get their attention."

Erin's smile screamed mischief.

"Honey, you already have their attention. If what you told me is true, it sounds like they're trying to prove something. Believe me, if men in this town avoid sex, there's a reason."

Gathering the material against her, Alison eyed the flaming-red number with strategic cutouts hanging on a nearby rack.

"That doesn't make any sense. Our relationship is just *supposed* to be sex. I have to leave at the end of the week, and chances are, when I do, I'm going to go to jail."

Instead of the look of surprise Alison expected, Erin waved her hand, shaking her head. "Men are idiots sometimes. Look, Dillon and Ryder must have told you already that the attorney they hired has enough evidence gathered to prove you're innocent of any wrongdoing. They have taped witness accounts and surveillance tapes, not to mention the one from the police car. Plus, they have a magnificent witness, who won't be shaken a bit."

Alison's mouth dropped. "You? You're going to the trial?"

Erin frowned. "Of course. A lot of us will be there. You're one of us now, and I, for one, sure as hell don't want to miss the show if that asshole decides to lie on the stand. I'm going to enjoy watching him make an ass of himself."

Seeing a chair close by, Alison dropped into it, staring up at Erin, completely stunned.

"You're going to be there?"

"Of course. You've turned white. Do you want a glass of water or something?"

"No. I can't believe it. Are Dillon and Ryder planning to be there?"

"Of course."

"And the attorney didn't take this case pro bono?"

Erin grimaced. "Uh-oh. Look, please don't tell Dillon and Ryder that I told you, but they're paying the attorney. They were scared to death for you and wanted to make absolutely sure you had everything you needed to win."

Dropping her head in her hands, Alison groaned. "No. It's not supposed to be like this. I just came here because it got to be too unbearable to live there with the threats every day. His friends and family kept calling and leaving nasty notes, slashing my tires, knocking down my mailbox, rocks through my window, and telling me that if I testify against Danny, they'd make me pay. I knew I couldn't live there anymore."

Erin knelt beside her and slid a hand over her hair.

"That sounds awful. Nobody helped you?"

Lifting her head, Alison took a deep breath.

"They were afraid to. I don't blame them. His family practically runs the town. He's related to, or has slept with, most of the town. His family's been there forever. Hell, he's even distantly related to the judge. I can only imagine how many people he knows on the jury."

Patting her hand, Erin stood.

"I'm sure it'll be taken care of by the attorney. Stop worrying so much. It's going to be a hell of a show. Now, did you tell me that what's between you and your men is just sex?"

Blowing her bangs, Alison sat back in the chair.

"Yes. When I researched this town and learned about the women's club, I figured I could kill two birds with one stone. I could hide, and at the same time learn how to please a man so that the next one wouldn't have any reason to cheat on me."

The look of fury on Erin's face made her feel better.

"Bastard. That doesn't wash in Desire. It's a sign of weakness that turns the town against the men, or women for that matter, who do it. I've heard of men who have been run out of town because they cheat. No one frequents their businesses, and people shun them on the street. It makes it almost impossible to live here. So, they leave. Dillon and Ryder aren't like that."

She frowned thoughtfully. "I can't think of any man in town that would be like that, except maybe those two Sikes brothers who just moved in across town. They look like trouble to me."

Shaking her head, she smiled. "They're not my problem. I'm sure they'll be dealt with if the need arises. Back to you. So, let me guess. Because you didn't get the seminar you'd signed up for, Dillon and Ryder offered to help you?"

Alison's face burned. "Something like that."

"And you've told them it's just sex?"

"Of course."

"And what do they say about a future with you?"

"I keep telling them I don't want to talk about it."

"Ahhh. Wow, I'm good. Alison, Dillon and Ryder have to be frustrated if you refuse to talk about a future with them. I'll bet this week's till that they want to show you that there's more between you than sex, and that's why they want to avoid it. They want you to see that. Oh, men always think they're so clever. Have they been cold to you?"

Alison thought back to all the hugs and light kisses, the arms around her and their solicitousness. "No. They've been very...affectionate."

"See? I'm right. And how do you feel about them?"

Alison popped up from her chair and strode to the counter, dropping the nightgown on it and digging through her purse for her wallet.

"I can't think about that."

Moving to stand on the other side of the counter, Erin put her hand over hers, waiting until she looked up.

"You can't *not* think about it, can you? Honey, I've been there. I know what it feels like to fall for these men. It's not easy. No one ever promises easy. But, it's real."

Tears blurred Alison's vision.

"It can't work. It's not possible."

"Oh, honey." Erin handed her a tissue and smiled. "Do you know I came to this town when my sister, Rachel, got pregnant. I thought for sure this town was only about sex and that my little sister would end up getting hurt. Boone and Chase put on a good show, but I knew if I stuck around long enough, they would slip up and Rachel would be hurt. I was all ready to whisk her away from here and start all over again."

Alison no longer felt so stupid. "You told me that. It's good to hear that someone else had the same doubts I do."

Erin laughed. "Sure did. And I waited. And while I was waiting, I fell in love with three men who wouldn't take no for an answer. Three! Every time I think about it, it scares me to death, but then as soon as I see one of them, I know I could never have made any other decision. Sometimes, I feel like I'm waiting for the other shoe to drop, and they know it."

Smiling serenely, she leaned forward. "They also know how much I love them. Dillon and Ryder need to hear that from you. Otherwise, they think they're spitting in the wind. You tell them how you feel. Tell them how worried you are about the trial. *Talk* to them. Tell them how much you're leaning on them to help you get through this. Believe me, there's nothing the men of Desire love more than knowing they're taking care of their women. You won't believe how good it'll make them feel to know you're counting on them."

Taking out her wallet, Alison looked up and smiled.

"It's been my experience that the opposite is true. You start counting on a man and they run the other way."

Ringing up the sale, Erin grinned.

"You're absolutely right about that. I always felt the same way. The men who live in Desire, though, are a breed all their own."

* * * *

Alison used the time walking back to the apartment to think about all that Erin had said. Surprised at the number of people who waved to her, she couldn't help but wonder how many of them would be coming to the trial on Friday to listen to the gory details of a relationship that had gone bad.

She'd lived in a small town her entire life, a place where everyone knew everyone else's business, but she'd always known everyone else. To think that strangers would know such intimate things about her and would be witnesses to Danny's garbage made her decidedly uncomfortable.

She'd just turned the last corner when her cell phone rang. Holding her breath, she looked at the display, frowning at the unfamiliar number, until she saw the name.

With a smile, she answered.

"Hi, Ryder. Did you get the tractor working?"

"Almost. I'm gonna come pick you up and drive you back to the apartment. Are you almost done?"

"I already left. I'm walking back."

"What? Why are you walking? Didn't you realize one of us—forget it. Where are you? I'll come and get you. Damn it, is your hip okay? Does your back hurt? Are you supposed to be walking that far?"

Surprised at his tone, she slowed her steps. "I'm fine, Ryder. I'm supposed to walk, remember? And it's not that far. Erin offered me a ride, but it's such a nice day, I wanted to walk back."

His voice lowered, taking on an intimacy that made her heart race.

"Did you buy some new bras?"

Alison winced. She hadn't and that's why she'd gone to the lingerie store in the first place. Caught up in her discussion with Erin, she'd forgotten all about them. Not that she really needed them, but after the excuse she'd used earlier, she hadn't figured out how to get out of buying new ones.

"Of course." The lie tasted bitter in her mouth. She had no use for them, but figured this one wouldn't hurt anyone.

"What color?"

Alison came to a halt, looking down the street toward the garage. "What?"

After a brief pause, one in which she could hear Ryder moving around, he spoke into the phone again. His deep, low tone held an underlying tension that had her shifting her feet.

"Just because I haven't been as hard on you as Dillon, don't think for one minute you're going to get away with lying to me. I don't see why you feel you have to lie about buying bras, but I'm going to find out. If I've learned one thing, it's that lies have no place in a relationship like the one Dillon and I want with you. I won't lie to you, and I sure as hell won't tolerate lies from you."

Tapping her bag against her leg, Alison smiled sarcastically.

"Is that why you told me the attorney was working for free?"

A string of harsh curses followed.

"Erin needs a spanking. I never told you that and neither did Dillon. The attorney did."

"But you knew and didn't tell me. Isn't that lying by omission?"

"You want to talk to me about omission? Let's talk about the way you avoid talking about anything past Friday."

Alison opened her mouth, only to snap it closed again, inwardly cursing. She heard a shuffling on the other end of the phone as though Ryder had put his hand over the receiver.

After a few seconds, he came back.

"Are you almost home?"

Thankful that he'd dropped the subject, Alison nodded, forgetting momentarily that he couldn't see her. Damn, he shook her up, and she hated like hell to lose an argument. "About a block away."

"We'll be home soon. Lock the door when you get inside."

"I was going to take a bubble bath."

"Good. Then you can put on whatever you bought to show Dillon and me when we get home, and we can talk about whatever has you so upset."

"How did you know—"

He disconnected, cutting her off abruptly.

Staring at the phone, she frowned. "How the hell did he know I bought something and that I was upset? Hell, I'm never going to get used to this."

Chapter Nineteen

Sitting on the sofa with her legs curled under her, Alison looked up when the back door opened. Not sure of their moods, and more than a little nervous about what she had to do, she pulled the shawl she'd wrapped around herself closer.

She heard both of them in the kitchen, comforted by the familiar sounds they made as they took off their jackets and boots. Staring at the doorway, she waited.

Ryder came through the door first, his eyes searching hers.

"Are you okay?"

The tenderness in his smile relieved some of the knots in her stomach and brought a lump to her throat. Not trusting herself to speak, she nodded.

Not looking at all convinced, he nodded once before heading to the bedroom. "As soon as we get all the grime washed off of us, we'll talk."

Dillon came out of the kitchen, bare chested, drying his hands and arms. "I like the new nightgown. It suits you." He started toward her, reaching for her, but cursed and straightened.

"I'm too grimy. Stay put." He went into the bedroom, and a few seconds later she heard him banging on the bathroom door, yelling at Ryder to hurry up.

Alison sighed and pulled her knees to her chin, wrapping the shawl around her cold feet.

Trust wasn't easy for her, but she trusted Erin's advice, trusted her own heart, and more than that, trusted Dillon and Ryder.

Blowing out a breath at the enormity of what she was about to do, Alison leaned against the back of the sofa and closed her eyes.

She hadn't realized the weight hanging over her until now. She didn't know how they would react to what she had to say, but all she could do was, as Ryder said, lay her cards on the table.

She owed them that.

Dillon and Ryder were like no men she'd ever met before. They lent their strength when she needed it and had never been intimidated by her own.

She grew stronger every day, but she knew she still had a long way to go, both physically and emotionally.

Smiling to herself, she thought about Dillon and Ryder dealing with the Alison she knew she could be. If nothing else, it would be a hell of a lot of fun.

But would they like that Alison?

Sighing, she tucked her legs under her and folded her arms over the back of the sofa, propping her chin on them, listening to the sounds coming from the other rooms, trying not to picture them naked as they showered. She'd watched them dress and undress many times now, and it never ceased to fascinate her.

How the hell could men be so sexy and erotically decadent, and still maintain such old-fashioned views?

Amazing men. Men she would love to spend the rest of her life getting to know.

They both oozed masculine dominance, something she found exciting in the bedroom but, she could imagine, would cause innumerable skirmishes in the years to come.

In the years to come.

God, she wanted this so badly she could almost taste it, the dream of it so breathtaking she was afraid to hope.

After several minutes of water turning on and off and a hushed conversation, both men emerged.

Facing the bedroom with her hand perched on her fist on the back of the sofa, she watched them approach, their tall, imposing figures so comforting and stable.

Taking a deep breath, she lifted her head and said the first thing that came to mind.

"I'm scared."

Their response to her admission proved to be more than she'd bargained for and convinced her more than anything that she was doing the right thing.

The panic on Ryder's face disappeared almost as soon as it appeared, leaving him frozen in place for a second or two before leaping forward.

"I won't let anything happen to you, I swear."

He lifted her over the back of the sofa, pulling her into his arms and burying his face in her hair.

"I won't let it. Everything'll be fine. I promise. I swear I'm going to kill that son of a bitch for putting you through this."

Dillon's warm hand settled over her back and began to caress her.

"Just what she needs, Ryder. Violence."

Alison lifted her head and smiled.

"Actually, it makes me feel better to imagine Ryder pummeling Danny's face."

Ryder grinned and patted her bottom. "Just say the word, darlin'."

Dillon reached for her. "Give her to me."

Ryder turned away, rounding the sofa and sitting with her on his lap. "I've got her."

A look passed between them before Dillon nodded and lowered his big body to the sofa, sitting beside her and drawing her legs across his lap.

"I know you're worried. I can see it's been eating at you, and it's been frustrating as hell that you wouldn't talk about it. No more, okay?"

Nodding, Alison placed her hand in his outstretched one. "Okay." Leaning against Ryder, she blew out a breath. "I didn't want to talk about it. I just wanted it to go away."

She held up a hand when Dillon started to speak.

"I know. It's not going away. It's been such a nice fantasy to be here with both of you. I just wanted to enjoy every minute of it. I didn't want that other stuff to intrude on what we have here."

Dillon lifted her hand to his mouth and placed a warm kiss in her palm, sending a shiver up her arm.

"And what do we have here, Alison?"

Sucking in a breath, Alison let it out slowly and stared at his hand resting on her knee.

"I think I've fallen in love with both of you."

Before either one of them could speak, she jumped off of Ryder's lap and around the coffee table, putting several feet between them. She couldn't sit anymore and couldn't think when they touched her, and she needed to get this right. Pacing back and forth, she waved off their outstretched arms.

She couldn't look at either one of them, afraid she wouldn't be able to say what she needed to say if she looked at them.

"I know you think we haven't known each other long enough. I feel the same way. I didn't want to say anything because, number one, this was only supposed to be about sex. I needed to get some of my self-confidence back that Danny destroyed. Number two, I thought it was stupid to get you involved in my problems. After all, they're *my* problems. Not yours. I still don't know what's going to happen at the trial. I might end up in jail."

She ran a hand through her hair, and stopped her pacing. With her hands on her hips, she turned to face them.

"How the hell can I promise anything to anyone when I might not even be free after Friday?"

Ryder sat forward. "Ally, your attorney has all he needs to deny any claim that Danny might make."

Alison whirled, throwing her arms in the air, and started pacing again, fighting the urge to throw herself in their arms and make them promise that everything would be all right.

"You don't know these people. They're crazy. Danny's not going to go to jail peacefully. When I go there, they're all going to come at me. They're trying to scare me so I don't testify. They'll do anything!"

Dillon stood and stepped around the coffee table, his quick movement enabling him to grab her before she could avoid him.

"Damn, you're riled up. Come here."

Lowering himself to the sofa, he tightened his arms around her when she would have stood again.

"Settle down before you hurt yourself."

Fighting the urge to lay her head against his chest and beg him to make it all go away, she pushed at him.

"Stop coddling me!"

Dillon nudged her back over his arm and laid a hand on her belly.

"Get used to it. Baby, I plan to spend the next fifty years or so doing just that."

Alison stilled.

"Fifty years?" Her breath hitched when the endearment registered. "You called me baby."

Running a hand over her thighs, he frowned.

"You have a problem with me calling you baby?"

Shrugging, she slid a glance at Ryder as he moved closer. "No. It's just that you never call me that except ...well, you know."

"Except when we're having sex?" He looked thoughtful for a minute, his hand moving in circles over her knee.

"You may be right about that. Interesting. I hadn't really paid attention. Maybe it's because I feel closer to you then and consider you mine."

Her breath caught at the bubble of happiness that started to form inside her.

"Yours?"

"Ours." Ryder lifted her foot to his lips and placed a kiss in the arch, smiling when she shrieked and tried to pull her foot back.

Laughing, she kicked at him with her other foot, only to have it caught in his other hand. "Stop! That tickles."

Grinning, he leaned toward her, parting her legs and making a space for himself between them.

"It seems I'm learning more about you all the time. I wonder what else I can discover."

Leaning against Dillon, she reached out to touch Ryder's long, damp hair, wishing she could give them more.

"I'm scared. I'm scared that Danny's going to win. I'm scared that I want you both so much and won't be able to have you. I'm scared that even if Danny loses, you won't want me. I'm scared that when I get stronger again, you won't want the *real* me. I'm scared that the relationship you want with me won't work. I know it works for some of the people here, but will it work for *us*?"

Sitting up, she looked at each of them in turn.

"I'm scared because I love you."

Both stilled, their slow smiles filling her with joy.

And fear.

Dillon smoothed back her bangs, bending to kiss her forehead.

"It's about damned time. I love—"

"No!" Scrambling off of his lap, she took several steps backward before turning and moving to the other side of the room to stand behind a chair.

Meeting their almost identical looks of confusion, she dug her fingers into the soft material.

"I don't want you to say anything. I'm not ready for this. Please try to understand. I left home to find the person I was before. I'm still recovering both mentally and physically. I need to get this trial behind me and get this weight off my shoulders before I can think about anything else."

Dillon held out a hand for her.

"Come here."

Ryder frowned. "We sure as hell don't want to push you into anything, but it made me mad as hell that you wouldn't talk to either one of us about this. Why the hell did you keep this all bottled up?"

With a sigh, Alison stepped forward, sitting on the arm of the chair.

"Erin made me realize that I wasn't being fair to either one of you. I love both of you, at least, I'm pretty sure I do. I want to come back here to both of you if I can. If you want me to."

"Of course we want you to." Dillon stood. "Now are you going to come here, or do I have to come get you?"

She stood and took another step forward.

"I just wanted you to know how I feel. I felt that I owe you that."

Dillon cursed and lunged for her, lifting her high against his chest and striding back to the sofa. He sat, settling her on his lap with a warning glare.

"Stay where the hell I put you."

His glare softened as he ran a hand through her hair.

"Now, about these fears of yours—"

"I know. I hate them. I was never like this before, but being with Danny changed me. I want to be me again. I was never—"

Ryder slapped a hand over her mouth.

"Good God, she's wound up, isn't she? Ally, no one is criticizing you. We just wanted to know that we meant something to you. Do you want to come back here after the trial?"

She nodded, unable to speak with his hand still covering her mouth.

Ryder removed his hand and bent to touch his lips to hers. "That's all we needed to know."

Dillon put a finger over her lips when she would have spoken.

"I understand your fears and we'll all get through them. We're in this together, baby. I know you won't believe me until you see for yourself, but Danny's not going to be able to prove it was self-defense. If your attorney is as good as he seems to be, Danny will probably get laughed out of the courtroom if he even tries. He'll probably go to jail, at least for a little while. We'll know when he gets out, and if he decides to retaliate, we'll be ready for him. The entire town will be on the lookout for him."

Thinking about what Erin said, that several people from Desire would be going to the trial, Alison sighed. "That's a lot to expect from people who hardly know me."

Dillon tucked a strand of hair behind her ear in a gesture so tender it brought tears to her eyes.

"You're a part of this town now, Alison. We all watch out for each other."

"I thought I was part of a town before. Then they turned on me. What happens if I fight with you and Ryder? Would the people here turn against me?"

Ryder laughed. "Some of these people are married now. They fight. We stay out of it, and I have to admit, that up until now, I thought it was funny as hell. But if any of the men in this town, even ones who are my friends, mistreated their woman, I'd be mad as hell. We protect women here, Ally. We live by that. I have to admit, I didn't really understand how important it was until now."

Dillon smiled. "In other words, if anyone thought we mistreated you, we'd have our asses handed to us. Feel any better?"

Still skeptical, Alison nodded hesitantly.

Dillon pulled her close, tucking her head beneath his chin.

"As for your other fears, we both love you, Alison. We want you here with us. We want to marry you."

Easing her back, he lifted her chin. "But we'll wait. When you feel safe with us and feel like yourself again, just let us know."

Ryder ran his hand up her leg. "And let us know if we can do anything to hurry it along."

Dillon hugged her close again. "In the meantime, you'll live here with us, sleep between us every night, let us love you, and help us design the house we're going to build next door."

Pushing against his chest, Alison sat back to stare at him. "What house?"

Ryder grinned and pulled her across to sit on his lap. "The house we're going to live in with you and make babies. Dillon insisted that we buy it when we bought the garage. I have to admit, I never thought we would ever have the kind of relationship this town was built on, but now I'm looking forward to it."

"Babies?"

Dillon kissed her hair and frowned. "Of course. You *do* want children with us, don't you?"

Thinking back to the day she arrived, she giggled. "Then *I'll* be the one pushing a baby stroller and having strangers look at each other and ask which one of *you* is my husband!"

Ryder tumbled her back over his arm, his fingers already busy on the row of pearl buttons.

"No one is going to doubt for one minute who you belong to."

* * * *

The day of the trial came far too soon, and not soon enough. She'd ridden with Dillon, Ryder, and Devlin Monroe, the man she'd met in the bar in what seemed a lifetime ago, to a hotel outside her hometown the night before.

She'd been shocked to learn that Dillon and Ryder had hired Devlin and his partners, Lucas Hart and Caleb Ward, as her bodyguards until they got back to Desire.

Staring out the window of the hotel room, she met Caleb's eyes, waving when he lifted his hand in greeting.

"This is crazy. I don't need bodyguards. I'm here with you two."

Ryder came out of the bathroom, one towel wrapped around his waist while he swiped his hair with another.

"I agree. No one is going to get past Dillon and me to hurt you, but Dillon felt you'd feel better with more protection."

Going to the window, he acknowledged Caleb's wave with one of his own, gesturing that they'd be out in a few minutes.

"Plus, Lucas, Devlin, and Caleb make a hell of a presence when they want to, and the attorney agreed that it would look better for you if you look like you're afraid of Danny."

Going to her suitcase, she pulled out her low-heeled shoes, lamenting the fact that her injury to her hip kept her from wearing high heels. Slipping them on, she eyed Dillon as he finished knotting his tie.

"Damn, you look good enough to eat."

Turning from the mirror, Dillon winked. "I was just thinking the same thing about you. Difference is, as soon as we get home, I'm eating you."

Wondering if she'd ever get used to their outrageous statements, she pressed her thighs together at the inconvenient rush of juices that dampened the panties she'd just slipped on.

"Damn it, Dillon. Stop saying things like that. This is serious. I don't want Danny to see I'm scared of him and his friends."

Ryder tossed the towels aside and started dressing in a dark suit. "When nobody's looking, stick your tongue out at him."

She plopped on the bed and just as quickly jumped up again. "I can't sit here. I'm going outside."

Dillon turned from the mirror and came toward her, taking her arm. "Good idea. You're wound up tight. Ryder, we'll be outside. Hurry up."

Caleb straightened as soon as they came through the door. When she'd met him the night before, he hadn't looked nearly as intimidating as he did now. Dressed in a dark suit and wearing dark glasses, he looked cold and formidable. Walking toward her, he ruined it by whipping off his glasses and smiling playfully.

"She's jumpy, isn't she? She must have walked back and forth from the window about fifty times in the last hour."

Keeping an arm around her waist, Dillon sighed. "She didn't even sleep last night. Every time Ryder and I thought we had her settled, she jumped up again."

"I'm standing right here, you know?"

Caleb sighed. "I checked again. Everything's on time. Some of his boys showed up here earlier. Got a good look at Lucas and took off. Pussies. I half expected the son of a bitch to skip bail."

Alison shook her head. "He'd never leave Muskogee. He's a big deal here. No, he's convinced he can worm his way out of this." Shrugging, she looked away. "Who knows? Maybe he can."

She blinked when she saw Devlin and Lucas approach from the side, struck speechless by the display of dangerous male and deadly threat the two of them made.

She already knew Devlin, but the easygoing male she'd ridden with on the way here looked nothing like the dark-haired man with the cold expression who walked toward her now.

Beside him, Lucas Hart, also dressed in a dark suit, his gaze continuously sweeping the area, looked downright lethal.

It didn't surprise her at all that Danny's friends had taken one look at him and left.

Even though she knew them, knew that they were here to protect her, she felt a chill go through her and moved closer to Dillon.

Dropping a kiss on her head, he tightened his arm around her.

"They make quite a statement, don't they? You're safe with them, and they'll scare the hell out of Danny."

Caleb leaned closer and whispered conspiratorially. "Lucas practices that look in the mirror every morning."

Trying to imagine the grim faced man coming toward her making faces at himself in the mirror startled a giggle from her, the reaction she would bet had been Caleb's intention all along.

Shooting him a grateful smile, she smiled at Ryder as he approached and looked up, meeting Dillon's watchful gaze.

"I'm ready now. No matter how this turns out, I want to get it over with."

* * * *

If she hadn't been such a nervous wreck, she might have enjoyed the next several minutes a lot more.

Instead she just fought not to throw up.

Flanked by Dillon and Ryder, Alison walked into the courtroom, meeting the prosecutor's encouraging smile before her gaze automatically flew to Danny. The supreme look of confidence in his eyes made her stiffen, the muscles in her back tightening one by one. Her stomach churned, burning and making her feel ill.

It was the same smile he'd given her right before he pushed her down a flight of stairs.

Surrounded by his family and friends, who took up the entire half of the courtroom behind him, he turned to nod at something one of them said, his look cool and amused when he turned back again.

Dillon's hand, already warm on her back, began to move, his fingers kneading the tense spot he already knew so well. Shifting his body, he kissed the top of her head, momentarily blocking her view of Danny.

"You're not alone, baby."

From the other side of her, Ryder slid his hand to her shoulder, bending until his lips touched her ear.

"You let this asshole scare you and I'll paddle your ass good."

The shock of Ryder saying such a thing in the middle of the courtroom had a giggle escaping before she could prevent it.

Danny's smile fell, his eyes hardening and his jaw clenching. He turned his head slightly, glaring at Ryder. Paling at whatever he saw on Ryder's face, he shifted his attention to Dillon.

If possible, he paled even more, his eyes widening before he hurriedly looked away.

Intrigued by Danny's reaction, and pleased to see him looking uneasy, she didn't want to turn away, but the others coming into the courtroom behind her drew her attention.

And the attention of everyone else in the courtroom.

Lucas, Devlin, and Caleb, each imposing figures on their own, tripled the impact by walking in together.

They drew every eye in the courtroom, the sounds of sharp intakes of breath echoing through the room.

Turning slightly in her seat, and grateful for the arm Ryder wrapped around her shoulder, she swallowed heavily when all three men removed their dark glasses. As one, they stared directly at Danny as they took their seats behind her, the icy disdain in their eyes sending a chill through her.

Dillon reached for her hand, cradling it in his, and leaned closer, smiling conspiratorially.

"Scary, aren't they?"

Giving him a distracted nod, she divided her attention between Danny and the back of the courtroom, swallowing the lump that kept forming in her throat at the number of Desire's residents who continued to pour in.

Ace Tyler, an intimidating figure in his uniform, glanced at Danny in disgust, just as quickly dismissing him, shifting his attention to the attorney defending him. His lips twitched slightly before he turned away, but not before the attorney paled and then turned red, the red becoming even darker when his movements became so clumsy he knocked several files to the floor.

Alison watched closely, a little amused at the look of anger on Danny's face, apparently for being dismissed so carelessly.

Brimming with confidence and authority, Ace surprised her further by removing his glasses and giving her a slow wink, taking a seat at the end of the row closest to the other attorney and turning to watch as the man fumbled and dropped another stack of papers.

Erin Preston talked animatedly while walking in with two of her husbands. Her glare, filled with revulsion, didn't appear to faze Danny at all, but the threatening look from Jared's piercing stare did.

Reese shook his head in resignation at whatever Erin said and grabbed her hand, bending to say something to her and hustling her to a seat.

Erin shot him a look and tried to pull her hand away, but he held firm and whispered to her again, this time earning a soft laugh. Looking her way, Erin smiled and waved before Reese tugged her arm, pulling her down to sit in the seat beside him.

He responded to Erin's glare by leaning close and whispering something in her ear, something that had her eyes going wide and her face coloring before she shifted in her seat and hurriedly looked away.

Through it all, Jared never stopped glaring at Danny.

Linc Barrett, the deputy who'd arrested Danny in Desire, came through the door next with Nat and Charity, followed closely by Beau, the man who'd helped her in the club.

Jesse came through the door with Rio, followed closely by Michael from the bar.

She recognized the next man through the door from the diner, one of Gracie's husbands, who walked in speaking in low tones to another man, one more muscular than any man she'd ever seen in person before.

A touch to Dillon's arm got his immediate and undivided attention.

"Yes, baby?"

Warmed by his attentiveness, she tried to ignore Danny's threatening looks from across the room and gestured toward the man who'd just walked in.

"Who's that man? I don't remember meeting him. Does he live in Desire?"

Turning in his seat, he nodded a greeting to the growing crowd behind them and squeezed her hand.

"That's King Taylor. He's one of the owners of Club Desire, and if you don't stop ogling him, *I'm* going to be the one paddling your ass."

Leaning into him, she tried to give him the smile she knew he wanted, but nerves kept her from pulling it off. Unable to keep her gaze from sliding to Danny, she clung to Dillon's hand.

"I just want this to be over with. If I end up getting arrested, will you come and see me on visiting day?"

Ryder closed his arms around her from behind, pulling her close and bending to touch his lips to her ear.

"I wouldn't let them take you. You and I would make a run for it. We could be outlaws together." He paused, thoughtfully. "Hmm, we'd have to get nicknames, though."

His outrageous teasing eased some of her nerves, and she looked up over her shoulder, smiling gratefully.

"I love you, you know?"

"All rise!"

Purposely turning away from Ryder's look of surprise, Alison's gaze flew to the front of the courtroom, and with Dillon and Ryder's help, she forced her shaky legs to support her.

With her stomach tied up in knots, she watched the judge carefully for any signs of friendliness toward Danny.

When he took his seat without showing any signs of recognition at all, Alison glanced toward Danny, who looked madder than hell.

"What's going on?"

Even though she'd whispered, Dillon and Ryder both seemed to hear her.

Helping her to sit again, Dillon gestured toward the man sitting on the other side of Ryder, a man Alison hadn't even noticed until now.

"Alison, this is Mark Reynolds. He's *your* attorney. No matter what happens here today, he's looking out for *your* interests. And from what I understand, he's a shark."

Nervously, Alison leaned across Ryder to speak softly to the expensively dressed attorney. He even smelled expensive, making her wonder just how much all this was costing Dillon and Ryder.

"I'm glad you're on my side. I have a feeling I'm going to need a shark. What's happening? Why does Danny look so mad?"

Mark Reynolds leaned slightly toward her, glancing at her briefly before returning his attention to the proceedings. Except for the amusement in his eyes, his face remained devoid of all expression.

"It's nice to meet you, Alison. I don't know about a shark, but I'm very good at what I do. As for what's happening…well, I unearthed a few photos of the defendant and the local judge drinking beer together at a family reunion, hunting together, even attending a strip club together. Those kinds of photos sent to the right places…"

Ryder rubbed her shoulder, unobtrusively straightening her in her seat and away from the other man.

"And we get a new judge."

Unable to stop trembling, Alison looked in Danny's direction to see him still scowling, talking animatedly in loud whispers to his lawyer.

His parents, sitting right behind him, didn't look much happier.

Gripping Dillon's and Ryder's hands, she turned her attention away from Danny and sucked in a breath as the trial began.

The prosecutor began his opening statement, giving a clear picture of Danny's womanizing and drinking, his tendencies toward violence, and his drunk-driving record.

It made her feel even more like a fool.

She'd grown up in the same town and hadn't been aware of half of the things the prosecutor named.

When he started to talk about her and her injuries, she had to swallow several times, fighting back nausea.

Aware of the anger coming off of Dillon and Ryder, she forced back tears and let her own fury surface.

She'd been stupid, of course, because she'd trusted the wrong man, but she'd be damned if she let Dillon, Ryder, and the other people from Desire see her as a victim.

She was strong. She'd come to testify, hadn't she?

Straightening her spine, she listened to the prosecutor finish his opening remarks and to Danny's attorney begin.

Several times his eyes darted toward where Ace sat at the end of the row behind her, and as she feared, he started his opening statement by blaming the entire incident on her.

"My client didn't set out to hurt the woman he loved. It was self-defense."

To Alison's shock, everyone on the side of the courtroom where she sat burst out into laughter.

The warmth and camaraderie settled even more of her nerves, and she found herself smiling at the look of mortification and anger on Danny's face.

The judge pounded his gavel.

"I won't put up with any more outbursts like that in my courtroom."

But the damage had already been done. Even several of the jury members smiled.

Danny's attorney floundered as he tried to get back on track, appealing to the jury, while looking nervously toward Mark Reynolds as her attorney calmly opened his briefcase and began to pull out a number of file folders.

"It's true! She came at him with a knife."

He went on to tell the jury that several witnesses would convince them of his client's innocence, all the while keeping a careful eye on Mark.

* * * *

Sitting on the witness stand, Alison blinked at how much the courtroom had filled on her side since she'd last looked. Warmed by the support of people she'd never even met, she kept glancing at Dillon and Ryder.

Their smiles of encouragement and the absolute trust and love shining in their eyes gave her all the courage and motivation she needed to get through this.

The attorneys, including Mark Reynolds, approached the bench and spoke in low tones. Danny's attorney argued vehemently, but she couldn't make out what he was saying, but in the end, he and the prosecutor both sat, leaving Mark Reynolds to question her.

"So, Miss Bennett, let's go over the events of that day."

Everyone that had come to support her, even Lucas, Devlin, and Caleb, smiled at her encouragingly.

Her gaze slid around the courtroom, stopping when she got to the two women who'd been friends all of her life.

She'd known Tracy Johnson and Beth Gibson since kindergarten. They'd had sleepovers together, giggled about boys, and copied each other's homework.

As they got older, they'd shopped together, borrowed each other's clothing, and spent hours talking about boys.

They'd been best friends and confidants, but had backed away from her as soon as she started having trouble with Danny.

Even when they'd visited her in the hospital, they'd been in a hurry to get away. The years they'd been friends, however, remained sharp in her mind, and she couldn't be angry with them. Disappointed, yes, but not angry. They never wanted to leave their hometown, and so had to conform.

They stood in the back with several of Danny's friends, looking decidedly uncomfortable.

Alison smiled at them, silently acknowledging that she understood their dilemma, and turned back to Mark Reynolds.

"Okay."

"You and Mr. Peller were very close at one time, weren't you?

"Yes. He was my boyfriend for almost a year."

Turning her head, she met Mark's gaze and, for the first time, caught a glimpse of the woman Danny had been with that day sitting in the row right behind him.

"Did you have a key to his house?"

"Yes. He gave me one about six months ago. He liked to come home from work and find me there and a hot meal on the table."

"So is that why you went over to his house that day? To cook for him?"

"No. I went over to get my sunglasses. I'd forgotten them there."

"And when you walked into the house, what happened?"

Alison drew a deep breath and let it out slowly, hoping to loosen the knot in her stomach.

"I heard voices from the bedroom, so I started to go there, until I heard what was being said. Then I stopped and just stood there kind of frozen for a minute."

"What did you hear?"

"I heard Danny asking a question over and over in a rough voice. It took me a minute to realize what he was saying."

Mark Reynolds crossed his arms over his chest.

"What was he saying?"

Alison smiled at the groan from the other woman and spared a glance at Ryder. "Who's your daddy?"

Ryder laughed so hard he had tears streaming down his face, making it difficult for Alison to keep a straight face.

Even Dillon looked like he was about to burst, and Erin had her face hidden in Jared's shirtfront, her shoulders shaking.

Alison didn't dare look at anyone else and turned back to the attorney, whose eyes danced with mirth.

Shaking his head, he faced her fully.

"So what did you do then?"

"I started upstairs."

"Did you go to the kitchen first to get a knife?"

Alison shook her head and glanced at Danny.

"No. I didn't stop anywhere. I'd left my glasses in the hall table upstairs. I wanted to get them and leave without him even knowing I'd been there."

"Had he cheated on you before?"

"Several times."

"So you must have caught him before."

"Several times. He wasn't very discreet."

"But you didn't know who he was with?"

Shaking her head, Alison glanced at Danny. "No. He liked variety. I never caught him with the same woman twice."

"Were you angry?"

"No."

"You suspected your boyfriend was in his bedroom with another woman, and you weren't angry?"

Crossing her arms over her chest, she stared at Danny, surprised to find that the fury on his face no longer had the power to intimidate her.

"He wasn't my boyfriend anymore. I'd broken up with him earlier in the week. He didn't like it and told me that I was still his, I had no business telling him who he could screw in his own bed, and he'd give me a few days to come to my senses."

Mark Reynolds's brows went up. "So when you heard his voice, what did you do?"

"I listened for a minute or two and laughed. Then I went upstairs because that's the last place I'd seen my sunglasses. Danny turned as soon as I got to the top of the stairs. He'd left the bedroom door open."

The knot in her stomach grew as memories of that day came back with a vengeance. The remembered pain sent cold chills down her spine.

Mark Reynolds came closer, turning his back on the others and smiling at her encouragingly.

"What happened next?"

Although she appreciated the support from those on that side of the courtroom, she hated that they would be witnesses while she was forced to rehash the entire incident.

Without thinking about it, she lifted her gaze to Dillon's.

"He stopped what he was doing and pushed the woman he was with aside. He was still naked when he started toward me and…aroused."

"Did he say anything?"

"Yes. He asked me if I was there because I wanted him."

"What were his exact words?"

Remembering the look on Danny's face, she closed her eyes and took a deep breath. Opening them again, she blew it out slowly.

"Miss it, bitch? Is that why you came back? You want me to fuck you again?"

Assuming Mark Reynolds blocked her view of Dillon and Ryder on purpose, she blinked back tears and smiled her thanks.

He nodded once, keeping his expression and voice cool.

"What did you say, or do?"

Keeping her voice steady had to be the hardest thing she ever did. "I laughed and told him I wouldn't have him on a silver platter and told him to go back to his new girlfriend. He got mad, called me a bitch again, and came at me. He pushed me down the stairs before I could even react."

Her voice broke on a sob, despite her best efforts, the shock and pain she'd felt that day slamming into her with a force that made it difficult to breathe.

"I hadn't expected it. He'd never even hit me before. It happened so fast."

Mark seemed pleased with her reaction even though his eyes filled with regret.

"What did he do then? Did he run to help you?"

Alison accepted the handkerchief he offered, grateful when he took a step sideways, allowing her to see Dillon and Ryder again, the looks of anguish on their faces reminding her that she was no longer alone.

She loved them. They loved her.

All that stood in her way of having a life with them were Danny and his lies.

Turning her head, she stared straight at Danny. She'd be damned if she'd let what he did to her ruin the best thing she'd ever had in her life. Keeping her eyes on his, she shook her head, straightening in her seat.

"No. He didn't run to help me. At the time, I didn't know it, but he'd broken my hip. All I knew was that I was in pain and couldn't move. I heard him laugh. He went back into the bedroom, and from the noises I heard, it sounded like he was finishing what I'd interrupted. I screamed for help, but no one came. After what seemed like a long time, he came down the stairs with his girlfriend. Both were dressed. He kicked me in the back as he passed me and told me to stop crying and to get the hell out before he came home."

She turned to Mark Reynolds. "Then he laughed and walked out the door."

She'd ignored the gasps of the jury members and turned now to face them, surprised that their images blurred. It surprised her again when tears started running down her face, tears that seemed to come out of nowhere.

Once they started, she couldn't stop them.

Lowering her head, she let them fall, wiping them away with the backs of her hands.

The disbelief of having Danny walk over her as though she were no more than a pile of garbage hit her all over again, as did the anguish of hearing the door close behind him and the fading laughter as he walked away.

She remembered the light in the living room changing as the afternoon wore on and her throat sore and raw from crying and screaming for help.

She heard Mark Reynolds's deep voice mingling with the angry tones of Danny's attorney and the calm tones of the judge, but it was as though it came from a distance.

She needed Dillon and Ryder.

Raising her head, she looked directly into Ryder's eyes.

He looked mad enough to spit nails, and Lucas had moved to sit beside him, holding a hand on Ryder's shoulder, apparently the only thing keeping Ryder in his seat. Her throat clogged at his anger.

Her warrior eager to defend her.

She slid her gaze to Dillon, unsurprised to find him staring at her, his jaw clenched. Even from this distance she could feel his strength, strength she readily latched on to.

The look of confidence and love in his eyes calmed her, the message in them clear even at this distance.

You're not alone.

Her eyes went to the residents of Desire who'd come to support her, pausing on each one of them.

They all looked at her, silently offering her support, the compassion and anger on her behalf warming her.

As she met the eyes of each person, one by one, her confidence grew. By the time she'd met the eyes of the last person, the sheriff, she felt part of Desire and more convinced than ever that she should make a new life for herself there.

"Miss Bennett, how long did you lie there, in pain, in *agony,* waiting for someone to come to your rescue?"

Meeting Dillon and Ryder's gazes again, she smiled her thanks before turning back to Mark Reynolds.

"Almost three hours."

The questioning continued as Mark Reynolds drew a clear picture of what had happened to her, going over it again and forcing her to recall details she hadn't remembered.

After that, she answered Danny's attorney's questions, firmly resisting his efforts to try to get her to change her story.

By the time she could finally leave the witness stand, she was exhausted and her back hurt, the muscles tight and painful.

To her surprise, a grim-faced Mark Reynolds came forward to help her from the stand. Bending close, his expression solicitous and full of concern, he allowed a hint of victory to creep into his low tone.

"You did beautifully. No one will believe a word he says now. Don't smile. Nod your head and wipe your tears. Dillon and Ryder are waiting."

Dillon and Ryder stood waiting at the end of the aisle, both looking at her in concern.

Mark led her to them, bending low again. "You were magnificent."

Standing with his back toward Danny's side of the courtroom, Dillon gathered her against him, turning toward the exit.

"She certainly is. She's had enough. We'll be outside."

"No."

Shaking her head, she laid a hand on his chest. When she realized that Dillon had positioned himself to block her view of Danny, she smiled, and for the first time since she'd walked into the courtroom, she felt warm.

Ryder stood next to Dillon and slightly in front of her, blocking her view of the rest of the other side of the courtroom.

The only people she could see lived in Desire, each and every one of them eyeing her in concern.

Even without standing within Desire's city limits, she felt at home.

Smiling her appreciation, she blinked back tears of joy and gratitude and straightened, her eyes lingering on the two men who had, in an amazingly short time, come to represent home to her more than anything.

"I'm good now. I need to finish this."

Ryder didn't look completely convinced, but nodded anyway and bent to kiss her hair, taking her arm to lead her back to her seat between them. Once she was seated, he leaned close.

"Mark's right. You *are* magnificent. But Dillon and I knew that all along."

Nestled between the two men she loved, Alison smiled, took a deep breath, and settled back to watch the rest of the trial.

Erin remained cool and composed on the witness stand, much to the frustration of Danny's attorney, who kept trying to get her to change her story.

Linc's testimony and the video of Danny's arrest in Desire had those sitting on Danny's side looking decidedly uncomfortable, some squirming in their seats.

Danny came off cocky and arrogant, and it quickly became obvious that the jury didn't believe a word of his claims that he'd only pushed her away in self-defense.

Things got even worse for him after that.

With the help of Mark and his files, the prosecutor went though each of Danny's witnesses with a thoroughness that astounded her. Those who said they were with Danny immediately after he'd left the house that day and said that he'd been shaken and upset had their stories torn to shreds.

The prosecutor had proven several of them to be liars, security footage from different places in town showing they couldn't possibly have been with Danny at all.

Sitting between Dillon and Ryder, Alison felt remarkably detached as she listened to it all.

This wasn't her life anymore.

She just wanted to get out of here and get back to her new life in her new home.

Ryder squeezed her hand. "Darlin', are you okay?"

Nodding, she smiled and dropped her head against his shoulder. "I am now."

It took very little time for the jury to find Danny guilty.

The shock on his face made it clear he hadn't expected it at all.

Mark Reynolds leaned close.

"Since there was no premeditation, he'll get off easy, but he'll have to take part in an anger management class."

Dillon stood, pulling Alison up beside him. "I don't give a damn what happens to him as long as he stays away from Desire, and Alison."

Ace came to his feet behind him.

"I doubt he comes to Desire again, but if he does, we'll be ready."

Unable to hide her curiosity any longer, she touched Ace's sleeve as they all started out of the courtroom.

"Sheriff, why did Danny's attorney look like he saw a ghost when he saw you?"

Ace gave her what she assumed to be a rare smile.

"A ghost from his past, anyway. Let's just say I know more about him than he'd like me to know and leave it at that."

Dillon lifted a hand when she would have pressed for more.

"Consider yourself lucky Ace told you that much. He's probably feeling a little soft toward you after hearing what you went through. Our sheriff is known for being tight lipped."

Feeling as though a huge weight had been lifted from her shoulders, she walked outside with the others, shading her eyes against the afternoon sun.

Surrounded by her new friends and absently listening to the conversations going on all around her, she hugged Ryder's arm and leaned against him.

"Thank God that's—"

"You bitch!"

Straightening, she looked toward where the angry voice had come from, unsurprised to see Danny's younger brother, Paul, running toward her.

Lucas moved fast for such a big man, placing himself between her and Paul before he could get anywhere near her.

Ryder leapt forward. "No!"

Blocking Paul from getting closer, Lucas held out a hand for the other men who'd started forward, his voice like a whip, telling them to keep their distance.

Stepping aside, he glanced at Ryder.

"Let Ryder have him."

Alison grabbed Dillon's arm, horrified at the scene unfolding in front of her. "Dillon, stop him. Do something."

Instead of being worried, Dillon leaned against the railing, wrapping his arms around her from behind.

"Are you kidding? Ryder hasn't been in a fight in a long time, and he's been building up steam ever since Danny assaulted you in Desire. Let him get it out."

Alison winced when Paul shouted his rage and came forward, swinging at Ryder.

Ryder ducked his swing with plenty of room to spare and shot a fist out, landing a punch into Paul's belly.

Two more of Paul and Danny's cousins came forward and jumped into the fray.

Fighting Dillon's hold, Alison struggled to get free.

"Ryder!"

Ryder turned at her scream, allowing one of the other men to get past his guard and hit him in the face.

Dillon held firm. "Don't distract him, baby. Look, Devlin and Lucas are keeping the others back. Ryder loves fighting. Just watch. Damn, he's pretty quick, isn't he?"

Ace leaned against the railing beside them.

"I'm glad this isn't my jurisdiction. It's kind of fun to watch Ryder fight, especially when I don't have to worry about breaking it up."

Caleb came to stand at her other side, pointing to where Erin stood, Jared and Reese each holding on to her as she jumped and shouted, urging Ryder on.

"Erin's bloodthirsty. If Jared and Reese didn't have a good hold on her, I think she'd be in the middle of it. It's kind of nice to be able to watch Ryder beat on someone, huh?"

Dillon chuckled. "One down, two to go."

Alison couldn't believe Ryder had already knocked Paul out. Fascinated, she watched Devlin release the man he was holding and started to shout again to Ryder.

Remembering what had happened last time, she snapped her mouth closed, putting a hand over her eyes.

"I can't watch. Dillon, he's gonna get hurt."

Watching the action, Ace glanced at her. "Are you kidding? I've never seen Ryder lose a fight." He shrugged, allowing a small smile. "Of course, he's never fought with me."

It took even less time for Ryder to finish with the next man, and then the next.

Relieved that, other than what would probably be a black eye, he didn't seem hurt at all, Alison broke free of Dillon's hold and ran toward him.

Accepting slaps on the back, smart remarks, and congratulations from the other men, Ryder turned toward her and grinned, catching her when she flung herself at him.

"Hey, darlin'. I finally got to hit somebody."

Now that her fear for him had subsided, her temper flared. Leaning back, she slapped his shoulder.

"Are you out of your mind?"

Ryder's grin fell. "Hey!"

Ignoring several "uh-ohs" as they all started toward the parking lot, Alison hugged Ryder, loving his solid warmth and relieved that he hadn't been hurt, before rearing back and slapping his shoulder again.

"You scared me, damn it! Don't you ever do anything like that again."

He ran a hand over her bottom before he set her on her feet. Sliding his hands into her hair, he bent to kiss her, wincing.

"Did you get scared for me, darlin'?"

He grinned, wincing again and touching his lip that had already started to swell.

Dillon wrapped an arm around her shoulder and drew her along with him as they all made their way to the parking lot.

"Serves you right. Tonight you won't be able to kiss Alison."

Ryder scowled and ran a hand over her hair. "I'll find a way."

The others had gone ahead of them and gathered in the parking lot.

Jesse leaned back against Rio, who towered over her and held her protectively from behind.

"Alison, are you okay?"

Standing there, surrounded by people who cared about her, Alison experienced a sense of camaraderie she never thought she would. Thinking back to the day she'd first arrived in Desire, she found it hard to believe that she now fit in with people, just a few weeks earlier, she hadn't understood at all.

Looking over to see Rio holding Jesse, Jared and Reese with Erin, and Beau staring lovingly at Charity when he thought she wasn't looking, Alison smiled and looked up at Ryder and then Dillon.

"I'm fine now. I'm just glad it's all over. I can't thank all of you enough for being here today. It means so much to me."

Jesse smiled and touched Rio's arm. "You're one of us now. If there's one thing I learned about Desire, it's that everyone sticks together."

Nodding, Alison leaned into Dillon. "I like that."

Looking up, she met Dillon's searching look and smiled. "It's been a long day. Can we go home?"

Dillon's eyes lit up, the love in them impossible to miss.

"Absolutely, baby. Let's go *home*."

Chapter Twenty

Singing along with the radio, Alison grinned at how well her truck took the last corner and patted the dashboard in admiration.

"Good girl. You're something now, aren't you?"

She looked over to what had used to be an empty lot, shocked to see how much work had been done with the framing of their new house since she'd left early that morning.

Boone shook his head in resignation as she passed, while Chase smiled and waved, giving her a thumbs-up.

With an enthusiastic wave, she turned into the garage parking lot and hit the brakes, stopping just inches from the closed garage door.

Damp tendrils of hair that escaped from her ponytail clung to her neck, and the tank top and shorts she'd slipped on earlier felt damp and hot. She couldn't wait to get inside the apartment and take a cool shower.

But first she had something to do.

Ryder came out from the garage through the open bay door to her left, wiping his hands on the rag he always kept in his pocket. His brows went up when he looked behind her truck, to the police car pulling in behind her.

Scrambling from the seat, she shut the door, which closed without protest, and turned, hands on her hips, just as Linc got out of the SUV.

"You already gave me a ticket. You didn't have to follow me home."

Linc glanced at her with a frown and approached Ryder.

"She's a menace. She drives like Hope. What the hell kind of engine did you put in that thing anyway?"

Alison leaned into the hand Ryder placed at her back.

"A big one."

Ryder laughed.

"Have fun, darlin'?"

"How fast was she going?"

Alison stilled at Dillon's question, coming from somewhere behind her, a little uneasy at his tone.

Glancing at her, Linc grinned, apparently happy now that she was going to be in trouble. "Seventy-six on the road into town."

She'd learned well in the last four months how these men stuck together, but she'd also learned a few other things.

She'd learned that the more she became herself again, the better her relationship with Dillon and Ryder got.

She'd also learned to be on her toes when Dillon adopted that tone.

Looking up over her shoulder, she leaned into Ryder and grinned, depending on his fun loving nature to help get her out of this.

"It runs so great, and it's so pretty. Everybody stares when I go by. It's so much fun to drive. You and Dillon are the best."

Ryder laughed and hugged her.

"It is fun to drive, isn't it, especially on the road into town. When you get to the straight—"

"Ryder, damn it! Will you stop doing that? Stop encouraging her. Christ, she gets more like you every day." Dillon yanked her out of Ryder's arms. With a hand on each of her shoulders, Dillon placed her in front of him, bending to get in her face.

"You were told to keep it under the speed limit. Speeding is dangerous, Alison."

Linc folded his arms over his chest, lifting a brow.

"You've been here long enough to understand that, Alison."

Alison understood, all right. With some advice from the other women in town, she'd even learned how to play the game.

Looking up at Dillon through her lashes, she pouted.

"It was fun. I thought you wanted me to have fun."

Dillon's eyes narrowed. "Damn it, Alison. Of course I want you to have fun but not in a way that's dangerous."

Shrugging, she glared at Linc over her shoulder and cuddled against Dillon, flattening her hands on his chest and looking up at him, her happiness and excitement making it nearly impossible to stand still.

Reaching for his shoulders she jumped up, secure that he would catch her.

He did.

Nuzzling his jaw, she couldn't hide her grin at the shudder that went through him. Touching her lips to his ear, she kept her voice at a whisper.

"Guess what I did today?"

A big hand smoothed over her back.

"What did you do today? You said you were going shopping."

Leaning back to see his face, and aware of Linc's eavesdropping, she reached out a hand to Ryder when he stepped closer.

"I ordered my wedding dress."

Although she stared at Dillon, she could feel both men become still, the surprised delight on Dillon's face bringing tears to her eyes. Smiling at Ryder's whoop, she cupped Dillon's jaw.

"I love you, Dillon."

Dillon gathered her close, his arms warm and strong around her.

"I love you, too, baby. Christ, I love you." Lifting his head, he leaned back, forcing her to meet his eyes.

"So you're ready now? You're ready to become Mrs. Tanner?"

Throwing her arms around his neck, she dug her heels into his tight butt.

"Absolutely. You should see my dress. It's gonna knock your socks off."

Dillon's hand went to her butt. "You already do."

Linc came forward, all smiles, and congratulated them.

"Another wedding. Congratulations. Looking forward to my own one day. Well, Alison, looks like you've been hanging around the other women too much. It appears you already know how to twist your men around your little finger."

Taken aback at the sadness in his eyes, she lifted her head.

"You'll find the right woman, and she'll do the same thing to you."

Nodding, he took off his hat and wiped his forehead, before donning it again.

"We already did. And you're right. She does. Good luck. And no more speeding."

Watching him walk away, Alison yelped when Ryder plucked her from Dillon's arms.

"I want my kiss." Capturing her lips with his own, he kissed her with a thoroughness that made her toes curl. By the time he lifted his head, hers was spinning and she wanted him more than ever.

"So you're gonna marry us? It's about time."

"You said you wanted me to be sure, remember?"

She heard Linc pull away as Ryder carried her into the garage. As soon as they got inside and away from any prying eyes, Dillon came up behind her, sliding his hands around to cover her breasts and nuzzling her neck.

"And what made you so sure that you had to get up this morning and rush out to order your wedding gown?"

Alison took a deep breath and let it out slowly.

"We've been arguing a lot lately."

At first, their fights had scared the hell out of her.

Dillon and Ryder had wanted to get the house started as soon as possible, and called Boone and Chase to start planning it.

Once the Jacksons told them about places online where they could look at houses and floor plans, Dillon and Ryder spent every night on their laptops, gathering an assortment that they liked, constantly asking her opinion.

Uncomfortable with making decisions about something she wouldn't be paying for, she avoided answering as much as possible. She couldn't get used to them paying for everything. It made her uneasy, and she told them so.

They gave her money every week for working in the garage, money she'd put aside for the truck. When they'd finished the truck and she'd tried to pay them, they'd had their first big fight.

Since then, she'd refused to take any money from them for working in the garage, and the issue of money had been a sore subject between them, especially when she hadn't yet agreed to marry them.

Dillon pulled her closer now, running his hand over her ponytail.

"Damn it, Alison, we're not rich, but we're more than able to provide for you. Ryder and I *want* you to buy the things for you. You're not *using* us, damn it!" Pausing, he leaned back and turned her face to his.

"We love you, you know? Just because we've been arguing doesn't mean we don't love you anymore. Never think that. Never."

Alison nodded, smiling at the frustration in his tone. "I know. That's why I'm marrying you. Last night when we were arguing, when you and Ryder got so mad at me because I ran over the box of tools, I knew. I realized that no matter how much you yelled at me, I wasn't scared that you'd hit me. I wasn't afraid that you didn't love me anymore. I yelled back. I screamed at both of you. I cursed at both of you."

Ryder set her on her feet, pushing her bangs back out of her eyes and grinned.

"You're real good with that mouth. Loud, too. My ears were still ringing when I got up this morning."

Alison nodded, smiling, so happy she wanted to dance in the street. "And last night you both made love to me real slow. And held me."

Running her hands down their chests, she looked from one to the other, grinning impishly. "No matter how much you yell, you love me. You're both soft on me, aren't you? How can I not marry two men who love me so much?"

Dillon ran his hand over her ass, the threat unmistakable.

"I'll still paddle your ass for speeding."

Alison let her hand go lower, cupping him, and giggled when his cock jumped against her hand.

"Yeah, but we'll both enjoy it. So am I going to be Mrs. Dillon Tanner or not?"

Holding her hand pressed against him, Dillon swooped down to take her lips with his, his eyes glittering with possession.

"As soon as possible. I can't wait until you wear my name. In the meantime..."

He pulled a box out of his pocket, smiling when she gasped.

"I've been carrying this around for months now. It's about time you put it on."

Alison clapped a hand over her mouth, her eyes swimming with tears as she watched Dillon open the box to reveal a sparkling ring with two square diamonds resting side by side.

"A reminder that you have two men who both love you so much they want to spend the rest of their lives making you happy." Wiping away her tears, he smiled and slipped the ring on her finger. He hugged her against him again and released her, running a hand over her hair while nudging her toward Ryder.

Alison had noticed that although Ryder kept touching her, he'd been unusually quiet. Cuddling against him, she stood on her toes to kiss his jaw, loving the feel of his hard body against hers.

"I can't wait until you're my husband."

Tugging her ponytail, he flashed her that bad-boy grin she loved so much, and bent to touch his lips to hers.

"Neither can I, darlin'."

Hardly able to contain her excitement, Alison giggled again.

"Well, if you're going to be my husband, I should be branded with your name, too, don't you think?"

Ryder's smile fell.

"Alison, we told you, it's the older male who—"

Nodding, Alison glanced at Dillon, who looked a little shaken.

"I know, and Dillon's three months older than you, but I wanted to wear your name, too. So…"

Backing away from both of them, she sent a nervous glance at the garage door to make sure no one was coming and reached for the fastening of her shorts. Aware of both men's confusion and rapt attention, she lowered her shorts and panties, slowly revealing the tattoo she'd gotten only hours earlier.

Dillon shared a secret smile with her and winked, nodding his satisfaction.

Ryder had a different reaction, one that shocked her to her core.

Instead of the wild bad boy she expected, Ryder lifted his eyes to hers before looking back down to his name she'd had tattooed above, and to the right, of her mound—in exactly the spot he'd teased her about getting tattooed before.

Moving toward her, he never took his eyes off of it. As soon as he got close, he surprised her even more by dropping to his knees in front of her and running his fingers over the letters of his name.

She winced, the area still a little sore.

He jerked his hand away, looking up at her and, to her utter amazement, had tears shining in his eyes.

"I love you so damned much. I can't believe you did this."

Wrapping his arms around her, he pressed his head again her belly. "You have my name tattooed on you."

Over his head, Dillon winked again before adopting a stern expression.

"I thought I told you no tattoos."

Alison grinned down at Ryder.

"Yeah, but a woman taking on two husbands has got to learn to be a good wife to both. This suits Ryder and me perfectly."

Ryder stood and lifted her against him and, with a hand on her bottom, urged her to wrap her legs around him, giving her that bad-boy grin that never failed to excite her.

"It sure as hell does. I have a yearning to eat a pussy with my name on it."

Dillon patted her ass as Ryder carried her toward the open garage door.

"You've done it now, baby. You've created a monster."

Tangling her hands in Ryder's long hair, she worked it free of the band he'd confined it with. She wanted to laugh and cry at the same time, and the promise of pleasure in Ryder's eyes had her body tightening with arousal.

"I wouldn't want him any other way."

Dillon laughed and called after her.

"Just because you're marrying us doesn't mean you're getting out of an ass whippin' for speeding."

Hugging Ryder, she swallowed the lump in her throat to see the yearning in Dillon's eyes despite his lighthearted bantering.

She knew him well enough to know how much he wanted her, and how much he cared about her relationship with Ryder.

It only made her love him more.

As Ryder started up the stairs, she raised her head and met Dillon's eyes.

"I wouldn't have that any other way either."

Wrapped in Ryder's arms, she smiled when Dillon cursed and hurriedly closed the garage door and started after them, his eyes on hers filled with love and promise. As they climbed the stairs, she looked over to the house that had begun taking shape, running her thumb over the ring that proclaimed their love for her.

And knew she'd finally found home.

THE END

WWW.LEAHBROOKE.NET

ABOUT THE AUTHOR

When Leah's not writing, she's spending time with family and friends or plotting out new stories.

Leah Brooke also writes historical erotic romance under the pseudonym Lana Dare.

Also by Leah Brooke

Ménage Amour: Dakota Heat 1: *Her Dakota Men*
Ménage Amour: Dakota Heat 2: *Dakota Ranch Crude*
Ménage Amour: Dakota Heat 3: *Dakota's Cowboys*
Ménage Amour: Dakota Heat 4: *Dakota Springs*
Ménage Amour: Desire, Oklahoma 1: *Desire for Three*
Siren Classic: Desire, Oklahoma 2: *Blade's Desire*
Ménage Amour: Desire, Oklahoma 3: *Creation of Desire*
Ménage Amour: Desire, Oklahoma 4: *Rules of Desire*
Everlasting Classic: Desire, Oklahoma 5: *Dark Desire*
Siren Classic: Tasty Treats Anthology, Volume 2: *Back in Her Bed*
Ménage Amour: *Alphas' Mate*
Ménage Everlasting: *Crescendo*

Also by Leah Brooke writing as Lana Dare

Ménage Everlasting: *Beaumonts' Brand*
Ménage Everlasting: *Amanda's Texas Rangers*
Ménage Everlasting: Desire, Oklahoma: The Founding Fathers 1: *Untamed Desire*

Available at
BOOKSTRAND.COM

Siren Publishing, Inc.
www.SirenPublishing.com

Lightning Source UK Ltd.
Milton Keynes UK
UKOW031413071211

183362UK00011B/165/P